PUSHKIN CHILDREN'S BC

The Song of S

'A cracking adventure... so nail-biting you'll need to wear protective gloves'

The Times

'A magical, strange, gripping tale'

Spectator

'Draws the reader seductively along its spiralling paths... the language... is beautifully lucid, with a clear sense of playfulness and urgency... a wandering, winding ballad with occasional joyous percussion, to the spell of which the reader can't help but succumb'

Guardian

'A lovely present for a young person from 10 upwards and beyond to grown-ups who will be as enchanted as I was!'

Reading Zone

'Brilliant imaginative storytelling... *The Song of Seven* is sure to go down as a classic in children's literature. It's only a shame it wasn't translated into English sooner'

BookTrust

'A fantastic new book from a legendary writer... gloriously written with tons of plot twists and turns, and a barrel-load of excitement'

Read it Daddy

THE SONG OF SEVEN

TONKE DRAGT

Translated by Laura Watkinson

PUSHKIN CHILDREN'S BOOKS

Pushkin Chlidren's Books
71–75 Shelton Street
London, WC2H 9JQ

The Song of Seven was first published as *De Zevensprong* in the Netherlands, 1967

First published by Pushkin Children's Books in 2016
This edition first published in 2017

Nederlands letterenfonds
dutch foundation for literature

This book was published with the support of the Dutch Foundation for Literature.

10 9 8 7 6 5 4 3 2 1

ISBN 978 1 78269 142 6

Designed and typeset by Tetragon, London
Printed by CPI Group (UK) Ltd, Croydon, CR0 4YY

www.pushkinpress.com

Always for Cornelijne

Contents

I

Frans receives a mysterious letter

And now the story has begun

THIS IS ONE

It was boiling hot, even though the windows and the door into the corridor were all open. The children had been silent for an hour, but that probably had more to do with the heat than with the tongue-lashing their teacher had given them at the beginning of the afternoon. Now that they'd nearly all finished the dull grammar exercises he'd told them to do, the noise was creeping back, little by little – whispers, a cough, quiet giggles, feet shuffling, desks creaking, paper rustling.

Frans van der Steg, sitting at his desk on the platform at the front of the classroom, tutted and looked up. His stern look didn't make much impression on the class though, perhaps in part because his spectacles had slipped down to the tip of his nose. But he didn't say anything. He simply wasn't in the mood.

In the class of first-years at the end of the corridor, the little ones were singing.

Do you know the Seven, the Seven,
Do you know the Seven Ways?

What a tedious tune, thought Frans van der Steg.

People say that I can't dance,
But I can dance like the King of France.
This is one…

"Well, I know I certainly couldn't dance at this tempo," he said out loud. "By the time they get to seven, I could have counted to a hundred."

The buzz and bustle in the classroom increased, but Frans banged his hand on the desk and put a stop to it before it became a din. Twenty-five pairs of eyes looked at him. Frans stared back and then pretended to go on marking the books in front of him. He looked at the red line he'd drawn beneath the title of Marian's essay, THE SEKRIT TRESURE, and gloomily wondered why he tried so hard to teach his students to spell. As he glanced at his watch, he heard Maarten's voice: "Sir?"

Frans van der Steg looked up again. He still wasn't used to being called "sir". He hadn't been working in this village for long, and in town he'd just been "Mr Van der Steg". What he should have said to Maarten was: "Did I give you permission to speak?" But instead he said, "What is it, Maarten?"

The chattering began again. The children could tell their teacher wasn't really angry with them anymore, and besides...

"It's twenty-five past three," said Maarten.

Twenty-five past three was packing-up time, and Frans van der Steg's group of ten- and eleven-year-olds could pack up faster than any other class. It had been like that almost since the first day back to school after the summer holidays. At first, the class had been very noisy when twenty-five past three came around, but that hadn't lasted for long. Kai, one of the most boisterous boys in the class, had – accidentally on purpose – dropped a big box of coloured pencils, much to his classmates' secret delight. Mr Van der Steg had just shaken his head and said with a serious look on his face, "Kai, Kai, you probably think there's no harm done and it'll be easy enough to pick up the pencils and tidy them away, but I've seen for myself the terrible consequences of such clumsiness. A friend of mine once did the same thing, only it wasn't pencils he dropped, but two whole armfuls of lances and spears."

Kai had just gaped at his teacher, but Maarten, who always spoke without being spoken to, had squawked, "Huh? Lances and spears? But how come?"

"Lances and spears," his teacher had repeated, "with sharp iron points, which don't break as easily as pencil points. It made such an incredible din! And it had to happen just as we were sneaking through the palace at night..."

"Palace? What palace?"

"The King of Torelore's palace. We were caught like rats in a trap. We'd worked so hard to steal those spears from the armoury. And then that idiot let them go crashing to the floor! Well, of course, everyone woke up: the King of Torelore, the Queen of Torelore, and all their soldiers with their sabres. And then the fun really started..."

As the teacher continued his tale, you could have heard a pin drop. But when the bell went, the class exploded with questions. "And then? What happened next?!"

Their teacher couldn't let them go home until they'd heard how he'd managed to escape from the deepest dungeon in the royal palace, where he was tied up with thick ropes and guarded by a hungry lion, could he? But Frans van der Steg had simply told Kai to pick up the pencils and sent them home with a promise to continue the story another day.

And he'd done exactly that. He'd been teaching the class for three weeks now and, at the end of every day, from twenty-five past three to half past, as they packed up, he told them a story, and on Saturday mornings, when the children also had lessons, the stories went on for much longer, sometimes for as long as three quarters of an hour.

His class had heard the tale of his adventures in the Kingdom of Torelore, and his account of his journey back home, complete with a shipwreck and a desert island. They knew all about his stay in the haunted castle, and about the time he'd faced the Abominable Snowman in the Himalayas.

"But it's not true, is it?" Maarten sometimes said. "You're just making it up."

The other children knew that too, but that didn't make them any less interested in their teacher's tales. Somehow, in their imaginations, he was two people – one was just their teacher, Mr Van der Steg, but the other was a kind of fearless knight, with hair like flames, FRANS THE RED, a hero who could take on anyone.

And now the only thing that could save this hot, boring afternoon was a new adventure. Yesterday Frans the Red had returned safe and sound from an expedition to the rainforests of Urozawa, and he had a few minutes left today to set off on his next escapade.

Mr Van der Steg straightened his glasses, ran his fingers through his hair and then slowly shook his head.

"Um, chaps," he said (he always called them that, even though there were girls in the class too), "I'm tired." He knew he was disappointing his students, but he really had no idea what to tell them. "The thing is..." he continued, "I'm waiting for..."

"For what, sir?" (there's no need to explain who asked that question).

"For a letter," said the teacher. It was the first answer that came to him. "A very important letter," he added. "It might arrive this evening. The sender is... something of an enigma... And I hope," he concluded, "that it'll be the beginning of a new adventure, with a mysterious and perilous mission."

They'll have to make do with that, he thought. When all the books had been handed in, it would be time to go home anyway. He leant back in his chair, stifled a yawn and absent-mindedly hummed along with the first-years, who were singing the Song of Seven again.

Phew, this weather! thought Frans van der Steg, as he cycled home. *It didn't get this hot all summer holiday. I really should have taken the class outside, instead of being annoyed with them for not doing their work properly.*

When he got home, to the house where he rented a room, he found his landlady in the conservatory with a big pot of tea.

"Ah, there you are," she greeted him. "I bet you could do with a nice cup of tea."

"I most certainly could, Mrs Bakker," he said. "You know just what a person needs after a hard day at work. Shall I get the deckchairs out of the shed? Then we can sit outside."

"Oh no, don't bother," his landlady replied. "There's a storm coming, and we'll only have to bring everything back in."

Frans opened his mouth to point out just how brightly the sun was shining today, but then he heard thunder rumbling in the distance, and he changed his mind.

"Once it starts raining," his landlady said, "that'll be the end of the summer."

Frans looked out to see thick black clouds rolling towards the sun. He didn't reply.

"Would you like a biscuit, Frans?" his landlady asked. She was old enough to be his mother, so he didn't mind her calling him by his first name. When he spoke to her, he was always polite and called her "Mrs Bakker", but whenever he thought about her, it was as "Aunt Wilhelmina". He knew that was her first name, and he thought the title of "aunt" suited her. She was rosy-cheeked, plump and perky, and she was a wonderful cook.

"I'm going out this evening," she told him. "The neighbours have asked me to go round and watch something on TV with them. Some kind of drama. It's supposed to be good. So you can work at the big table in the dining room if you have lots of paperwork to do."

"Thank you," said Frans. He sat down, stirred his tea and sighed again. "I still have another nineteen essays still to mark," he added, "and twenty-five spelling tests. And I've got to do my own homework for tomorrow too."

"That's the biggest nonsense I've ever heard! Schoolteachers are supposed to give out homework, not do it themselves."

"Ah, but I want to get ahead," said Frans, "which is why I'm studying for another qualification."

His landlady gave him a look of disapproval. "You should be satisfied with the job you have! My son was always interested in getting ahead too, and where did that get him? All the way over there on the other side of the globe! In Australia! My only son, and he's all I have."

"But he writes you lots and lots of letters," Frans said, to cheer her up, "and he sends you photographs of the grandchildren."

"That's true," she said. "I'm expecting one today, in fact. I suppose that's better than nothing. But the postman's late though."

"I'm waiting for a letter too," said Frans with a smile. "And it's a very important one, or at least that's the story I told."

"Have you been making things up again? I hear you've got those children's heads spinning with all kinds of crazy stories. Mind they don't return the favour. Would you like another cup of tea? Ooh, look how dark and cloudy it's getting now! I'm glad I only have to go next door this evening. Looks like we're in for a terrible storm."

Mrs Wilhelmina Bakker was right: that evening, after dinner, the rain came hammering down against the window panes. Frans was sitting at the big table, with all his papers spread out over the plush red tablecloth. The wind blew so hard that the curtains were rippling, even though the windows were closed. The whole house was creaking; at times it sounded like someone was walking up and down the hallway, sighing and groaning. But of course there was no one there; Frans was all alone in the house. He tried to concentrate on his work, but after a while he had to get up to look. Opening the curtain, he peered outside. A flash of lightning blinded him for a second, followed, a moment later, by an almighty clap of thunder.

I hope that lightning didn't strike anything important, he thought.

But then other sounds filled the air – windows rattling away, doors banging and flying open.

"What on earth...!" said Frans, dashing into the hallway.

A gust of wind blasted towards him; the front door had blown wide open. The brass lantern in the hallway swayed to and fro, and strange shadows danced across the walls. Rain lashed Frans's face as he struggled to close the door. It was only then that he spotted the letter on the mat. He picked it up; the envelope was damp and the writing was smudged. Yet he could still clearly make out his own name and address.

"My goodness me," he said to himself. "It seems my story has become reality – a letter for me, and it just blew in with the storm."

He checked that all the other doors and windows were properly closed, before going back into the dining room and sitting down at the table to open the envelope. After reading the letter, he sat there for a while, staring at it in amazement. Written in strong, confident handwriting, the letter said the following:

> *Tuesday 22 September*
>
> *Dear Mr Van der Steg,*
>
> *In response to your letter of the eighteenth of this month, I should very much like to meet you. As I live in a somewhat remote spot in the woods, I shall send my man to pick you up, on Friday 25 September, at exactly half past seven.*
>
> *Respectfully yours,*

The signature was illegible. All Frans could make out was two large letter G's, each followed by a small *r*. *Gr… Gr…*

But that wasn't why he'd raised his eyebrows. He was most surprised because he had not in fact written a letter on the eighteenth of this month.

Then he began to laugh. It was obviously just the children playing a joke on him.

But which of his students had handwriting like that? One of their fathers must have written it, or an uncle, or a big brother.

Do I know anyone who's called Gr... Gr... *something?* he wondered. *No, I'm certain that person doesn't exist. Someone's deliberately made the signature impossible to read.*

He studied the letter and then the envelope. They were made of beautiful, expensive-looking paper, with a small coat of arms in the corner, which had another G on it, with a cat's head inside.

Frans put down the letter and opened his textbook. After a couple of minutes, he caught himself thinking about the letter again. *What nonsense,* he told himself. *It's just the children having a joke, that's all. I'll have to do something about this tomorrow though. I'm the one who makes up my adventures, and they shouldn't be getting involved. "In response to your letter of the eighteenth of this month..." However did they come up with that? What day is it today? Thursday the twenty-fourth. And the letter's dated the day before yesterday... Ha, they might as well have written April the first! And of course there's no stamp... No, wait a second, there* is *a stamp on the envelope...*

He took a closer look and got another surprise. The stamp had been franked in the nearby village of Langelaan on 23 September!

"How can that be...?" he murmured. "That was yesterday, and I didn't say anything to them about a letter until today. They must have faked it somehow... but they can't possibly be *that* clever. I can't imagine how they might have done it. The envelope's dirty, but it doesn't seem to have been tampered with. Hmm..."

He took off his glasses and thoughtfully polished the lenses. That rain! It was coming down so hard and the wind was howling away!

"A fine beginning for a ghost story," he said to himself, shaking his head. "A letter that was franked on a date it couldn't have been sent. Written by someone with the grim and gruesome name of Gr... Gr... And tomorrow he's sending his 'man' to pick me up, at half past seven precisely. Who on earth does he think he is, ordering me about like that?"

THAT WAS ONE *and now for Part Two*

2

Frans goes for a ride in the dark

In a carriage through the rain

THIS IS ONE

It wasn't Maarten who was the first to ask if their teacher's new adventure had begun yet. Marian beat him to it, at quarter to three, when they were drawing.

"Sir," she said, "what was in the letter?"

Frans gave her a piercing stare. Marian looked like an angel, but a very mischievous one, and she wrote wildly imaginative essays about secret treasures hidden away in even more secret passages. But her handwriting and spelling were so bad that the letter couldn't possibly have come from her.

"What are you talking about, Marian?" he asked.

"About the letter that was going to arrive yesterday," she said. "You told us that..." Then she fell silent and blushed.

Mr Van der Steg looked around the class. The children stared back at him. *They're all in on it,* he thought. *They know more about this whole business than I do – I'm sure of it!* And he said slowly, "Yesterday evening, with a flash of lightning and a crash of thunder, the letter came blowing into the house. I found it lying on the mat."

The children looked as if they were really interested to find out what would happen next. "I was astonished," he continued, "because I have no idea who sent it, but he knew my name and address and..."

"But you told us he was going to write to you," said Maarten, interrupting him. "So you must know him! I mean..."

"Don't interrupt when I'm speaking, Maarten," said Frans van der Steg. "I was expecting a letter, that's true, but not this one..." He paused, not quite sure what to say next. Until now, he'd always had complete control of the adventures he'd invented. But even if the children were somehow involved, it wouldn't have been kind of him to keep quiet about the letter. So he said, "According to the person who sent this letter, I wrote to him too, last week. But I didn't."

"Ooh, it's so mysterious," whispered Marian. Her eyes were sparkling and there was a smudge of green paint on her nose.

"Who..." began Maarten. Then he put up his hand and asked politely, "Who sent it, sir?"

"I don't know. He calls himself Gr... Gr..." Frans turned around and wrote the name on the board in big letters. He was beginning to enjoy himself. "It sounds like a growl or a groan, don't you think?" he said. "He must be a grisly grump. Or maybe a griping grouch. Gr... Gr... Do you think his surname's Grumplestiltskin?"

"He's a greasy grotbag," said Kai.

"A grim grizzly bear!" cried Maarten.

"He wants me to pay him a visit this evening," Frans continued. "He's sending his man to take me to his house in the woods... But," he added in a brisk tone, "his man will have a wasted journey, because I won't be at home." That was true. On Fridays he always went into town for his evening classes.

But the children thought that was wrong of him. Imagine not being at home when a gruesome grouch is sending his man to pick you up so that you can pay him a visit. Surely their teacher didn't mean it...

It took Frans some time to calm them down.

"This Mr Gr... Gr... mustn't think he can boss me around!" he declared. "If he's so keen to speak to me, then let him come to me. And I shall tell him exactly what I think of him."

At twenty-five past seven that evening, Frans van der Steg put his books in his bag. Then he wrapped his scarf around his neck, wondering if he should go on his bike or take the bus into town. It was still raining, so he decided on the bus. *I'll have to run,* he thought, *or I'll miss it.*

As he stood in the hallway, putting on his coat, the doorbell rang. "I'll get it!" he called to Mrs Bakker, who was washing up in the kitchen. "And then I'll be off."

On the doorstep stood a large man in a dark coat. He'd put up his collar and pulled his cap down almost over his eyes. Frans couldn't see much of his face, just a big red nose. He stood there in the storm, rain and hail, and said bluntly, "Are you Van der Steg?"

"Yes, that's me," replied Frans, and then he saw a carriage on the road in front of the house – an old-fashioned coach with a black horse.

"It's half past seven," said the stranger. "I'm here to fetch you."

"Yes, but..." Frans began.

His landlady called from the kitchen, "Close the door, Frans! Do you want me to blow away?"

"Get in," said the man. Then he turned around and walked to the coach.

Frans headed outside, closing the door behind him. He wanted to tell the stranger that he had another appointment and so he couldn't go with him. But the man didn't give him the opportunity. He climbed up front into the driver's seat and pointed his long whip at the coach door.

"Get in!" he ordered.

"Do you think I'm mad?" replied Frans van der Steg. But suddenly the adventurous spirit of his own stories took hold of him. *Why not?*

He climbed in, closed the door – and sat there in the carriage, with his bag full of books beside him. They moved off – the wheels rattling, the horses' hoofs click-clacking on the road, the wind whistling through the gaps around the windows, and the rain drumming on the roof. The coach sped up, going faster and faster, swaying and wobbling, and it was pitch dark inside.

"Ah, yes, it would seem that I am in fact mad," Frans said to himself. "I'm skiving off my classes and I don't even know where this grumpy coachman is taking me."

Frans couldn't see anything through the windows. He tried to open one, but it wouldn't budge. For a moment, he just sat there. Then he raised his voice and shouted, "Hey, coachman! Coachman! Where are we going?"

There was no answer. Just the sound of rain and wind, of wheels and hoofs. He fiddled with the windows again, tugging and banging on them. And as he did so (with no luck), he realized he wasn't enjoying himself at all. Then the carriage suddenly rounded a bend, and he fell off the seat. When he'd picked himself back up, he noticed that the thud of the horses' hoofs sounded much duller now. They seemed to be riding along a dirt track, so they must have left the village behind. *As I live in a somewhat remote spot in the woods...*

But of course he couldn't be afraid – not Frans the Red, the Hero of Torelore and the Vanquisher of the Abominable Snowman!

But I do wish I could see something, he thought. Again he tried to open a window. This time he realized that he needed to pull it down; it was stiff, but he finally managed it. The wind blew about his ears, but at least he could look outside now.

Yes, they were riding along a dirt track. A lantern hung on the outside of the coach, but its light was weak and it kept swaying, so he couldn't make out very much at all. He could vaguely see fields and a dark sky above. There was no sign of the village – no houses, no barns, no farms. Frans leant out of the window and yelled at the coachman, "Hey, you! Where are you taking me?"

The coachman didn't appear to hear him; he just cracked his whip and the carriage went even faster.

Frans sat back down. The coach was shaking him about, and he was beginning to feel rather cold. He couldn't get the window closed again, so he just sat and looked outside.

"A nice little ride in the countryside," he muttered to himself. "In a coach that must be over a hundred years old... the suspension isn't in great condition and I wouldn't be surprised if a wheel fell off. And all at some ungodly hour... But no, it can't be much later than eight o'clock..." He tried to remember if he'd ever seen this coach before – as far as he knew, there was nothing like it in the village. They were riding through a copse of trees now. The village was surrounded by plenty of woodland, and Frans had already been for a few bike rides, but it was too dark to make out anything that might have been familiar.

As the coach slowed down, he leant out of the window again and thought he could see a light through the trees. Then they swung around another bend, bounced across a pothole and, with a jolt, came to a stop.

Silence. Only the sound of the rain.

"Are we there?" Frans called to the coachman.

"Not yet," came his gruff voice. "This is Sevenways."

"And where exactly are we going?" asked Frans.

The coach jerked forward before stopping again. They'd come to a clearing. Frans could see a signpost nearby. "Where are we going?" he asked again.

"Don't have to tell you that, do I?" was the grumpy reply.

Now Frans felt a flash of anger. He turned the door handle, which – wonder of wonders! – opened right away. Then he leapt out of the coach, walked to the front and yelled, "What kind of way is this to treat a person? I refuse to go any farther until I know where we're going."

"Sir!" barked the coachman. "Don't tell me you know nothing about it!" He waved his whip in the air.

Frans looked around. They'd stopped at a point where a number of paths met and he could see the outline of a house nearby. There was light in one of the windows.

"If you don't get back in," said the coachman, "you're going to get soaked." He clearly didn't say it out of concern for Frans though, as it sounded more like a threat when he continued, "And you'd better be quick about it, or we'll be late."

Frans took a step backwards and trod in a puddle. For the second time, he felt something that was a little like fear. He glanced at the house again and saw the glint of a sign. It looked like a pub, which meant he couldn't be too far from civilization. So, firmly, he said, "I'm not getting back into this carriage until I find out who you are and what our destination is."

"As you wish, sir!" called the coachman. "If you don't want to go beyond Sevenways, then you can stay at Sevenways! Good evening."

He cracked his whip and shook the reins. The coach moved off, narrowly missing Frans and splashing him with mud, before heading down one of the tracks.

"If this is a joke, it's gone too far!" Frans muttered angrily, and he stared after the coach until it disappeared from sight. "Leaving me in the pouring rain at Sevenways. The Seven Ways! I thought that was just a song or a dance..."

But there was the pub, where he could shelter and have a hot drink. He'd have to walk back home, but he didn't want to think too hard about that for now.

The light in the window moved and, as he walked towards the building, it went out. Frans paused for a moment. It was so dark! The pub couldn't be closed, could it? He felt his way through the dark, groping for the door. It was open, and so he went straight in. The place was even darker inside, but at least it was dry.

"Hello?" he called. His voice echoed strangely. "Hello!" he called again. "Anyone home?"

No one answered.

Frans shivered. Suddenly he knew he was in an abandoned building, in a room without furniture or people. He couldn't see his hand in front of his face, but there had been a light just now... It hadn't been an ordinary light though, he realized, more like a torch or something similar. So there must be someone else inside the building... He listened carefully, but the pouring rain drowned out any other sounds.

Hesitantly, he took a few steps. He felt another door and went into a second room. And he found himself standing in the rain again... No one could live in this building; the roof wasn't even intact.

He went back to the first room, where he leant against a wall, clenching his fists inside his coat pockets. If this had happened in one of his stories, he'd definitely have had some kind of weapon in one of those pockets.

He held his breath for a moment. Above his head, he could see light through the cracks in the ceiling. It shifted, disappeared... and a second later it shone directly into his face. He blinked. There was a staircase in front of him and someone was coming down, with a torch in his hand.

On a scooter with a biker boy

THIS IS TWO

"What are you doing here?" asked the stranger, coming closer. He was quite short and slight, and he was wearing a crash helmet. His voice sounded young and not at all surprised. Frans was sure he'd never met him before though.

"I'm sheltering from the rain," was all Frans said.

"Yeah, it's chucking it down," the young man replied. "Look, it's raining bricks." He stopped next to Frans and gave the wall a couple of whacks. A couple of bricks came tumbling down.

Frans leapt out of the way. "Hey, watch out!" he yelled.

"This whole place is going to collapse before long," the young man said cheerfully. "Hey, Jan!" he called, with one hand up to his mouth. "Bring us something to drink!" He turned back to Frans and said, "You didn't really think this was a pub, did you?" And he shone his torch in Frans's face again.

Frans thought this was very unpleasant – not just because he couldn't see anything now, but also because he felt ridiculous. "But it used to be a pub though," he said.

"Yes, it used to. Tooreloor's Tavern."

"Torelore's?" said Frans with surprise.

"Tooreloor, Jan Tooreloor, what are we all waiting for?"

chanted the young voice in the darkness. "But he's gone now and this is a haunted house... or a haunted pub."

Frans stepped aside to avoid the irritating beam of light. But the torch followed him and the voice asked, "So who are you and what are you doing here?"

"My name is Frans van der Steg," Frans answered coldly. "Will you stop shining that light in my eyes? And, if I might ask, who are you?"

The young man in the crash helmet turned the torch on himself. Frans saw he was just a boy, around sixteen years old, and that he was wearing a black leather jacket.

"And jeans and biker boots with pointed toes," said the boy, shining the light on them. Then he showed Frans his face again, looking at him with a mocking sneer. "That's right," he said. "I'm a biker."

"Oh," replied Frans. "And what's your name?"

"I call myself the Biker Boy and that's what I am," the boy replied. "My scooter's outside."

"And what are you doing here?"

"That's my question," said the Biker Boy. "I asked first. Why did you come here in that stupid old coach? You meeting a date here or something?" He grinned and added, "Don't think she'll come all the way out to this spooky hole. There are ghosts here after sunset."

"What nonsense," snapped Frans. "You know, my business here is actually none of your concern. But maybe I should be concerned about what you're up to."

"Oh yeah?" said the Biker Boy. "Whatever you say. Actually, as it happens, I could do with some help. I've been looking all over for a packet of cigarettes I left lying around here..."

"And I'm sure you'd like me to help you look, wouldn't you?" said Frans sarcastically. He didn't believe a word of the Biker Boy's tale.

"You can try," said the Biker Boy. He swept his torch around the room. It had clearly once been the pub's main bar, but now it was empty and bare, dirty and rundown. "But you won't find it," the Biker Boy continued. "There are three cigarettes in the packet, and my mates drew a skull on it, with their signatures underneath."

The circle of light paused at a hole in the ceiling, illuminating a cobweb and a big fat spider.

"It was a bet," the Biker Boy said. "We were out here this afternoon, me and my mates, and they said I wouldn't dare to come back after sunset. So I bet them I would. I'm supposed to bring back the cigarette packet they left here as proof that I came... Hey, you don't have it, do you?"

"Of course not," said Frans. "I got here after you."

Then there was a sudden bang above his head, as if something had fallen. Frans jumped.

"Ha, what a chicken!" the Biker Boy scoffed. "It was just the storm blowing off another roof tile. No need to tremble like that!"

Frans looked up at the ceiling. Was that a footstep he'd heard?

The Biker Boy grabbed his arm. "Listen here," he said. "I have to get back before the second showing and..."

"The second showing? What showing?" asked Frans.

The Biker Boy looked at him with round, dark eyes. "We're going to the cinema," he said, "and if I win the bet, they're going to pay. You can at least prove I was here, so you'll have to come with me as a witness."

"Why would I ever...?" Frans began.

"I'll take you on the back of my scooter. So you'll have a lift into town. Or were you planning to walk home?"

"You don't even know where I live!"

"You're right, and I don't care," said the Biker Boy. "Come on. We'll be there in twenty minutes."

Maybe it's not such a bad idea, thought Frans. He didn't really trust the Biker Boy, but once he was in town, it'd be easy enough to get home. It was too late for his evening class now anyway. Then he cursed under his breath.

"What's wrong?" asked the Biker Boy.

"I left my bag in the coach, with all my books in it," said Frans, "and that wretched coachman's driven off with it. Do you know who he is?"

"Why are you asking me?" said the Biker Boy. "You're the one who went for a ride in that thing, not me! Did anyone ever tell you you're a bit weird?"

He's not wrong, thought Frans. But what he said out loud was, "If you want me to be your witness, you'll need to be a bit more polite."

"Fine. Okay!" said the Biker Boy. "Come on."

Soon after that, the boy climbed proudly onto his scooter. He revved the engine and the bright beam of the headlight lit up the sheet of falling raindrops.

Frans got on behind him. There were supposed to be seven paths here, but he had no idea which one went into town. It was actually a stroke of luck that he'd run into the Biker Boy – how else would he have found his way home?

But as they noisily sped off, he began to change his mind. Not just because he was getting colder and wetter by the second,

but mostly because he was worried every moment might be his last. The Biker Boy rode his scooter hard, racing faster and faster, and tearing around the bends.

"So irresponsible," Frans said to himself, as the trees flashed by and the wind whistled around his ears. His ride in the coach had actually been a lot calmer. Sometimes he thought he could hear the Biker Boy singing above the din of the engine. He seemed to be enjoying himself.

That's just what I'd expect of him. He's trying to frighten me, thought Frans van der Steg. However, the Hero of Torelore gritted his teeth and spoke fiercely to himself, "But he won't succeed!"

Even so, he sighed with relief when they reached a road with a tarmac surface and a sign with a speed limit. The Biker Boy slowed down (although he must still have been above the speed limit) and called back over his shoulder, "It's not quite ten to nine by the church clock. I've beaten my record!"

"And you didn't break your neck doing it!" Frans shouted back to him. "Congratulations!"

Shortly after that, they rode into town, and by nine they'd stopped at a chip shop. There was a cinema across the road, with a few young men in leather jackets hanging around outside. One of them saw the Biker Boy and gave a loud whistle.

"Are they your friends?" asked Frans.

"The film won't have started yet," said the Biker Boy, ignoring Frans. "I'm going to get some chips first. This weather! Come on."

They both had a bag of chips. Frans rubbed his glasses clean, put them back on, and looked carefully at the Biker Boy. For the first time he could see him properly. The Biker Boy stared back at him too, weighing him up. Then he said, "Wait here a moment for me," and he walked off. Frans watched him cross the street and start talking to the boys in leather jackets outside the cinema.

"Right then," said the man in the chip shop. "So that was two bags of chips..."

Frans paid for the chips, and when he looked up again, there wasn't a soul in front of the cinema. He waited a couple of minutes before crossing the street and heading into the cinema lobby. The Biker Boy and his mates weren't there either. The man behind the ticket desk looked at him expectantly and asked, "Want to buy a ticket, sir?"

"No, thank you," said Frans. "I'm waiting for someone."

He chose a spot where he could keep an eye on the chip shop, and stood there a while. The scooter was still there, but the Biker Boy didn't show up. He could hear dramatic music coming from inside the auditorium. The film must be starting.

Frans went to the man at the ticket desk and said, "Did a couple of... young men in leather jackets just go inside?"

"The cinema's full of yobs in leather jackets these days," the man replied sadly. "I'm a father, sir, and there's no way I'd ever let my children go to the second showing. And if they ever get a scooter, I don't want them racing around aimlessly like that bunch of hooligans. Those things should only be used for getting from A to B, don't you think?" His face had brightened up now that he had someone to talk to. "I might work at a cinema," he said, "but how often do you think I watch films? Never! I'm all for healthier ways to spend your time. Camping, for instance. A tent in the woods, away from civilization, that's what you want! But these youngsters nowadays, they're all too lazy for that..."

Frans listened to him for a while, still keeping an eye out for the Biker Boy, even though he was sure he wouldn't turn up. He was probably watching the film with his mates.

Well, he needn't think I'm going to hang around here waiting for him, he thought to himself. *He can have those chips in exchange for the lift. But I'll be happy if I never see him again. Ignorant lout!*

Frans said goodbye to the man at the ticket desk and walked to the nearest stop to catch the bus back to his village. He was chilly and wet and disappointed with himself. In one of his own stories, this evening would have turned out very differently. *But*, he thought, *I can't quite imagine how...*

THAT WAS TWO *and now for Part Three*

3

Frans finds out who Gr... Gr... is

He follows the carriage's trail and ends up at the Thirsty Deer

THIS IS ONE

The next morning the wind had blown away all the rainclouds. The weather was cool, but fine, and the sun was shining as if summer still lingered. But Frans van der Steg cycled to school with a frown on his face.

He had the growing feeling that he should have acted differently the night before. The children would be sure to want to hear about his adventures, but the role he'd played had been anything but clever or heroic. *I shouldn't have got into the coach,* he thought. *No, I shouldn't have got out of it. I really should have made that coachman answer my questions and boxed the Biker Boy's ears... Oh, and I wish I'd never made up that story about a mysterious letter.*

It was Saturday, which meant the class would be expecting at least half an hour of stories. Frans had brought a book to school with him, and when it was time he read out one of the stories. As he reached the last page, he kept glancing at his watch and he went as slowly as he could. But the story was still finished before twelve. The bell wouldn't ring for another three minutes... and, of course, the children asked the question he'd been dreading.

"Sir, did you visit Gr... Gr... yesterday?"

"No," answered Frans truthfully, and he wondered yet again if that person actually existed. He raised his hand to fend off more questions. "Listen, chaps," he said in a serious tone. "I'm afraid I'm on the trail of a strange and dangerous secret. I can't tell you any more than that at the moment... And now I'd like to ask you a question. Do any of you know or suspect the actual identity of Gr... Gr...? Because the man must have a name!"

The classroom was very quiet. Some of the children stared at him with wide eyes, while others deliberately looked away. Marian, who blushed easily, went bright red.

Frans van der Steg cleared his throat. He really did feel very uneasy... just as if there actually were some dangerous secrets involved! Or was it because he felt like he was somehow fooling his class? But there was no way back now, and he had to break the awkward silence.

"Perhaps it's better if anyone who knows something about this speaks to me in private," he said. "You can always talk to me after school."

Now they all started whispering, and somehow it sounded different... *Don't start imagining things*, Frans told himself. *You just caught a little chill yesterday, that's all.*

Then, fortunately, the bell went, and he could send them on their way.

As he was marking books in the empty classroom, Marian suddenly appeared beside his desk. "Sir..." she began shyly.

Three boys were standing in the doorway – Maarten, Kai and Arie.

"What is it?" asked Frans.

The boys came over to the desk as well. "Sir," said Maarten – of course he was the first one to speak – "it's about what you just said in the lesson..."

"Gr... Gr..." Kai growled softly.

"Do you know who Gr... Gr... is?"

"Oh, no, no," the children answered at the same time.

"No, sir," said Maarten. "But we want to help you if we can. Could we... can we... We'd really like to take a look at the letter!"

"That's right," said Marian. "Maybe we'll see something useful. Would you mind?"

Frans took the letter out of his pocket, where he'd slipped it that morning. Without saying anything, he placed it on the desk and watched as the children studied it. He couldn't see their faces, but they seemed to be completely serious. Marian was the first to look up; she was blushing again, but that didn't necessarily mean anything.

"No idea," she said breathlessly.

"Me neither," said Kai and Arie. Maarten just shook his head.

"Well, that's a shame," said Frans as casually as possible. "But thanks anyway."

The children shuffled their feet and looked a bit embarrassed.

"Do any of you know a biker?" asked Frans.

Now the children looked puzzled. "A biker?" repeated Marian. "What do you mean?"

"One of those yobs in leather jackets who race around on scooters," said Maarten. "That's what you mean, isn't it, sir?"

"My brother's got a scooter," said Kai. "But he's not a yob."

"That's what you say!" said Arie.

But Maarten asked, "Is this biker part of the secret too?"

"Maybe," replied Frans. "He rides along the roads in the dark, talks about ghosts and then disappears without saying goodbye."

"And then?" asked Marian, like it was a story.

"I don't know yet," said Frans. "Well, maybe you'll get to hear more about it, and maybe not. We'll just have to wait and see. And if you have anything to report, come and talk to me! See you on Monday."

The children left, but Maarten popped back and whispered, "This is for real, isn't it, sir?"

"Yes, Maarten," Frans said, with a nod, "it's for real." And, as he spoke those words, he meant what he said.

Just a moment later, though, he'd changed his mind. If it was for real, there had to be some logical explanation, and he couldn't think of one.

"It's a conspiracy," he said to himself, "and those four children are part of it – maybe even the whole class!"

But as he cycled home, he whistled a happy tune. Now he knew what he needed to do! He was free that afternoon, so he'd go back to Sevenways and take a good look around in daylight. He'd follow the trail of the carriage and find the solution to all these puzzles. On Monday he'd tell the children the end of the story – and he was sure they'd all be amazed.

*

After lunch, he asked his landlady, "Have you ever heard of Sevenways?"

She looked at him with some surprise, or at least he imagined she did. "Seven Ways?" she repeated. "People say that I can't dance..."

"No, I don't mean that Seven Ways," said Frans. "It's just... I... Well... Apparently there's, um, a crossroads near here with seven paths..."

"It sounds to me like you're all at sixes and sevens," his landlady said. "Why are you interested in Sevenways?"

"I'd like to go there," said Frans. "Just for a bike ride."

"That's a good idea," she replied. "It'd be nice for you to get out and about a bit. Sevenways isn't hard to find: down the high street, left at the petrol station, and then take the first turn-off after Dijkhof's farm. Have fun!"

Soon after that, Frans was cycling along the route that the carriage had taken the evening before. After the farmyard, the road got worse and worse, all mud and huge puddles, but he didn't let that put him off. The weather was still fine and he could see the tracks the coach had left. He didn't know the countryside around him, but it was beautiful and very quiet, with not a single house in sight.

After cycling for half an hour, he came to Sevenways, the point where so many paths met in the middle of the woods.

He got off his bike. The abandoned building was on his right, the haunted pub, as the Biker Boy had called it. It was indeed little more than a ruin; in this bright afternoon light there was no mistake about it.

In front of him was the signpost. It pointed in seven directions. He'd just come along one of those roads, and another went into town. That was the path he'd been along yesterday with the Biker Boy; the tracks of the scooter were clearly visible. The marks left by the carriage were much deeper. It had driven on along a third path, which, according to the signpost, led to the village of Roskam. The fourth way went to Langelaan. The fifth arm of the signpost was very narrow and was simply painted blood red. The sixth went to the "Herb Garden", and there was no seventh way.

Frans counted them again – yes, there really were only six ways. The seventh arm of the signpost pointed at the ruin. There had once been something written on it, but most of the letters were gone. He could make out a T at the beginning and then an O... no, it wasn't Tooreloor... And there was an S and a T... with an R and an S at the end.

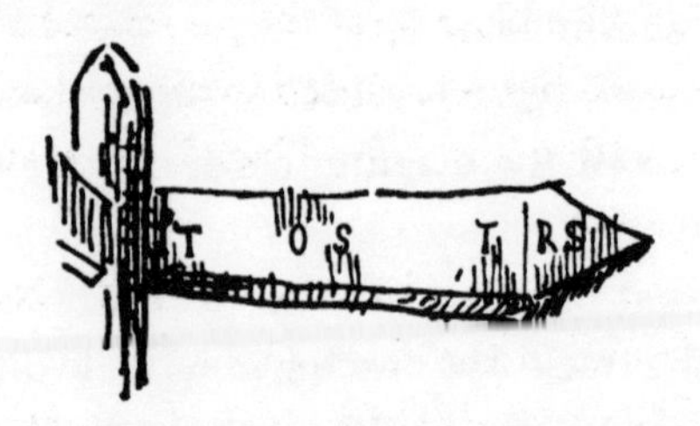

"I don't understand why a place with six paths would be called Sevenways," he said to himself. "Aunt Wilhelmina's right about me being at sixes and sevens."

He leant his bike against the signpost and walked over to the building. It had two sections. One part had clearly been the pub. Above the door, which was still open, the pub sign banged away on its last hinge. The other part of the building had probably been used as a garage or shed. Its large double doors turned out to be locked.

Frans went through the open door and headed up the creaking stairs to the first floor. The whole place looked so rickety that he didn't dare to venture any farther. Cobwebs brushed his face and he could see footprints on the dusty floor... the Biker Boy's, of course. But then he saw that someone else must have been walking about up there. There were tracks left by two pairs of shoes, one with more pointed toes than the other. He remembered the bang he'd heard upstairs the night before... Had there been someone else in the building with them?

"Don't start pretending you're a detective now," said Frans van der Steg to Frans the Red.

He went back down the stairs, and saw nothing out of the ordinary, not even the cigarette packet that the Biker Boy had been looking for.

Back outside, he looked up at the pub sign. He could vaguely make out a human figure, painted in red, but a skull had been daubed over it with a few angry black lines. Haunted or not, it was a sinister place.

Frans got back onto his bike and took the road to Roskam, following the route of the carriage.

First he rode through a dark wood, which already smelt like autumn, and then past fields and meadows, before he saw the village ahead. It was very small, with a squat church at its centre. The muddy track became a brick road, which curved into the village. On the bend was a pub – not a haunted one this time. It looked like an old-fashioned inn for travellers. The name suited it: "The Thirsty Deer".

And thirsty's what I am! thought Frans. *I'll stop for a drink.*

He parked his bike and took a quick look around before heading inside. On the other side of the road was a majestic chestnut tree and, behind it, a coach house. As he stood there, the doors opened wide and a carriage came rattling out.

The very carriage he was looking for!

It was definitely the same man sitting up front. He looked less mysterious now, but just as unfriendly. He'd knotted a scarf around his head that was even redder than his nose and made him look like some kind of highwayman.

The coachman paused for a moment and saw Frans hurrying towards him. Then he cracked his whip and urged his horse on.

"Hey, wait a moment!" Frans called.

But the coach continued on its way, and Frans had to jump back or it would have rolled right over his toes. Frans ran after it. "Stop, stop!" he yelled.

The coachman ignored him. And the coach drove on, faster and faster, into the village, before disappearing from sight.

Frans walked back to the Thirsty Deer. He was furious.

Would he be able to catch up with the coach on his bike? He could try, but if he didn't make it, he'd just feel even more stupid. He thought he could see lots of people at the windows of the pub, all of them looking at him. He decided not to worry about it and to go inside.

Inside the pub, it looked just as you would have expected from the outside: quaint and very cosy. The room had a tiled floor and a dark wooden ceiling. There were small tables with red-checked cloths and one large table with untidy newspapers and rings left behind by glasses. There was lots of copperware, and one corner had a billiards table with some men playing. A jovial landlord stood behind the bar, drying cups with a brightly coloured cloth.

The pub had no radio or television. The only sounds were the click-clack of the balls, the clink of glasses and the murmuring of the guests. It was quite busy, and all of the customers were men. Some of them glanced up when Frans came in, but most paid him no attention.

"What will it be, sir?" the landlord asked chirpily.

"A beer, please," said Frans, and then he continued, "By the way, I just saw an old-fashioned carriage out there across the street. I wanted to speak to the driver, but he drove off. Do you have any idea where he's from?"

"Oh, that'll have been Jan," replied the landlord. "He's Count Gradus Grisenstein's coachman."

"Count Gradus Grisenstein?" repeated Frans.

Everything in the pub suddenly stopped. The silence was so unexpected that Frans looked around in surprise. The men at the tables stared at him. The billiard players turned their backs on their game. Only one man, a grey-haired man with a beard, who was sitting at the large table, calmly went on playing patience.

Frans didn't know what to do with himself. But then everyone looked away and started behaving completely normally again. He wondered if he'd just imagined it, and so he said once again, raising his voice a little, "Count Gradus Grisenstein's coachman, eh?"

No one reacted. The balls calmly click-clacked again. The guests went on playing, drinking, smoking and talking and paid no attention to Frans.

"There you go, sir," said the landlord, pulling up a chair for him. "I'll just bring your beer over." Then he hurried off, as if to avoid more questions.

Frans sat down, still not entirely recovered from his surprise. *Gradus Grisenstein's coachman. Gradus Grisenstein...*

Gr... Gr...! He took out the letter, opened it up and looked at the signature.

Yes, now that he knew the name, he could clearly make it out. It definitely said *Gradus Grisenstein*!

Suddenly he felt someone's eyes peering over his shoulder. He glanced back to find someone standing there, brazenly trying to read the letter.

As Frans glared in speechless fury, the young man, not at all flustered, gave him a friendly smile and said, "Good afternoon!" He had a pleasant face, although his straight brown hair was far too long for Frans's liking. His large, dark eyes studied Frans with obvious interest. "Cigarette?" he said, holding out a packet.

Frans was so surprised that he accepted. The young man didn't take one himself. He pulled his chair over, threw the packet on Frans's table and looked for some matches.

"Here, I've a light for you," said a polite voice. The man with the grey beard had appeared beside them. In one hand he held a pack of playing cards and in the other was a lighter with a huge blue flame.

"Thank you," said Frans. Silently, he took a few drags. The young man sat there as if expecting Frans to do something. Who was he? He seemed so familiar...

Suddenly he realized. It was the Biker Boy. He looked very different, without his crash helmet and leather jacket, but it was definitely him.

"I know you," said Frans.

The boy raised his eyebrows. "I'm sorry. You're mistaken," was his reply. "I'm sure I don't know you."

"Yes, you do!" said Frans. "We met yesterday evening."

And he gave the Biker Boy a stern look, as if he were one of his naughtiest students.

"Yesterday?" said the boy, with a puzzled expression. "Where?"

"At Sevenways," replied Frans.

"I was here last night, at the Thirsty Deer," the boy said, so firmly that Frans started to doubt himself. "Everyone here can be my witness."

But the word "witness" just reminded Frans of the Biker Boy and his bet. "That's not true!" he said sharply.

The boy, however, was just as calm as before. "You might think you've met me," he said, "but I've never seen you before. Honestly. I'll swear it by all six paths of the Seven Ways."

Now the man with the beard joined their conversation. "Then we can only conclude, Roberto," he said, "that you have a double." He sat down at Frans's table, gave them both a friendly nod and shuffled the dog-eared cards with clean, white fingers.

"Roberto!" called one of the men at the billiards table. "Are you coming? It's your turn!"

Roberto smiled at Frans, jumped to his feet and went over to join the players. Frans watched him until the landlord arrived with his beer. Putting the letter back into his pocket, he asked, "So who is this Count Grisenstein and where does he live?"

"Ah, I'm needed elsewhere, sir," said the landlord. "Be with you in a moment." And he scuttled off.

A conspiracy, thought Frans. *The longer this goes on, the more it seems like a conspiracy... Whatever next?*

"Take a card," said the man with the grey beard. He fanned out the pack and held them out to Frans. "Choose one," he ordered, "and look to see what it is."

Frans did as he was told. It was the seven of hearts.

"Don't show it to me," said the man, "and put it back in the pack. That's right." Again he shuffled the cards, put them on the table and gave them a tap. "Now reach into your right trouser pocket," he said.

Frans did so and pulled out a playing card. "Seven of hearts!" he exclaimed.

"Let's do it again," the man said cheerfully. "And pay closer attention this time. No, don't think too long about it."

The same ritual was repeated. This time Frans took the jack of spades from his left inside pocket.

"In the art of using playing cards to predict the future, the jack of spades is the villain," said his peculiar companion. "That's food for thought, eh?" He stood up and bowed. "It was a pleasure," he said. And, in a low voice, he added, "You'll find something else in your left inside pocket."

Then he calmly walked off, exchanged a few words with

the landlord at the bar and left the pub. Frans stared after him, reaching into his pocket to find that there was indeed something else in there. It wasn't a playing card, but a business card, a rectangular piece of white card with the following words printed on it in a nice, neat font:

J. THOMTIDOM
Magician

As he looked at the card, other letters took shape beneath the name – handwritten letters. At first they were hazy and red, then they gleamed in grass-green and finally turned pitch-black before his unbelieving eyes. They formed three sentences:

> *You'd better not say the name Grisenstein out loud. If you'd like to find out more about him, come and visit me tomorrow after church. My house, "Appearance and Reality", is on the road from Sevenways to Langelaan.*

"This is all too much!" Frans said to himself, and he slipped the card back into his pocket with slightly trembling fingers. "First a doppelganger and then a magician..."

Someone tapped him on the shoulder, making him jump. It was Roberto.

"Don't forget your beer," the young man said. "See you around."

"Are you off?" asked Frans. "Hey, wait a moment..."

"I have a suspicion we'll meet again before long," said Roberto. "For the second time." He didn't wait for a reply, but quickly headed for the door.

A number of the other guests called goodbye as he left. "See you, Roberto!"

No, that friendly young man couldn't possibly be the Biker Boy.

Deep in thought, Frans drank his beer. *Is Gr… Gr… really such a grotesque and grisly grouch,* he thought, *that no one's allowed to say his name out loud? I'll have to visit that magician. I just hope he's not trying to fool me somehow…*

Without thinking, he took a cigarette from the packet on the table, and then realized it didn't belong to him. Roberto had left it there. Roberto's packet... A skull was drawn on it in biro, with three messy signatures around it. So the story about the double wasn't true. Roberto and the Biker Boy were indeed one and the same person!

And now the young man had disappeared for the second time.

Frans stood up, and then sat back down. *I can spare myself the trouble of going after him,* he thought gloomily. *I'm sure I won't find him. All the people I meet keep popping up and then vanishing like characters in a puppet show! And they act about as strangely as puppets too.*

He looked around the bar, suddenly feeling ill at ease, even though it seemed so cosy. He felt as if the other men were giving him sidelong glances, and secretly watching him, and he imagined they were nudging one another behind his back and whispering about him. The landlord was still behind the bar. He didn't look cheery now, and had an impenetrable expression on his face.

If I asked him another question, thought Frans, *I'm sure he'd just give me a mysterious look and his answers would all be vague or false.*

So he downed his beer, paid, and went home.

He visits a magician and finds out that appearances are deceptive

THIS IS TWO

"Rrr...! Rrr...!" trilled the alarm clock.

"Grr...! Grr...!" went Frans's thoughts. "Count Grisenstein... don't say the name out loud... Grr... Rrr...!"

He reached out to turn off the alarm.

"Gr... Gr... Grisly greybeard... No, that's the magician... Magician? Pah. He just knows a few conjuring tricks..."

Frans stayed in bed, his eyes half closed. "Invisible ink, that's what it is!" he said to himself. "It only becomes visible when it's heated up... I read something about it once. So it was the warmth of my left inside pocket..."

He threw off the covers. He'd set the alarm clock for a reason; he had to get up and dressed, as he was going to pay a visit to Mr Thomtidom, magician, conjurer or prankster.

A quarter of an hour later, he was downstairs.

"Good morning," said his landlady, who was standing in front of the mirror in the hallway, trying different hats on top of her grey curls. "It's very early for you to be up and about!"

"I'm going out," said Frans. He went into the kitchen and took some bread from the cupboard. On Sundays he always made his own breakfast.

"That's nice," his landlady said. "I'm glad you've finally realized you can't spend all day with your nose stuck in books."

"I don't have any books now," grumbled Frans, as he buttered the bread. "So I'll have to stick my nose into other things." With a thoughtful look on his face, he ate a piece of cheese. "Does this Count Grisenstein actually exist?" he wondered to himself. "I really should find out. Hang on a moment..."

With a piece of bread in his hand, he walked to the telephone. It was in the hallway, under the stairs. As usual, he bumped his head. "Ow!" he yelled.

"I always think it's handy having the phone there in the hallway," his landlady said. "But you're so clumsy. You keep banging your head. Every single time! Which hat do you think suits me better, the black one or the purple?"

"The black one," said Frans, even though he thought they were both equally unattractive. "And I'm not clumsy, Mrs Bakker. I'm just too tall." He sat down on the chair by the telephone and started flicking through the phone book.

F... G... Ga... Go... Gr... Graf with one f and Graff with two fs... Gravenstijn... Green... Grisenberg... No Grisenstein.

"I'll wear the purple one," Mrs Bakker decided. "I don't see why I should always wear a black hat to church. Oh, and Frans, lunch today is at half past one precisely. You'll be back by then, won't you?"

He nodded.

"Then make sure you're on time," she said. "I want to go out at two. I'm off to visit my sister and it's quite a walk."

"I'll be there," said Frans, not really listening. No, it wasn't in the phonebook. "So where does this Count Grisenstein live?" he wondered out loud.

His landlady said something about a "house" and "stairs" and added, "See you later."

The front door closed behind her.

Frans stayed where he was sitting. "So Count Grisenstein's house is on the stairs, is it?" he muttered. "Where exactly? In the cupboard under the stairs or on the landing? No, Count Grisenstein doesn't exist... not really. But, in that case, how does Mrs Bakker know about him?"

He stood up, banged his head again, and said with a sigh, "No, I'm not going to think about it anymore. First I'll finish my breakfast and then I'll visit Mr Magician. And let's hope, once I'm inside his house, I'll learn to tell the difference between Appearance and Reality."

The weather was sunny and calm, and church bells were ringing in the distance. For the second time, Frans cycled to Sevenways. He was singing an old song from days gone by:

Green, green, so green the grass
the grass beneath my feet.
Oh, where's my friend, my oldest friend,
so dear and oh so sweet?

At the signpost he got off his bike and walked around a little. It was early and the invitation had been for "after church".

Six ways, he thought. *Well, I know where three of them lead now, and I'll be going along the fourth one before long. Maybe I'll take a look at the fifth and sixth paths at some point too. But there isn't a seventh way, and that's decidedly strange.* He started singing again:

Green, green, so green the grass,
What do I seek to find?
A mysterious count and my missing books.
You have them? Oh, *so kind…*

Frans moved on to a different song:

In The Hague there lives a count –

and then he started again:

In a house there lives a count
and his…

Then he faltered and stared at the seventh arm of the signpost. Was it just a coincidence? He could read it very clearly: the T, and the O and the S, and the T, R and S he'd seen before – and he could fill in the rest of the letters now. HOUSE. STAIRS. The House of Stairs. That was it!

He looked at the ruin and shook his head. "Maybe the pub was called the House of Stairs," he said to himself, "although it doesn't seem like a very suitable name. I only found one staircase in there and it wasn't very impressive. And I'm certain there's no count living there!"

He climbed back onto his bike and set off on the way to Langelaan. The road was wide and straight, with tall trees on either side, and it looked very grand and well-kept, the sort of lane where you might expect to find country mansions, though after half an hour's cycling Frans still hadn't seen any such houses. But then, ten minutes later, he spotted his destination.

On his left, some way back from the road, stood a large house. A plaque on the wall announced that its name was "Appearance and Reality". A gravel path, lined with pots of geraniums, led to the front door.

Frans leant his bike against a tree and looked at his watch. It was exactly quarter past eleven. The magician's house looked different than he'd expected; he'd been imagining something old and mysterious. This house, though, was new – brand new, in fact. All he could see was the brick front of the house, with its neat, straight lines. The windows were all closed with yellow shutters, which gleamed as if the paint were still wet.

He walked up to the front door, read the nameplate – *J. THOMTIDOM, Magician* – and pressed the bell.

A few seconds later, he heard a click and a metallic voice said, "Push the door and come in."

Frans did as he was told, and the door opened inwards. He took two steps before stopping to stare, open-mouthed. He could never have imagined the sight that greeted his eyes! Not a corridor, not a hallway or lobby... the door opened onto a stretch of grass in the open air, with trees on both sides. And at the other end of the field, at the foot of a hill, was an old army tent.

Frans glanced back; the door was still there. The wall was just a façade. "Which just goes to prove," he said out loud, "that appearances are indeed deceptive."

"A very astute observation!" a voice called. And Mr Thomtidom appeared from the tent.

Both men walked across the field and stopped, facing each other. The man who called himself a magician gave Frans a look of approval.

"Welcome," he said. "We've already met, so there's no need for formalities."

"I know your name," Frans began, "but you don't..."

"I know you're called Frans van der Steg," Mr Thomtidom said, interrupting him. "You're a teacher, you're twenty-four years old, you're just over six foot one inch tall, and you have red hair."

"The part about the hair isn't so hard to guess," Frans said drily. He decided that he was not going to let anything else surprise him.

"To a colour-blind person, your hair might just as easily be green," said Mr Thomtidom. "But I think it's a very fine red. A proper dark red... not that carroty colour. Come along, the coffee's ready."

"So this is actually your home? In, um, reality?" asked Frans, when they reached the tent.

"Well, it's true that the ugly wall at the front is just for appearances," replied Mr Thomtidom, "and that this accommodation is a better match for my reality. But to be honest I'm not yet entirely acquainted with my own true reality, even though I've studied both philosophy and psychology."

"That all sounds very academic," said Frans. "I thought you were a magician."

"Yes, that is my *real* profession," said Mr Thomtidom. "White magic mainly – although I'm sometimes forced to delve into the Dark Arts." He looked up at Frans with a smile. His eyes were a very pale blue and it was impossible to tell if their gaze was hazy or, in fact, extremely sharp.

"Don't let that frighten you, though, Mr Van der Steg," he added. "Go on in. You'll have to duck your head. There we go! I'll open up the front of the tent, so we'll have more light."

Frans looked around. He saw an airbed with a couple of blankets, a camping stove, a frying pan and a folding table, with two cups on, next to a coffee pot and a bowl of sugar. That was all.

"Please take a seat," said the magician.

Frans sat down on the airbed, thinking to himself, *The man lives like a hermit!* But Mr Thomtidom's appearance completely contradicted that impression. He seemed far too well-groomed. All his impeccable black suit was missing was a top hat.

"What are you thinking about?" the magician asked unexpectedly.

"I'm still trying to tell the difference between appearance and reality," replied Frans.

"Aha," said Mr Thomtidom, "I imagine that's the influence of the Seven Ways."

"Yes. And that's another example of appearance and reality," said Frans. "Why is the place called Sevenways? There aren't seven ways. There are only six!"

"That is a most profound question," said the magician, sitting down beside him. "Do you take sugar? You haven't lived in the area for long, so of course you're not familiar with our local history. Centuries ago, on the spot where the signpost now stands, there was once a hermit's cell..."

"So were there seven ways back then?" asked Frans, who wasn't really in the mood for a lecture on local history.

Mr Thomtidom answered this question with another question. "Answer me this, how many paths meet at a fork in the road?"

Frans thought for a moment. "Three," he replied. "It's a road that splits in two, so it's three different paths in total."

"Exactly. And how many ways are there when three paths meet?"

"Three, of course," Frans replied. "That's three ways, too," he added, feeling rather surprised after all.

"So what conclusion can we draw?" said the magician in his lecturing voice. "If two roads can be three, then it follows that seven ways can be six, not seven."

Frans frowned and didn't say anything.

"Just think about it," the magician continued. "You get Sevenways by adding together a fork in the road and a crossroads. A crossroads is four roads and a fork in the road is both three roads and two, so therefore we can demonstrate that six ways are in reality the same as seven."

Frans almost choked on his coffee as he tried to follow the magician's logic. It all sounded very clever, but he was sure something wasn't right. To his annoyance, though, he couldn't quite spot the flaw in the man's reasoning. A little sharply, he said, "With that kind of thinking, you could undermine our entire system of arithmetic."

"Do you really think so?" said the magician with a smile. "I'm delighted to hear it. You know, I'm not one of those people who is always at sixes and sevens or in two minds or who does everything at the eleventh hour. And that's as sure as two and two doesn't always make four."

But Frans wasn't in the mood for a lecture about maths. "Mr Tomtidom..." he began.

"THomtidom, please, not Tomtidom," the magician corrected him, pronouncing the TH in his name very clearly.

"Mr THomtidom," said Frans, "you asked me to visit to..."

"...to give you the chance to ask me something," the magician said, completing his sentence for him. "Or rather, to give me the chance to tell you something."

"About Count Grisenstein," said Frans, "who lives on the stairs."

"At the House of Stairs," repeated the magician. "So you already know!"

"I don't know anything!" cried Frans. "Where on earth is the House of Stairs? It can't be that old ruin by the signpost and..."

"Please, Mr Van der Steg, not so loud," said the magician. "The building at Sevenways obviously isn't the House of Stairs, but the ruin of Jan Tooreloor's tavern."

"But the signpost says..."

"Once upon a time, many years ago, the pub was on the road to the House of Stairs."

"Oh," said Frans. "So it's a real place, then?"

"But surely you never doubted that, Mr Van der Steg? Otherwise you'd never have come here to ask me about Count Grisenstein!"

"To be honest, I'm not convinced he exists either," said Frans. "I received a letter from him and..."

"Well, non-existent people don't send letters, do they?"

"The letter was a reply to a letter from me, one that I never wrote!"

"A reply to a letter from you? And what did your letter say?"

"I just told you. I never wrote a letter!"

"Please calm down, Mr Van der Steg," the magician said in a soothing tone. "Maybe you just forgot. Some people are simply forgetful by nature."

"Not me," said Frans angrily.

The magician downed his coffee and stood up. "We have secrets to unravel and mysteries to solve," he said. "And now that we've finished our coffee, it's time to begin. Please accompany me to my house."

"Your... *house*?!"

"Yes, my house," said the magician. "As the façade proved merely to have the appearance of a house, you thought this tent was in reality my home. In fact, I only spend time here when I need to meditate. My real house is a good deal more comfortable. Come with me, and I shall reveal the heart of the matter."

He hears about a hidden treasure and a rhyme written in stone

THIS IS THREE

On the other side of the hill, between a copse of birch trees and a pine grove, stood a small wooden bungalow with a huge chimney. *That* was his real house, the magician said.

Unless he has another house hidden away somewhere nearby, thought Frans. But when he went inside the bungalow, his doubts vanished, because everything looked just as it should.

There were shelves full of books, and more books piled up on the chairs and the floor. Hanging on the walls were thermometers and barometers, old engravings and faded maps, and shelf after shelf of the strangest objects. A first quick glance revealed lots of bottles filled with all kinds of coloured liquids, four or five hourglasses, a crystal ball, an octahedron, a Bunsen burner, a rack of test tubes, a black hat, three pinecones, a bird's skull and a terrarium with salamanders inside. The room was pretty packed, but still fairly neat and tidy. In the middle was a round table with a colourful tablecloth woven with the signs of the zodiac.

"Please sit down over there," said the magician.

Frans looked around, trying to find a chair that had nothing on it, until his host freed one up for him by removing a stack of books.

"Actually," he said, "these are your books. I've been keeping them for you."

"But where on earth did you get them from?" asked Frans. "Oh, of course," he continued. "I don't really need to ask, do I? You must know that rude coachman, and the young man who calls himself the Biker Boy."

"The Biker Boy?" repeated the magician, clearing another chair and joining Frans at the table.

"I mean Roberto," said Frans. "Does he have a scooter?"

"Roberto? No, he definitely does not have a scooter," replied the magician.

"I don't know if I believe that, Mr Thomtidom," said Frans. "Thank you for looking after my books, but what I'd really like to know now is why that coachman disappeared and abandoned me at Sevenways in the dark."

"Oh, you mustn't hold that against him," the magician said. "Poor Jan hasn't had the easiest of lives, so he can sometimes be a little difficult to get along with. Besides, you're the one who got out of the coach. I believe you actually refused to go any farther."

"Yes, but..." began Frans.

"Oh, I forgive you completely," the magician said, interrupting him. "As you said, it was dark, and our courage can fail us at such times."

"You've got it all wrong," said Frans, with a chill in his voice. "I'm not the cowardly type, but I don't see why I should meekly allow myself to be carried off to... who knows where?"

"Who knows where? You know where!" the magician said. "Your destination was the House of Stairs. Which brings us to the heart of the matter. I shall begin with the House of Stairs.

First, though, I'd like to ask you something. Why are you so curious about Count Grisenstein?"

"Why?!" exclaimed Frans. "You're asking me... Now that really is the last straw! It seems as if everyone's conspiring against me!"

"Please don't be angry, Mr Van der Steg," said the magician. "You're a stranger to these parts, so you don't know that there are some subjects we discuss only in whispers around here. And one of those subjects is the House of Stairs. Before I take you into my confidence, I would like to know: firstly, why you accepted Count Grisenstein's invitation; secondly, why you changed your mind when you reached Sevenways; and thirdly, why you then decided to go exploring and went to Roskam."

Frans did not reply.

"And to convince you that the House of Stairs is not some fantasy, I'd like to show you this," the magician continued. He handed Frans a well-thumbed book. "Turn to page 77," he added.

The book was called *Historic Houses* and page 77 began as follows:

> *The House of Stairs is one of the oldest and most remarkable buildings in this region. It owes its name to the large number of staircases it possesses.*

"So many steps! Stairs and ladders and fire escapes..." said the magician. "The building's a maze. No two rooms are on the same level. So..." he continued, "will you answer my questions now?"

Frans realized it was the only way he'd find out anything. And so he told the magician the whole story, starting with the letter. He even mentioned the children and that he'd suspected them of being involved.

When Frans had finished, the magician gave a satisfied nod and said, "Now it's my turn, Mr Van der Steg. Close the book. You can read it at home later. I shall now give you a brief account of the history of the House of Stairs."

Frans settled back and prepared to listen. He was sure the magician's tale would be a long one and would involve plenty of learned words.

"The House of Stairs," said Mr Thomtidom, "has belonged to the Grisenstein family for centuries, and even today it is inhabited by members of that illustrious clan, although they are not as powerful and eminent as they once were. Once upon a time" – and now he sat up straight – "everyone would prick up their ears at the sound of that name. There was Count Gregorius, for instance, also known as Gregorius the Mad, who had nine cats to guard his castle and raced through the woods on his horse at night, singing at the top of his voice. His daughter Griselda was... but I mustn't get side-tracked. I'd better go back to the Middle Ages, and the days of Sir Grimbold, a knight who..."

"Do you really have to go back that far?" asked Frans. "I came here to find out about the Count Grisenstein who's alive today! I'm sure all those ancestors are very interesting, but I don't have much time..."

Just then, the clock on the mantelpiece began to make a grinding sound, as if to lend force to his words. Frans had never seen such a peculiar clock. It looked like a castle with towers, and each of the towers had one or two windows, like a cuckoo clock. The clock's face was where the gate of the castle would be, its hands pointing to twelve. As Frans studied the clock, the window in the tallest tower opened and, instead of a cuckoo, a wooden owl popped out, looked at him with glassy yellow eyes and said "Hoo-hoo!" twelve times, in a deep voice.

"I made that clock myself," said the magician, when the owl had vanished back into the tower.

"What a fine piece of work!" said Frans.

"You really think so?" said the magician, sounding flattered. "It's not quite finished yet. That owl should only appear at twelve midnight. I have another bird in mind for noon – what do you think of a lark? At one o'clock a hummingbird hums, and two turtledoves coo at two... Oh, it was quite a job carving all those birds! At first I was only going to use mythical creatures, but the problem is that I don't know what kind of sounds they make. The phoenix, for instance, and the garuda and the roc and the griffin... I don't suppose you happen to know their calls, do you?"

Frans replied that unfortunately he didn't.

"That's a shame," said the magician. "Well, maybe I could keep them silent and just use them for the half-hours. But to get back to the House of Stairs... Where was I again? Oh yes, Sir Grimbold. Now I definitely need to tell you about him. Sir Grimbold went on a crusade, and he was away for seven years. He returned with many tales of dangerous adventures and a large chest made of ebony. That chest contained a treasure of inestimable value, but he told no one how he came to have it, and no one was allowed to look inside the chest. Sir Grimbold's family lived near here in a house made of grey stone, which is where the name Grisenstein comes from, but for himself he built a lowly hovel at the point where the Seven Ways meet. He lived there as a hermit for the rest of his life, and he kept the chest with him. However, after his death, it simply vanished..." The magician looked at Frans and repeated the word: "Vanished!" Then he stood up and said, "All you've had is coffee. How about something a little stronger?"

"Oh, please, don't trouble yourself," said Frans.

"No, no. It's no trouble at all. You'll have a glass of port with me, won't you? It's very good, a lovely deep-red glow, like the blood of rubies." The magician put two crystal glasses on the table and brought out a dusty bottle. As he poured the drink, he continued his story.

"A couple of hundred years later, Sir Grimbold's great-great-great-grandson Gregorius enlarged and embellished the grey stone house, and named it the House of Stairs. When they were working on the cellars, a secret passage was discovered, which led to the spot where the hermit's cell had once stood." The magician raised his glass and said, "To your health and to the success of your new venture."

New venture? thought Frans. *What venture?* but all he said was, "Thank you," and drank some port. It was indeed very good.

The magician also took a sip. "In the library at the House of Stairs," he said, "there is still a document that was written and signed by Count Gregorius Grisenstein. He reveals that he found Sir Grimbold's chest, and the treasure inside it – which was 'exquisitely fine'. Then he had the passage bricked up and the treasure hidden once again, this time in the House of Stairs itself. He does not say where, and he concludes with the following lines:

"Words written in stone with a good, true knife
Will last far longer than my own brief life."

The magician emptied his glass. "So, what do you think?" he asked.

"A secret passage and a hidden treasure," said Frans. "It's almost too good to be true." He noticed that his glass was full again; his host must have topped it up. Frans took a sip, looked at the clock (it was quarter past twelve) and asked, "And then what happened?"

"The treasure was never found," the magician said in a hushed voice. "All the Grisensteins have searched for it, and that may be one of the reasons why the House of Stairs has seen so much demolition and rebuilding. It truly is a remarkable building! The following words are carved into the stone lintel of the back door. Listen closely, Mr Van der Steg!

"The Treasure shall be hidden out of Sight
Until found by a Child who has the Right.
The Fiendish Foe will watch and wait
But a Song will seal his sorry Fate."

A silence fell. Frans emptied his glass and politely refused when the magician offered him a refill. Then he asked, "Why are you telling me all this?"

"It's the inscription that Count Gregorius was referring to in his document," said the magician, "the words written in stone. Count Gregorius hid the treasure. And Count Gregorius was, of course, none other than Gregorius the Mad, who was in the habit of infuriating everyone with his mysterious utterances and incomprehensible rhymes, which he liked to refer to as prophecies."

Frans glanced at the clock again. It was almost twenty-five past twelve, and he needed to leave at half past. His landlady had told him not to be late for lunch. The magician's story really did seem to be taking a long time. Was it his voice that was making Frans so sleepy?

When, he thought, *is he finally going to get to the "heart of the matter"?*

"That's why," continued the magician, "some people claim there never was any treasure, and that Gregorius the Mad made it all up! However, there is another account..." His voice became quieter and quieter until it was just a vague buzzing.

Then Frans heard nothing more.

THE SEKRIT TRESURE... that was the title of Marian's essay. No... No, it was Mr Thomtidom the magician who'd been talking about treasure...

Frans opened one eye and realized his head was lolling on the table.

Oh dear, he'd fallen asleep!

With a jolt, he sat up. He blinked and felt his face turning red.

The magician was sitting opposite him, looking at him with a sympathetic smile. "Did you hear what I said?" he asked.

"N... no... yes..." stuttered Frans.

"You're not tired, are you?" said the magician. "I do hope my story didn't bore you. Sometimes I do rather stray from the point."

Frans saw that it was only one minute before half past twelve, so fortunately he'd fallen asleep for just the briefest of moments, although he still didn't understand how it could have happened. He took a deep breath and smelt a scent of pine trees and freshly mown grass, with a hint of something else: pepper and peppermint... Suddenly he realized he was hungry. "I'm not tired in the slightest," he said, and he sneezed.

"Bless you," said the magician. He'd taken off his black coat and didn't look nearly as elegant now that he was in his braces and a green shirt.

Frans straightened his glasses and said, "It was most interesting. Please go on. You told me about the treasure, but you haven't told me about Count Grisenstein yet. I mean the Count Grisenstein who wrote to me." As he spoke, he thought: *How strange that I'm so hungry.*

"The man calls himself Count Grisenstein, and he is undoubtedly a Grisenstein," said the magician. "His first name is Gradus. But the true and legal Lord of the House of Stairs is Geert-Jan, even though he's only ten years old. He's the heir to the house and the owner of the treasure, should it ever be found. And if there's any truth to the old story I just told you, he's the one who holds the key to the secret."

But Frans hadn't heard the story the magician had just told. He didn't dare to tell him that, though, but just nodded at the other man, trying to look as intelligent as he could. His stomach had started rumbling. He blushed again and hoped his host wouldn't notice.

The magician stood up and started pacing the room. He had to step over the occasional pile of books, but he didn't stumble once. As he paced, he continued his story, "Count Gradus Grisenstein is the great-uncle and guardian of young Geert-Jan, who is an orphan. They live at the House of Stairs, with a couple of grumpy manservants and a bad-tempered housekeeper. Geert-Jan has a weak constitution, they say, and he hardly ever comes outside. But that," he continued, "is absolute nonsense! The Grisensteins have always, without exception, enjoyed perfect health – so why not Geert-Jan? His uncle says he's not allowed to go to school. But he still has to learn, of course." He stopped and asked Frans, "So can you guess now why Count Grisenstein wanted to speak to you?"

Frans slowly shook his head.

"But I'm sure you can," said the magician. "Count Grisenstein is looking for a tutor for his young nephew, a teacher who can educate him. And that teacher is you!"

"Why would you...?" began Frans.

"You read the advertisement that he placed in the local newspapers..."

"I most certainly did not!"

"Asking for someone to give private lessons," the magician persisted. "And you wrote a letter in response."

"Oh, did I really?" said Frans indignantly. "Then I'm sure I must have done it so that I could search for the treasure, eh?"

"No, searching for treasure isn't your job. And besides, you didn't know anything about the treasure at that point."

"There are a lot of things that I don't know anything about!" shouted Frans. "Now, would you finally tell me why you asked me to come here?"

"To warn you," said the magician calmly. "Count Grisenstein is a dangerous gentleman, but that mustn't stop you from going to the House of Stairs and becoming Geert-Jan's tutor."

"But that's out of the question!" said Frans. "I already have a job, at the village school. I work there every day of the week, except Sunday."

"But you have Wednesday and Saturday afternoons off!" said the magician. "And you'll do this for the sake of little Geert-Jan, won't you? That poor boy, who's never allowed to play with other children..." He took a step closer to Frans and suddenly he looked very serious. "Think about the rhyme," he said, "the rhyme written in stone:

"The Treasure shall be hidden out of Sight
Until found by a Child who has the Right.

"That child is Geert-Jan. For the first time in hundreds of years, the terms of the prophecy have come to pass.

"The Fiendish Foe will watch and wait
But a Song will seal his sorry Fate.

"That Fiendish Foe is Count Gradus Grisenstein, with his grasping, greedy heart and his grim and gruesome plans. But he won't get what he's after."

Frans leapt to his feet. He spoke in a loud voice in an attempt to shake off his vague sense of fear. "That's enough!" he said. "Prophecies, legends, mysteries and secrets! I wouldn't even dare tell such a crazy story to the children in my class!"

"Oh yes, the children," said the magician with a nod. "Ask them for advice. They'll tell you to write Count Grisenstein a letter saying that you're sorry his coachman didn't find you at home on Friday evening, and that you'd like to make another appointment. With your good references, you stand an excellent chance of getting the position."

Frans was speechless.

"And of course this conversation was just between the two of us," the magician added. "And by all that's good and holy I implore you never to mention Sevenways. The Count must not suspect that you have ever set foot there."

"If only that were true," muttered Frans.

"Don't say that," said the magician. "How else do you intend to beat the Dragon?"

Dragon? That was the final straw. Frans knew he couldn't stay a minute longer. He took a step back, nodded stiffly and said, "My thanks for your wise advice and enlightening words. But now I really do have to go."

Frans practically fled. He thought he heard the magician shout something after him, but he didn't look back. Quickly he climbed up the hill, then back down, and ran past the tent, across the field of grass and to the front door.

He jumped onto his bike and rode off, pedalling so hard that he flew along as if he were on a motor scooter.

THAT WAS THREE *and now for Part Four*

4

Frans discovers that there's a conspiracy

He makes friends with Roberto

THIS IS ONE

After a while, Frans slowed down so that he could think more clearly.

Right then, he thought, *at least now I know for sure that the magician is mad, completely round the bend, as mad as that Count Gregorius he was talking about, or maybe I've gone mad myself – but that's still not going to get me anywhere! Whatever is at the bottom of all this?*

His visit to Mr Thomtidom suddenly felt like a dream. The lane he was riding along looked strange too – he didn't know why but something was not as it should be.

"Frans, just keep calm," he said to himself. "You'll feel better later, when you've had something to eat."

There was Sevenways already. He wasn't far from home now. But then Frans glanced at his watch and had such a shock that he almost lost control of the handlebars. He looked again... and a few seconds later he was at the signpost, with his bike lying beside him on the ground. He held his watch to his ear; it was still ticking. He'd wound it up that morning and checked that it was right – and now it was quarter to five!

Not one o'clock, but quarter to five!

There was no doubt about it. Now he understood why the lane had seemed so strange: the light had changed, and the sun was already low in the sky. So he'd left the magician's at around quarter past four... That meant he'd been asleep for almost four hours instead of just a few minutes!

The magician had turned back the hands of his bird clock and then acted like everything was normal.

He must have put something in the port, thought Frans. *But why? Why?*

He didn't get the chance to think about the answer to that question, though, as he heard someone call his name in a loud and indignant voice.

"Frans van der Steg!"

His landlady came striding towards him from the direction of the village. She was wearing her purple hat and a coat with a fur collar, and holding an umbrella in one hand and a bag in the other. Her face was red and angry.

"Well, aren't you a fine one!" she said. "I waited for you for a good hour at lunchtime. And now I find his lordship taking the air at Sevenways, as calm as anything."

"Aunt Wilhelmina..." Frans began. "I mean, Mrs Bakker... I'm terribly sorry, but I..."

"Please, no excuses," she interrupted him. "You'll have to heat up your lunch yourself, and I hope for your sake that you have your key with you. The front door's locked and I'm not giving you mine."

She turned and, without looking back, strode off along the track leading to "The Herb Garden". With dismay, Frans watched her go; he knew he didn't have his key.

"Oooh!" said a voice behind him. "That's tough luck on an empty stomach. Unless you want to come and eat at my place."

Frans spun around. It was Roberto... or the Biker Boy.

Of the two, he looked more like the young man Frans had met at the Thirsty Deer. He was dressed flamboyantly, in a brightly checked shirt and dusty khaki trousers, with a red handkerchief tied loosely around his neck and a wide-brimmed straw hat perched on the back of his head. He was standing hands on hips and legs apart – with tall muddy boots on his feet, and his right hand resting on a big penknife that was hanging from his belt. He looked at Frans with a challenging grin.

"Well?" he said. "Say something! Are you up for it?"

"Up for what?" said Frans coldly. Then he walked closer and said, "So what are you now? A cowboy?"

The young man raised his eyebrows. "I'm Roberto," he replied, "as you well know. And I was just kind enough to invite you to come and eat at my place."

"Yes, very kind indeed," said Frans sarcastically. "But please don't feel obliged to do something in return for the chips. You were very welcome to them."

"Now what are you talking about?" asked Roberto with a look of surprise on his face.

"Stop trying to make a fool of me," said Frans. "I know perfectly well who you are."

"Of course you do, I just told you," the boy said. "I'm Roberto, adventurer and idler."

"And Biker Boy," Frans added.

"First cowboy, now Biker Boy," said Roberto. He sounded annoyed. "Listen, you can't go around saying all kinds of things about me! What's your problem with me, schoolteacher?"

"All these mysterious goings-on... and your friends, that's my problem!" said Frans. "Why are you acting as if I've never been on the back of your scooter?" He pointed dramatically at the tumbledown pub. "That's where we first met, in Torelore's Tavern... I mean Tooreloor's."

"Mysterious goings-on?" said Roberto. "So Mr Thomtidom didn't tell you anything?" He pronounced the magician's name correctly.

"Mr Thomtidom..." repeated Frans. "So you're both involved in the same conspiracy!"

"That's right," said Roberto, nodding calmly. "The Conspiracy of Seven. And you're one of us..." He held up his hand and continued, "Don't interrupt! You will be one of us as soon as you're initiated. But you mustn't be so suspicious and you have to stop going on about scooters and chips. I really don't know what you're talking about."

"Well, how do you think I feel?" wailed Frans. "I don't have a clue what's going on! What am I supposed to make of you, for instance? Please don't try telling me some tired old story about a twin brother who's your double."

"I don't have any brothers," said Roberto. "Anyway, that's enough chatting. Are you coming? I live nearby and I'd like to remind you that I just invited you round to eat."

Frans remembered just how hungry he was, but he said, "And do you intend to slip me some kind of sleeping potion too, so that I'll wake up in a few hours with no idea what's happened in the meantime?"

"What do you think I am?" exclaimed Roberto, staring at him with big, innocent eyes.

"That's exactly what that friend of yours, Thomtidom the magician, just did."

"Oh, him!" said Roberto, shrugging his shoulders. "It may not have been a sleeping pill. Could have been hypnosis. He says he has hypnotic powers, and he does like to experiment."

"You seem to think it's perfectly normal," Frans said abruptly. "Well, I don't! I refuse to be someone's guinea pig."

"Well, I don't have hypnotic powers in any case," said Roberto. He took off his hat, turned up the brim, put it back on, and said, "And if you come to visit me, there are sausages for tea!"

Frans frowned thoughtfully. He suddenly realized that he quite liked Roberto, even though he didn't trust him one bit.

"Sausages with mustard," said the boy.

That settled it. "Fine," said Frans. "I accept your invitation."

"Just leave your bike here," said Roberto. "It'll only be a nuisance on the path to my place. It's this way." He pointed at the blood-red arm of the signpost.

"The way to the robbers' den..." muttered Frans. He picked up his bike, leant it against the wall of the pub, and then followed his new acquaintance, wondering if he would soon get to find out more about this Conspiracy of Seven.

Roberto led the way along the muddy path, which was so narrow that they had to walk in single file. It wound around, taking them through hilly woodland. Roberto strode ahead in his big boots, whistling quietly to himself. For Frans, who was not wearing boots, the walk wasn't as pleasant. They went over a number of ditches and streams, across rickety plank bridges. Frans counted the bridges; there were five in total. Twice they came to a ditch that they had to jump over. Roberto was right; this was no path for a bike – and certainly not for a scooter.

Now and then Roberto looked back, and one time he said, "It's not far now."

That wasn't quite true though, and they walked on for a long time, mostly in silence. Frans was surprised at himself. He really should have been asking all kinds of questions. *But,* he thought, *I wouldn't really know where to begin. I'm just going to wait and see what happens. I do hope he was telling the truth about those sausages though.*

"We're nearly there," Roberto suddenly announced. "Stand there and wait until I call you." He quickened his pace, ran on ahead and disappeared into the trees.

"As you command," Frans muttered to himself. "And I will obey." He shifted from one leg to the other, feeling how wet his feet had become. He glanced at his watch a few times (it was already after half past five) and when two whole minutes had gone by, he began to get impatient.

"Hey, Roberto!" he called. "Where are you? I'm coming!"

"Give me a moment!" came Robert's reply. His voice was clear and came from somewhere nearby. So at least he hadn't run away.

Frans waited for a minute. Then he decided he'd had enough; he gritted his teeth and started walking.

But suddenly, there was a big bang, and the ground shook. Frans gasped and froze for a moment. Then he broke into a run. "Roberto!" he yelled.

He could smell something – it was just like gunpowder! And as he raced around the bend in the path, the first thing he saw was a cannon.

It was a real cannon, and Roberto was standing beside it, with a look of triumph on his face.

"A salute for you!" he called to Frans.

Frans stopped in his tracks and said, "That's a dangerous game you're playing!"

"Don't worry. It was just a blank," said Roberto. "What do you think? Isn't it amazing?"

Frans couldn't help but agree. When he took a closer look at the cannon, he was really impressed. It must have been well over a hundred years old, but it was still in good condition. "A very fine cannon indeed," he said. "How did you get your hands on it?"

"Oh, I just found it lying around," Roberto replied casually.

Frans didn't ask any more questions. It seemed that he'd ended up in a part of the world where antique cannons were as easy to find as buttons and marbles – a place where magicians could use their powers to send a person to sleep and eccentric counts lived in castles filled with staircases and hidden treasure.

He saw now that they were in a clearing. There was a tent like Mr Thomtidom's near the cannon. Behind it, half hidden among the trees, he saw a small, round building, the kind of thing you might find in a park. It was even more tumbledown and moss-covered than the pub at Sevenways.

Roberto took a primus stove from the tent, lit it and put a kettle on top. Spreading a canvas sheet on the ground, he invited Frans to sit down. Then he began to prepare their meal, laying all kinds of things on the ground beside Frans: two bright red plastic cups and a cracked plate, bags of sugar and tea, some bread, a jar of mustard and two tins of hotdog sausages. "Could you open them?" he said, putting his penknife in Frans's hand. Meanwhile he disappeared into the little building and returned with his arms full of wood.

"I hope it's not too damp," he said, as he skilfully started to build a fire.

A campfire in the woods... at the end of a path marked by the blood-red arm of a signpost, and a tent that was guarded by an ancient cannon...

Frans and Roberto sat together like old pals, enjoying the meal of heated-up sausages, with a side dish of bread, which they toasted on a stick over the fire, and strong, sweet tea.

By then, the light was turning reddish gold, and the shadows beneath the trees were becoming dark and mysterious.

"So have I been initiated into your conspiracy now?" asked Frans, when he'd finished the last sausage. He said it half joking, half seriously. If he'd been just a few years younger, he might have spoken entirely seriously, even if he'd known it was just a game.

"No, not yet," replied Roberto, and there was no sound of amusement in his voice, although he spoke quite casually. "First I need to know if you're prepared to carry out your part of the plan, and if you'll keep our aim secret from our enemies and from the uninitiated."

"And what is that aim?" asked Frans.

"Ssh!" said Roberto. "Don't talk too loud. We're close to the territory of the Fiendish Foe."

"The Fiendish Foe?" repeated Frans. "Who? Where?"

"Count Grisenstein's estate," whispered Roberto. He gave Frans a sideways glance before continuing, "Why are you asking about things you already know? Mr Thomtidom must have told you all this! About Sir Grimbold, who brought the treasure here, about Count Gregorius, who hid the treasure, about Count Gradus, who wants to have the treasure, and about Count Geert-Jan, who's the rightful owner of the treasure... Geert-Jan, who's imprisoned in..."

"Imprisoned?" said Frans. "Who by?"

"By his uncle, of course, you dope! Count Gradus Grisenstein."

"Ah, it's a classic story, told a thousand times," murmured Frans, ignoring that remark about "you dope". "The Wicked Uncle, the Innocent Child, in a house filled with stairs and family secrets..."

"It's not some kind of fairy tale!" said Roberto, his voice rising in indignation. "How would you like being locked up in that house, not even allowed to put your nose outside?" He leant closer to Frans and added in a whisper, "If the boy finds the treasure now, his life will be in danger! Then Count Grisenstein will no longer have to act the concerned uncle..."

Frans sat up with a start. "What are you saying?" he exclaimed, half incredulous, half horrified.

"Don't be alarmed. Geert-Jan won't find the treasure, not on his own... not if the prophecy is right."

"Prophecy?" said Frans.

"So you don't know anything about it?"

"I did hear something... *Words written in stone with a good, true knife...*"

"No, that's about the rhyme on the lintel," said Roberto. "I mean the other story, the one from the Sealed Parchment."

"Sealed Parchment? I don't know anything about that. I was asleep at the time... But it's all nonsense anyway!"

"Nonsense?" said Roberto quietly. "So why do you think the count suddenly moved into the House of Stairs? Why do you think he watches and spies on Geert-Jan like a jailer? Because he's after the treasure! Only the boy can find it, and he knows that as well as we do."

"I really don't know if..." began Frans.

"Count Grisenstein is a villain," Roberto continued. "The estate isn't far from here. He's put barbed wire up all around it and signs saying 'No trespassers', and there are gamekeepers patrolling with loaded guns. Don't go thinking you can just walk right into the House of Stairs! It's a big, creepy building, with cold, old rooms and corridors..."

"And stairs," said Frans with a nod, "and dark, gloomy dungeons. Very spooky, but also rather interesting..." He shivered; it was getting cold.

Roberto looked at him, his eyes glinting and his face glowing in the light of the fire. "But someone has to find a cunning way to get into the House of Stairs," he said in a low voice. "Before it's too late."

Frans van der Steg felt a slight sense of unease in spite of himself. "But," he mumbled, "that kind of thing doesn't happen nowadays, does it?"

"Doesn't it?" whispered Roberto.

Frans shivered again.

"Are you chilly?" said Roberto. He jumped to his feet and disappeared into the tent. A moment later, he threw a raincoat around Frans's shoulders. Then he sat back down beside him and said, "You're not scared, are you?"

"No," replied Frans. "What is there to be scared of?"

"I just mean... Because you keep changing your mind. First you got into the coach and then you got back out. Sometimes you nod your head and then you shake it. Are you in or are you out?"

"In or out of what?"

"Our conspiracy."

"Listen," said Frans, in a loud voice, "before I go nodding or shaking my head, I want to hear what this conspiracy of yours is all about..."

"Stop shouting!" said Roberto. "I'll tell you, but you need to know that you can't go back! That you'll have to continue on... on your way."

"My way? And which way's that?"

"Well, let's just call it the Seventh Way. The seventh path from Sevenways."

He hears about Seven Conspirators

THIS IS TWO

Frans and Roberto were both silent for a while. Above their heads, a bird plaintively called its own name. A long-eared animal jumped out of the bushes and, startled to see them, disappeared.

Then Frans said quietly, "There are only six paths from Sevenways."

Roberto prodded the fire with a stick until it burst into flames. "Six paths," he said, "and the Conspiracy of Seven has six members. But there should, of course, be seven – and there will be, if you join us. Our aim is to free Geert-Jan from the clutches of Count Grisenstein. And he has to find the treasure. One thing can't happen without the other; it says so in the Sealed Parchment."

"The Sealed Parchment," repeated Frans. "What's that?"

"If Mr Thomtidom hasn't told you about it, then I'm not going to either," said Roberto.

"Well, that's nice!" said Frans indignantly. "It's not my fault I fell asleep!"

"Perhaps that's why he sent you to sleep," said Roberto, "because you weren't allowed to find out about the existence of the Sealed Parchment yet."

"If I wasn't supposed to hear about it, then he shouldn't have started talking about it," said Frans. "So WHY did he send me to sleep?"

"Stop changing the subject," said Roberto. "I was telling you about the Conspiracy of Seven. Mr Thomtidom and I want to nominate you as a member..."

"I'm most honoured," said Frans.

"But it's our President who will decide if you should be initiated," Roberto pressed on.

"President! And who might that be?"

"The Herb Lady – Miss Rosemary."

"Not some kind of witch!"

"Don't be so insulting," said Roberto. "She's the youngest of three sisters..."

"Rosemary, the youngest of three sisters," Frans murmured to himself. Suddenly he had a vision of a beautiful young woman, who would bring a touch of romance to this mysterious story... No, this wasn't a story. It was real life. He looked around; the sunlight had gone, and dusk would soon give way to darkness.

The fire was burning less brightly now. "Maybe we should just let it go out," said Roberto. "It could lead spies this way." He hugged his arms around his knees and went on telling Frans about the conspiracy. "The youngest of three sisters often has special gifts or powers, or at least that's what Mr Thomtidom says. Miss Rosemary grows herbs, and she lives at the Herb Garden. You have to go and see her tomorrow. I'm sure you've seen the path from Sevenways. Mr Thomtidom is our Secretary and General Advisor..."

"What about you?" asked Frans. "Are you the Treasurer?"

"No, we don't have any money. I am the First Liaison Officer. The Second Liaison Officer is Jan Tooreloor."

"Jan... Tooreloor? Does he exist too? And who's he? Oh yes, the landlord of that abandoned pub."

"He used to be. Now he's Count Grisenstein's coachman."

"That villain?" said Frans. "Well, a fine liaison officer he is, abandoning his passengers in the wind and rain!"

"Stop going on about that! You're the one who wanted to get out."

"And how do you know that?" asked Frans. "Are you sure you weren't at the pub, disguised as the Biker Boy?"

Roberto ignored his question. "The other two conspirators are spies," he went on. "So I need to conceal their names from you for the time being."

"I'm not going to join a conspiracy if I'm not fully informed about all of its secrets," said Frans firmly.

"Only the President can do that," said Roberto, just as firmly. "Aunt Rosemary."

"Aunt?"

"Yes, she's my aunt. Is that so strange?"

Rather regretfully, Frans dismissed his vision of the beautiful young woman. Instead, an older woman appeared in his mind's eye. She was wearing a straw hat like Roberto's and gazing intently into a crystal ball. He shook off this fantasy and asked, "And what part have I been given in this conspiracy?"

"I could call you our Secret Agent," replied Roberto. "You have to infiltrate the House of Stairs."

"I see," said Frans. "And what am I supposed to do when I get there?"

"You'll be Geert-Jan's tutor."

"Mr Thomtidom already told me as much. Ah, of course, he's the one who wrote the letter! He's our Secretary, after all."

"Which letter?"

"The one I didn't write," said Frans. "So I have to become Geert-Jan's tutor, but Count Grisenstein mustn't know that I'm infiltrating the House of Stairs with a specific purpose... and that I'm a member of the Conspiracy of Seven."

"Finally you're talking sense," said Roberto. "And now let's just hope you get the job..."

"And that I want it!"

"And that you're brave enough to do it," Roberto added.

"It doesn't require much bravery," said Frans. "All I have to do is write a letter to Count Gradus Grisenstein and ask him for an interview. I think I'll just do it myself, before your secretary does it for me. You know, I prefer to manage my own business."

"Fine, you manage away," said Roberto. "Just as long as you remember one thing: we've eaten sausages together, so I trust you'll remain silent about everything I've told you." His face looked very serious in the fading glow of the fire. "Promise!" he said.

"I swear, on the sausages!" said Frans.

Roberto stood up. "It's dark," he said. "You need to go."

"So that's all you wanted to say?" asked Frans.

"Yes. But you should come and visit again. And you can always use my tent as a shelter, even if I'm not at home."

Roberto picked up the dishes and carried them into his tent, where he also stashed the canvas and the coat he'd lent Frans. A couple of minutes later, he was back beside the smouldering fire, now hatless and holding a torch in his hand. "I'll walk you back to Sevenways," he said, as he carefully stamped out the fire.

"And then?"

"Then you can cycle home."

"And what about you?" asked Frans. "Where do you live?"

"Here!" replied the boy, and his tone made it clear that he thought the question was ridiculous.

"Here? In this tent? All alone? At your age?" said Frans. "And your parents or guardians don't mind?"

"Stop being such a schoolmaster," said Roberto.

"If I weren't a schoolmaster," said Frans, "I wouldn't be able to infiltrate the House of Stairs, which you and your friends are so keen for me to do."

"Keep close behind me," said Roberto. "This torch doesn't give off much light. If I were on my own, I'd walk this path in the pitch dark, and no spies would slip past me."

"Are there..." began Frans, but Roberto interrupted him.

"Sssh!" he ordered. "We're not at my place now, so we need to keep our mouths shut."

They walked on in silence. Frans could see little more than what was lit up by the beam of the torch, but the darkness around him seemed to be full of life. He wasn't at all scared, even though he thought more than once about spies, who could be

lurking nearby... Spies! There were two spies involved in the conspiracy, and he wasn't allowed to know their names... "But I *do* know!" he whispered.

"What?" Roberto whispered back.

"Those spies of yours... I know where they are."

"You should be paying more attention to *his* spies!" Roberto hissed.

Frans didn't need to ask who Roberto meant – it was obviously Count Grisenstein. He didn't say anything for a while; he was concentrating hard on the path. But a little later he whispered, "It's the children! Two of the children in my class."

Roberto snorted quietly. "The strange ideas that schoolmasters get into their heads," he said.

"So the children aren't involved in the conspiracy?"

"Of course not! But you can tell them about it if you like."

"I thought it was a secret!"

"Not from the children," said Roberto. "Feel free to tell them about it."

"Oh, come on," said Frans, "I'm sure they've known about it for a long time!"

"Watch out," said Roberto. "There's a ditch here."

For the rest of the walk, they didn't talk about the conspiracy. Roberto didn't mention it again until they reached Sevenways.

"Write that letter to the count," he said, "and report to Miss Rosemary as soon as possible. I think Geert-Jan is going to like you."

He turned the light of his torch on the pub. "There's your bike," he said. "Cycle home safely. Bye then."

He turned around and, as he was walking away, he switched off the torch. Within a few moments, the darkness had swallowed him up.

"Hey, Roberto!" Frans called in a low voice.

"See you!" came Roberto's voice. "I hope Aunt Wilhelmina gets home soon and lets you in."

Frans heard leaves rustling, but saw no one else in the dark woods. "He's acting like a real conspirator," he muttered. Then he walked slowly to his bike and thought, *Aunt Wilhelmina? How does he know I call her that? Or is Mrs Bakker another of his aunts?*

Then he hopped on his bike and started cycling home. "Well, this has been a very eventful Sunday," he said to himself. "I set out to uncover a conspiracy, and now I'm almost part of it myself!"

He braked when he heard a sound that didn't belong there. The drone of a motor scooter. He looked around. Was that a light speeding along one of the paths from Sevenways?

Secret Agent! he thought, as he rode on. *No, I'm sticking to my original plan. I'm going to join that conspiracy, just so I can unmask the conspirators!*

Frans the Red didn't stand for any nonsense – and he was always the master of any situation.

Aunt Wilhelmina has something to say

Half an hour later, Frans van der Steg was standing in front of the house where he lived. He was anything but the master of this situation, unless he intended to break a window and climb inside. Frans the Red would perhaps have done exactly that... No, he would never have ended up outside a locked front door in the first place; he didn't let landladies boss him around, no matter how good their cooking was!

Frans looked around. It felt as if all the villagers were peering at him from behind their curtains, and making fun of him. It was ridiculous. He couldn't sit waiting on the doorstep, just because he'd been stupid enough to leave the house without his key!

Again he heard the sound of a scooter. A beam of light appeared and disappeared at the end of the dark street. A few moments later he heard brisk footsteps, and his landlady came walking down the road.

"What are you doing out here?" she said. "You're not waiting for me, are you?"

"I didn't have my key, Mrs Bakker," said Frans coldly, "and I was just wondering what I should do: smash a window or ask to spend the night at the police station."

"No need," said Mrs Bakker, putting her own key into the lock and turning it. "I left the back door open."

"You didn't tell me that!" said Frans.

"I'm allowed to be angry for once, aren't I?" his landlady said. "At least you didn't have long to wait. I was right behind you. My nephew dropped me off on the corner."

She went inside and Frans followed her. In the hallway she turned on the light and looked at the mirror, shaking her head. Her hat was askew, and her grey curls were nowhere near as neat as before. "It's such a long walk," she said to her reflection. "Otherwise I'd never ride on a thing like that."

"A thing like what?" asked Frans.

"A motor scooter."

"A motor scooter?" repeated Frans with some surprise.

"Yes, my nephew gave me a lift to the village, as he often does. But the wind blasts about your head and it's not the most dignified place to sit. I'd never do it in daylight." Mrs Bakker took off her hat and continued, "Oh, and I've gone and left my umbrella behind! Don't gape at me like I'm the eighth wonder of the world! Haven't you ever been on the back of a motor scooter?"

"No, yes, of course," said Frans, helping her out of her coat.

"Rob's a very good driver," she said, "although I do have to keep reminding him that he doesn't need to go that fast on my account."

"Rob?" repeated Frans. "Is he your nephew? Did he give you a lift back from Sevenways?"

"From my sister's house," said his landlady, looking in the mirror again. "It's near there."

"Rob... Roberto... and a motor scooter," muttered Frans. "Is he a biker? I mean... are Rob and Roberto one and the same person and does he have a scooter and does he dress like..."

"He does sometimes look like a bit of a yob, or a biker, or whatever you want to call it," his landlady replied. "But he's a good boy really. It's a difficult age, of course, but he'll grow out of it." She started combing her hair.

"Does he live in a tent in the wood?" asked Frans. "Roberto, the adventurer with the cowboy hat?"

"That may well be true," his landlady replied. "But in actual fact he lives in town. He's my other sister's only son. Do you know him then?"

"I certainly do!" said Frans. "I've met him as the Biker Boy and as Roberto. But Roberto claims he doesn't know the Biker Boy!"

"Oh well, why should that matter?" said Mrs Bakker. She turned away from the mirror and looked at Frans. "Why shouldn't the boy be two people? It's perfectly normal! Every sensible human being is made up of more than one person – as a schoolteacher, you of all people should know that!"

"Yes, but..." said Frans, feeling rather flabbergasted.

"If Rob wants to lead a couple of different lives, then let him!" his landlady continued. "Soon enough he'll learn how to unite all those different fellows – bikers, cowboys, adventurers, and boys who have to go to school – in just one life. Aren't you more than just Frans van der Steg? I'm made up of several different people, you know – certainly more than just two."

"Mrs Bakker... Aunt Wilhelmina..." said Frans.

"You can call me Aunt Wilhelmina," his landlady replied. "Come on. Go and turn on the lights in the dining room. I'll make some tea and cut us a couple of slices of cake."

Frans followed her into the kitchen. "Aunt Wilhelmina!" he exclaimed. "I've got it! You're one of the spies!"

"A spy? Me?! Hardly! That's one thing I'd never want to be..."

"You're part of the conspiracy. The Conspiracy of Seven!"

Aunt Wilhelmina put the kettle on the gas and rinsed out the teapot. "Oh, if that's what you mean, you're right," she said. "But calling me a spy... That sounds like something Rob would come up with. He watches too many of those detective films."

"But why have you never told me anything about it?" asked Frans.

"Conspiracies are always secret, my boy."

"When you saw me at Sevenways, you just got angry with me," Frans continued. "But you should have known that magician of yours had sent me to sleep."

"That magician certainly doesn't belong to me," said Aunt Wilhelmina. "And I don't approve of his magic either. Why on earth did he have to send you to sleep? A conspiracy's no excuse for being late for lunch. All that silliness just confuses what it's really all about: freeing Geert-Jan Grisenstein. You seemed like the right man for the job. That's what I told my sister – and that's all I did."

"Is your sister Miss Rosemary?" asked Frans.

"Yes, she's the youngest of the three of us, and she was always the most beautiful, but she never married. I'm the eldest, and my other sister, Cornelia, is Roberto's mother. Would you like me to heat something up for you?"

"No... yes, no, thank you," said Frans. "But is all of this for real? Why is everything so strange and complicated, with all these prophecies and family secrets?"

"Well, that's the fault of the dear departed Count Gregorius," said Aunt Wilhelmina. "I mean Gregorius the Mad. He's the one who started setting all those riddles. And Jan Thomtidom isn't much better." She pronounced the name correctly too. "I think all that magic business is very dangerous indeed. You're better off sticking to reality."

"Did Mr Thomtidom write that letter?" asked Frans. "I mean the reply to the advert, the one Count Grisenstein answered."

"What are you talking about now?" his landlady asked.

"Aunt Wilhelmina, please don't pretend you know nothing about it! You told the President of the Conspiracy that I was the right person to infiltrate the House of Stairs as the tutor of Count Grisenstein's nephew. So you must know all about the letter."

"Oh, you mean the letter you were waiting for on Thursday. Well, Frans, you must know more about that than I do, because you knew it was coming before it even got here."

"Aunt Wilhelmina!" cried Frans. "I also told you that I made that story up!"

His landlady turned to him and put her hands on her hips. "Young man," she said sternly, "if you want to go making up events and incidents and presenting them to other people as if they're true, you'll have to bear in mind that they may well indeed come true! Perhaps this will teach you to keep fantasy and reality apart."

"But you're turning things all around," Frans began, feeling rather flustered.

"How about you turn around?" his landlady said. "And go and put the lights on, as I asked, and get the cups out. Then I'll bring the tea through."

Soon after that, they were sitting at the dining table. Aunt Wilhelmina poured the tea and put a plate of thick buttered slices of fruitcake in front of Frans.

Frans thanked her and started eating. Between bites of cake, he muttered, "Roberto and his aunts make three, and Mr Magician, that's four, and Jan Tooreloor, that's five..."

"Are you singing the Song of Seven?" his landlady asked.

"I'm counting the members of the conspiracy," said Frans. "There should be seven of them, and if I include myself, I get six. So who's number seven? I mean the other spy – Roberto said there were two."

"I still don't like to think of myself as a spy," said Aunt Wilhelmina.

"Oh, but you're perfectly suited to it," said Frans. "No one would ever suspect you, and that's just how it should be in a good mystery. But who's the other one?"

Aunt Wilhelmina put on a thoughtful expression. Then she chuckled and said, "That's just typical of Rob. He insisted there should be seven members of the conspiracy. The second spy is already at the House of Stairs."

"At the House of Stairs? I've already counted Jan Tooreloor."

"Jan the coachman? Oh, he's not a spy."

"No, that's true, he's a liaison officer... and what a good job he does! But then who's the spy?"

"You'll have to find that out for yourself," said Aunt Wilhelmina. "Like me, he's someone you'd never suspect."

Frans pushed his plate away. "But then why do I have to get inside the House of Stairs if a spy's already there?"

Aunt Wilhelmina gave him a mysterious look.

"Ivan can't do what you can do," she said, "and you can't do what Ivan can."

"Ivan? His name is Ivan?"

"That's right. You're sure to meet him if you get into the House of Stairs."

"Ivan..." murmured Frans. "Ivan the Spy... He certainly sounds like a character from a spy movie. I don't suppose he's Russian, is he?"

"As far as I know, his parents are local," his landlady said.

"Please tell me more," asked Frans.

"Absolutely not."

"I think these spies are there just to spy on me!" said Frans, banging the table with his fist. "Well, I won't put up with it! I'm not going to be part of this ridiculous conspiracy."

"Don't get so upset," said Aunt Wilhelmina. "You know, there's some truth to what they say about redheads being short-tempered. Ivan is dark and silent, and he's good at sneaking around."

"A sneaky spy. Of course," said Frans. "And Ivan isn't his real name, is it? That's just an alias, isn't it?"

"I'm not telling you anything else," said Aunt Wilhelmina. "You'll have to talk to my sister. Rosemary holds nearly all the strings, even though Jan Thomtidom thinks he does."

"To the Herb Garden," said Frans. "The sixth path from Sevenways, and the last. But why are there six paths and not seven? Go on, Aunt Wilhelmina, tell me now that there's a seventh path, all invisible and forgotten."

"Your imagination is truly astounding," said Aunt Wilhelmina. She stood up and rummaged around in one of the drawers of the sideboard. "Look," she said, "here's a map of the local area. Sevenways is on it too."

Frans looked at the map. "Six paths," he said, "and not a single one more."

"Someone once wrote a book about the area," said Aunt Wilhelmina. "It explains what it used to be like here and what it's like now, and why it was different back then and why it's as it is now. I believe Jan Thomtidom has a copy."

"The book!" said Frans. "I forgot Mr Thomtidom's book, and my own books are still there too."

"Oh, you might as well just leave them there," said Aunt Wilhelmina. "Jan Thomtidom won't notice a few extra books."

"But I need them for my studies!" said Frans.

"You have better things to do," his landlady replied.

"Running up and down stairs, I'm sure," muttered Frans, looking at the map. "Yes, there it is. The House of Stairs, close to Langelaan. I don't understand why Jan Tooreloor went via Sevenways – it takes longer that way. Aunt Wilhelmina, what secret does Sevenways hide?"

"Now don't get yourself all entangled in mysteries," said his landlady. "That will make you easy prey for Count Gradus Grisenstein."

Frans sighed and said in a grave voice, "Count Grisenstein, the Fiendish Foe, the Dragon, the grim grizzly bear..." He pictured some kind of wild man, even more terrifying than the Abominable Snowman.

"He's a villain all right," said Aunt Wilhelmina, "but he's also a gentleman, that has to be said."

In his mind's eye, the wild man transformed into a gentleman in a dinner suit. He had raven-black hair, a dark expression and a gleaming smile in a shadowy face. A blood-red cape was wrapped around his shoulders and a sword flashed in his hand.

"He's as cold as ice," his landlady said. "Would you like another cup of tea?"

The cruel face of Frans's imaginary count grew colder and colder, and the red cape was replaced by a fur coat.

"If you don't want any more tea, you'd better go to bed," said Aunt Wilhelmina. "It's Monday tomorrow, a tiring day."

"I've already slept enough today," said Frans. "But fine, I'll follow your advice. I could do with a few dreams to take me back to reality. Could I borrow this map?"

"You can keep it," said Aunt Wilhelmina. "Please don't spend too much time pondering it though. Think about that poor, innocent child instead. Good night."

As Frans reached the door, she called out to him. "Oh, in case I forget to mention it tomorrow," she said. "When you go to Rosemary's, would you bring my umbrella back with you?"

"If I go, I'll bring it back," Frans replied. "And I shall go. It seems there's no getting out of it. Good night, Aunt Wilhelmina."

He didn't go straight to bed though, but first looked again at the map and added a few notes himself, including Roberto's tent and Mr Thomtidom's house, "Appearance and Reality". "Once upon a time, there were seven paths," he mumbled, drawing a dotted line from Sevenways to the House of Stairs. And then the map looked like this:

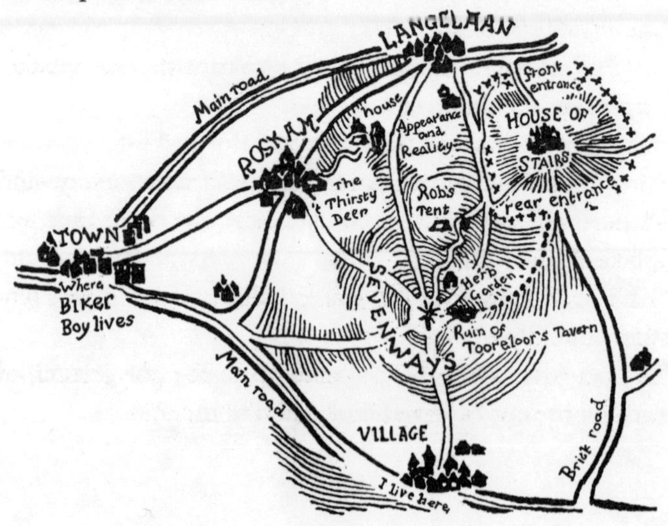

And now even the children get involved

THIS IS FOUR

That Monday, Frans woke earlier than usual, and he was in his classroom long before school began. As he was writing sums on the board, Marian came in, with her friend Jo. They said they were there to water the geraniums.

The two girls set to work with the watering can, but Frans was sure they had another reason for coming in early. After a while, he turned his back on the sums and said, "So, Marian, have you found out who Gr... Gr... is yet?"

"N...no, sir," she said, blushing.

"Well, I have!"

"Have you, sir? Really?" Marian exclaimed.

Jo didn't say anything, but she was so excited that she splashed water all over the floor.

"So who is he?" asked Marian.

Frans crossed his arms and said seriously, "You know very well!"

Marian went even redder. "Y... Yes, sir," she confessed. "But I wasn't allowed to tell. I..."

"Aha!" said Frans. "So you weren't allowed to tell! And who was it who told you that?"

"A man with a beard – he came up to the playground, on Saturday morning, before school. Didn't he, Jo?"

Jo nodded. "A man with a grey beard," she added in a quiet voice.

"He said you might ask us something about a letter," Marian continued. "And that we weren't to tell you anything, even if we knew, sir. He said you had to find out for yourself. We thought it was a bit strange, but we promised, all of us. But we didn't know who the letter was from..."

"You just said that you did know!"

"Only after you showed us the letter," said Marian. "At least I did, and Maarten. The coat of arms was on the letter..."

"Coat of arms?"

"The stairs and the cat's head... Count Grisenstein's count of arms."

"I see," said Frans. "Everyone around here seems to know more about that gentleman than I do... Count Gradus Grisenstein. And the man with the grey beard was, of course, also a friend of yours!"

Marian and Jo shook their heads.

Maarten's voice suddenly echoed around the classroom: "He's a magician."

"My goodness, Maarten, you made me jump!" said Frans. "You sneaked in here just as silently as if you were Ivan himself."

"Who's Ivan?" Maarten immediately replied.

"Do you know Mr Thomtidom?" asked Frans, ignoring his question.

"Thomtidom? Is that his name?" said Maarten. "I didn't know that. But he came to school once and did some magic for us. He can do these great tricks with cards."

"He has some even better tricks up his sleeve," said Frans. "So you all knew Gr... Gr... was Count Grisenstein, and you didn't tell me."

"Not all of us knew," said Maarten. "Kai and Arie know, of course, and Marian, and Jo."

"I told Chris and Lisbeth too," whispered Marian.

"And Kai must have told Hanna and Hans," said Maarten.

"In secret, of course," said Marian.

"In other words," said Frans, "the whole class knows now."

"But how did you find out, sir?" asked Marian.

"Oh, that's a long story," said Frans.

"Will you tell it to us?" pleaded Maarten.

"I'm not sure," replied Frans. "You haven't told me anything yet, have you?"

"Oh, that's so mea- um, I mean, oh, that's not fair," said Maarten, and then he fell silent because the bell rang.

Soon after that, all the children were sitting in their seats. They knew they had maths, because they always did on Monday mornings, but they were looking at Frans as if they were expecting something completely different. Maarten put his hand up and asked, "Sir, who's Ivan?"

"That question, Maarten, has nothing to do with our lesson," said Frans.

"But you said I was like him, sir!"

"You're nothing at all like him," said Frans. "It's just that you crept into the classroom as silently as he would. Ivan is a spy. He's dark and clever, cunning and crafty... Sometimes they call him Ivan the Terrible," he added, "and no one suspects he's a spy, which is, of course, very dangerous for his enemies."

"Who are his enemies?" asked Maarten in a whisper.

"I don't know for sure yet," replied Frans. "And now we're going to do some sums."

Ignoring the disappointed whispers, he told the children to open up their maths books. Then he said in an almost threatening tone that they had three quarters of an hour – and not a second longer – to finish all the sums, without making a mess or any mistakes.

While the children were working, Frans thought about the magician and his peculiar views on arithmetic. He smiled to himself as he wondered what his students would say if he gave them a question about a six-way crossroads that had the same number of paths as a seven-way crossroads.

He didn't mention Mr Thomtidom though, and tried not to think about what had happened to him. And that was probably why he was so strict with the class that Monday morning. He made the children work, work, work! After sums, he gave them a dictation, and then some reading-comprehension exercises, and he yelled at anyone who stopped paying attention for just a moment. After the break, he went on in the same way, ignoring the dirty looks his students were giving him (no one dared to say anything). He made them do mental arithmetic so quickly that they could barely keep up, and when they'd finished that, he announced that they were going to study some grammar.

Frans wrote on the board the first sentence that came to him: *The wicked uncle held the innocent child captive in his house.*

When he saw the words written there, in white on black, he already regretted it, but he said calmly, "Kai, please analyse the grammatical structure of this sentence."

Kai stuck out his bottom lip and, after some serious pondering, he said, "Well, *held* is the verb, and *the wicked uncle* is the subject..." Then he fell silent; grammar wasn't really his strongest point.

Kai bit his lip and fidgeted in his seat, but his teacher pressed on. "And what's the object?"

Kai didn't say anything. He was listening carefully to a quiet murmur behind him.

"Maarten!" roared the teacher. "If you're so sure of the answer, then say it out loud!"

"*The ch... child... The innocent child* is the object, sir," replied Maarten.

As Frans looked at the board, he realized for the first time that the innocent child was so much more important than the wicked uncle. Geert-Jan was just an innocent little boy, not some object – and he was a prisoner. If Count Gradus Grisenstein was truly that dangerous, someone needed to put a stop to the situation – and soon!

"No," he said slowly. "Geert-Jan is not an object."

He turned to the class and saw curious astonishment on all their faces. "Geert-Jan..." he repeated.

And then he forgot all about grammar and nouns and verbs. He had to tell them what had happened to him.

There was one problem with this story though. Were they the adventures of Frans the Red or of Mr Van der Steg, the schoolteacher?

Frans the Red had claimed he was waiting for an important letter, but then Mr Van der Steg had been amazed to receive that letter. Frans the Red had said he knew nothing about Gr... Gr..., a gruesome gremlin who lived in the wood. But Mr Van der Steg knew that he was called Gradus Grisenstein, a man whose name was familiar to all the locals.

All the children in the class had heard of the House of Stairs before, and even the story about the treasure wasn't news to them. They didn't know anything about the conspiracy though (or they pretended not to), and none of them were aware of any other mysteries surrounding Count Grisenstein's home. Was a child really imprisoned there? Was a Sealed Parchment hidden there as well as the treasure? Was there some dark spy creeping up and down the stairs of the house?

Frans told them the story, and not even the bell at twelve o'clock stopped him. Fifteen minutes later, he solemnly swore to his class that he'd given them a true account of all his experiences. And then it took a little while for them all to leave the classroom, whispering excitedly, and go outside.

"Ah, I see you all had to stay behind, did you?" said the headmaster, who was standing outside the door. "Most disappointing. Mr Van der Steg is doing his utmost to get you youngsters to learn something."

Frans felt guilty when he heard those words. Instead of teaching the children, he'd been telling them stories for three quarters of an hour, and it wasn't even Saturday.

But his class didn't give him away; they pulled faces as if all they'd been doing, all that time, was analysing sentences. They were good children and he knew the secrets of the conspiracy were safe with them.

*

At twenty-five past three that Monday afternoon, half the class put up their hands at the same time, and the other half began to whisper.

"I know what time it is," said Frans, who was looking out of the window, with his hands in his pockets. "And you can go on working until half past three."

"Yes, sir," said Maarten. "But you... Can't you just quickly write that letter? That's what you were planning to do, isn't it? The letter to..." And he lowered his voice... "Count Grisenstein."

Everyone chimed in and noisily agreed with his suggestion.

"Geert-Jan has to be freed as quickly as possible," said Marian.

"And the treasure has to be found," said Kai.

Frans walked slowly to his desk, picked up a sheet of paper and said, "Fine, I'll do it. Quieten down, all of you."

The children did as they were told. And Frans wrote:

To Count Grisenstein
The House of Stairs
Near Langelaan

Monday 28 September

Noble sir,

To my great regret, I received your letter of the 22nd of this month too late, and as a result your coachman did not find me at home.

Then he thought, *I just hope Jan Tooreloor hasn't told him anything different. No, no, he's part of the conspiracy, so he'll have done what he had to do.* He went on writing:

I sincerely hope you do not hold this against me, and I would very much welcome the opportunity for a conversation with you. I am at your disposal every evening this week...

But then he thought, *If I say "every evening", I might end up missing my evening class next Friday too, but then I suppose that if I get the job I won't be doing much studying anyway.*

I await your response with interest.
Respectfully yours...

Then it was half past three, and the children crowded around his desk to read the letter and to give it their approval. They were all gabbling away at the same time, and asked the same question over and over again, "Are you going to see Miss Rosemary now?"

"Go on! Scram! The lot of you!" shouted Frans, suddenly realizing what a strange situation it was. Who was in charge here? Him or the children?

When he was alone in the classroom, he read through the letter again and noticed he'd signed it as FRANS THE RED. That wouldn't do, of course, so with a sigh he picked up a blank sheet of paper and wrote out the letter again. He found an envelope in his desk drawer, wrote the address on it and said, "Right, so that's that."

It was almost four by the time he left the school with the letter in his pocket. He'd expected to see a few children still hanging around outside, but the playground was deserted; there wasn't a child in sight.

"And it's just as well," he said to himself. "Those children are getting far too big for their boots – it's as if I'm a puppet in some play they've made up. And as for the letter, I may have written it, but I'm not going to post it yet. First I want to... Yes, what do I actually want to do? I want to talk to Miss Rosemary first... No, I don't even know if I want to do that. I don't like the thought of her holding all the strings. But I suppose I have no choice! Then I might as well head straight there, and I'll be home in time for tea."

The road to Sevenways was quiet and peaceful, as it had been the previous times, but as Frans got closer, he became aware of sounds he'd never heard there before – lots of high-pitched voices, all speaking at the same time.

The children! He should have known. Of course they wanted to go and see the place where his strange adventures had taken him.

At the clearing, Frans had to brake to avoid an obstacle: a messy pile of bikes that had been thrown down onto the ground. The children were all there, the whole class. They were chattering and screaming, and some of them were singing:

Do you know the Seven, the Seven,
Do you know the Seven Ways?

Most of them had gathered around the signpost. A few were staring at the path that led to Roberto's tent and the cannon guarding it, while others were investigating the tumbledown pub. Two boys were struggling to get the big double doors open, and Kai was perilously leaning out of a window on the top floor.

"Hey!" shouted Frans, climbing off his bike. "Kai, get back inside and come downstairs this instant!"

The children by the signpost were delighted to see him. The girls started dancing around and singing:

"This is one, this is two, this is three..."

Kai yelled something and waved his arms. Maarten came running up triumphantly, holding the pub sign.

"Calm down!" called Frans. "And come here! That includes you, Kai!"

Soon they were standing around him, but they were all talking at the same time, and it was impossible for Frans to speak or to make any sense of what they were saying.

But suddenly there was silence – a silence broken only by the rattle of wheels and the crack of a whip.

Down the road from Roskam, the old coach came rolling towards them, with Jan Tooreloor sitting up front.

THAT WAS FOUR *and now for Part Five*

5

Frans becomes entangled in the conspiracy

He is initiated by Miss Rosemary

THIS IS ONE

The coachman brought the carriage to a halt close to the signpost. As Frans and the children stared at him, he responded with a sneer. Then he jumped down from the front and opened the door.

Frans and the children stared even harder, although the person who climbed out of the coach was not who they'd expected. It was a woman with a small build, as dainty as a porcelain figurine. Her face was white and pink, with large dark eyes. She'd wrapped a colourful flowery scarf elegantly around her head, and a snow-white curl had slipped out from under it, just over her left eyebrow. She was wearing a black coat with white dots and had a large basket on her arm. The coachman swiftly took it from her, so it seemed he did in fact know how to be polite. She thanked him with a radiant smile and said, "It was very kind of you, Jan, to bring me here." Then she took a sugar lump from one of her pockets and gave it to the horse.

"I'd happily take you all the way home, Miss Rosemary," said the coachman. "And as for this commotion here..." He glowered at Frans and the children.

"There's no need to worry, Jan," said Miss Rosemary, as she looked at the children. "Please put my basket down. I shall just..."

She didn't finish the sentence. The coachman put the basket on the ground, and then pounced on Maarten and snatched the pub sign from his hand. "How dare you?!" he yelled furiously. "Destroying my property!"

Maarten gaped at him, scared half to death.

"Calm down, Jan," said Miss Rosemary. She walked up to him and laid a hand on his arm.

The coachman backed off. "Only because it's you who's asking," he growled. "Otherwise I'd..."

"I'll make sure nothing else unpleasant happens here," said Miss Rosemary, interrupting him. She stood on tiptoe and whispered something in his ear.

The coachman tapped his cap, returned to the coach without looking back and climbed up, with the sign clutched firmly under his arm. Then he drove off in the direction of Langelaan.

Miss Rosemary turned to Frans. "So you're Mr Van der Steg," she said, holding out her hand in a gesture that made Frans feel the urge to plant a kiss on it. But he didn't (kissing her hand seemed so ridiculous with all those children standing around); he simply shook her hand.

"And you must be his students," Miss Rosemary said to the children. "Luckily I can see now that you know how to be quiet too. The din you were making just now could be heard almost all the way to the House of Stairs... Imagine if it had reached the ears of Count Grisenstein."

It was so quiet now that Frans could hear an insect buzzing and the wind gently rustling the leaves.

"Now leave your bikes nice and neatly by the Red Man," said Miss Rosemary.

"The red man?" whispered Maarten.

"That's what this pub used to be called: 'The Red Man', Tooreloor's Tavern. Didn't you see the man on the sign? Put down your bikes and come with me, all of you. I'd like to have a word with you all. That includes you, Mr Van der Steg."

Shortly after that, Miss Rosemary was lightly treading the path to the Herb Garden, with the children following her. They walked two by two, without being asked, and Frans, who was bringing up the rear, noticed that any whispering was silenced as soon as the small woman put her finger to her lips.

He was almost jealous. *She barely comes up to my waist, but she has my whole class under her thumb*, he thought enviously.

First they walked some way through the wood, and then the path took them through a field where a few patches of heather were still in bloom. About ten minutes later, they reached Miss Rosemary's house. The path didn't end there, but carried on. The house was small and white, with a thatched roof. Climbing roses and creepers grew up the walls, and boxes of geraniums hung beneath the windows with their pink shutters. There was a large garden all around, divided into sections by low, neatly trimmed hedges. In front of the house was a lawn with glorious borders of colourful flowers: late roses and Michaelmas daisies, chrysanthemums and dahlias. A flagstone path led to the front door.

Miss Rosemary opened the wooden gate, which had the words "The Herb Garden" painted on it. "This is my flower garden," she said. "The herbs grow around the side of the house and behind it. Can you smell them?" And indeed, all kinds of vague but delightful scents drifted through the air.

A big sheepdog ran up, barking. "Be quiet, Chive," she said. "These are our friends." The dog wagged his tail and jumped up her. "Welcome, welcome, my dears! Come on inside," said Miss Rosemary. Then she suddenly let out a quiet gasp. "Oh, my goodness, how foolish of me!" she said. "I've gone and left my basket of groceries back at the signpost."

"Shall I..." three boys began at once. But Miss Rosemary looked over the tops of their heads at Frans. "Mr Van der Steg, would you please fetch it? You have the longest legs of all of us."

Frans was, of course, happy to do so. But as he walked back to Sevenways with large strides, it occurred to him that she hadn't asked him because of his long legs.

*

His suspicions grew even stronger when he returned to the house in the Herb Garden. It was less than fifteen minutes later; he'd ridden his bike on the way back. Miss Rosemary thanked him and took the basket before leading him to a room that was not large, but where all the children had somehow managed to find a place to sit. They were on chairs and on the floor, with glasses of lemonade and cinnamon biscuits. When Frans came in, he felt as if he'd interrupted a conversation, even though they all said hello nicely.

She must have told them something I'm not allowed to know, he thought. *Maybe she really did leave the basket behind on purpose! That's not right! Who's supposed to be part of this conspiracy? Me or the children?*

He looked at his hostess, who was standing in the middle of the room. She'd taken off her coat and was wearing a grey silk dress with a large white lace collar. Her age was hard to guess; she was much younger than her sister Wilhelmina, but her hair was as white as snow. She reminded him of a lady from the days when aristocrats wore wigs; she really should have been dressed in a hoop skirt and surrounded by courtiers in knee-breeches and velvet jackets. But she looked perfectly at ease with the children gathered around her.

"Finish your lemonade, my dears," she said in her lilting voice, "because you really need to be off now. You're far from home and you have to be back in the village before dark."

It no longer surprised Frans that his students instantly obeyed her. They got up without too much fuss and didn't break a single glass. Then they followed her to the front door and shook her hand, one by one.

"Your teacher's going to stay here for a little while," said Miss Rosemary. "He'll bring you up to date later. And there's already something you can do to help him." She looked at Frans and said, "Do you have the letter with you? Then they can post it."

A murmur went up among the children.

"Can I do it...?"

"Can I...?"

"Let me...!"

"The letter to Count Grisenstein," said Frans. "Here it is. But it doesn't have a stamp."

"I'll put one on it for you," said Miss Rosemary. She took the letter from his hand and left the room.

Returning just a moment later, she looked around the crowd of children and gave the letter to Jo. "You can post it," she said, "and the others will make sure you don't forget."

"How could she ever forget something that important?" said Maarten, a little enviously.

"And now off you go home, my dears," said Miss Rosemary. "Remember what I told you."

The children said goodbye to her again, and waved at Frans as they dashed off.

Then Frans asked, "What did you say to them, Miss... um..."

"My name," she said, "is Rosemary Grysenstein, but you can call me Miss Rosemary, like everyone else."

Frans stared at her, the children forgotten. "Your surname's Grysenstein?!" he said.

"That's Grysenstein with a Y," said Miss Rosemary. "I'm not related to the count. It's just a coincidence that our names sound the same. Or maybe it isn't a coincidence. My father always said we were distant relations, the Grisensteins with an I and the Grysensteins with a Y... through our great-great-great-grandmother, Rosemary the knife-grinder's daughter..."

And suddenly a couple of silly lines of verse popped into Frans's head:

Rosemary, Rosemary, have a fine day!
Knife-grinder's daughter, toorelay!

But of course he didn't sing them out loud. He just said "Oh."

"But that story isn't the point right now," said Miss Rosemary. "Let's go inside." She walked ahead of him into the front room, where she briskly began collecting the glasses on a tray. "I do know them, though, the Grisensteins with an I," she continued. "When I was a girl, I often played with the previous count – in the gardens and woods around the House of Stairs. And I helped him to search for the treasure."

"The previous count?" asked Frans.

"Yes, Geert-Jan's father, Gilbert Grisenstein. We were the same age, and when I was ten or eleven years old – that's longer ago than you might think – he was my best friend."

Miss Rosemary picked up the tray and said, "Please, sit down, and I'll go and make a cup of tea."

Frans did as she asked, and for a short while he was alone in the room. The furniture was old-fashioned, with a few slightly worn but comfortable chairs, a couple of tables that had been polished to a shine, a bulbous cabinet and an antique sideboard. On the floor was a rug with birds and flowers on it; the wallpaper was striped and the curtains had flounces. Small oval paintings hung on the walls, there were plenty of potted plants scattered around, and the sideboard was covered with little ornaments. It was a friendly room, and a good match for his hostess's appearance.

And yet, thought Frans, *no matter how friendly she looks, I have no doubt that she's capable of holding and tugging all the strings!*

The dog suddenly appeared from under a table, stretched, and sat down opposite Frans, studying him.

"Chive wants to get to know you better," said Miss Rosemary, coming back in with the tea. "He guards my house."

"Do you live here on your own?" asked Frans.

"Not entirely alone," she replied. "I do have Chive, after all." She sat down too, and the dog lay at her feet. "A man sometimes comes in the morning to help me with the heavy work," she added. "But otherwise I do everything myself."

"I've heard that you grow herbs," said Frans.

"Yes, it's a nice little business," she said with some pride. "I sell them in all the villages hereabouts, and in the town too. I work in my garden every day, but obviously I wear different clothes then, and my rubber boots."

Frans tried to imagine her with boots on her feet and a spade in her hands, but found that he couldn't.

"But you haven't come here about my herbs," continued Miss Rosemary.

"No," said Frans, "your nephew Roberto and Aunt Wilhelmina sent me to you to... to be, um, initiated, I believe."

"Oh, but that's already happened," said Miss Rosemary.

"Already happened? But how? And when?"

"When I told the children to post your application letter. That makes you one of the seven conspirators." Miss Rosemary offered Frans a chocolate from a silver dish, took one herself, and began to tell him more about the House of Stairs and the previous Count Grisenstein.

"When we grew up, we remained friends, Gilbert and I," she said. "But we lost touch during the war, and after that we rarely saw each other. Gilbert was a rather adventurous type, just like his ancestor, Sir Grimbold. He was nearly always travelling, and I'd receive the occasional picture postcard from the strangest locations in the world..." She paused and gazed thoughtfully into space.

She must have been a very beautiful young woman, thought Frans. *That adventurous Gilbert was a fool to go travelling and just send her picture postcards.* And he asked her, "So who was living in the House of Stairs back then?"

"The House of Stairs remained empty for a long time," replied Miss Rosemary. "It might sound strange, given the shortage of housing after the war, but you'd have to be a Grisenstein or a little bit crazy to want to live there. It's too big for any ordinary family, and it's no good for any other purpose, such as a hotel or an office. All those stairs... far too impractical. But then Count Gilbert wrote to say that he was coming back. He was in love with a girl from Honolulu or Rio de Janeiro, or maybe from Torelore..." She smiled briefly and said, "He'd fallen for a girl he'd met on one of his journeys and he wanted to bring her to his ancestral home as his bride. But the House of Stairs had been terribly neglected, and restoring it was going to take some time. So he stayed abroad and married her there."

I wonder if Rosemary was sorry about that, Frans thought to himself.

"But Gilbert's wife never lived in the House of Stairs," Miss Rosemary continued. "She died a year after the birth of her son, Geert-Jan, the boy you're interested in. Poor motherless child, poor Gilbert..."

Miss Rosemary sighed. "Count Gilbert returned," she said quietly, "but only so that he could entrust Geert-Jan to my care. Then he went off on his travels again, more restless than ever. I took care of his son – he was such a sweet child."

She looked around the room, as if she could see a little boy toddling about. Frans followed her gaze and saw the fragile ornaments on the sideboard: green and white horses, spotted dogs, rainbow-coloured birds and animals he didn't know the names of. Most of them, though, were damaged and missing ears or legs, and he spotted a few tin soldiers standing among them. Geert-Jan Grisenstein must have had fun here.

"So you looked after him?" he said. "Then why is he living with his uncle in the House of Stairs now?"

"His father planned to return one day," said Miss Rosemary. "The heir of the Grisensteins should live in the house of his ancestors. But Gilbert never came back. He died in a plane crash."

They sat in silence for a short while, Miss Rosemary stroking her dog. "It's more than five years ago now," she said. "Have another chocolate; this one has a nut in... No, Chive's not allowed any." She sat up straight and continued, "A relative, Gradus Grisenstein, became Geert-Jan's guardian. And, according to the law, it was his decision to make. Gradus Grisenstein took Geert-Jan away from me, and there was nothing I could do about it."

She looked at Frans, her fine eyebrows drawn together. "The boy was six at the time," she said, "and he'd just started school. But Gradus was his guardian and he took him to The Hague."

"To The Hague? Not to the House of Stairs?"

"No, Gradus lived in The Hague, as he thought that was an appropriate place for a count to live. He never liked the House of Stairs, not even as a child. I knew him when I was younger too. He sometimes came to stay with Gilbert, and of course he searched for the treasure with us. But Gilbert never told him what was in the Sealed Parchment..."

Aha, thought Frans, *it's that Sealed Parchment again.*

Miss Rosemary continued. "I never trusted Gradus. Oh, he took good care of Geert-Jan, with nannies and what have you. But I'd have brought up the boy here for free! I'd even have gone to The Hague for him. But Gradus didn't want me to. Firstly because he didn't like me, and secondly because... but I didn't realize that until later."

She stacked the empty cups and stood up.

"You'll stay for dinner, won't you?" she said.

"It's very kind of you to offer," replied Frans. "But I'm afraid I can't. Aunt Wilhelmina is counting on me to be home on time."

"My sister will most certainly be counting on you to eat here with me," she said. "I'll give her a call to let her know you're staying."

"Do you have a telephone?" said Frans with some surprise. He hadn't expected to find such a device in this house.

"Of course," said Miss Rosemary. "I simply couldn't do without one." She left the room and Frans heard her having a brief telephone conversation in the hallway.

"Good, now that's all arranged," she said when she came back, and she began laying the round table in the corner of the room.

"But Count Grisenstein – I mean, Count Gradus Grisenstein – lives in the House of Stairs now, doesn't he?" said Frans.

"That's right," replied Miss Rosemary. "But only since last year. He moved in just before Geert-Jan's tenth birthday... His tenth birthday!" she repeated. "That makes you think, doesn't it?"

But Frans had absolutely no idea what it was supposed to make him think.

"And of course I immediately paid them a visit," his hostess continued. "Geert-Jan was pleased to see me, but Count Gradus couldn't get rid of me quickly enough. And now he refuses even to let me visit. He says I'm a bad influence on his nephew." She scowled as she added, "Well, I'm not keen on his influence either! From what I've seen and heard..."

"And what is that?" asked Frans.

"You know very well!" Miss Rosemary's expression changed, her eyes becoming anxious and concerned. "I sincerely hope you'll be Geert-Jan's tutor," she said in a whisper. "Sometimes I'm scared that..."

Frans stood up and went to stand beside her. "Scared that what?" he asked quietly. Miss Rosemary straightened the silverware. "Count Gradus does not like children," she said. "If he goes looking for a treasure, it's only so that he can become rich, not for the fun of the search itself. But come along," she continued, "let's not spoil our appetites with shadows of things that are not yet here and that may never come."

Frans noticed now that she had laid the table for three.

"Yes, I've invited another guest," she said, following his gaze. "But we'll be able to speak freely, as he's another member of the conspiracy."

"Is it Ivan?" asked Frans, looking at her expectantly.

"No, Ivan is very attached to his home," replied Miss Rosemary. "And besides, he doesn't get along with Chive."

"Who is it, then?" asked Frans. "Roberto?"

Chive gave a quick bark and trotted to the door, which opened. Mr Thomtidom was standing there on the doorstep.

"No, it's me," he said with a bow, "the Secretary of the Conspiracy. Although I prefer to call myself a magician."

He hears about the Sealed Parchment

THIS IS TWO

The magician stepped into the room and walked towards them. He removed his top hat and pulled a bouquet of red roses from it.

"Beautiful Rosemary," he said, "I know that bringing flowers to the Herb Garden is as foolish as taking coals to Newcastle or owls to Athens or water to the sea... but I could think of no better tribute."

Miss Rosemary thanked him warmly, and Frans felt sorry for a moment that he hadn't thought to bring flowers for her too.

The magician turned to him. "Nice to meet you again, Mr Van der Steg." He put his hat back on, took it off again – and this time he pulled out a pile of books, which he gave to Frans. "Here you go," he said, "you left them at my place yesterday, when you departed in such a hurry."

"Thank you," said Frans coldly. "You know, I found your little tricks really quite surprising."

"Could you perhaps phrase that a little differently?" said Mr Thomtidom. "How about this, for instance? 'Mr Thomtidom, your magical gifts are a marvel.' The way you fled from my house, Mr Van der Steg, made me think you were trying to free yourself from one of my magic circles! But let me reassure you: most magic is about appearance rather than reality, and all magic obeys the laws of logic."

"Well, I'll let you men entertain each other for a moment," said Miss Rosemary. "And then I can go to the kitchen."

"Ah, now she's going to perform more powerful magic than my own," said Mr Thomtidom, when Miss Rosemary had left. "The preparation of a delicious, nutritious meal."

"But your own magic powers are quite something," said Frans, still in a chilly tone. "Or was it just an ordinary sleeping pill that knocked me out for four hours yesterday afternoon?"

"Hmm, that was indeed a strange business," said Mr Thomtidom. He sat down and added, "I was most surprised when you suddenly drifted off. I tried to shake you awake, but it was no good!"

"I'm sorry, but I find that hard to believe," said Frans, sitting down opposite him.

"You think it was me who sent you to sleep?" exclaimed Mr Thomtidom. "Why on earth would I do that? To secretly snip off a lock of your hair perhaps? Or do you have a better suggestion?"

"My imagination fails me," said Frans. "But I'm keen to hear what you'll tell me. Why did you turn back the hands of your clock?"

"So that you wouldn't feel uncomfortable," replied Mr Thomtidom. "I wanted to spare you the embarrassment. It's rather impolite, you know, to fall asleep when you're visiting someone, even if the conversation isn't very interesting."

He smiled amiably at the younger man.

"But the conversation was extremely interesting!" said Frans with a friendliness he didn't feel. "The story of the Sealed Parchment, for example... I'd have liked to hear more about that."

"Really?" said Mr Thomtidom. "Well, they say that Count Gregorius, almost two hundred years ago now, gave his grandson a letter on his tenth birthday, closed with many wax seals. That was the Sealed Parchment, and it contains clues about where the treasure is hidden. Count Gregorius allowed the grandson until his eighteenth birthday to look for the treasure; if he hadn't found it by then, he would no longer have any right to it. Then he would have to reseal the parchment and keep it until his eldest son was ten. That boy would then be permitted to go in search of the treasure, also until he was eighteen, and then he would pass it on to his eldest son. Because, or so Count Gregorius said, only a child has a right to the treasure. And so the parchment, opened and resealed over and over again, passed from father to son. Only the eldest son of a Grisenstein has ever been allowed to read it..."

"And where is the parchment now?" asked Frans.

"If all has gone according to custom and tradition, Geert-Jan must have it," replied Mr Thomtidom. "Although his father was sadly unable to pass it on to him." He leant forward to Chive, who had come to stand beside him, and began talking to him in such a quiet mumble that Frans couldn't make out a word. The dog pricked up his ears and wagged his tail, as if he were listening to a particularly enjoyable story.

"So you speak the language of dogs, do you?" said Frans sarcastically.

"Not fluently," replied the magician, with a modest expression on his face. "The language of cats is more my thing. But luckily dogs are good listeners."

They soon sat down at the dinner table, and Miss Rosemary served up the soup, which smelt delicious and tasted even better. Then she brought out dishes of floury potatoes and tender meat in a fragrant gravy, with peas and fresh salad. A separate meal in a deep bowl was put on the floor for Chive.

Mr Thomtidom said contentedly, "Rosemary, I would fast six days of the week so that I could feast on the seventh with you." And he added, "Ah, if Geert-Jan could live with you for just a week, he'd be the healthiest boy for miles around."

Frans decided it was time to bring up the subject of the Sealed Parchment again.

"No one knows what it says," said the magician. "But legend has it that the treasure can be found only with the help of the prophecies in that document."

"More prophecies?" said Frans.

"Yes, the prophecies of Gregorius the Mad," said Miss Rosemary. "My sister Wilhelmina calls them riddles without an answer. But Jan Thomtidom believes they're interesting problems with a logical solution. Have some more gravy, Mr Van der Steg."

"Well, in any case there's certainly one problem that can be solved with logical reasoning," said Mr Thomtidom. He took another bite, waited until his mouth was empty and continued, "And it's this: why did Count Gradus Grisenstein suddenly go to live in the House of Stairs last year, leaving The Hague, even though he found it much more to his liking there?"

"So why is that?" asked Frans.

Mr Thomtidom looked at him as a kind-hearted teacher would look at a particularly slow pupil.

"Count Gradus is Geert-Jan's guardian," he said. "He will manage the Grisenstein properties until the boy comes of age. As the executor of the will, of course, he has also taken possession of the Sealed Parchment, in order to pass it on to his nephew on his tenth birthday, in his father's place... and without breaking the seals."

"But you think he broke them?" asked Frans.

"It is a certainty that Count Gradus broke the seals and read the parchment before sealing it back up again."

"And why did he seal it back up again?" said Frans.

Mr Thomtidom shook his head at Frans's lack of understanding. "So Geert-Jan wouldn't realize his uncle had read the parchment," he said.

"So the count *has* given the document to his nephew!" cried Frans.

"Of course," said Mr Thomtidom. "On his tenth birthday, as I already said. That's why that scoundrel Gradus moved into the House of Stairs: to give Geert-Jan the opportunity to search for the treasure."

Frans put down his knife and fork and said, with a mixture of surprise and irritation, "Are you telling me that this scoundrel, as you call him, has gone to live at the House of Stairs to help his nephew find the treasure?"

"Exactly," said Mr Thomtidom with a nod.

"Well, I don't think your reasoning is very logical at all," said Frans. "If the count wanted the treasure that much, he'd look for it himself."

"Now your reasoning is illogical, Mr Van der Steg," came the reply. "The boy has to look for the treasure; he has the Sealed Parchment."

"If the count is such a rogue and a scoundrel, he would never have given the parchment to his nephew!" said Frans. "Or he must be more of a fool than a scoundrel."

"Oh no, Gradus certainly isn't stupid," Miss Rosemary said. "But I have to say that Jan Thomtidom's reasoning does indeed sound illogical to anyone who doesn't know what's in the Sealed Parchment."

"But no one knows, do they?" said Frans.

"Have a little more salad," said Mr Thomtidom. "Then some for me, please. Rosemary, you make the best salads ever – I dare say in the whole world. Don't you think, Mr Van der Steg?"

"That's one thing we agree on," said Frans. But his mind was elsewhere as he helped himself to more salad. It was only when he passed the bowl to Mr Thomtidom that he noticed he hadn't left very much for him.

The magician looked as if he was about to mention it, but Miss Rosemary didn't give him the chance.

"No one but a child who was the eldest son of a Grisenstein has ever seen the Sealed Parchment," she said.

"Except for Count Gradus," said Mr Thomtidom.

"Even though he had no right at all!" He looked disapprovingly at Frans. "The lengths a man will go to for the sake of greed," he muttered.

"The boy who has the Sealed Parchment may show it to no one," continued Miss Rosemary. "But he can, of course, tell someone else what it says... Geert-Jan's father told me, in utmost secrecy, when we were both ten years old."

"So you know what's in the letter!" whispered Frans.

"She knew once," said Mr Thomtidom. "But she may have forgotten..." He looked at Miss Rosemary as if hoping she'd agree.

Miss Rosemary, however, replied, "I haven't forgotten, Jan Thomtidom, as you well know! And what's more, I haven't kept the secret... as Mr Van der Steg could see from the colour of your shirt."

The magician put his hand on his chest as if trying to hide the colour of his shirt – which was green – and said rather stiffly, "My dear Rosemary, I would ask you not to stray into the subject of my research in the field of colour theory. That subject is of no importance at the moment; it is completely irrelevant, and could even seem irrational and unreal to Mr Van der Steg."

Frans stared at him. The conversation had taken a turn that was beyond irrational and unreal. It was completely incomprehensible!

Miss Rosemary laughed brightly. "There's no need to be afraid, my dear Jan," she said. "I truly won't try to interfere with your magic circles. I wouldn't think of tangling up the ribbons and bows of your visionary plans. But you must see that poor Frans the Red doesn't understand a thing!"

"His name," said Mr Thomtidom, "is still Frans van der Steg. And he must think he's already stepped into a magic circle or fallen into a trap. And that's not fair. I want him to be able to start out upon his mission without any worries, without feeling that he's surrounded by magic circles."

"To be honest," said Frans, looking from one to the other, "I already feel encircled or entangled or whatever. How am I supposed to start out upon my so-called mission without any worries, as you put it, if I don't know what conclusions to draw from the circles that you're drawing... I mean, from this conversation... Hang on. What exactly *are* we talking about?"

"The conversation," said Miss Rosemary, "is about the Sealed Parchment – and that's all."

"A subject that would appear to be rather weighty," muttered Mr Thomtidom, "and therefore bad for the digestion."

Frans looked at his plate, which was piled high with salad, and started eating again. He didn't know what else to do, and the food was excellent.

"But we still need to tell him about it, Jan," said Miss Rosemary. "He knows a lot, but not enough. I still think you should have explained it all to him right away."

"I disagree," said Mr Thomtidom. "Besides, what's done is done... Or in this case, not done. Whatever he knows or doesn't know; he's still an *outsider*... and that is the point of the whole story."

"I am running out of patience!" said Frans, raising his voice. "Would you both please talk as if I'm actually here?"

"But of course you're here!" said Miss Rosemary with a friendly smile.

"And as the guest of honour too," said Mr Thomtidom. "Empty your plate. A good meal is the best medicine for a person who's feeling muddle-headed and forgetful."

"Then I suggest you'd better empty your plate too, Jan," Miss Rosemary chided him.

Mr Thomtidom fell silent and concentrated on his dinner. Frans went on eating too, but he kept glancing at his hostess.

Miss Rosemary played with her napkin and said thoughtfully, "Gilbert whispered the prophecies of Sealed Parchment in my ear. He recited all the rhymes for me. And I remembered them. I may have forgotten a word or two here or there, but not the essence! It was a secret, but when Gilbert's son was imprisoned in the House of Stairs, I knew I could reveal it to his friends... To you, Jan Thomtidom, and to all the other conspirators."

Frowning, the magician looked up from his plate, which was now empty. Frans forgot about his salad and waited eagerly to hear what she would say next.

Miss Rosemary folded the napkin in four and slowly recited:

Try, my Child, and my Child's Child's Children
To unravel this tangled Rhyme.
One alone will never find me,
Together you must beat the Time.

Scale the heights, head down below,
The steps will show you where to go.
In this house with many a stair,
Follow the steps to lead you there.

The magician raised one lecturing finger. "A tangled rhyme indeed..." he said. "And what were those words? *One alone will never find me*... Do you see now why Gradus Grisenstein had to give his nephew the parchment?"

"He knows he can't find the treasure on his own," said Miss Rosemary. "We mustn't forget the prophecy on the lintel either," the magician added. "The treasure will be found by a *child*."

"I understand it now," said Frans. "But what's all that about steps to show you where to go?"

"It's a clue to where the child must seek the treasure, of course," replied the magician. "It's clearly connected to steps and stairs or even ladders maybe, anything that would allow a person to scale the heights and head down below. Any of the steps in that house might show the seeker where to go..."

"A most illuminating clue," said Frans, "when the treasure's hidden in a house with a hundred staircases. No wonder no one's ever found it!"

"There's more in the parchment," said Miss Rosemary, folding out the points of her napkin. And she said:

These Words are the Sign:
All the Children must be your Friends,
If you are to beat the Foe.

"And so we've solved the next puzzle," said the magician. "Why does Count Gradus Grisenstein claim that his nephew is in poor health, so that he has to keep him indoors? Because then the boy doesn't have to go to school! If he were to meet other children, they'd become his friends. And the count is scared of that happening."

"Because he's the Foe," said Miss Rosemary.

"The Fiendish Foe that the other prophecy also warns about," said the magician in a hushed voice. "Yes, Count Gradus Grisenstein is the Dragon that must be beaten..."

Miss Rosemary recited:

These Words are the Sign:
The Stranger who will defeat the Dragon
Must travel over Sevenways.

"And here we come to the heart of the matter!" said the magician. He picked up the napkin, which Miss Rosemary had now put down, and waved it around. "*The Stranger who will defeat the Dragon*... the Dragon is the Fiendish Foe, and only an outsider can eliminate him. You, Mr Van der Steg, are a Stranger! You have not been living here long, and the day before yesterday you had never heard of the House of Stairs. You are the one who will beat and defeat Count Grisenstein..." He flapped the napkin at Frans, making him blink. "That's why Jan Tooreloor drove the coach – with you in it – via Sevenways to the House of Stairs," he continued. "I mean, if you hadn't got out, you'd have travelled over Sevenways to Count Grisenstein, just as it says in the prophecy." Mr Thomtidom raised his hands; they were empty. "The napkin," he said, "is under your plate."

But Frans wasn't impressed by this conjuring trick. "As it says in the prophecy?" he repeated. "So I need to go to the House of Stairs because, according to you, it's been predicted?"

"Precisely. Because it was predicted and prophesied by Gregorius the Mad," said the magician.

Gregorius the "Mad", Frans thought to himself. *So what does that say about people who believe his rhymes are true? And what does it say about me if I do as they tell me?* He didn't really want to answer those questions, so he emptied his plate in silence.

"Your letter to Count Grisenstein has been written and posted," said Miss Rosemary, apparently reading his mind. "If he sends for you, you can't refuse. There's no going back!"

She stood up. And suddenly she seemed like the good fairy from a children's story, with her mysterious eyes and her silver hair. She smiled at him and added, "Didn't you tell your students you were longing for a new adventure and an important mission?"

Frans smiled back at her. "I am at your service," he said. "Frans the Red is ready for duty."

"Excellent," said the magician. "Then our business is concluded."

"Concluded?" said Miss Rosemary. "Whatever you say. Then I'll fetch the pudding. It's semolina, with redcurrant juice, as red as our hero's hair." She gave the magician a meaningful smile and left the room. *They're hiding something else from me!* thought Frans. He turned to the magician and said, "There's one more thing I don't understand."

Mr Thomtidom looked at him with a frown, stroking his beard. "What's that?" he asked.

"What," said Frans, "does the Sealed Parchment have to do with the colour of your shirt?"

He ventures into forbidden territory

THIS IS THREE

"And of course he didn't answer my question," said Mr Van der Steg.

It was the next day. The bell for half past three had already gone, but his students had all stayed behind so as not to miss any of his story about the visit to Miss Rosemary's.

"Oh no!" Frans continued. "Mr Thomtidom just began telling me some long and complicated story about how difficult it is to find a tie to go with a green shirt. Then he magically made my tie *and* his tie disappear, and had them both reappear in a finger bowl. And when Miss Rosemary came back with the pudding, it was so delicious that we forgot about our deep and meaningful conversation."

Frans got up and went to stand among the desks. "After dinner, Miss Rosemary washed up," he continued in a quieter voice. "Mr Thomtidom dried and I stacked the plates and bowls on a tray and took them to the front room. When I went back into the kitchen though, I heard the magician whispering something. 'It's just as well we didn't tell him everything,' he was saying. 'We might have scared him off...' Then he stopped. I think it was because he heard me coming."

The children looked up at him, with questions on their faces.

"So what happened...?" whispered Maarten.

"Well, I'm part of the conspiracy now," said Frans, "but I think there's another conspiracy within that conspiracy, a conspiracy that I'm not in on. And I'm determined to expose it! No prophecy, no matter how threatening, is going to scare me off!" He put his hands on his hips and looked defiantly at his students.

They seemed impressed. That was how the real Frans the Red should act. But then Marian asked, "So how are you going to do that, sir?"

Frans the Red disappeared, and Frans van der Steg gave a sigh. "I don't know yet," he said. "I was planning to pay Miss Rosemary another visit, when that meddlesome magician's not around, with his mysterious mumblings."

Marian nodded. "Yes, you should watch out for Mr Thomtidom," she said. "He could enchant you, sir."

Maarten snorted, but Frans said, "I think you're right, Marian. You see, I've forgotten my books again. And I'm sure it's down to his magic...! And I left Aunt Wilhelmina's umbrella there too. She'll have to fetch it herself now, as Miss Rosemary has told me I can only visit her again if she sends for me."

When Frans got home from school that afternoon, his landlady was, as always, sitting in the conservatory with a pot of tea. This time there was someone with her, a boy in a leather jacket and a crash helmet. "Roberto!" Frans exclaimed.

"Are you talking to me?" the boy said. "My name's Rob. That's what my mum and dad call me anyway, and Aunt Wilhelmina."

Frans looked at him with some surprise. This boy seemed more like the Biker Boy than the Roberto he'd eaten sausages with.

"Are you sure you won't have a cup of tea, Rob?" asked Aunt Wilhelmina.

"No, thanks, auntie. I should be going," her nephew said.

"Such a hurry!" said Aunt Wilhelmina.

"I need to be somewhere," said Rob. "Got a practice with my mates."

"Homework?" asked his aunt.

"No, we've got a band. I play the guitar. You know that already!"

"Well, not too fast, please. And keep the noise down!" said Aunt Wilhelmina.

"You'd better tell that to the drummer," said Rob with a laugh. "Those drums go right through everything. The neighbours keep banging on the wall. But you've got to let your hair down sometimes, you know?"

"I was talking about your scooter, not the band," said Aunt Wilhelmina. "But now that you mention it, the music that you young people play! What a noise! I saw some band on the television the other day, a few longhaired louts playing and singing for a room full of youngsters. Well, it seems the crowd enjoyed it so much that they demolished the place and smashed everything to pieces. Absolutely scandalous! We're lucky we don't have parties like that in our village. I'm sure your class would never behave like that, would they, Frans?"

"I do hope not," said Frans.

Aunt Wilhelmina's nephew gave him a mocking look. "So you're a schoolteacher, are you?" he said.

"I thought you knew that," Frans muttered uneasily.

"Well, I'm off then," said Rob, "before I have to listen to another lecture about the youth of today. Bye, auntie."

"Well, I simply don't understand young people today," she said. "But it'd be strange if I did! Bye, Rob, say hello to your mum from me."

The boy gave Frans a casual nod and left the conservatory. Frans followed him to the front door.

"Hey," he said, "I was at your Aunt Rosemary's yesterday..."

Rob raised his eyebrows. "Seems like you're pretty popular with my aunts," he said. "What have you been talking to them about? Surely not my good behaviour?"

"Stop being silly," said Frans. "I just wanted to tell you that my letter's written and posted."

"Yeah? So what?" the boy said.

"I thought you were interested," snapped Frans. "The letter to Count Grisenstein!"

"Well?" came Rob's reply. "What's that got to do with me?"

Frans understood now: this wasn't Roberto, but the Biker Boy!

"Don't be so childish," he said. "You're part of the conspiracy too."

"No, I'm not, that was just a joke," said the Biker Boy with a sneer. "I just went to Tooreloor's Tavern on my own for a bet. Ask the children in your class to join in with your games. I don't have time for this!" He headed outside and got on his scooter, which was in front of the house. A moment later, he roared off, without glancing back at Frans, who watched him go with a bewildered look on his face.

"I think your nephew is taking that double life of his too far!" he said angrily, when he was back in the conservatory with Aunt Wilhelmina. "Now he says he's not part of our conspiracy."

"You shouldn't talk so much about that," said his landlady. "I've already told you conspiracies are supposed to stay secret.

And as far as Rob's concerned, he was obviously in a bad mood because his mother sent him over with a message for me."

"No, it's the motor scooter," said Frans. "Rob with a scooter is a Biker Boy, and Rob in the woods is Roberto the adventurer."

"It's not that simple," said Aunt Wilhelmina. "Rob with a scooter rides through the woods too. But I'm afraid he's going to have to repeat a year at school if he carries on like this. He only just got through last year and he's more interested in having fun than in studying."

The next morning, the children in Frans's class seemed to have the same attitude as Rob. They weren't paying attention, and they kept whispering, as if they were plotting and planning.

It's my own fault, thought Frans. *I've told them too many sensational stories. From now on I'll have to focus more on actually teaching them.*

He straightened his glasses and peered around the classroom. In the back row, Arie was showing something to the boy beside him.

"Arie," Frans said sternly. "What have you got there? Bring it to me."

The boy was about to protest, but did as he was told. Silently, he handed a toy pistol to Frans.

"Playing during your lessons? That's not good," said Frans. He put the pistol in his pocket and then said, "Back to your seat."

Arie looked at him unhappily. He knew only too well that there was no point asking his teacher to return his property. He'd hang on to the pistol until Arie's good behaviour changed his mind. Arie gave a deep sigh as he took his seat again; that could take some time.

Frans looked at his watch and said, "You can start packing up... I don't have any stories to tell," he continued, as the expectant silence fell. "I haven't received an answer from Gr... Gr... I doubt I'll hear from that gentleman again. And the conspiracy is falling apart. Roberto's disappeared and the Biker Boy thinks it's all just a silly game."

"But Roberto and the Biker Boy are the same person, aren't they?" called out Kai, before Maarten had the chance to say anything.

"Yes. But Roberto has turned into the Biker Boy," replied Frans.

"Do you think he's been enchanted?" asked Marian.

"There's no such thing," said Maarten. "Mr Van der Steg isn't telling fairy tales!"

"Well, maybe I am," said Frans slowly. "You know, I'm no longer entirely sure that the Story of the Seven Ways really happened..."

"Sir!" said Maarten, with a gasp. "But you didn't make it all up, did you? About Gr... Gr... and the treasure... And Roberto and his cannon, and..."

Frans shrugged his shoulders. "No comment," he said. And he thought: *And if this story's made up, it certainly wasn't me who invented it! I'd think up something better than this. But then who did come up with it? And how is it possible that all these strange things have happened to me of all people?*

It was Wednesday. A long, free afternoon stretched out in front of him.

"It's about time I paid some attention to my studies," Frans said to himself. "But I've left my books at Miss Rosemary's...

She may have told me not to visit her, but I'm surely allowed to go and pick up my own property from her house!"

So, after dinner, he hopped onto his bike and rode off, without following Aunt Wilhelmina's wise advice, who said he should take a raincoat. "The sun's shining!" he called back over his shoulder. "And if rains, I can always use your umbrella. I won't forget it this time."

By the time he arrived at Sevenways, he was sorry he hadn't listened to his landlady. The sky was grey as lead and filled with ominous clouds. The woods around the signpost looked dark and gloomy – almost threatening. The six roads were deserted.

"But it's not raining yet," Frans said out loud. He looked at the old pub, which really did seem like a haunted house now, and wondered what Jan Tooreloor had done with the sign.

Hmm, no, Jan's name can't really be Tooreloor, he thought. *No one could have such a strange name. It's like something from a fairy tale or a song. Or an insult – he's completely doolally, toorelally, Tooreloor!* Then he looked at the blood-red arm of the signpost. In his head he heard Maarten's voice saying, "You didn't make it all up, did you?... About Roberto and his cannon..."

Frans left his bike and set off along the path to Roberto's sanctuary. "I just want to see it with my own eyes," he said to himself, "so that I know I didn't make it all up!"

It was growing darker and darker beneath the trees, but he went on walking. When he'd crossed three bridges and a ditch, drops of rain began to fall. *But I'm already halfway,* he thought, so he carried on. After the second ditch and the fifth bridge, the drips became an actual rain shower. He stepped up the pace and soon reached where he was heading.

The tent had gone, but the cannon was still there. Frans realized it was nowhere near as fine as he'd thought at first. It certainly was old – but age had taken its toll and there was no way anyone could have fired it, not even using blanks.

"So I didn't make up the cannon," he said to himself. "But what about the shot... Did I imagine that? And where's Roberto's tent?"

The rain became a downpour. He fled into the small round building, which was luckily still there among the trees, so it wasn't just his imagination. It had no door, just a rope across the entrance, with a rather ragged piece of paper hanging from it, which said NO TRESPASSERS in big letters, with a skull drawn beneath. Frans wiped his glasses and read the small letters scribbled below: *Except for the Seven.*

"Well, that's nice," he said. He untied the rope and went inside.

Inside the building, it was dark and not very cosy. The roof was leaking in several places, but he found a dry spot and stood and looked around. The first thing he saw was the tent, neatly folded. Then he spotted a bundle of wood, a primus stove, some empty cans and a few boxes. He opened one and found some firecrackers inside.

"Well," he muttered to himself, "at least that solves the mystery of the cannon shot."

So Roberto really had existed. And his big straw hat and an old raincoat were hanging from a hook on the wall.

Frans reached into his pockets for a packet of cigarettes, but all he found was Arie's pistol. *I hope,* he thought, *that it stops raining soon. I don't feel much like sheltering in here all afternoon...*

Ah, but there's no need for that, he thought a little later. *I can always borrow that raincoat. And if Roberto objects, it serves the Biker Boy right.*

He pulled on the coat and, after a moment's hesitation, put the hat on too. Dressed in his new outfit, he stepped outside. Now he saw that the path didn't come to a dead end here – it wound deeper into the woods.

Now that he was equipped to face the rain, he felt the urge to explore his surroundings. So he continued his walk along the winding path, emerging, fifteen minutes later, on a wide dirt track.

He stopped and looked left and right, regretting that he hadn't brought Aunt Wilhelmina's map with him. If he remembered it correctly, this should be the road that led from Sevenways to the Herb Garden, and then onwards to somewhere near Langelaan. So, if he turned right, he'd get to Miss Rosemary's. He decided to do exactly that; he'd be able to pick up his books and walk back to Sevenways, and then cycle home from there on his bike.

As he walked along, he began to wonder what Miss Rosemary would say when he turned up in this old coat and ridiculous hat, with wet and muddy shoes.

He told himself that it would be silly not to go on though, after he'd come so far. When the rain stopped, he didn't take off the hat, as water was still dripping from the branches. Trees lined the path on both sides; to his left they leant over a barbed-wire fence. Before long, he spotted a path leading off on that side, but that was closed too, and there was another sign saying *NO TRESPASSERS*, with different words beneath it this time: *Article 461, Criminal Code.*

Frans stopped again. He remembered Roberto's words: *He's put barbed wire up all around it and signs saying "No trespassers"...*

This must be the Grisenstein estate!

Frans walked on. He'd have liked to take a closer look, but the path was too well secured. A little later, though, he saw a hole in the fence, where the wire was twisted and broken. He looked around; there was no one in sight.

It was starting to rain again but he realized this would be the perfect weather for getting into the estate without being noticed. He wanted to see the House of Stairs for himself!

Frans looked around once more, and then slipped through the hole. Roberto's raincoat snagged on the fence, but fortunately it was only a small tear. Then he found the path and started walking parallel to it; he knew the House of Stairs must be somewhere in that direction. His coat was getting more and more soaked by the drizzle and by the wet bushes as he battled his way through. There was no sign of any buildings and the wood seemed just like any other wood.

This estate appears to be rather large, he thought, as he stopped and considered whether to go on. Frans the Red would probably climb a tree, so that he could at least take a peek at the chimneys of the House of Stairs. Frans the Red had climbed the slopes of the Himalayas and the towers of Torelore. But Frans van der Steg didn't like heights. And poor Frans van der Steg was about to get a fright...

He heard the sound of voices and a moment later he saw someone moving among the trees directly ahead. A big man was coming towards him – and another one! Most likely the gamekeepers who patrolled the estate with loaded guns...

Frans turned around. The bushes rustled as he retraced his steps.

Behind him he heard someone shout: "Hey, you!" He glanced over his shoulder. One of the men had seen him and was waving at him to stop.

Frans took to his heels. Now he could hear both the men shouting.

"A trespasser!"

"I'll get him!"

"Stay where you are!"

That only made Frans run all the faster. He raced through the wood, with the men following close behind.

There was the barbed wire. Now he just had to find the hole he'd sneaked through. Should he go left – or right? He looked back again, but no one was coming. He hurried along the fence, searching for the opening... There it was!

Panting, he dropped onto his knees and quickly crawled through. The coat he'd borrowed must be in a terrible state! But he was safely off the count's property, and if the gamekeepers came after him, it'd be up to them to prove he'd ever been there. They appeared to have given up the chase, though, as he couldn't see or hear anyone.

Frans picked up the hat, which was lying on the ground beside him; it was a miracle he hadn't lost it sooner. *It's just as well the children didn't see that,* he thought with a wry grin. *Frans the Red running like a coward!* Putting the hat back on, he resumed his walk.

He'd only gone a short distance when he heard rapid footsteps behind him. And then a low voice said in his ear, "Stop right there, thief!"

Before Frans could decide whether to do as he was told, someone leapt onto his back. He turned around and tried to shake off his attacker. But the man seemed to be mad with rage.

He gave Frans a whack on the jaw that made his teeth rattle and a thump on his head that made him see stars. It wasn't just his hat that went flying, but his glasses too, and the attacker got in another punch before Frans could even see who it was. Pulling himself out of the man's iron grip, he blindly hit back. Then he stumbled, or was tripped, and he fell...

He is wounded in combat

THIS IS FOUR

When Frans came round, he was sprawled on the ground, gasping for air, and he could still see stars. He heard voices above his head; at first they seemed to be coming from a long way off. Then he made out two pairs of legs, planted in two pairs of boots. The voices were growing louder and angrier...

Carefully he tried to stand up. One pair of legs knelt down beside him... and he saw it was Roberto... Roberto who took hold of him and asked in a worried voice, "Frans, are you all right?"

Frans sat down, rubbed his throbbing head and said weakly, "I'm still in one piece, I think."

Roberto turned to the other man. Frans could still see no more than his legs. "You idiot!" he said furiously. "You're going to regret this!"

Frans looked up. "Where are my glasses?" he asked, not sure if he could trust his eyes.

A weather-beaten hand held out Frans's glasses; the lenses were still intact, but one of the arms was broken. When Frans put them on, all he could see was splashes of mud, so he took them off and began to clean them. He could hear Roberto yelling at his attacker.

"If you did that by accident, you're an amazingly, stupendously, incredibly idiotic imbecile! And if you did it on purpose, you're a snivelling sneak, a treacherous traitor, a slimy..."

Roberto's insults grew more and more colourful and creative. Frans meanwhile put his glasses back on and looked at his attacker, who was listening to the torrent of words with a guilty look on his face. And when Frans recognized that face, he was speechless. It was Jan Tooreloor, Count Grisenstein's coachman!

The man was confused and dishevelled. "I'm sorry, Roberto. I really am," he said, when Roberto finally fell silent. "I saw him walking along in your hat and coat, and I knew right away that it wasn't you. I thought he'd stolen your things, so I sneaked after him and I..."

"Attacked me without any warning," Frans said with clenched teeth.

"I didn't know it was you!" cried Jan Tooreloor. "Not until your hat came off and I recognized your red hair."

"You could have looked first before you started hitting him," said Roberto, placing his hand on Frans's shoulder.

"But I did it for you, lad!" said Jan Tooreloor. "And it's not as if I hurt *you*, even though you came at me like a madman. I didn't even hit *him* that hard..."

Roberto leapt up and it looked like he was going to attack the coachman again, even though the man was twice his size. "You're asking for such a beating!" he began furiously.

"Wait!" said Frans. "If anyone should do that, it's me."

He tried to stand up, but a stab of pain made him wince. So he sat back down, clutching his ankle.

Both Roberto and the coachman were staring at him.

"But I'm afraid," Frans continued, with a grimace, "that it's going to have to wait a little while."

Roberto knelt down beside him, but Jan Tooreloor said, uneasy, but still defiant, "No one ever died from a bump on the head and a scratch on the cheek."

Frans took a deep breath and said, "And I hope I get the chance to repay you for both of those injuries! But it's actually my leg that's the problem."

"Well, that's not my fault," growled Tooreloor. Then he sank down onto his knees and looked at Frans's leg with a gloomy face. "Twisted or sprained," he said. He untied his red scarf and started to wrap it around the injured ankle.

"Hands off!" said Frans. He went to pull his leg away, but the pain removed any desire to protest.

Then he made another attempt to stand up, this time with Roberto's help. He managed, but he could only stand on one foot. The other foot, now shoeless and tightly bandaged with the red scarf, was useless.

"He can't walk," said Roberto. "Jan, you're going to have to carry him on your back. We'll take him to Aunt Rosemary's. It's not far."

"Absolutely not!" said Frans. "I can't let her see me like this. Besides... I'm sure it'll be better soon." Those last words didn't sound very convincing, although he didn't mention that his head had started thumping so badly that he felt dizzy. The others seemed to have realized anyway, as they ignored his protests. Before he could object any more, Jan had hoisted him onto his broad back.

"Now put your arms tightly around his neck," ordered Roberto. "And forward march!"

"Don't forget your hat," mumbled Frans. "I'm sorry I borrowed your things."

"And for more than one reason, I bet," said Roberto.

"I'm sorry too," growled Jan Tooreloor, as he lumbered slowly into motion. "He's blasted heavy."

"You deserve for him to be ten times heavier," Roberto rebuked him. "You should feel weighed down by guilt." But then he added with a smile, "If it weren't so sad, it'd actually be really funny!"

That's true, thought Frans, sitting on Tooreloor's back – he must look quite a sight. Luckily it was Roberto and not the Biker Boy who was walking along beside him.

The short distance seemed endless, but eventually they reached the Herb Garden. In the garden Frans saw the sight he'd found so hard to imagine before: Miss Rosemary in boots and with a shovel in her hand. She dropped the shovel and was soon busy taking care of Frans's injuries with her "potions, plasters and poultices", as Roberto put it.

Miss Rosemary worked quickly and capably, and still managed to tell all of them off as she did so – Jan Tooreloor, Roberto and Frans himself. Her nephew was the only one who said anything in reply; he launched into an animated account of the events, but Miss Rosemary interrupted him. "Just go and put the kettle on!" she snapped. "And fetch some pillows from upstairs. No, Jan, you're not leaving until I've spoken to you. There you go," she said as she finished, giving Frans a long, hard look.

Frans was sitting in an armchair with his leg up on a stool. He felt as if he were seeing her face through a haze of pungent and heady spices.

"Do you have a headache?" she asked.

"It's not too bad," he answered, making a failed attempt to smile. "I'm so sorry to have caused you all this bother..."

"If you sit there quietly, you won't be any bother at all," she said. "Now just close your eyes and lean back."

Frans did as he was told. He felt something cool on his forehead and a little later someone slipped a pillow under his ankle. When he opened his eyes again, he saw Roberto, who gave him a nod. Miss Rosemary and the coachman had left, but he could hear their voices in the hallway.

"I never wanted to bring in some outsider!" barked the coachman. "And certainly not some lily-livered city-boy, who doesn't know anything about anything, some gutless bookworm..."

Frans shot up, the damp cloth sliding from his forehead. Was that what Jan Tooreloor thought of him?

"Calm down," said Roberto, pushing him back into the chair. "Wait and see what Aunt Rosemary has to say!" He carefully laid the cloth back on Frans's bump.

Frans couldn't hear what Miss Rosemary said, though, and

Jan just went on grumbling, "What's he supposed to be doing in the House of Stairs anyway, him with that red hair of his? If it was me, or Roberto..."

Miss Rosemary interrupted him, and her tone was very stern. But then the two of them must have walked off, because their voices faded away.

"Now she's giving him what for!" whispered Roberto.

"I don't understand," Frans said flatly, "why that untrustworthy man was ever allowed to join the conspiracy."

"We can't exclude him," said Roberto. "The Conspiracy of Seven, the Secret of the Seven Ways and Jan Tooreloor – they're all wrapped up together."

"Secret?" repeated Frans. "A secret...? Yet another one?"

"But you're right; he is untrustworthy," Roberto continued. "And he seems to have something against you. You should keep an eye on him!"

"Thanks for the warning," said Frans, catching the wet cloth as it slipped from his forehead again. "But why is Jan Tooreloor wrapped up with Sevenways and what's his secret?"

"You'd better not mention the name Tooreloor from now on," Roberto advised him. "He's hidden it and buried it away. I mean, he has a different name now..."

"I already suspected that name wasn't real," muttered Frans.

"No, that's not what I meant," said Roberto. "Jan Tooreloor was the innkeeper at the Red Man. And now he's the coachman of the Fiendish Foe and..."

"I'm going to call Wilhelmina," said Miss Rosemary, returning, "to tell her you're staying here tonight, Frans."

"Oh, please, no, don't do that," Frans replied. "I'll be able to go home soon."

"You most certainly will not!" said Miss Rosemary firmly. "You can't use that leg of yours today. We'll have to see how it looks tomorrow."

"But..." began Frans.

"I have a guestroom," she said cheerfully. "Roberto, come with me for a moment, would you?" and she left the room again, so Frans couldn't protest. Her nephew followed her.

So Frans was Miss Rosemary's guest again, and he was sitting at her table, this time with Roberto as a dining companion. He wasn't very hungry though, and Miss Rosemary said he should have an early night.

Mr Thomtidom came round after dinner; he brought a pair of his pyjamas for Frans to borrow, and a pot of ointment that he said was the best medicine for sprained and twisted ankles. Frans had to admit that most of the conspirators seemed to mean him well, but they did treat him rather like a little boy. Miss Rosemary gave him a cup of steaming herb tea, with orders to drink it all up, while the magician spirited away his glasses to repair. And soon after that Roberto helped him up the stairs to the guestroom.

"Can I tell you something in confidence?" said Frans, with a thick tongue. "I'm not a member of your conspiracy. I've just somehow become entangled in it!"

There must have been some kind of strong sleeping drug in the herbal tea, because he couldn't remember the rest of the evening.

When Frans woke up, it took him some time to work out where he was. He'd never slept in a bedroom with pale-blue blobs on the walls before, wearing green silk pyjamas with sleeves that only just reached past his elbows.

It was broad daylight, and the sun was shining in through the open window.

Miss Rosemary appeared beside his bed and put down a fully laden tray. "Good morning," she said brightly.

"Good morning," said Frans, sitting up and rubbing his eyes.

"I've brought your breakfast," said Miss Rosemary, "and your glasses."

Frans thanked her and asked what time it was.

"Ten thirty," his hostess replied.

"My goodness!" gasped Frans. "What about school? Morning break time is already over."

"Wilhelmina already called the headmaster," said Miss Rosemary, "and told him you're ill."

"But I'm not ill!" said Frans. He put his glasses back on and looked at her guiltily.

"What was she supposed to say? That Mr Van der Steg trespassed on private property and then got into a fight?"

Frans lowered his eyes; he didn't know how to reply. The wallpaper, he saw now, was not covered with blobs at all, but with blue roses and forget-me-nots.

"I'll have a look at your ankle in a moment," Miss Rosemary continued. "If you take it easy today, maybe you'll be able to walk a little tomorrow. Finish your breakfast first; then you can come downstairs. I've ironed your suit. It's in the wardrobe."

Frans wondered what his students would say if they could see him sitting in the Herb Garden in a comfortable chair as if it were the holidays. He was sheltered by the tall hedges, which were full of intricately woven cobwebs, with drops of water clinging to them and glistening in the sun. Summer seemed to be lingering in this spot, where lavender grew, and thyme, chives, fennel and celery, and of course the plant that shared its name with the lady of the house.

"Roberto's coming this afternoon after school," Miss Rosemary told him. "He said he'll take you home. Jan Tooreloor took your bike to the village yesterday, because you can't use it anyway."

"So I'm going to have to ride on the back of the Biker Boy's scooter again," muttered Frans.

"No, it's Roberto who's taking you home," said Miss Rosemary. "But you never know, he could suddenly change... it really is most annoying. He hardly ever comes here on his scooter; he usually leaves it at Sevenways. This time he'll need to ride it all the way here. We'll just have to hope for the best..."

The afternoon was cold, so Frans had to sit inside, still with one leg up on a stool. He saw Miss Rosemary occasionally; she was busy with her work in and around the house. He decided to make good use of the time and picked up his books and tried to study a little. But that just gave him another headache.

"Maybe you'd better help me prepare the vegetables instead," said Miss Rosemary, coming back into the front room. She put down a pan of beans and a bowl beside him and left without waiting for a reply.

"They say I'm their Secret Agent with an Important Mission," mumbled Frans. "And what am I doing? Preparing vegetables. Well, never fear. This Secret Agent is not going to spill the beans!"

Later that afternoon, Mr Thomtidom turned up, with a big box under his arm. He looked at Frans's ankle and gave a satisfied nod, as if he were the one who had healed it. "I've brought my backgammon set," he said, opening the box. "Shall we play a game? Activity is the best medicine."

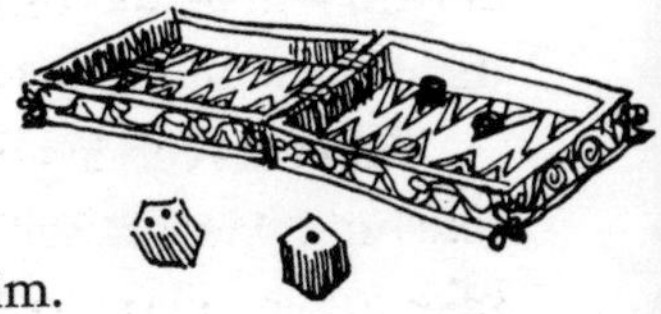

Frans was glad of the company, but the backgammon wasn't a complete success. The magician must have enchanted the dice, as they definitely favoured him. There was no doubt that he was going to win. He gave Frans a lecture about backgammon past and present, in the near and far east, going into great detail about how it was played by the Saracens at the time of the Crusades, before finally moving on to the rules for tournaments and duels. He'd just embarked on a story about old weapons when Miss Rosemary came to join them. She handed Frans a pistol and said, "I found this in your jacket."

"I do hope it's not loaded," said the magician, sounding rather worried.

Frans laughed. "It's just a toy gun. It belongs to one of my students," he said, putting it back in his pocket.

Mr Thomtidom gave a small, embarrassed cough and then quickly said, "What's that noise I hear? I thought this road was off limits for scooters."

"Not off limits, but as yet undiscovered," said Miss Rosemary. "I think it's Roberto."

"Yes, here he comes," said Mr Thomtidom, looking out of the window. "But... is that really Roberto?" he continued. "He looks almost like a stranger."

"Please, Jan, just say hello to him as if it's Roberto," said Miss

Rosemary, now sounding rather worried herself. "And if it's not him, then use your magic powers to transform him back into Roberto."

"I fear that young man will have no respect for my grey beard," said Mr Thomtidom, still looking outside. "Look. He's got off now, and he's studying his bike."

Frans stood up and limped over to the window. In front of the garden gate, the Biker Boy was tinkering with his scooter.

Then the phone rang in the hallway.

A few moments later, Miss Rosemary put her head around the door. "Frans!" she said. "It's Wilhelmina on the phone. The postman just delivered a letter for you."

Frans forgot about the Biker Boy. "From Count Grisenstein!" he said, walking towards her much faster than was good for his ankle.

Miss Rosemary nodded and passed him the phone.

"Hallo, Aunt Wilhelmina," said Frans. "Oh, I'm fine, thank you... Would you open the letter and read it out to me?... Yes, I'll wait..." Miss Rosemary and the magician looked on eagerly as he waited for his landlady to fetch her reading glasses and open the letter.

Just then, Chive rushed into the hallway and ran barking to the front door. The door opened to reveal the Biker Boy on the doorstep, regarding them all with a haughty, bored expression. The dog stopped and wagged his tail.

Frans heard Aunt Wilhelmina's voice down the phone again. Frans repeated out loud every sentence that she read:

Wednesday 30 September

Dear Mr Van der Steg,

In response to your letter, I would like to inform you that I would still be most pleased to welcome you. I shall send my coachman for you on Thursday the first of October, so that we can have a discussion at my home. Please await my carriage outside your house at half past seven.

Respectfully yours,

Gr... Gr...

"That's Gradus Grisenstein," Aunt Wilhelmina added. "His signature is about as easy to fathom as a map of the House of Stairs."

The Biker Boy took off his crash helmet and ran his fingers through his long hair. The dog jumped up him, tail wagging.

"Thursday the first of October!" said Frans. "That's... that's today! What time is it now?"

"Half past five," said Mr Thomtidom. "So you have two hours to..."

"Jan the coachman is going via Sevenways!" Roberto said, interrupting. He turned to Frans; the Biker Boy was gone. "He can pick you up there, as long as you make sure you're at the signpost by eight."

Frans spoke into the telephone: "Aunt Wilhelmina, thank you so much! Would you tell the coachman I'll be waiting for him at Sevenways?... Yes... Fine... I'll remember. See you soon." He put the phone down.

"And now," said Roberto, his eyes gleaming, "the adventure can begin!"

The Secret of the Seven Ways is revealed

THIS IS FIVE

"But we won't talk about the conspiracy yet," said Miss Rosemary, when the four of them were sitting at the table and tucking into mince and beans. "We don't even know if Frans will get the job and we shouldn't count our chickens before they're hatched..."

"Or put the carriage before the horse," said Roberto.

"Or enter the House of Stairs before we've found the Seventh Way," said Mr Thomtidom.

Frans raised his eyebrows and said, "But there *are* only six ways."

"And that," said Roberto, "is the Secret of the Seven Ways."

"What did I just say?" said the President of the Conspiracy. "We won't meet up until our Secret Agent can report back to us. Then I'll call all the conspirators together – except one."

After dinner she wrapped a fresh bandage firmly around Frans's ankle and said that he could walk as long as he didn't go off on any long hikes.

"He'll hardly have to take a step," said Roberto. "I'm taking him to Sevenways and after that he'll be in the coach."

"The count is sure to send you home in the coach too," said Miss Rosemary. "So we should say goodbye. And don't forget – we've never met each other!"

"And remember to take your books," said Mr Thomtidom.

Frans went and stood in front of the mirror in the hallway, straightened his tie and looked rather sorrowfully at his face. The bump on his forehead was purple and he had a big plaster on his cheek. He wondered what kind of impression he'd make on Count Grisenstein.

The telephone rang. Miss Rosemary answered and said, "Wilhelmina!"

"She wants to make sure I remember her umbrella this time," said Frans.

But that wasn't the case. Miss Rosemary said, with some surprise, "Huh?" and then, a little angrily, "What?" and then in dismay, "No, but..." Then she added, "Thank you. Yes, we'll think of something."

She put the phone down. "Now I'm really annoyed!" she said. "Jan Tooreloor went round to Wilhelmina's house, but when he heard that Frans wasn't in, he acted like it was a really bad thing. He said he'd return to the House of Stairs by the proper road and tell the count. He refused to go via Sevenways!"

The other three stared at her.

"This is the last straw!" cried Roberto. "There's always something up with Tooreloor. He's enough to drive anyone toorelally! And it was all his fault that Frans couldn't be at home."

"This is most unpleasant," said Mr Thomtidom. "It's nothing less than sabotage!"

"I did rather haul Jan over the coals yesterday," said Miss Rosemary quietly.

"That's no reason for disobedience and insubordination," said Mr Thomtidom.

"But what will we do now?" said Roberto. "Frans has to go to the House of Stairs, and he needs to travel via Sevenways and no other way."

Frans nodded. He had become convinced that the conspirators were right and that he had to go to the house by that route – and by that route alone. Hmm... But...

"But I don't need to go there by coach, do I?" he said, looking at Roberto.

"Of course not," said Mr Thomtidom. "And there's a fast vehicle in front of the door... a motor-assisted pedal cycle, I believe they call them..."

Miss Rosemary shook her head and said, "A vehicle that's too fast for my liking."

"Roberto can go slowly though," said the magician. "Even though that conveyance of his is still alarmingly loud and dangerous."

"No more dangerous than that ancient coach," said Roberto, annoyed. "Why shouldn't I take Frans? You people need to move with the times. My scooter's fast and safe."

"Well, we have no other choice," said his aunt with a sigh. "Frans can't miss his appointment again, so Roberto will have to take him to the House of Stairs."

"We'll be there before Jan!" said Roberto.

"Not before him," said Frans. "We'll be going faster, but it's longer via Sevenways than along the proper road."

"No, it's closer," said the magician.

"I saw on the map that..." Frans began.

"The track from Sevenways is the shortest," the magician said, interrupting him. "I mean, of course, the Seventh Way."

"Seventh Way?"

"Yes, Sevenways wouldn't be called Sevenways if there weren't seven ways, would it? That would fly in the face of all logic," said Mr Thomtidom.

Frans had no answer to that. "But we still need to leave right away," said Roberto. "If you don't want me to go too fast..."

"You can't go too fast on that road anyway," said the magician, "even if you want to. You don't have a death wish, do you?"

"It's a perfectly good road," said Roberto. "I hope we see Jan. Then we can throw him out of the conspiracy!"

"Only I have the authority to do that," his aunt said, putting him in his place. She placed her hands on his shoulders and continued, "I'm not going to say 'Be careful', Roberto, but I will say 'Be sensible'! And stay who you are!"

Then she held out her hand to Frans like a noble lady sending a knight out on a perilous quest.

"I'd like to go along too," said Mr Thomtidom.

"No, you need to roll up your sleeves for the heavy work," said Roberto. "Like casting spells, for instance."

Then he said they needed to hurry and, less than three minutes later, Frans was sitting up behind him on the back of the scooter. It was a cloudy evening, and the wind was blowing, but it wasn't raining. At a calm pace, they set off. Frans looked back again at the lighted windows of the house in the Herb Garden. *I didn't even thank Miss Rosemary properly for her hospitality*, he thought. *And I've forgotten my books again.*

Within a few minutes they were at Sevenways. Roberto drove up to the pub, stopped in front of the big double doors and turned off the engine.

"This is the old coach house," he whispered. "And now I'll reveal the secret to you, and show you the Seventh Way."

He took a key from his pocket and slid it into the lock. Then he opened up the doors and said, "Come on." After they'd taken the scooter inside, he shut the doors behind them and switched on his torch.

Frans looked around. The room they were in was completely empty, with an uneven stone floor. Opposite the entrance he saw two other large doors, which were also closed. Roberto walked over to them and unlocked them too. Then he opened them with a ceremonious gesture and shone his torch outside. "Behold!" he said. "I present the Secret of the Seven Ways: the Seventh Way!"

And yes, there behind the second pair of doors a path began, which meandered into the woods and disappeared in the darkness.

"I should have known..." Frans said in a surprised whisper. "I can't believe I didn't notice it before!"

"Yes, it really was rather unobservant of you," said Roberto. "This way leads directly to the House of Stairs. It used to go around the coach house at one time, and everyone knew where to find it. Now it's hidden and forgotten. The Fiendish Foe has allowed the road to become overgrown with nettles. Jan and I spent days clearing a way through... What time is it?"

"Nearly eight," replied Frans.

"It takes me less than quarter of an hour," said Roberto. "If I go quickly."

"You promised to go slowly," said Frans.

Roberto switched off his torch. "But that would be even more dangerous," he said. "Aunt Rosemary said, 'Be sensible,' not 'Be careful.' If we go slowly, the gamekeepers are sure to catch us."

"Gamekeepers?" repeated Frans.

"Yes, this area is off limits too. The Seventh Way is the property of the Fiendish Foe, as is this ruin."

"The Seventh Way belongs to the count?" said Frans. "And this pub too? I thought Jan Tooreloor..."

"You're not very good at thinking, are you?" came Roberto's voice from the darkness. "Did that whack on the head damage your brain? Jan Tooreloor used to rent this place from some rich gentleman in Langelaan. Years ago the Fiendish Foe bought it from that gentleman and he threw Jan out... Why? To leave it unused and to let it collapse! To make sure the Seventh Way would be forgotten, and disappear... You see, if there's no Seventh Way, no one can follow it. Because someone who comes along the Seventh Way could defeat him, as he well knows!"

Frans's eyes were getting used to the darkness; he could see the path again, gleaming with puddles. The trees swayed and rustled. "So he had great foresight, this count..." he mumbled. "Years ago, you say?"

"Yes. But Mr Thomtidom says that he first bought the Red Man – that's the name of the pub – for a different reason," whispered Roberto. "This is where the secret passageway began where Gregorius the Mad once found the treasure." He gently tapped the ground with his foot, and Frans thought he heard a quiet echo from below. "Gradus Grisenstein had the whole place torn apart," Roberto continued. "But he didn't find anything. Gregorius the Mad had sealed up the passageway, and the treasure's now inside the House of Stairs..."

"That's a pity," said Frans. "This forgotten Seventh Way is all very well and good, but I was hoping to end up in an underground passage at some point, preferably a haunted one."

"Oh, there are plenty enough ghosts here," said Roberto cheerfully.

"Yes, you told me that before, when I met you here the first time."

"The first time we met was at the Thirsty Deer," said Roberto.

Frans didn't reply. It was pretty tiring, spending time with someone who was made up of two people. Then Roberto hopped back onto the scooter, and Frans climbed up behind him.

"Jan Tooreloor could tell you a lot of ghost stories," Roberto added. "And so could I... But I don't have time right now; we need to get going. Hold on tight. I want to go fast."

"Would you please..." Frans began, but his words were lost in the roar of the engine.

And then they raced off along the Seventh Way.

The path was full of bumps and potholes, so it sometimes seemed as if they were leaping forward in bounds, rather than riding along. It also had plenty of bends – but Roberto just went

faster and faster. Frans wondered if it was still Roberto sitting there in front of him, or if the Biker Boy was steering the scooter.

It was a rollercoaster ride, alarmingly loud and dangerous, to use the magician's words. Frans was shaken and jolted about, and branches whipped into him, all of which combined to give him a splitting headache. When he tried to look around, he just saw trees flashing by. Finally he closed his eyes and didn't open them until Roberto braked sharply, and stopped.

The path opened onto – or rather, merged with – a brick road, which led to a tall metal gate, about twenty feet away.

Frans climbed down from the back of the scooter, with a quiet "ouch", because he could feel the pain in his ankle again. The engine went on thrumming away.

"Are we there?" he shouted above the noise.

Roberto's only reply was to drive on slowly towards the fence. Frans followed him, limping. Through the railings, he saw a driveway, which seemed to lead nowhere. There were trees along both sides, waving to and fro in the wind.

"Hey!" he called to Roberto. "Turn off your engine."

Roberto didn't do as he was asked, but started riding around in circles instead.

"Stop that right now!" said Frans angrily. "You've already performed enough daredevil stunts for one evening." As he spoke, his suspicion was confirmed. Roberto had turned back into the Biker Boy.

The young man came to a sudden stop in front of him, silenced the engine and switched off the lights.

"I seem to remember," said Frans coldly, "you telling me something about gamekeepers. If you carry on like that, you'll be sure to attract their attention."

"So what?" came the voice of the Biker Boy. "We're on a public road now, and I've as much right as anyone to be here. I'm not scared of some dull old count. Who cares if he lives in a massive house?"

Frans tried to open the gate, but it was locked. He could just about make out the house now; it was quite a way from the road. He saw lights in some of the windows. "How are we going to get in there?" he muttered.

"It's not that hard!" said the Biker Boy. "Are you feeling brave enough to climb over the fence and into his garden? Yeah, that's a great idea! We're going to give that count a proper fright..."

"No. Absolutely not," said Frans. "If you remember, I came here for a job interview. So you can forget about doing anything that'll make me look bad."

The Biker Boy whistled through his teeth. "He's worried about his job!" he shouted to the trees and the clouds above. "Hah!" he scoffed. "You're just as fake as Count Grisenstein himself. As soon as you get inside his house, you'll be sitting up and begging and giving him your paw, just like everyone else. Well, just so you know, you can count me out!"

"Shut up!" said Frans angrily. "You brought me here and you can't let me down now."

Neither of them spoke for a moment. The Biker Boy had got off his scooter; he was holding it with one hand and rattling the gate with the other – it made a nasty squeaking noise. Then he turned to Frans and began singing in a mocking tone:

"Oh dear, what can the matter be?
The gate's locked up and we don't have a key..."

By accident – or maybe on purpose – he let go of the scooter, which fell over and banged into Frans's ankle.

The sudden pain made Frans even angrier; he lashed out and clipped the Biker Boy on the ears.

The young man swore. "You're going to regret that!" he said. "I'll show you. I'll..." He stopped.

The wind drove the dark clouds apart and the moon appeared – a ghostly white full moon.

The Biker Boy's face was very pale in the moonlight; he wasn't looking at Frans, but staring through the bars of the fence. Frans followed his gaze and held his breath for a moment.

Now he could see the House of Stairs very clearly: an insane house, a house out of a nightmare... all towers and turrets, with jutting angles and protrusions, with crooked chimneys and strange structures on the roofs. It looked as if it had grown rather than been built, as its silhouette was so very peculiar. And above it the sky was like a wild sea; scraps of clouds with glowing edges flapped and fluttered across the moon.

"So now you can see it..." said the Biker Boy in a slightly shaky voice. "You'll have to..."

"Just shut up!" said Frans again. "Why don't you clear off? You're only confusing matters."

"Quiet!" said the Biker Boy. "I can hear something."

"Why should I care?" said Frans grumpily. "Go on. Get out of here!"

But still he turned his back on the House of Stairs. The sound was coming from the other direction – the rattle of wheels and the click-clacking of hoofs on the road.

Then he looked back at the Biker Boy, who was slowly picking up his scooter.

"Go on. Get out of here!" he repeated, but suddenly he felt a little unsure of himself. Which of the two was he talking to now? Had Roberto come back?

The young man was already on his scooter though and, in a gruff voice, he said, "I'm off! That old coach of yours is coming, so you don't need me anyway."

"Roberto..." began Frans.

But the boy had already started the engine, and soon he was riding off without looking back. He swerved onto the Seventh Way, and Frans saw the light of the scooter flashing through the trees and finally disappearing. Suddenly he regretted sending him away.

Now he was all alone in front of the closed gate, and in the distance the coach was approaching.

THAT WAS FIVE *and now for Part Six*

6

Frans enters the House of Stairs

He becomes acquainted with Count Grisenstein

THIS IS ONE

The clouds swept across the moon again, their edges still glowing. Shadows fell across the path, and Frans could only hear the coach now. He wondered what Jan Tooreloor would say when he saw him, and he stepped to one side, so that he was standing close to the gate, almost invisible to anyone who was not looking closely.

Now he saw the coach looming out of the darkness – it was completely black; the lanterns on the sides were not lit. The coachman was driving quickly. He must know the road well. And he brought his coach to a stop just in time, right before the gate.

Frans watched as Jan Tooreloor climbed down and started fiddling with the gate. He must have had a key, as it soon swung open with a creak. The horse pawed the ground with one hoof, as if to say it wanted to continue on its way, but Tooreloor showed no sign of climbing back up. He just gave a gloomy grunt and said, "Yes, we're here. But what should we do now?" He took off his hat, scratched his head and went on muttering to himself. Then he turned, wandered around and finally stood staring at the Seventh Way, as if he were expecting someone to appear from that direction.

Maybe he's waiting for me, Frans suddenly thought. But it didn't seem very wise to reveal his presence. Then he had an excellent idea: *What if I hop in? Perhaps he'll take me where I want to go…*

Frans crept towards the coach, cursing his painful ankle.

The horse raised its head and snorted. Frans carefully opened the door. He had to get inside the coach before Tooreloor spotted him. After all, it was likely that the man still didn't want to take him to the House of Stairs. So his best chance was to go along with Jan as a stowaway. Very cautiously, he struggled into the coach. Then he settled contentedly into the darkest corner – just in time, as the coachman was returning. He drove his coach through the gate, which he then locked again. Then he climbed up front and cracked his whip.

"Well, well," said Frans to himself. "Count Grisenstein really doesn't make it easy for people to get inside his home. Is that gate always locked? I wonder what he does about deliveries."

Frans slid the window down so that he could look out, but he could no longer see the House of Stairs. He noticed that Jan Tooreloor was going very slowly, as if he were still in two minds about something. But they couldn't have been moving for longer than ten minutes when they made a sweeping curve and came to a stop.

Jan Tooreloor climbed down. Frans put his head out of the window and asked, "Are we there?"

He almost laughed out loud at the coachman's surprise. The man took a step back and gasped. "I-i-is that you?" he stammered.

"Yes, it's me," Frans answered in a cheerful voice. "And you should be grateful for this opportunity to make up for your mistake and to take me to the House of Stairs as agreed."

Jan Tooreloor swore under his breath. But then he said, almost politely, "Yes, sir." And he even helped Frans out of the coach. "However did you get here?" he asked.

"Roberto brought me as far as the gate," Frans replied. "Along the Seventh Way. So you're not the only one who can do that!"

"Sssh!" hissed the coachman. "Not too loud." He cast a nervous glance at the House of Stairs.

Frans said nothing. Somewhere a window was rattling, and a cat wailed, mournful and off-key.

Now that he was standing in front of it, the House of Stairs looked less threatening, but just as strange. Even in the dark he could see just how complicated its construction was – with alcoves and extensions, and canopies and balconies, and so many windows and bays, with chimneys like turrets, and turrets like chimneys, and weathervanes on the roofs. At the front was a sweeping staircase, where two lanterns cast a dim, flickering light.

"You can go in through the back door," said the coachman.

"Is this the back?" asked Frans, as he began to limp up the stairs.

"Yes, sir. I see you're having trouble walking," said the coachman. He looked as if he wanted to help Frans, but Frans pretended not to notice.

Fortunately, the first flight of steps wasn't very long and Jan Tooreloor was soon pulling on the rope that hung beside the back door. The sound of a bell echoed through the house. The coachman tipped his cap, grunted a goodbye, and returned to his coach.

*

Frans waited; he heard footsteps but it was a while before the door opened.

A thin woman with a sour face grumpily told him to come in. Frans suddenly thought about the threshold he was crossing, but he had no time to see if any words were written on the lintel. The woman warned him to mind the step down and silently walked on ahead of him. Frans followed her through a stone hallway, up a short flight of stairs, along an oak-panelled corridor, down a narrow staircase, along another oak-panelled corridor and then up a wide flight of stairs, which opened onto a bare landing with a tiled floor. All the rooms were badly lit, most of them with gas lamps. They passed many doors; some of them were open, and Frans saw yet more staircases through them, some going up and some going down. At times he thought he could hear footsteps, ones that didn't belong to him or to the silent woman – footsteps behind them and in front of them, scurrying above them and walking below. His thoughts turned briefly to Ivan, the spy who was so good at sneaking around, and he wondered where the child might be who was imprisoned in this house...

After crossing an empty landing, he had to go up nine steps – he'd started counting by that point – and then he stopped to rest. The thin woman gave him a disapproving look, pulled a red velvet curtain aside and said, "Through there. The count is waiting for you." She turned around and disappeared.

"And now," said Frans to himself, "I am placing myself in the power of Gr... Gr..., who is lying in wait at the centre of all these staircases, like a spider sitting among the threads of his web. And I feel like the fly who is wondering how it will ever get back out again."

After a few steps, he stopped again and stared, with his eyes open wide.

He was in a huge room with a magnificent wooden floor. Galleries ran all around, with open wooden staircases leading up to them. This room was better lit, with long candles in tall brass stands. He saw suits of armour all lined up, standing there motionless, and a slender gentleman in grey, who came towards him and greeted him with a bow. Count Grisenstein!

He looked so different from the man Frans had imagined that, for a moment, he found it hard to believe it was really him – the Fiendish Foe, as Roberto called him.

A slim man in a finely tailored suit, with a rather bland face, blond hair and grey eyes. There was nothing mysterious or eccentric about him, and he didn't suit this house at all – he'd have been much more at home in The Hague, among the politicians and the diplomats.

"Mr Van der Steg?" he said, with a cold, yet pleasant voice. "My name is Grisenstein. Welcome to the House of Stairs."

Frans suddenly felt awkward and untidy, although the count was far too much of a gentleman to show any surprise about his bump and his sticking plaster.

Instead he just said that he hoped the ride to the House of Stairs had not been too unpleasant. "My coach is rather old-fashioned," he said, "but one should travel in style, don't you think?"

"Oh, it was an extraordinary ride," said Frans, smiling to himself.

"I hope you mean that in a good way," said the count.

"Of course, sir," said Frans. "Jan Tooreloor is an exceptionally good coachman."

"Jan Too-re-loor?" repeated the count slowly. The expression on his face was neutral. And yet something had clearly caught his attention and he needed to stop and think for a moment.

"Tooreloor?" said Count Grisenstein again. "Is that my coachman's name? Tooreloor? And how would you know that?"

Frans remembered that Roberto had told him not to mention that name again. "Oh, actually, I'm not so sure about it now," he replied uncomfortably. "Well, I think that's what he said... No, it was someone else, I believe... I just thought it was such a strange name that I remembered it. But I must have heard it wrong."

"Yes, I think you must have," said the count, with a fleeting smile. "I don't believe it's a name that one would find in any parish registers." He turned away from Frans and looked around the room.

Frans was about to add something, but then decided to keep quiet. *I wish those conspirators had been a bit clearer!* he thought. *What would Count Grisenstein say if he knew the whole story? He'd probably raise his eyebrows and calmly ask about the location of the nearest lunatic asylum. Although... someone who lives in a house like this is probably not that easily surprised by anything... This one room is enough to make anyone's head whirl!*

Frans looked around again. On every side, wooden staircases led up to the galleries, and more wooden stairs went from those galleries to galleries above, and from there other staircases went up to even higher galleries, with more stairs leading up to arched openings in the walls. High, high up overhead, he could see the dark rafters of the roof.

"This is known as Gregorius's Small Banqueting Hall," said Count Grisenstein.

Frans wondered what the large banqueting hall must look like.

"The room's been beautifully restored, don't you think?" said the count. "But it's not suitable for a quiet conversation. Come with me."

As they walked across the room, he stopped for a moment and said, "All these stairs... They're not too much for you, are they, Mr Van der Steg?"

"Oh, please don't be concerned," said Frans. "I just sprained my ankle a little, yesterday. That's all."

"I do hope it wasn't anything serious," said the count.

"Oh no," Frans quickly replied. "I took a tumble down some stairs."

He could have bitten his tongue. That was the stupidest answer he could have come up with! "But please don't think I do it regularly," he added quickly. "In fact, it's the first time in my life that I've ever fallen downstairs."

"And unfortunately I must ask you to climb another flight of stairs," said the count, opening a door. "Please lead the way. It's only twenty-two steps."

Frans warily climbed a stone spiral staircase, which opened into a room that felt like an oasis – all blue and white and tastefully furnished in a Rococo style. A cosy fire burned in the small hearth, and when the count had closed the door, there were no stairs to be seen.

Soon the two men were sitting opposite each other in elegant chairs. A coffee pot was on the table between them, with a small candle under it to keep the coffee warm.

"I shall pour it myself," said the count. "My housekeeper is free after eight. Climbing up and down stairs all day tires her out."

"Your house is a most remarkable building," said Frans.

"To be more accurate, it's ghastly," said the count. "A monstrosity of poor taste and improbable architecture, and most uncomfortable too, but," he continued, "living here for a while is good for the health. In this streamlined age with its efficient buildings, the soul is often neglected. Everyone needs a little mystery – even if it comes in the form of stairs, corridors, hidden doors and revolving panels."

"There's some truth to that," said Frans. Count Grisenstein seemed like a sensible man... perhaps the first reasonable person, he suddenly thought, that he'd met in a week.

"But let's get down to business," said the count. "You are offering your services as a tutor. The boy you'd be teaching is my great-nephew and my ward. As you'll have read in my advertisement, he's ten years old – he's about to turn eleven, by the way. His name is Geert-Jan Grisenstein; he's an orphan and I'm his only living relative." He steepled his fingers and gave Frans a searching look. "So why," he asked, "did you respond to my advertisement?"

"I..." began Frans. *If only I knew what I wrote*, he thought. "It sounded like an attractive position," he said, "and I wanted to earn some extra money."

He wished he hadn't said those last words, but the count nodded in agreement and said, "Your references were particularly good, so I was a little taken aback at first that you appear to be so young."

References! thought Frans. *That magician's thought of everything! Does that make me an accomplice to fraud?*

"You teach at a nearby village school," the count continued. "So do you have enough time to take on this position as tutor too?"

"Oh yes, sir," said Frans. "I have every Wednesday and Saturday afternoon off, and every evening too, except for Friday."

"I don't think the evenings would be appropriate," said the count. "I should mention that my nephew's health leaves a lot to be desired, which is why he can't go to school for the time being. And of course he has to go to bed early."

"If his health is poor, I think it would be a very good idea not to bother him with lessons every day," said Frans. "Wednesday and Saturday afternoons should be enough. He should also spend plenty of time playing outside in the fresh air."

"Geert-Jan doesn't like fresh air," said the count stiffly. "He prefers to play his funny little games indoors."

"You could maybe invite some other children to visit," began Frans. "If they play together..."

"No!" said Count Grisenstein, abruptly interrupting him. In a milder tone, he continued, "Geert-Jan is far too nervous! He needs a quiet, protective environment. I'm concerned now that you might not have the tact and wisdom to teach him..."

A vague feeling of suspicion crept over Frans. Maybe the conspirators were right after all!

"But the boy has to learn something," he said. "I don't know if I have much wisdom, or tact, but I am at least a schoolteacher by profession."

Count Grisenstein gave him a friendly smile. "You seem like a sensible, level-headed kind of man," he said. "And, as I mentioned, your references..." As he reached for the coffee pot, a large signet ring glinted on one of his fingers.

"Well then," he said, as he poured two cups, "I'll take you on for a trial period. Let's say until the Christmas holiday, with no obligation on either side. If we get along, we'll continue the arrangement. Agreed?"

"Absolutely, Count Grisenstein," said Frans.

"So every Wednesday and Saturday for now," the count continued. "And what about Sunday? Or do you object to working on Sundays on principle?"

"Well... I do think Sunday should be a day of rest," said Frans hesitantly.

"You could come and play some games with Geert-Jan," said the count. "You said yourself that playing would be good for his health. It doesn't have to be every Sunday of course."

They agreed that Frans would begin the following Saturday afternoon, and that he'd come and visit at least on that first Sunday too. The coach would fetch him and take him home.

It worked! thought Frans. He was very glad that he'd got the job, even though he'd never applied for it. He'd also be earning good money. He'd have liked to meet Geert-Jan, but of course the boy was already in bed.

*

When it was time for Frans to leave, Count Grisenstein walked with him to Gregorius's Small Banqueting Hall. Most of the candles had gone out.

"I'll just call my coachman," said the count. "Wait here a moment."

Frans was alone in the semi-darkness now, but after a few moments he began to sense that he wasn't on his own at all... He peered around. He couldn't see anyone on the stairs, and yet the steps were creaking, and there, right at the top, in an alcove, something seemed to be moving. Ivan? Who was he, this unknown spy? One of the servants Frans hadn't met yet? It wasn't the coachman, and it couldn't be the housekeeper either...

He heard the count's voice, somewhere else in the house: "Jan! Jan Tooreloor..."

Then there was another creak, somewhere nearby, above his head. He turned around, and this time he definitely saw

something! A small figure ducked below the balustrade of the lowest gallery. The figure was not dark, but white... So it wasn't Ivan, but it could be a child, a boy in pyjamas.

"The coach is waiting," said Count Grisenstein, unexpectedly appearing behind him and making Frans jump.

"Thank you very much," he said quickly. He didn't mention the small figure behind the balustrade, but he understood that Geert-Jan might want to take a peek at his tutor. When he glanced up again though, before leaving the room, there wasn't a soul to be seen in the gallery.

He argues with Jan Tooreloor

THIS IS TWO

Frans lingered for a moment at the back door; there were indeed letters written on the lintel, half obliterated and hard to make out.

The Treasure shall be hidden out of Sight...

Then he walked – or rather, limped – to the coach, which was waiting by the steps. Jan Tooreloor turned to look at him; he looked decidedly disgruntled. But maybe it only seemed that way, and perhaps the sinister glint in his eyes was just the light of the moon. The wind had chased away the clouds and it was very cold. Frans climbed in, and the coach started moving even before the door had closed. The coachman urged on the horse with a wild roar and cracked his whip again and again.

After a short delay at the gate, they headed down the brick road. *So we're taking the normal route home,* thought Frans.

A few minutes later though, the coach slowed down and made a U-turn. Frans looked outside, wondering if the coachman had forgotten something. But then the coach turned again, and he saw they were taking the Seventh Way. Reassured, he made himself a little more comfortable and rested his injured leg on the opposite seat. His brief visit to the House of Stairs had proved more tiring than a long walk.

Count Grisenstein! he thought. *Last week he was just Gr… Gr… I still can't believe he's a fearsome fiendish foe, a wicked uncle… Yes, it was exactly a week ago that I received his first letter, but it seems much longer…*

He tried to view his recent experiences like the sensible, level-headed schoolteacher that the count believed him to be. But it was still a most peculiar sequence of events. Mr Thomtidom had responded to the advertisement on his behalf, without bothering to tell him about it, which was impolite to say the least...

Frans looked outside again. They were going more slowly now, as the road was only just wide enough for the coach. Where was the Biker Boy? Had he raced into town to go to the cinema? Or had he changed back into Roberto and was he at his Aunt Rosemary's, or in his tent? *Last week,* he thought, *Roberto was obviously waiting in Tooreloor's Tavern to open the doors, so that the coach could drive through the coach house. And when I refused to go any farther, he was probably so disappointed that he turned into the Biker Boy. The coachman went to drown his anger at the Thirsty Deer. You can tell by his nose that he's a regular there…*

The coach halted again, but he soon realized they'd reached the ruin and that Jan Tooreloor had to open the double doors. They rattled through the coach house, and came to a stop at Sevenways. The clearing was brightly lit by the moon. There were two signposts now – the second was the shadow of the first.

Frans heard the coachman climb back down, and a moment later the door flew open. Tooreloor loomed before him, a dark, menacing figure. He raised his whip and barked, "Out!"

"Out?" Frans repeated in astonishment. "We're only at Sevenways. You were supposed to take me home."

"Yes, I was supposed to take you home," said the coachman. "The count called me and he said, 'Take him home, Jan Tooreloor.' You blasted traitor!"

"Traitor?" said Frans. He was baffled, but also a bit worried. "What's up with you this time?"

"You! That's what!" Tooreloor answered furiously. "Yes, you're what's up with me! I've never understood why they were all so mad about you. So what if you're a schoolteacher and an outsider? But fine, they knew better than I did. Or at least they thought they did! Turns out I was right. You call yourself Frans the Red, but you couldn't care less about my tavern, the Red Man! You just trample all over everything and kick a man when he's down. Well, I wish you'd broken that foot of yours, Red Frans, and that I'd given you two black eyes to go with that bump on your head!"

Frans pulled his leg off the seat and shot bolt upright.

"That's enough, Tooreloor!" he said.

"Tooreloor, Tooreloor!" the coachman repeated angrily.

Frans made a defensive move, as he genuinely thought the other man was about to attack him. But then he pulled himself together and said, "What is it about that name? I wasn't the one who gave it to you! As far as I'm concerned, you can call yourself whatever you like."

"That does it!" said the coachman, his voice almost shaking. "Get out!"

Frans van der Steg called on Frans the Red to help him. "Not until you tell me why!" he said firmly. "Surely I have a right to a full explanation for your rude behaviour."

His attitude seemed to calm Jan Tooreloor a little.

"I don't know much about rights," he said, "but I can give you an explanation: I think you're a gutless coward! First you were scared to go down the Seventh Way, and yesterday you let me swat you like a fly. You may be a schoolteacher, but you couldn't even stop your children from destroying my property. That's one thing, Mr Frans the Red, but betraying me to the count... that really is the limit! And talking of limits: the door to the House of Stairs is closed to me, and that's thanks to you! Go on! Get out!"

"But... how?" cried Frans.

"So you didn't tell the count my name?"

"No... yes..." stammered Frans. "But I didn't know..."

"I didn't know!" the coachman mimicked him. "So you didn't know I have a bone to pick with the count, and a score to settle? He took the Red Man from me, my tavern, the best pub between Roskam and the House of Stairs. He threw me out and I swore to take my revenge. He knows that just as well as you..."

"But I didn't know," Frans protested.

"Count Grisenstein knows only too well," said the coachman. "Did you think I'd go and work for him under my own name? Of course not! I'd call myself Pietersen, or Bakker, or even Doolally, but not Tooreloor!"

"Now I see," said Frans. Why had none of the conspirators explained the situation to him?

"And now the count comes to me," the coachman went on, "with that mean little smile of his and he says, 'Tooreloor, take Mr Van der Steg home.' Bang goes my chance of revenge! Because later, when I get back and I've unharnessed the horses, the count will smile that smile again and he'll say the same thing as I'm about to say to you: 'Get out!'"

"I'm really sorry," said Frans. "I didn't do it on purpose..."

"Get out!" roared the coachman.

"But I can hardly walk! That's all your fault and..."

"I don't care," said Jan Tooreloor, interrupting Frans. "Go and cry like a baby at Miss Rosemary's door and let her take care of you. If you dare! Or you can stay overnight at the Red Man for all I care – oh, it's full of ghosts, by the way..." With an air of grim satisfaction, he went on, "There's the Grey Hermit, also known as the Shade of Sir Grimbold... And then there are all the ghosts of the customers who can't drink there anymore..." And he continued, "As for me, I'm off to Roskam, to get drunk at the Thirsty Deer. So for the last time: GET OUT!"

Frans put his hands in his pockets and didn't budge. "No," he said. "It's late. You're taking me home as you should, Tooreloor!"

Frans looked around the class. They were absolutely silent. His students were waiting with bated breath to find out how his clash with the angry coachman had ended. Their teacher had obviously survived, as he'd returned to school this Friday, even though he was limping and had a bump on his head that was all the colours of the rainbow. Now he was sitting quite comfortably at his desk. He gave them a brief smile, for the first time since he'd started telling them about Jan Tooreloor.

It hadn't been pleasant confessing to the children that Frans the Red had been humiliatingly knocked down. That had never happened to the hero of his stories. He'd hoped to surprise the children by revealing something better: the Secret of the Seven Ways. But that had been a disappointment...

Kai had interrupted him in the middle of the story, jumping up from the front row, where he was sitting on his own. "Sir! Sir!" he'd cried excitedly. "I knew that! I've seen it, the Seventh Way!"

"You've seen the Seventh Way?" Frans had said. "But when? And why didn't you tell me?"

"When we were at the Red Man on Monday afternoon," Kai replied. "I tried to tell you, sir, but you didn't listen. You just told me to come down."

It had been a big shock for Frans when he realized that the whole class had known about the Seventh Way for days. That took some of the fun out of his storytelling, and it didn't return until he was describing the House of Stairs and his meeting with Count Grisenstein. Then he told them about his ride home and the hold-up at Sevenways.

"I said: 'It's late,'" Frans told them, "'you're taking me home as you should, Tooreloor!'" He put his hands in his pockets and paused for a moment.

"What happened next?" cried Maarten, who couldn't bear to wait any longer.

Frans acted as if he hadn't heard him. He fixed his gaze on the back row and said, "Arie! I should really come back there to you, but as I'm still finding it hard to walk, could you please come up here?"

Arie did as he was told, with a look on his face that said he was wondering what he'd done wrong this time. When Arie reached the front, Frans held out the pistol.

"Arie," he said solemnly, "I'm returning your property, with my thanks for the loan."

"Huh?" said Arie.

"This pistol saved me," said Frans. "I pointed it at Jan Tooreloor, like this – and I said, 'So, will this little plaything make you do as I say?'" He went on with his story. "Jan Tooreloor leapt back. I wish you could have seen his face! He was speechless. 'Drop your whip,' I said, 'and put your hands up!' He did as he was told. Then I got out of the coach, which was quite an effort, and climbed up front – which was even more difficult, as I had to keep the gun on him. At first I was going to drive myself home and leave him at Sevenways. That was what he deserved. But then I thought, no, this coach doesn't belong to me and besides I can't... Anyway, that's beside the point. 'Jan,' I ordered him, 'pick up your whip and come and sit up here beside me.' I waved the gun around a bit and the coachman swore at me, but he did as I said. When he was sitting next to me, I rammed my pistol – I mean, Arie's pistol, into his ribs and said, 'Take me home!' And wham bam whoosh, we were off!"

Frans laughed. "We flew along," he said. "Sometimes it all got a bit much for Jan, and he asked me kindly to point the pistol elsewhere. Or I might shoot him by accident..."

The class laughed out loud. Arie took hold of his pistol and looked at it with respect, as if it really were a dangerous weapon.

"And so," Frans ended his story, "I got home, safe and sound."

Arie gave a little cough and nobly said, "You can borrow the pistol for a while, sir. You might want to use it again."

"That's a very kind offer," said Frans, "but there's no need, Arie. I'm sure I won't have any call to use it at the House of Stairs. Count Grisenstein is a gentleman..."

Arie looked relieved, but Maarten said, "No, Gr... Gr... is just pretending. I bet he's got a gun too, a real one!"

Marian asked, "And what about Jan Tooreloor, sir? What happened to him?"

"I don't know," replied Frans. "I think he went back to the House of Stairs."

"Did the count fire him?" whispered Marian. The serious look on her face made Frans feel a bit guilty. *You have absolutely no reason to feel guilty*, he told himself. *Jan Tooreloor really isn't a man you should feel sorry for...* And he said, "I'll find out tomorrow – I'm going to see Geert-Jan."

Marian sighed. "So you won't be able to tell us until Monday," she said.

Frans actually found out what had happened to Jan Tooreloor before he went to the House of Stairs though. When he got home from school the next day, Aunt Wilhelmina was waiting for him with a letter. "From the count!" she said. "I wonder what it says?"

Frans had a bit of a fright. Count Grisenstein surely hadn't changed his mind! What if Jan Tooreloor had given away the conspiracy...

He tore open the envelope and read out the letter:

Friday 2 October

Dear Mr Van der Steg,

Unfortunately I am unable to send for you on Saturday as promised, as I currently have no coachman available. You will have to find your own way here.

As we have agreed that you will also visit us on Sunday, I should like to invite you to stay at the House of Stairs on Saturday night.

That means you will not have to waste so much time travelling to and fro, and maybe Geert-Jan will become accustomed to his new tutor more quickly.

Respectfully yours,

Gr... Gr...

"So Jan Tooreloor has been fired," said Frans.

"I know," said Aunt Wilhelmina. "I heard the news from Rosemary. As soon as he got back to the House of Stairs, the count sent him packing. There was Tooreloor, without a penny in payment, without a roof over his head! But fortunately they were able to cheer him up a little at the Thirsty Deer, and he's staying with Jan Thomtidom now." She looked at Frans and shook her head. "You men do little more than complicate things!" she continued. "One gets fired, another's walking around with a limp, and the third one has a black eye."

"Third one?" said Frans. "Who's that?"

"Rob, of course! Oh, but you haven't heard about that yet," said Aunt Wilhelmina. "He was going too fast again, and crashed into a tree. So Rosemary had another patient to take care of. That was on Thursday evening. Oh, there's barely anything wrong with him. He's already up and about. His scooter wasn't so lucky, but it's a good thing that he'll have to do without it for a while."

"Yes, that's a very good thing for the Biker Boy," said Frans, "but I'm sorry for Roberto."

"And now you're going to spend the night at the house," said Aunt Wilhelmina. "Is that really necessary? You're never at home these days! Well, I'm sure the place will disappoint, just you wait and see!" She frowned and added, "Whatever has happened to poor little Geert-Jan? Has he really become so afraid of strangers that he's going to need time to get used to a new tutor?"

Frans once again saw the little figure hiding behind the balustrade. In his mind's eye, he could see the boy's face now too. A delicate, pale little face with big black eyes looking at him, anxiously pleading...

He gives Geert-Jan his first lessons

THIS IS THREE

Frans's ankle had not yet healed well enough for him to cycle to the House of Stairs. So he'd have to go on the bus, which went the long way round, via Roskam and Langelaan.

"Not via Sevenways," he said to his landlady. "The conspirators will just have to accept that."

"Well, it's fine by me," said Aunt Wilhelmina, "and I think I can speak for the others. When you went to the House of Stairs the first time, you travelled along the Seventh Way. The count gave you the job and I think that should be enough. Just take the bus."

The journey felt very long to Frans, as there were lots of stops and the bus didn't miss out a single one. In Roskam someone he knew got on. It was none other than Mr Thomtidom, armed with a walking stick and a briefcase.

"Good afternoon, Mr Van der Steg," he said, raising his hat. "You didn't expect we'd see each other again so soon, did you?" He sat down beside Frans and added, "And I just so happen to have your books in my bag. Isn't that a fortunate coincidence?"

Frans didn't think it was a coincidence at all, but he gave the magician a friendly nod and reached for his overnight bag, which was in the luggage rack.

"Oh, no need, no need," said Mr. Thomtidom. "I have to get off at the same stop as you, and I'll give you the books then. Beautiful weather today, eh? A little chilly, but at least the sun's shining. That's all going to change tomorrow though: cloudy with showers..." He went on talking, about thermometers and barometers, about areas of high pressure and low pressure and oceanic depressions. He didn't stop until it was time for them to get off.

"If you walk straight on, you'll come to the gate to the Grisenstein estate," he said, when he was standing on the road with Frans. "It's not far, but I'll lend you my walking stick. That should save you some bother."

"That's very kind of you," said Frans, "but..."

"No, please don't argue," said the magician, interrupting him. "I brought this stick specially for you, Mr Van der Steg. Is it true that you're staying there tonight?"

"Yes, it's true," replied Frans, accepting the walking stick.

Mr Thomtidom nodded his approval. "That's a stroke of luck," he said. And in a low voice he continued, "Keep your eyes peeled! Make sure Geert-Jan minds his p's and q's and his sixes and sevens, and keep your seven senses about you too, even if a little black beast turns up at your window!"

"What?" said Frans.

"There's the bus going in the other direction," said Mr Thomtidom. "I need to catch it! You can find me tomorrow afternoon at the Thirsty Deer." He dashed across the road and hopped onto the bus back to Roskam.

He came out here just for me, thought Frans, as he began walking towards the House of Stairs. *He's a decent man, even though he is peculiar. Oh, and he didn't give me my books! But I don't have any time to study this weekend anyway. And I missed my evening class yesterday too. I should have asked Mr Thomtidom where he found my wonderful references. And where's Jan Tooreloor staying – in his house or in the tent?*

Mr Thomtidom was right; it wasn't a long walk to the estate. This time he approached from the front; this entrance, like the back, was barred with a large iron gate. It was opened for him by a surly, burly bald man in a gamekeeper's uniform, who then locked it up and trotted off, soon disappearing from sight.

It was still quite some way to the House of Stairs, and by the time Frans reached it, he was very grateful for the walking stick.

He paused for a moment on the lawn in front of the house, beside a pond with a fountain that wasn't working. He took another look at the building; it was as if someone had somehow taken a whole load of houses and castles, shaken and shuffled them all up together, and then made a new building out of the resulting mishmash. An intricate terrace of marble staircases rose from the garden to the front door, with stone flowerpots and large statues adorning the balustrades. But the marble was cracked and dirty, not a hint of green was growing in the flower pots, and most of the statues had lost their heads.

Frans climbed the steps and banged the knocker on the front door. The door opened instantly and a surly, burly bald man in a butler's uniform appeared. Frans realized right away that it was the very same man as the gamekeeper who had unlocked the gate for him. He must have changed his clothes quickly, as he was panting and looked red in the face.

"You must be the new tutor," he said. "I'll present you to the count; he's waiting in the Round Room." He took Frans's overnight bag in his large hand and led him into the hall. It was a very grand room with carpets and crystal chandeliers, and staircases on three sides, covered with elegant red carpets.

Frans limped upstairs after the butler, wondering how many servants the count must have. Probably not very many, if they had to do two jobs. And Jan Tooreloor had been sacked. The mysterious Ivan must still be somewhere in the house though. But this butler-and-gamekeeper couldn't be the dark and mysterious spy, as his eyes and complexion were pale.

After the elegant red carpets, their route took them through a less grand part of the house – across empty landings, along gloomy corridors and, of course, up and down lots of stairs. The butler stopped at a door and said, "Please enter. Shall I take your bag to the guestroom?"

"Yes, please. Thank you," said Frans. "Oh, if I could just take out the schoolbooks first." Then he knocked the door and went in.

Count Grisenstein was sitting at a desk in a round room, studying a complex drawing that looked like a map. When he saw Frans, the count quickly folded it up, rose to his feet and greeted him with a smile.

"Ah, excellent. You're on time in spite of the long journey," he said. "How's your leg?"

"Better by the day," replied Frans.

"Would you mind if I introduce you to my nephew right away?" said the count. "I'm sorry it'll mean climbing another flight of stairs."

"Oh, I'm starting to get used to it," said Frans. "Although finding my way around this house is proving a challenge. I'd very much like to see a map of the building."

"Unfortunately I don't have a map," said the count. "But rest assured, we live in just a small part of the building. We'd need too much money and staff to keep everything decently maintained. Geert-Jan, however, regards the entire house as his property... and his playground. He's waiting for you in the library. That seemed like the best place for your lessons. I see you've brought some books."

Frans walked with him and thanked him for the invitation to stay the night. He was starting to think though, that Count Grisenstein really might not be quite what he seemed. Although it could of course have been a different map that Frans had seen on the count's desk...

*

The library was large; three walls were covered with bookshelves and the fourth had windows looking out over the woods. On a table in the middle of the room, notebooks, pencils and pens had been laid out next to a huge pewter inkwell. But there was no sign of a boy.

Count Grisenstein frowned. "Geert-Jan!" he called.

No reply.

The count looked around the room, opened a door and called the boy's name again. "I told him to wait for you in the library," he said irritably. "He was here fifteen minutes ago."

"I'm sure he'll be back soon," Frans said calmly.

The count shook his head. "You don't know my nephew!" he said. "He's probably wandering around the house somewhere. If we wait for him, he won't show up until the end of the afternoon and then he'll claim, with an innocent look on his face, that he'd 'completely forgotten' you were coming." The look he gave Frans was half joking, half apologetic, but his eyes were cold and angry. "I'll go and look for him and then send him to you," he added.

So it would seem he's rather a spoilt little boy, thought Frans. "Let me help you look," he said.

"Absolutely not!" said Count Grisenstein firmly. "You'd only get lost." With large strides, he left the library.

Frans heard him calling, his shouts echoing along the corridors and in the stairwells: "Geert-Jan! Manus! Selina!" He heard footsteps going up and down – and then a woman's voice snapping, "I'm not going to risk my health again to go looking for that young man!"

Shaking his head, Frans put his books on the table and, as he did so, his eye was suddenly caught by the tablecloth that was hanging over it. It was moving! He bent down, lifted one corner and said, "Come out from under there!"

A slim blond boy emerged and looked up at him. For a moment, he didn't seem to know whether to laugh or cry, but then his features hardened and any emotion vanished.

"I imagine you must be Geert-Jan Grisenstein," said Frans. "I am Mr Van der Steg, your tutor. You must know your uncle's gone searching for you, so run along after him and make your apologies."

"Apologies?" said the boy, acting surprised. "He told me to sit in the library, and that's what I did."

Frans began to suspect that "poor little Geert-Jan" might not be the easiest of students.

"Excellent," he said calmly. "Then you can go and explain to your uncle that he's made a mistake. And be quick about it!"

The child didn't move a muscle.

"Well?" said Frans.

Geert-Jan walked around the table and sat down, as far as possible from Frans. "No, sir," he said in a clear voice. "If I go downstairs, Uncle Gradus will be going upstairs. If I go up one flight of stairs, Uncle Gradus will be going down another. If I go left, he'll go right... that's what always happens!" The shadow of a smile flitted across his face. "It'd be like looking for a needle in a haystack! A needle that's moving!" he concluded cheekily.

Frans walked over to him. He wanted to grab him by the scruff of the neck and repeat his order. But the boy ducked out of the way, flailing his arms.

"Oh, sir!" he cried out, in genuine or feigned horror. "Now you've gone and knocked the inkwell over!"

There was an awful lot of ink in the pewter inkwell, and a dark-blue puddle spread across the tablecloth. Frans picked up the inkwell and quickly started mopping up the ink with his handkerchief, while Geert-Jan stood and watched, without lifting a finger to help.

"If I do as you say," he continued cheerfully, "then I really won't be here when Uncle Gradus comes back. And he'll have to go and look for me again."

"If you don't hold your tongue, I'll empty this inkwell over your head!" said Frans furiously. "Go to the door and shout to let him know you're here."

"But you just told me to hold my tongue..." began Geert-Jan.

Frans looked up from the tablecloth. He'd never felt so tempted to give one of his students a clip around the ear. "Do the last thing I told you to do," he said icily. "And then go up or down a flight of stairs and fetch some milk to get this stain out."

"The ink will be dry before I'm back," said the boy. "It's a hundred and nineteen steps to the kitchen..." Then he took one look at his tutor and decided to get moving.

Frans looked at the tablecloth with a worried expression. This was not a good start!

Outside the library, Geert-Jan called out, "Uncle Gradus! Uncle Gradus! I've been found!"

Soon after that, Count Grisenstein returned. Frans told him with some embarrassment that there'd been a little accident with the inkwell. The count took it very calmly. "Oh, it doesn't matter," he said. "Now at least you know what to expect from your student. I hope you'll be able to teach him something." But he didn't sound very confident.

Frans didn't feel much confidence in himself either as he sat at the table, waiting for his pupil to come back.

The boy returned surprisingly quickly, but without the milk. "Selina wouldn't give me any," he told Frans. "She said we should just put a vase on top of it."

"Yes, do that," said Count Grisenstein. He was already at the door. "Well, Mr Van der Steg, your student's here now," he said. "So you can begin. Geert-Jan, do your best."

"Come and sit opposite me, Geert-Jan," said Frans, when the count had left the room.

The boy acted as if he hadn't heard. "Which vase shall we use?" he asked, walking around the library and looking at the various vases.

"Come and sit here with me right now!" said Frans.

To his surprise, Geert-Jan obeyed his order this time. "Ooh, sir, your handkerchief's absolutely soaked with ink!" he cried, barely containing his glee.

"That's not a problem," Frans replied abruptly. "I have an acquaintance who can turn it white again in a second."

"Do you?" said Geert-Jan. "No, you're just making it up," he added spitefully. "That's never going to come out."

"I'm not saying it'll come out," said Frans. "I'm just saying he'll make it white. The man I know can do the same thing in reverse too. He'll give you a sheet of blank paper, and when you look at it again a little later there'll be something written on it – in ink."

Geert-Jan opened his mouth to ask a question, but then changed his mind and tried to look bored. Frans studied him; this boy was not some sweet child with anxiously pleading eyes! Quite the opposite, in fact. The boy seemed arrogant and distant. He was tall for his age, thin, blond and rather pale. His eyes were dark blue, but he was looking down, as if trying to hide his thoughts.

"But let's not talk about my handkerchief," said Frans, wiping his ink-stained fingers, which only made them look worse. "I'm here to teach you something..."

"I don't like learning," said Geert-Jan.

"Well, that's a shame for you," said Frans calmly. "But I don't care." He opened a book and put it down in front of the boy. "Read to me," he said.

Geert-Jan looked at the pages, sniffed and began to read. He did it very quickly, but in a monotone, ignoring all the full stops and commas. Frans listened to him without making any comment, and waited for him to reach the bottom of the page before saying, "Go on."

The boy glanced up at him, a look of confusion and defiance on his face. Then he read on in the same way, for another whole page.

"Go on," said Frans again.

Geert-Jan frowned, but did as he was told. This time he read more slowly, and sometimes his voice began to rise or fall a little.

"Stop!" said Frans. "You're an excellent reader."

For a moment, Geert-Jan looked at him in surprise.

"Absolutely," said Frans. "Reading for so long while keeping up that drone is a real challenge. Do it properly this time, and pay attention to the full stops and commas. That should be much easier."

"Yes, sir," said the boy and he read, "The sun went down comma evening fell and a few stars appeared in the sky full stop the man said comma quotation marks it's getting late..."

"If you carry on like that, it's going to be really late by the time we finish," said Frans.

"I have to go to bed early," said Geert-Jan quickly.

"Why? You can always have a lie-in tomorrow," said Frans. "If you're that slow to grasp your lesson, we'll have to go on until midnight."

He immediately regretted his words, as Geert-Jan nodded happily and said in a bright and sinister voice, "Midnight! The witching hour... when all the ghosts come out... Great!"

"Read the first page again, and do it properly this time!" Frans barked.

Geert-Jan leafed through the entire book to find the first page, but when he'd found it he read it without making a single mistake. Then he jumped to his feet and said, "Now I can go and choose a vase."

"No," said Frans.

"What about these two?" said the boy. "This one's nicer, but this one's bigger." He put the biggest vase on the table. "Look, it covers almost all of the stain..."

"Geert-Jan," said Frans sternly, "listen to me! You will remain seated in that chair until we are finished, just as you would at school."

"May I just put back the other vase back?" asked the boy. "It might get knocked over too, and it's fragile."

"Sit down!" roared Frans.

Geert-Jan quickly sat back down. "From now on," he announced, "I'll act exactly as if I'm at school, sir! I won't say anything unless you ask me a question, and whenever I want to ask something I'll put my hand up." He crossed his arms and put on an obedient face.

Frans didn't trust this act at all, but he just said, "Excellent," and began asking him questions. Geert-Jan's answers were sometimes right, occasionally wrong, but mostly completely crazy. Frans soon realized he was giving the silly answers on purpose; his student seemed to enjoy pretending to be stupid. *Well, if you're trying to make me angry, it's not going to work!* he thought.

The boy sat opposite him with an innocent look on his face; he kept up his pretence of good behaviour, acting so extremely politely that it almost became cheekiness. Half an hour slowly crept by...

"Now let's see how good you are at sums," the tutor said finally.

"Whatever you say, sir," said Geert-Jan in a bored voice. "I'm very good at numbers. Including fractions and decimals too, sir."

"Good," said Frans, opening up a different book. "Then do these sums. The first five."

Geert-Jan put his hand up and said, "Will you check them straightaway, sir?"

"All right," said Frans, "I will."

Outside, in the distance, there was a bang.

"What was that?" said Geert-Jan, forgetting to put his hand up.

"Do your work," Frans ordered.

Geert-Jan looked at the sums and began to work them out, quietly mumbling to himself. Frans stood up and walked to one of the windows. He looked out over the woods – wasn't Sevenways in that direction? He heard another bang, and then another, and he remembered Roberto's cannon.

"Three!" whispered Geert-Jan.

"Have you already finished three sums?"

"Almost, sir," said Geert-Jan. "Did you hear that? What do you think it was? A cannon?"

"That's most unlikely," said Count Grisenstein, suddenly emerging through a hidden doorway between two bookcases.

Frans was a little shocked by this unexpected appearance, but Geert-Jan hardly paid any attention.

"Fortunately there are no military training grounds nearby," said the count, as he came to stand behind his nephew and took a look at his sums.

"But it could still be a cannon," muttered Geert-Jan, covering his book with one hand.

"There was once a cannon here in the garden," said the count. "Your father and I used to play with it sometimes, although you couldn't shoot with it. But when we returned last year, it had disappeared. It must have been stolen when the house was empty." He turned to Frans and said, "I've come to ask if you'll take tea with me in the Rococo Room later. Geert-Jan will show you the way."

"I have to finish my sums first," said his nephew. "Four!" he said at the sound of the next bang. "Four times seven is twenty-six..."

"Twenty-eight," corrected the count. "I'll see you later, Mr Van der Steg." He left the library.

"You mustn't watch me while I'm working," Geert-Jan said to his tutor. "I can't concentrate."

Frans didn't reply. He looked outside again and wished he were standing in front of a class full of children in a perfectly ordinary classroom without any hidden doors.

"Finished, sir!" said Geert-Jan.

Frans went back to the table and started checking the sums. They were very complicated, but Geert-Jan had worked out the first four without making any mistakes. The last one was wrong though.

"Geert-Jan," said Frans, "why didn't you do this sum properly?"

"Five!" said his pupil.

"The fifth sum is wrong. You just wrote down any old thing!"

Frans held the book under Geert-Jan's nose. "Would you please work it out now?"

"But I did, sir!" the boy noisily objected. "Six times eight is twenty-five, carry five – three times nine is thirty, plus five is forty... that's right, isn't it, sir?"

Frans banged his fist on the table. Outside, there was another explosion, like an echo. "That's enough!" he said. "You need to mind your p's and q's, young man – and your sixes and sevens – or otherwise..."

"Six..." whispered Geert-Jan. For the first time, he was clearly thrown off balance. "What did you say, sir?" he asked, staring at Frans with wide eyes. "I... I don't understand."

"You understand very well," said Frans abruptly. "The fifth sum works exactly like the others, and you could do them."

With a show of great enthusiasm, Geert-Jan went back to work, crossing out some numbers and scribbling others above. But after a while he whined, "I don't understand! That's not my fault, is it, sir? You're supposed to teach me!" His eyes were glistening when he looked at Frans. "Would you please explain it to me?" he asked.

"Do you think," said Frans, "you can make a fool out of me?"

"Six times eight is eighty... no, forty-eight," whispered Geert-Jan. "And three times nine... *That's seven!*"

Frans had heard the boom as well, and now he began to wonder if the boy knew about the Conspiracy of Seven as well.

"You said I should mind my sixes and sevens..." Geert-Jan began. *Actually,* thought Frans, *it was the magician who said that.* "Was that seven?" asked Geert-Jan.

"I think so," replied Frans, with a frown. He'd never felt quite so uncertain before. But he couldn't let it show, of course, so he said as sternly as possible, "I meant that you should pay attention to your sums!"

They both looked at each other equally curiously.

"Yes, sir," said Geert-Jan meekly and he went back to his book.

Three minutes later, Frans confirmed that the fifth sum had also been worked out correctly. He silently wrote a big tick beside it, without making any kind of comment like, "See? You *can* do it."

"Shall we go and have tea now, sir?" asked the boy.

"All right," said Frans.

"What's wrong with your foot?" asked Geert-Jan, when they were on their way to the Rococo Room. "There's a bump on your head too. Did you fall downstairs?"

"No, I was in a fight," said Frans, without thinking.

Geert-Jan stopped and looked at him almost with awe. "Who with?" he whispered.

"Oh, it was just a joke," said Frans.

"How silly!" exclaimed Geert-Jan indignantly. He opened a door, which led to Gregorius's Small Banqueting Hall. "It's over there," he said, pointing. Then he ran ahead of Frans and disappeared.

Before long, Frans was climbing the twenty-two stairs to the Rococo Room, where he had sat before with the count. As he put his hand on the doorknob, he heard the count and his nephew talking. He could clearly make out what Geert-Jan was saying, "...that new tutor's really horrible."

So he knocked before going in.

He wonders where Ivan could be

THIS IS FOUR

Frans sat, feeling rather awkward, in the blue-and-white Rococo Room, sipping tea and looking at the two Grisensteins. They resembled each other, great-uncle and nephew – both slim and blond, they had the same narrow and inscrutable face. But their eyes were different, and so was their behaviour.

The count made casual and pleasant conversation, and now and then he tried to involve his nephew. Geert-Jan, though, was wearing his blank expression again, and when he replied, he did his best to be as cheeky as he could while still being polite. He said nothing to his tutor, just sneaked the occasional look at him.

The count really should put him in his place! thought Frans.

Count Grisenstein kept chatting away pleasantly, but at one point Frans saw a flash of an expression that was far from friendly. That made it clear that he'd behave differently if he were talking to his nephew in private. The relationship between the two definitely left a lot to be desired.

Frans had a sudden, clear realization that his own sympathies were with Geert-Jan – in spite of the boy's bad behaviour. He felt hurt when he remembered his pupil's opinion of him. "That new tutor's really horrible." *If he only knew how and why I came here!* he thought angrily. But after some reflection he came to the conclusion that it would be best if he just pretended to be a completely ordinary tutor, with a completely ordinary student, in a completely ordinary house.

As they talked, he found out more details about the house. He didn't hear anything about family secrets or prophecies, let alone the treasure. He did discover though, that Count Grisenstein had three members of staff: Selina, the housekeeper; Manus, who did all kinds of little jobs around the place; and Berend, who was a butler indoors and a gamekeeper outside. The name Ivan was not mentioned.

Geert-Jan dropped his stand-offish attitude for a moment and asked, "Uncle Gradus, why did you fire Jan?"

"My dear boy, the man was dangerous!" said the count. "I can't have a coachman who drives the coach when he's drunk."

"Aha," said Frans, sensing an opportunity to find out more. "So now I understand why he was going so fast!"

"I liked him," said Geert-Jan.

"I believe, young man," said the count with a cold smile, "that it's time for you to continue your lessons. How did it go, Mr Van der Steg? Have you had to give my nephew lines for punishment yet?"

"Yes, uncle. A hundred lines," said the boy.

"Excellent!" said the count with satisfaction. "Finally something's being done about your education."

"Why did you say I'd given you lines?" asked Frans irritably when he was walking back to the library with Geert-Jan.

"I'm sure you were planning to," said the boy. "How else are you going to make sure I mind my p's and q's? And my sixes and sevens?"

"Maybe it's not such a bad idea," said Frans slowly. "But I'm not in favour of making students write down repeated lines for punishment."

"How about lines of poetry, then?" suggested Geert-Jan. "No, we have to go down these stairs, sir. I'd be happy to write out lines of poetry as punishment."

"Listen," said Frans, stopping. "Students must leave the choice of the punishment to their teachers. Perhaps I won't give you any punishment at all, if that's what I decide. But when I come to think of it, I should probably give you a good hiding."

Geert-Jan just laughed, then skipped down a flight of stairs and waited for Frans to catch up.

"Are we still not at the library yet?" said Frans. "I think we're going the wrong way."

Geert-Jan put his finger to his lips. "Shush!" he whispered.

"Will you just behave normally for once?" said Frans impatiently. And yet he wondered if it was possible to act normally in a house like this.

"It's Manus," said Geert-Jan in a hushed voice. "He always tries to eavesdrop on everything. Didn't you see him when we came out of the Rococo Room? He was going to sneak after us, so I went the long way round. But I'm afraid he's tracked us down."

Frans could clearly hear the sound of furtive footsteps. "Don't be silly!" he said loudly.

Geert-Jan didn't reply, but just beckoned him and walked on.

Whether what he says is silly or not, thought Frans, *it just goes to show that this environment is completely unsuitable for a boy of ten, even if he is bright for his age.*

He was glad when they finally got back to the library, where everything looked well-ordered and sensible. Geert-Jan walked around the whole room, rattling the handle of the hidden door and looking under the table before sitting down.

"Why all the precautions?" asked Frans.

"I already told you, sir," replied the boy. "It's none of Manus's business how many lines I have to write."

"Geert-Jan," said Frans, "you know very well that you're imagining this Manus sneaking around! He's only the chief cook and bottle-washer around here..."

"But that's just it," said Geert-Jan. "He does all the jobs that Selina and Berend think are beneath them. He spies and..."

"What does he look like?" asked Frans. "Is he dark and silent?"

"No..." said Geert-Jan, looking at him with some surprise. "He has brown hair with all these little curls, and eyes like... like a haddock's. Why do you want to know?"

"Oh, no reason," said Frans, who thought it was a good idea not to mention Ivan's name. "It just seemed like a suitable description for someone who sneaks around and spies... But why would Manus do that?"

"On Uncle Gradus's orders, of course," replied Geert-Jan.

Something's not right here, thought Frans. Had he stumbled upon some other intrigue? Then he reminded himself not to get entangled in mysteries. Hadn't Aunt Wilhelmina already warned him about that? He could only help this imaginative young boy by keeping all his seven senses about him.

"Well," he said calmly, "I have nothing to hide. I hope the same applies to you. Is there anything else you'd like to tell me? Or to ask me about?"

Geert-Jan picked up a pencil and began writing in his notebook. "No, sir," he said grumpily. "I thought you were the one who was supposed to be asking and telling me things."

Frans didn't let Geert-Jan see that his answer had disappointed him.

"Then we'll get back to work," he said.

In the second half of the afternoon, Geert-Jan behaved better, but he remained sullen and withdrawn. At half past five he went to the dining room with Frans for dinner. It was a dull and dreary room, but it was close to the kitchen so that Selina didn't have to walk up so many stairs. Frans now realized that Count Grisenstein and his nephew were not as fortunate as they seemed, even though they had aristocratic titles and lived in a huge house. Selina was definitely not a good cook. Geert-Jan just played a little with the food he had on his plate, and paid no attention to his uncle, who kept telling him to eat up.

"It's an early night for you!" the count barked finally.

"But I have to finish my work!" said Geert-Jan, looking at his tutor. "My lines."

"Nonsense!" said Frans. Even if he really had given Geert-Jan lines as punishment, he wouldn't make him do them in the evening. The boy looked pale and tired.

But Geert-Jan gave him a wicked grin. "You said you wanted to go on until midnight!" he said.

"You didn't think I meant it, did you?" said Frans, and he didn't know what was more annoying – the nephew's grin or the uncle's pitying smile.

After dinner, sour-faced Selina turned up to take Geert-Jan to bed. The boy said goodnight to his uncle, and then he asked Frans, "Why are you staying here tonight? I don't have to work on Sunday, do I?"

"I thought a little company would be fun for you, Geert-Jan," said the count.

The boy gave a scornful sniff and walked away. Selina followed him and began grumbling at him for some reason or other.

No, this place is anything but fun! thought Frans. *The boy really would be better off with Miss Rosemary.*

Suddenly he pricked up his ears. Selina's voice, outside the room now, spoke a few words very clearly, "If that Ivan doesn't..."

Ivan!

Then the count tapped him on the shoulder and asked him to accompany him to the Rococo Room.

*

Count Grisenstein held out a box of cigars, and Frans took one, even though he wasn't keen on them. His host lit one for himself too and asked, "So what do you think of my nephew? Not the easiest of boys, of course," he added, "but with careful education something could be made of him yet."

"Isn't he terribly lonely?" asked Frans.

"Lonely?" said the count, raising his eyebrows. "He has enough company here."

"But not the company of other children."

"Such a typical thing for a schoolteacher to say," said the count calmly. He puffed on his cigar before continuing, "Geert-Jan is not like other children. His health is weak, as I already told you, and he is an anxious child. He prefers to play alone." He leant forward in his chair. "I feel the need to warn you, Mr Van der Steg," he said. "You can't treat my nephew like the students at your village school..."

Frans shifted position; his ankle hurt but he couldn't rest his foot on a stool here. "So how should I treat him?" he asked.

"With great care," he said. "Although that doesn't mean you can't give him extra work as punishment. But Geert-Jan is no ordinary child. He has the most extraordinary imagination..." He was silent for a moment. "Maybe you've already heard that there's a story attached to this house," he continued, "a legend, a folk tale, a fairy story... They say there's a treasure buried here."

"I've heard about that," said Frans. "As you say, a legend, a folk tale, a fairy story..." He blew out a plume of smoke and let his gaze wander for a moment from the count to a painting of a lady in a hoop skirt and a powdered wig. She was very beautiful, but seemed somehow to be mocking him. A long-haired white cat sat on her lap.

"Geert-Jan believes in that story," said the count.

"Of course he does," said Frans. "That's hardly surprising at his age."

"I'm glad to hear you have such a sensible opinion on the matter," said Count Grisenstein. He looked at Frans through a cloud of blue smoke. "But Geert-Jan doesn't only believe the story – he's actually searching for the treasure. He spends all his time trying to find it! And that sometimes worries me..."

"Ah, he'll grow out of it," said Frans in a calm tone. "Send him outside to play a little more..."

"Well," said the count, "I thought you should know. Maybe you can keep an eye on him... and put the brakes on his imagination by giving him plenty of proper work to do."

"I'll do my best," said Frans.

"And I'd appreciate it if you could keep me informed," said the count. "Not just about his progress, but also about his fancies and fabrications."

"That goes without saying," said the tutor.

It goes without saying that I won't *keep him informed*, thought Frans the Red, when he was finally alone. *At least not until I know what the count's up to*, thought Frans van der Steg. *One spy is enough for poor Geert-Jan.*

Manus had led him to the guestroom; he was a slimy little man with curly brown hair and eyes that Geert-Jan had described accurately. But where was Ivan?

Frans looked around. There was only one door – he couldn't see any hidden entrances or secret windows, but there were alcoves and corners. The windows were open and it was cold. He'd have to get under the bedcovers as soon as possible. For the first time in his life he'd be sleeping in a real four-poster bed.

He soon blew out the candle and hopped into bed; there was no electric lighting in the House of Stairs. The bed was warm and soft and he went straight to sleep. But he had exhausting and confusing dreams about Geert-Jan and the count, and a whole bunch of spies, who all turned out to be his students.

He didn't know how long he'd been asleep when he awoke with a start. Still half in his dream, he'd heard a door opening. He sat up... Was that something rustling? The door seemed to be closed though. He felt around for matches to light his candle, but couldn't find any. He was too sleepy to make any more effort, so he lay back down and went on dreaming. Later he woke up again, this time because the moon was shining on his pillow. He turned to the window and rubbed his eyes.

On the window sill, sharply silhouetted against the bright sky, sat a black figure in the shape of a cat. It *was* a cat. Frans picked up his glasses from the bedside table and knocked over the candlestick. Oh well, it was light enough in the room.

The cat hadn't moved. He had the feeling the creature was staring at him.

"...and keep your seven senses about you too, even if a little black beast turns up at your window..."

Frans was wide awake now. He climbed out of bed and approached his unexpected visitor. A little black beast... no, it was a huge creature, a gigantic cat, and as black as pitch.

"Hey... puss, puss..." he whispered.

The animal glanced at him and went back to staring out of the window. Frans gave it a little stroke, but it remained as still as a statue.

"Fine, you just sit there," he said, returning to bed. "The window's open, so you can leave whenever you like." Now it seemed as if the cat were watching him again... "Mind your sixes and sevens!" he said to himself, with a chuckle.

And he went back to sleep.

When he awoke for the third time, he heard the rain. He looked at the window; it was already getting light. The cat was no longer there... had he dreamt that too? He soon discovered that he hadn't though, when the animal jumped onto the bed.

Like a magnificent panther, it prowled across Frans's stomach towards his face – its tail upright, its round green eyes wide open. Staring down enigmatically, it started kneading away with its front paws, digging its claws into the sheet.

"Good morning," said Frans, not feeling particularly welcoming. "It seems rather early to be getting up. It's Sunday today, don't you know?"

The cat snuggled down and bumped Frans's chin with its nose.

"Do you really have to lie right there?" Frans protested quietly. "You're rather heavy, aren't you?"

In response the cat yawned wholeheartedly, giving Frans a close look at its predator's mouth, with its pink tongue and sharp teeth.

"Exactly," he mumbled. "I'm tired too." He gave the creature a nudge, but it didn't take the slightest notice. It put its front legs around Frans's neck and launched into a purr that matched its size.

"You didn't purr when I stroked you last night!" said Frans. "So now that you wish to purr, I refuse to stroke you."

The cat squeezed its eyes into peering slits, purred even louder and affectionately dug its claws in and out.

"Ow!" said Frans. "Stop that." He struggled to sit up, and then deposited the animal on the floor. A wasted effort – because, as soon as he lay down again, the cat hopped back onto the bed and assumed the same position. With a sigh, Frans came to the conclusion that he shouldn't bother trying to get back to sleep. He stroked the animal a few times – and then he heard a different sound through the purring.

A doorknob quietly turning...

He felt around for his glasses, put them on and called sternly, "Come in here, this instant!"

Geert-Jan appeared in the doorway, in his pyjamas and with bare feet. Frans sat up and the cat slipped from its comfortable position.

The boy closed the door behind him and stood there motionless. He looked at his tutor, then at the cat, which indignantly slunk to the foot of the bed and started licking itself.

"Good morning. What are you doing here?" said Frans.

Geert-Jan stepped into the room. He looked much younger now, and seemed rather embarrassed. "I... I was looking for Ivan," he replied.

"Ivan?" repeated Frans.

The boy touched the cat, which deigned to glance at him and to respond with a quiet "Prrr!"

"Is the cat called Ivan?" said Frans.

"Sssh!" hissed Geert-Jan. "Yes," he said then, "this is Ivan. Ivan the Terrible."

He finds out more about the Sealed Parchment

THIS IS FIVE

Frans looked at the cat, who was now washing himself behind the ears, with an air of serious concentration. "Of course!" he said. "I should have known. Ivan is dark and silent... Ivan the Spy."

Geert-Jan stared at him. "How did you know that?" he whispered.

"Oh, that's quite a long story," said Frans. "I was warned about a little black beast turning up at my window..."

"Did he wake you up?" asked Geert-Jan.

"Did you let him in here?"

"Yes, sir."

"Why?"

"To... um, I just did... But how did you know that about Ivan?"

"His name," said Frans, "was mentioned to me as an... as an ally."

Geert-Jan was still staring at him. All of his aloofness was gone. His eyes were gleaming; his face was glowing.

Frans pushed off the covers and got out of bed. "But I didn't suspect for a moment that he was just a cat," he said.

"Just a cat? Ivan's a feline superspy," said Geert-Jan.

"Is that right?" muttered Frans. "And a cat burglar too, I've no doubt." He gave a shiver, walked to the window and closed it.

"How's your foot?" asked Geert-Jan.

"Fine," said Frans. "But your feet are going to get cold if you stand there. Go on, climb into my bed before you catch a chill."

Geert-Jan did as he was told. Pulling the covers around himself, he said, "I never get sick. Don't you want to go back to bed, sir?"

"No," said Frans, "I'm going to have a shave. That cat of yours has ruined any chance I had of going back to sleep." He gave his student a searching look. "You never get sick, eh?" he said. "So why don't you go to school?"

"Uncle Gradus says I won't learn anything at a village school," replied Geert-Jan.

"Ah, so that's what Uncle Gradus says, is it?" said Frans. He picked up his shaving equipment and added under his breath, "Of course, I'm just an ordinary village schoolteacher, after all."

"What did you say?" asked Geert-Jan.

"Nothing," replied Frans, pouring water from a jug into the washbasin.

"I think it would be much more fun to go to school," said Geert-Jan. "I went to school in The Hague, but I've always had tutors here. They never stay for long though."

"Why not?" asked Frans, spreading shaving foam on his cheeks.

"The first one didn't like climbing all the stairs," Geert-Jan told him. "The second left because there's no electric lighting here and he was scared of the dark. The third had to leave because Uncle Gradus didn't like him, and the fourth went because I didn't like him. You're the fifth."

Frans carefully began shaving. "And what..." he said between strokes of the razor, "will be the fate... of the fifth... tutor?"

Geert-Jan suddenly appeared beside him. "You have to stay!" he whispered.

"Be careful! Now I've cut myself!" said Frans. "Go on, get back into bed!"

For a while neither of them said anything. When Frans looked at Geert-Jan again, he was sitting on his pillow with the cat. "Ivan knew right away," he said quietly. "He purred, didn't he?"

"Like an engine," replied Frans.

"He never does that without a reason," said Geert-Jan.

"Hey!" said Frans. "Did you let that cat in here so he could judge me and decide if I'm allowed to stay?"

Geert-Jan nodded. "But I already suspected who you were," he said quickly. "Roberto told me he'd fire seven cannon shots to announce your arrival."

"My goodness me," said Frans. "Seven cannon shots just for me? So then, who exactly do you think I am?"

Geert-Jan flew off the bed. He raced to the door, pulled it open and looked outside. "I thought I heard something," he explained. "You mustn't shout like that. Manus always gets up early." He approached Frans and whispered, "You're my ally... aren't you?"

"Roberto announced my arrival and Ivan confirmed it," replied Frans. He turned away and started brushing his teeth.

"How was I supposed to know the ally would be a tutor?" said the boy apologetically. "And you mustn't expect me to become an obedient student, sir! If Uncle Gradus realizes who you are, he'll fire you too – like he did with Jan the coachman."

Frans rinsed his mouth and asked, "Was Jan the coachman an ally too?"

"Yes," said Geert-Jan. "Ivan slept with him in the room above the stable at first, because I didn't dare to show him to Uncle Gradus..."

"Doesn't your uncle know you have a cat?"

"I don't *have* Ivan," Geert-Jan said, correcting him. "He's my friend and my helper, but he doesn't belong to anyone. He wouldn't like that at all. Uncle Gradus didn't know he was here to begin with, but he does now. Ivan went exploring, of course. He sneaked into the Rococo Room and started rubbing his head on Uncle Gradus's leg. And then he let him stay."

"So he's a friend of your uncle's too."

"Of course he isn't!" said Geert-Jan indignantly. "Ivan only pretends to be his friend. He hates Uncle Gradus and Uncle Gradus hates him."

"You mustn't let your imagination run away with you, Geert-Jan," Frans chided him. "Count Grisenstein doesn't hate Ivan. After all, he let him stay..."

"Only because there's a cat's head on the Grisenstein crest," said Geert-Jan, "and of course because Ivan has green eyes."

"Because he has green eyes? Oh yes, of course. I understand."

"Why?" asked Geert-Jan. He put his hands on his hips and looked suspiciously at Frans. "Why did you say that? What made you think that?"

"Think what?" said Frans. "Well, Ivan rubs his head on your uncle's legs and he has green eyes. So apparently that's why he was allowed to stay. You just told me that yourself. What do you want me to say? That I *don't* understand?"

The cat jumped off the bed and rubbed against his legs, purring loudly. Geert-Jan crouched down and said in a whisper, "Ivan?" Then he looked up and said, "Roberto smuggled him in. Do you know Roberto?"

"I certainly do!" said Frans. "But how do you know him?"

"He sometimes sneaks through a hole in the barbed wire to bring me news from... from the outside world. He did it when Jan the coachman was patrolling in the park." Geert-Jan stood up and continued, "It's a shame he's been fired. My wicked Uncle Gradus chased him away! Why do you think he did that?"

Frans didn't say that he knew the reason why. And he wondered if he should allow a student of his to get away with calling his own uncle wicked. Before he'd decided, Geert-Jan was already walking to the door.

"I'd better be off now," he said. "See you later." He called, "Ivan!" Then he left the room and the cat followed him.

Was Count Grisenstein actually wicked? That was the question Frans was asking himself as he sat across from him at the breakfast table. His host was being very pleasant in his distant way. He fed the occasional piece of ham to Ivan, who sat beside his chair, staring at him with a hypnotic gaze. As for Geert-Jan, he was back to his unfriendly attitude of the day before.

The boy's a born actor! thought Frans. *And I think he's perfectly capable of running rings around everyone in this house, including me.*

After breakfast, they went to the library. Geert-Jan said he wanted to go outside, but the count wouldn't let him. "It's raining far too hard," he said. "Go and play a game with Mr Van der Steg."

Geert-Jan pulled a face, but he took out a backgammon set and put it on the table, next to the vase that was covering the ink stain. The count settled down in a comfy chair with a stack of newspapers.

Frans and his student played backgammon for a while, but their hearts weren't really in it. Geert-Jan kept looking at his uncle and Frans felt more and more as if the count were spying on them. Maybe he'd even made little holes in his newspaper to peep through. At one point, he put the paper down and said, "Don't be so rough, Geert-Jan! That backgammon set is a valuable antique. Our ancestor, Sir Grimbold, may once have used it."

Frans looked at the board with a little more interest and began to tell his student interesting facts about backgammon past and present, in the near and far east, and about how it was played by the Saracens at the time of the Crusades. But just as he was about to move on to the rules for tournaments and duels, Geert-Jan interrupted him.

"I'm not in the mood anymore," he said. "Shall I show you around the house instead?"

Count Grisenstein rustled his newspapers and said, "Your tutor probably isn't at all interested, Geert-Jan."

Frans replied that he certainly was interested though.

He followed his student to Gregorius's Small Banqueting Hall. Manus was sweeping the floor; he greeted them politely, but Geert-Jan walked by as if he weren't there.

The boy climbed one of the wooden flights of stairs to the first gallery. Ivan was sitting on the top step, with his tail wrapped neatly around his front paws, and his green eyes half closed. Frans bent down to stroke him, but the cat ducked under his hand and haughtily stalked off.

"Ivan doesn't want to be stroked," said Geert-Jan. "Except for when he asks for it."

"What a terribly snooty cat," muttered Frans.

They climbed the stairs to the second gallery and then went up to the third, where they stopped for a moment to look down over the balustrade. Manus was still sweeping away. When he looked up, Geert-Jan stuck out his tongue, turned around and quickly climbed the fourth set of stairs. This one had no hand-rail and it ended in an arched opening in the wall. Frans had to duck to get through, and then he gazed around in surprise.

They were in an enormous attic – on one side were small dormer windows that looked out onto the rear of the building. The room was empty and neglected; there were cobwebs everywhere. A rope ladder hung from a hole in the ceiling.

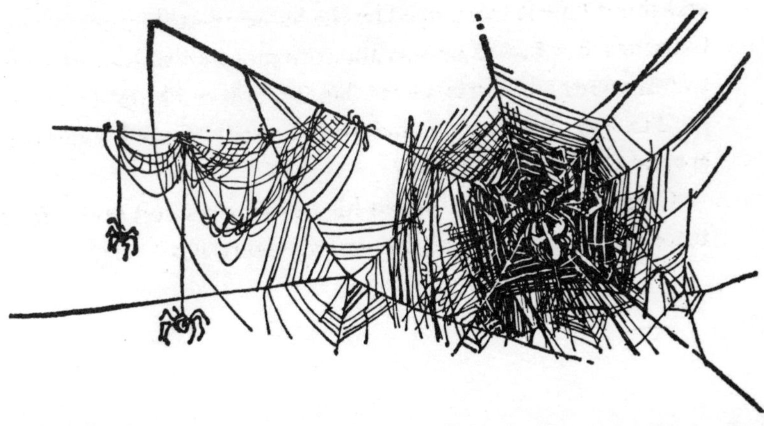

"Good," said Geert-Jan with a smile. "There's only one other way in here. And if Manus wants to take that route, he'll need at least quarter of an hour. He wouldn't dare to follow us... Why are you looking at that ladder? It goes up to the loft. Do you want to go up even higher?"

"No, no," said Frans – which was the truth, as he could feel his ankle hurting again. "You must know this house like the back of your hand," he continued. Geert-Jan shook his head. "I wish I did," he said. "But I've climbed every ladder and every flight of stairs inside the house, as far as I know, and I've also headed down below..." He gazed thoughtfully at a spider, which was dancing across the floor with its long, spindly legs. Then he looked up at Frans and said in a serious voice, "I want to tell you the Secret of the House of Stairs... You're an ally and I'm not going to be able to do it on my own."

They sat down together on the floor, and Geert-Jan told his tutor the story he already knew – the legend, the folk tale, the fairy story of the Hidden Treasure. The sound of the rain, tapping on the windows and the roof, accompanied his muted voice. He talked about the Sealed Parchment too, but he didn't say what was in it, and Frans thought it was better not to reveal that he knew.

"The treasure's mine if I can find it," said Geert-Jan. "But Uncle Gradus wants it too – and that's why he's spying on me. When we first moved in here, he wanted us to look together, and so we did..." He fell silent for a moment before continuing, "I can't find the treasure on my own, you see... maybe I'll tell you why later. Uncle Gradus knows that too. He knows a lot of things that he shouldn't. I'm sure he secretly read the Sealed Parchment before he gave it to me! Now

I'm looking on my own, and he's looking on his own... It's all very annoying..."

"Annoying? Looking for a treasure?" said Frans. "Then stop looking!"

"Never!" said Geert-Jan indignantly. "It'd be great if Uncle Gradus weren't here. He wants to have the treasure and to keep it for himself. He doesn't want me to find it, and if I do find it, he'll try to steal it from me... But he won't succeed!"

"Are you sure you're not being too hard on your uncle?" asked Frans.

"No," said the boy abruptly. "You'll see for yourself what he's like." He looked at his tutor with a frown. "Are you my ally?" he asked. "Yes or no?"

"Of course I am," replied Frans.

A warm smile lit up Geert-Jan's face. "Then you can help me look," he said "Just as long as you don't let Uncle Gradus find out. You teach at a school, don't you? How old are the children in your class?"

"They're ten and eleven," replied Frans, rather surprised by the change of subject. But he soon realized why his student had asked.

"I'd be in that class if I went to school," said Geert-Jan with some regret in his voice.

"You could be in that class now," said Frans. "You'll soon catch up if you do a bit of work. You're clever enough."

"Am I?" said Geert-Jan. "But I'm not going to school anyway," he added grumpily. "So why should I work?" Then he began asking Frans questions about his class. How many children were in the class? What were their names? What were they like? For every answer Frans gave, Geert-Jan had another question ready.

Suddenly, though, he stopped talking. Jumping up, he said, "I can hear Manus! Let's go back to the library."

Frans couldn't hear Manus at all, but he scrambled to his feet, brushed the dust from his clothes and followed his student. He paused for a moment in the arched opening. Only now did he realize quite how high they'd climbed – he could see the floor of the banqueting hall far down below. The first flight of stairs had no handrail, so he had to be very careful going down. His heart was in his mouth as he watched Geert-Jan, who took all the stairs at a run and then waited down below for his teacher.

There was no sign of either Manus or Ivan. Frans imagined them both sneaking around the building somewhere – along dark corridors and around twisting staircases, the servant going first, with Ivan following behind.

When they got back to the library, Count Grisenstein was waiting at the window, looking terribly bored.

"So, did you enjoy your little tour, Mr Van der Steg?" he asked.

"Not much, I don't think," said Geert-Jan, answering for his tutor. "He's terrified of going down stairs without a handrail."

Frans frowned. He didn't think his student had noticed, and besides he didn't like him saying so out loud, in such a sarcastic tone of voice. He knew that Geert-Jan considered him an ally now, but that didn't mean he could just say whatever he liked.

"The rain's almost stopped," said the count. "So if you'd like to go home, just say so. There's a bus every hour."

So my visit's obviously lasted long enough for his liking, thought Frans a little angrily.

But Geert-Jan said, "He can't go yet, Uncle Gradus! I still have to write my lines."

"That's not..." began Frans, but the child gave him such a pleading look from behind his uncle's back that he didn't finish his sentence.

"Well, well," was all Count Grisenstein said.

Geert-Jan quickly fetched pens, pencils and paper, sat down at the table, pushed the backgammon set aside and asked, "What do you want me to write?"

"Just write: 'I mustn't tell fibs'," said Frans.

Geert-Jan picked up two pencils and started scribbling away. "With one pencil," Frans told him sternly. "One line at a time – and neatly!"

The count stifled a yawn and said, "I'm going to take a look around the garden. I'll see you later." Silently, he left the library.

As soon as he'd gone, Geert-Jan stopped writing. "Sir!" he whispered.

"Finish your work first," said Frans. "You're the one who wanted to do it."

"It was just a trick!" his student objected.

"Not just a trick, but also a lie," said Frans coldly. "Carry on writing."

Geert-Jan did as he was told. A little later he asked, "Is one sheet of paper enough?"

"Make it two," said Frans.

"I thought you were against lines as punishment," said Geert-Jan.

"I am," said Frans.

"Can I write lines of poetry on the second sheet?"

"All right, then," Frans replied.

Geert-Jan swapped his pencil for a pen, dipped it deep into the pewter inkwell and studiously began to fill a second sheet. *Maybe there's a poet in him*, thought Frans. *It's in the family, after all. Count Gregorius wrote poetry too.*

After a while, Geert-Jan put down his pen, blew on the lines of poetry to dry the ink, covered them with the lines he'd had to write as punishment and asked, "So when you hand out lines at school, sir, what do you do with them afterwards?"

"I usually throw them in the bin," replied Frans.

"You don't read them?" said Geert-Jan in a shocked voice.

"Sometimes I do," said Frans reassuringly. "I'll certainly read your lines of poetry."

"Sir," said Geert-Jan in a whisper. "After you've read them, would you please not just throw them in the rubbish bin, but burn them? You mustn't let anyone else read them."

"There's no need to be ashamed..." Frans began.

"No, that's not it. It's just that... Well, you'll understand when you read them. Do you promise?"

"Young man, I will destroy your lines of poetry with fire as soon as I have read them," said Frans solemnly. "No one else will ever set eye on them."

Frans himself did not set eye on them until that afternoon when he was on the bus home; he'd left shortly after eating lunch with the count and his nephew.

He shook his head and smiled as he looked at the sheet of paper filled with "I mustn't tell fibs." But when he saw the next sheet, he raised his eyebrows and looked more serious. Now he understood what Geert-Jan had meant. The lines weren't by the boy himself – and Frans knew them already, more or less... This was what he read, and there was only one spelling mistake:

TOP SECRET AND CONFIDENTUAL.
THIS IS WHAT MY ANCESTOR COUNT GREGORIUS GRISENSTEIN WROTE IN THE SEALED PARCHMENT:

Try, my Child, and my Child's Child's Children
To unravel this tangled Rhyme.
One alone will never find me,
Together you must beat the Time.

Scale the heights, head down below,
The steps will show you where to go.
In this house with many a stair,
Follow the steps to lead you there.

These Words are the Sign:
All the Children must be your Friends,
If you are to beat the Foe.

These Words are the Sign:
The Stranger who will defeat the Dragon
Must travel all the Seven Ways.

Greensleeves will cast the Spell.
Greeneyes will find the Key.
Greenhair will beat the Dragon.

P.S. Please burn this now. G-J Gr.

He plays cards at the Thirsty Deer

THIS IS SIX

The bus stopped for what seemed like the hundredth time and the driver called out: "Roskam!"

Frans jumped up, banging his head on the luggage rack, and got out, with his overnight bag in one hand and Mr Thomtidom's walking stick in the other. He hadn't been planning to break his journey home in Roskam, but he actually wanted to talk to the magician now, and he'd be sure to find him at the Thirsty Deer.

He soon stepped into the pub for the second time. It was very full – warm and cosy, even though it was also rather smoky and stuffy. The first person to greet Frans was Jan Tooreloor, who was standing at the bar, ordering a drink. When he saw Frans, a peculiar mixture of awe and disdain, joy and fury flashed across his face.

"Well, who do we have here?" he said loudly. "It's Mr Frans the Red!"

A few of the guests looked up and stared at Frans. The landlord came towards him, pointed at a corner of the bar and said, "There's some space over there, sir."

Then Frans spotted a venerable head with a grey beard. He squeezed in between the tables and soon he was standing before Mr Thomtidom.

"Good afternoon," said Mr Thomtidom with a smile. "Please sit down. This is Roberto's seat, but he's playing billiards."

Frans glanced at the billiards table; the boy was leaning over it, entirely absorbed by the game.

"I've come to return your walking stick," he said to the magician. "Thank you for the loan."

"It was my pleasure," said Mr Thomtidom. "Do you mind if I borrow your books? Some of them are very interesting. Unfortunately I don't have them with me today. I hope that's not too inconvenient."

The landlord appeared at their table and asked Frans what he'd like.

"A coffee, please," he replied. "And one for you, Mr Thomtidom? Right, we'll have two coffees – and a candle."

"A candle, sir?" asked the landlord. "Need a little light refreshment?"

"Just bring me a candle, please," said Frans with a sigh.

The landlord shuffled off.

"Any news?" asked the magician quietly.

Frans looked around the bar again. He nodded at Roberto, who looked back at him with one normal eye and one with a purple ring around it. Jan Tooreloor was still standing by the bar, now gazing thoughtfully into his glass.

"You can speak freely," the magician continued. "You could cook up all kinds of plots and conspiracies in the middle of this din and no one would notice... Aha, that chair's just become free, so Roberto can come and join us."

The landlord brought the coffee and the candle, and Roberto abandoned his game of billiards at a signal from the magician.

He greeted Frans cheerfully; he seemed to have forgotten their disagreement at the gate to the House of Stairs.

"So," said Frans, "I see you haven't escaped without injury either. The job of liaison officer seems to have its own dangers."

"Who cares about danger?" said Roberto, as he sat down with them. "Certainly not the Seven."

"How is Miss Rosemary?" asked Frans.

"Excellent," replied Roberto. "Although she was angry with me for a whole day. She sends her greetings."

Mr Thomtidom tapped Frans on the arm. "Well...?" he asked in a conspiratorial tone.

Frans slowly took two sheets of paper from his pocket. "Here," he said, "I have some lines that Geert-Jan Grisenstein wrote as punishment."

"Lines?" said Roberto, raising an eyebrow. "Well, I see you're off to a good start. What did that poor boy do to deserve punishment?"

"You're the one who deserves to be punished," said Frans wryly. "For stealing cannons from other people's property."

"It was just the one cannon," Roberto objected. "Besides, I didn't steal it. I borrowed it, with the permission of its rightful owner, Count Geert-Jan Grisenstein, the Lord of the House of Stairs."

"Well, the Lord of the House of Stairs has chosen to write down some very interesting lines for me," said Frans.

Roberto tried to read them, but Frans rolled up the sheets of paper and held them in the candle's flame. "I promised him I'd destroy them after reading," he said. "It's a secret, don't you know?" He waited for the paper to go up in flames, without paying any attention to the magician, who was warning him about the fire risk. He almost burned his fingers, but he put out the flame, threw the burnt remains in the ashtray, and then looked at his co-conspirators with a smile. "You both know the contents," he said. "The Sealed Parchment... all the verses!"

"All of them?" said the magician, furrowing his brow.

"All five of them," nodded Frans. "I found the final one particularly enlightening. Now I understand why you always wear green shirts."

They were silent for a while. All around them was the chattering of the other guests, and the billiard balls click-clacking softly in the background. No one was paying any attention to them, except for Jan Tooreloor, who was eyeing them over the edge of a recently refilled glass.

"Well, nothing to say?" Frans asked the magician. "I'm Geert-Jan's tutor now, and I plan to remain so. No prophecy – no matter how insane – is going to scare me off. That's what you were worried about, isn't it?"

Mr Thomtidom moved his lips, but he spoke so quietly that Frans couldn't hear what he said.

"It's high time a reasonable person with some common sense became involved in this business," Frans said in a loud voice.

"And I suppose that person would be you?" asked Roberto.

Frans did not reply. "Anyone can buy green sleeves," he said, "and you see green eyes now and then. Just today I met a black cat who has green eyes..."

"Greeneyes will find the key," said the magician.

"Which key?" asked Frans.

"That can be interpreted in a number of ways," said the magician. "Literally or figuratively, whichever you prefer. But

I know that the treasure is kept in an ebony chest. And legend has it that only one key fits the lock, a key made of gold..."

"The magical key to the kingdom? Saint Peter's key to the gates of Heaven?" said Frans. "Hocus pocus! Open sesame! Greensleeves... all right, then. Greeneyes... fine! But as for Greenhair... I've never heard of any person or animal that has green hair!"

"Mr Van der Steg," said the magician, "you mustn't be so concerned about the prophecy! Prophecies come true or don't come true whether we human beings do anything about them or not..."

"Now that's simply not true!" Frans said, interrupting him. "You've done everything you can to make it all come true! Aren't I a stranger? Didn't I have to travel over Sevenways?"

"Ssshh!" whispered Roberto.

"Miss Rosemary didn't quite remember that line correctly, by the way," Frans continued in a quieter voice. "Although it boils down to the same thing. The place Sevenways isn't mentioned specifically.

"These words are the Sign:
The Stranger who will defeat the Dragon
Must travel all the Seven Ways."

Mr Thomtidom sat up straight. "Is that right?" he whispered. "Are you sure?"

"Absolutely certain. 'All the Seven Ways', not 'over Sevenways'," replied Frans. "It sounds better too, don't you think?"

"My goodness me," exclaimed the magician. "This is proof that prophecies come true, notwithstanding and in spite of our efforts. Seven Ways, you say?"

"Yes, and...?" began Frans.

"Think about it! Have you travelled all the Seven Ways? Yes or no?" The magician stood up and waved over at the bar. "Roberto," he said, "call Jan over. He needs to hear this!"

"Mr Thomtidom, everyone's looking at us," Roberto warned him.

"Why shouldn't they look?" replied the magician calmly. "The four of us are just playing a nice game of cards." He already had a pack of cards in his hand. "Ah, here comes Jan," he continued. "See if you can find another chair, Roberto." He began dealing the cards, quickly and neatly.

"I'd rather play billiards," said Roberto, when the four of them were sitting around the table, each with thirteen cards in his hand.

"What do you want from me?" asked Jan Tooreloor grouchily. "Am I here to play hearts or bridge or...?"

"No, there's more at stake! A treasure hunt, in fact..." whispered Roberto. "Our little *club* needs to grab a few *spades* so we can go in search of our *hearts'* desire and maybe even find a few *diamonds* too."

"It's about the fourth verse of the Sealed Parchment," the magician whispered confidentially to Jan Tooreloor. He repeated the lines as Frans had told them to him:

"The Stranger who will defeat the Dragon
Must travel all the Seven Ways.

"I bid spades," he added.

"Seven Ways?" said Jan Tooreloor sulkily. "All I know is that you lot treat me like I'm a few cards short of a deck. I've been dealt a bad hand. I'm no good at bridge. Let's play poker instead."

"Don't you get it?" said Mr Thomtidom. "We thought our Secret Agent" – he nodded at Frans – "had to travel over the crossroads at Sevenways; we didn't know he had to travel all of the Seven Ways."

"That's what *you* thought," said Jan Tooreloor. "But I was always against bringing a stranger into our conspiracy."

"So you abandoned him at Sevenways," the magician continued. "And what happened next? Mr Van der Steg, it's your turn."

"What game are we actually playing here?" asked Frans.

"Doesn't matter," said Roberto. "You can play bridge or poker, or bluff or cheat."

Frans laid a king of hearts on the table.

"Most appropriate," said the magician approvingly. "A Red Man..." He placed the king of spades next to it, picked up both cards and turned to Jan Tooreloor. "And what happened next?" he said again. "Mr Van der Steg didn't take it lying down, did he? Over the next few days, without anyone telling him to, he travelled all the Seven Ways, all those he had not been along before. The first was his way home... Then he went along the way to the town, in the company of a Biker Boy, as he puts it." He gave Roberto a wink. "Then he followed the road to Roskam all the way to this pub, that was the third... The fourth is the way to my home, the fifth is the way to Roberto's hiding place, the sixth goes to the Herb Garden..." For every way he mentioned, he laid an ace on the table; his pack appeared to have more than four of them...

And he concluded solemnly, "The seventh and final way is the one I do not want to mention out loud." He looked at the other three. "Play another card," he ordered.

When the others had done so, he scooped up all of the cards and said to Jan Tooreloor, "So do you still dare to deny that Mr Van der Steg is predestined, appointed and chosen to be our envoy in the house that I shall also not name out loud?"

"No, I don't dare to deny it," said Jan Tooreloor reluctantly. "But in the meantime it's left me without a job!"

"We'll find something for you," said the magician reassuringly.

"You're still part of our conspiracy," said Roberto, also in a comforting tone. "I bid four clubs and red is trumps."

Jan Tooreloor looked at Frans. "Well, he certainly knows how to use a gun," he said, with a hint of admiration. "Although I'd rather shoot the Fiendish Foe myself..."

"Guns?" said Roberto. "Do you have a permit, Mr Van der Steg? Otherwise it's illegal. You do know that, don't you?"

"Why don't we just put all our cards on the table?" said Frans abruptly. "This isn't a game! All I'm interested in is Geert-Jan's wellbeing..."

"Which is why you gave him lines," sneered Roberto.

"A bit of discipline would do you some good too," Frans flashed back. "A boy of your age shouldn't be hanging around in pubs playing cards..."

"Whatever you say, schoolteacher," snapped Roberto. He threw down his cards and stood up. "I'm off," he added. "Bye, everyone."

He walked away. Jan Tooreloor stood up and followed him.

Frans watched them go, feeling rather disheartened.

"I won," said Mr Thomtidom calmly. "Just let them go," he said to Frans, as he gathered up all the cards. "Roberto needs to be home in time for dinner, and if he misses the bus, he has to walk. His motor scooter's in for repairs... Speaking of scooters, have you ever thought about traffic lights?"

"Not particularly," replied Frans.

"Ah, then don't bother your head about that for now," the magician advised him. "But you should keep an eye on them, of course. And if you want to be home in good time, you need to get going too; the bus to your village leaves in five minutes." He smiled at Frans and added, "I'll pass on your report to our President. Give your landlady my best wishes, and all your class too... Yes, make sure you don't forget them. Goodbye!"

"And that's absolutely true," said Mr Van der Steg the schoolteacher, three days later. "Mr Thomtidom sends you all his best wishes."

It was Wednesday, almost midday, and he'd just told his class they could pack their things away.

"That magician," said Maarten. "Did you find out why he always wears green shirts?"

"N... no," said Frans hesitantly. He hadn't told the children that Geert-Jan's copy of the Sealed Parchment had an extra verse; after all, he'd promised the boy he'd keep it a secret. *Anyway*, he thought, *maybe it's just as well the children don't know about it*. How was his story supposed to end if there was someone in it with green hair? Even the Hero of Torelore had never met anyone like that.

Otherwise, though, he'd told them the truth about what had happened to him: the beginning of the story on Monday afternoon, with more on Tuesday. The children had listened very closely; they seemed particularly impressed by Geert-Jan's cheekiness. In fact, Frans had felt the need to tell them not to follow the boy's example – he thought one difficult student was enough.

Now all the children were looking at him; they'd noticed his hesitation. Maarten was already opening his mouth to say something.

"Listen to me, chaps," Frans continued. "If someone confides a secret in you, you don't tell it to anyone else, do you?"

Maarten closed his mouth, and the other children started to whisper. Then they all spoke at the same time: "No, sir!"

"Then you understand," said Frans. "My lips are sealed."

"And so are ours," said Maarten solemnly.

A silence fell. Frans looked around the class. He suddenly had the feeling again that the children knew more than he did – that it was *their* story, not his.

"Sir," said Marian, breaking the silence, "will you send our best wishes to the magician too? And say hello to Geert-Jan from us?"

"Yes, Geert-Jan too!" the rest of the class agreed.

"And Roberto," said Maarten.

"And Jan Tooreloor," said Arie, taking the pistol out of his pocket and looking at it.

"And Aunt Wilhelmina and Miss Rosemary," added Frans.

"And Ivan!" said Marian with gleaming eyes. "He'll be there too when you go to look for the treasure this afternoon, won't he?"

"What exactly are you imagining?" said their teacher. "That Geert-Jan the Treasure-hunter is going to set off on a search with Ivan the Terrible and Frans the Red, in and out of rooms, up and down stairs? No, no, no, Geert-Jan has to work, and if he doesn't do it properly, he can write some more lines."

He thought back to the lines of verse again. How could the other conspirators be so certain that Count Gregorius's Prophecy would come true?

THAT WAS SIX *and now for Part Seven*

7

Frans wonders about the prophecy

The tutor turns treasure-hunter

THIS IS ONE

On Wednesday afternoon Frans went on his bike to the House of Stairs, not via Sevenways, but along the normal road. When he reached the rear entrance and got off his bike, he found that the gate was locked. He gave it a few tugs, irritably wondering if he'd have to ride all the way round to the front entrance. Before he'd decided what to do, he heard a familiar sound; there was the old coach approaching along the drive. Had Count Grisenstein given Jan his job back? No, someone else was sitting up front; after a few moments, he recognized it was Manus. The man didn't look very comfortable up there; he was desperately clinging to the reins and looking rather worried.

Manus brought the coach to a stop just in front of the gate, and then he noticed Frans. "Oh, Mr Tutor, sir!" he said, jumping down from the coach. "How lucky that I happened to see you here. Now I can open the gate for you." He spoke soothingly to the horse, gave the whole carriage a distrustful look, and then took a large key from his pocket. "I should have thought you might come from this direction," he continued. "Now Berend's waiting for you by the other gate for no good reason." He let Frans in and looked at the coach again. "I was going for a practice drive," he said apologetically. "The count wants to go out soon, but he's fired the coachman. I don't suppose you know why, do you?" He looked up at Frans with something sly in his expression.

Frans shook his head and thought to himself that he didn't like Manus very much.

"It's because his name was *Tooreloor,*" Manus went on in a muted voice. "Does that mean anything to you?"

"No," replied Frans, looking as surprised as he could. "No, it doesn't mean anything to me!"

The man patted the horse on the neck. "And I'm not going to say anything either," he replied, "even though it's me who's the victim. There's no new coachman to be found, and who has to deal with it again? Me! As if I don't have enough to do already!" He looked sadly at Frans.

Frans didn't feel any sympathy for him at all, but he said in a friendly voice, "You're something of a jack-of-all-trades, aren't you?"

Manus gave him a fake smile – at least that was how it seemed, although he had no reason to be unfriendly. "I'm going to turn the coach around and drive back now," he said. "The count wants to leave at half past two. Would you like a lift? Oh, no, you've got your bike." He came closer to Frans and added in a whisper, "Good luck with your lessons, Mr Tutor. If you can't find the young gentleman, you should look for him in the Round Room."

Then he turned around, climbed up onto the coach and started moving. This was accompanied by lots of jolting and jerking and cries of "Giddy up!" and "Whoa!" and "Whoops!"

Frans cycled up to the house. The back door was slightly open, but he still rang the bell. As he waited, he studied the rhyme on the lintel. He had plenty of time to do so, as it was a while before the housekeeper appeared.

"Oh, it's you," she snapped. "Why are you standing out there? The door's open."

"I thought it'd be a little impolite to come in uninvited..." began Frans.

"Well, I think it's impolite to make someone walk for miles for nothing," said the housekeeper sourly. "It's my afternoon off!" She let Frans in. "You know where you're going," she added briskly, and then she strode away.

Frans headed for the library. He went up the stairs and down the stairs, wandering along corridors and through rooms before finally arriving at Gregorius's Small Banqueting Hall, where he met Count Grisenstein, who, dressed in his hat and his coat, was sliding a pair of immaculate gloves onto his fingers.

"Good afternoon, Mr Van der Steg," he said. "I'm just off for a little trip into town. But I hope to see you later, when your lessons are finished. You'll be staying for dinner, won't you?"

Frans accepted the invitation, although the prospect of the dinner itself wasn't exactly pleasant.

"My nephew is waiting for you in the library," said the count. He bid Frans farewell and left.

Finding the library wasn't too difficult now for Frans, but when he got there the room was empty. That was disappointing; he hadn't expected Geert-Jan to get up to his old tricks again.

He walked over to the table – the boy wasn't underneath it, but there were textbooks and notebooks on the table and a piece of paper propped up against the inkwell. *I'm in the Round Room,* Frans read in Geert-Jan's handwriting.

"So Manus was right," he mumbled, as he tried to remember where the Round Room was. He looked at his watch; it was twenty-five past two.

At twenty to three, he finally entered the room he was looking for. Geert-Jan was sitting where his uncle had been the last time, also studying a complex drawing. Ivan sat beside him, proudly enthroned on the desk. The boy looked up immediately; the cat showed no interest.

"Hello, sir," said Geert-Jan. "Look at this!"

"No, I won't look," said Frans sternly. "You should be in the library."

"Didn't you find my note?" asked Geert-Jan.

"Yes, I did," said Frans, "and Manus also said I'd find you here. But that's not the arrangement; you're supposed to have your lessons in the library. Children at school aren't allowed to arrive late to their lessons either."

"Manus?" said Geert-Jan, ignoring Frans's last words. "I told you he's a spy! But he's gone now. I just saw the coach heading out of the driveway; he was sitting up front and Uncle Gradus was inside." He gave Frans a gleeful grin and said in a confidential tone, "So now we have the whole place to ourselves! Selina won't move an inch unless she's called, and Berend's patrolling outside."

"And we have work to do inside," began Frans. "In the library..."

"Yes, but I just had to show you this!" said Geert-Jan, placing an index finger on the drawing. "It's the map of the House of Stairs."

"How did you get hold of that?" asked Frans, interested in spite of himself.

"It belongs to me, but it disappeared one day. Not really, of course. Uncle Gradus stole it."

Frans frowned, but didn't say anything.

"Ivan showed me where it was," Geert-Jan continued. "But obviously Uncle Gradus doesn't know that. The map was in his desk drawer. Just look!"

Frans glanced at the cat, who was sitting, large and regal, beside the map. Then he looked at the map itself – he'd never seen anything so complicated before; his student must be very bright to make sense of it. "Geert-Jan," he said, "I don't approve of you poking around inside your uncle's desk. Put the map away and come with me."

"But a map's not secret!" said Geert-Jan. "Besides, it's *my* map, and this house is *my* house. I'll put it back soon, sir. I promise. But please just take a look at it first!"

Frans remembered how the count had tried to deceive him: "*Unfortunately I don't have a map...*" and he did as his student asked.

"This is the Round Room, where we are now," said Geert-Jan, pointing.

Frans saw that the drawing was made up of more than one map, because, of course, the House of Stairs had many, many floors. He could see the library and the Small Banqueting Hall and he discovered that there was indeed a large banqueting hall too. The "Great Banqueting Hall" was completely dilapidated though, Geert-Jan said, and no longer in use.

"Do you see anything unusual?" the boy asked in a whisper. He quickly tapped various points on the map.

"Yes," said Frans. "I can see little crosses, drawn in pencil..."

"Those are the places where we searched, Uncle Gradus and I, when we'd just moved in," Geert-Jan told him. "But he's also put crosses by places where I've looked on my own! So now do you believe that he's spying on me?"

They stared at each other. Frans felt rather uneasy. He was becoming more and more convinced that Count Gradus was in fact after the treasure. That made the House of Stairs seem less and less like a mysterious mansion in a grimly gripping tale – it was turning into an unpleasant reality, a place that could prove dangerous for a ten-year-old boy...

Not that Geert-Jan looked at all scared. He was actually smiling when he said, "All those crosses to show where the treasure *isn't*! Great!" Thoughtfully, he added, "And I'll still need to search a lot of the places with crosses again..." He looked at Frans. "We can do it together, sir!"

Frans didn't reply; he had no idea what to say.

"It's in the Sealed Parchment," whispered Geert-Jan. "*One alone will never find me...*" He folded the map and put it back in the drawer. "Let's start right away!" he said eagerly.

"Listen," said Frans, "I came here to teach you, not to play games with you!"

"Games?" repeated Geert-Jan with an indignant howl. The cat jumped down from the desk and wound around his legs. "You have to help me!" the boy continued. "There's no one else who can do it. I have Ivan, of course, but he only wants to look when he's in the mood, and most of the time he's not in the mood... Please, sir," he begged. "We might never have another chance like this afternoon! No one will be spying on us! Go on, please! Before Uncle Gradus gets home..."

He walked over to a low door behind the desk, which Frans hadn't noticed before. When he opened it, Frans could see a dark space behind, and a metal ladder.

"*The steps will show you where to go...*" muttered Frans. "How many staircases and ladders are there in this building?"

"I've never counted them," replied Geert-Jan. "Shall we, sir?"

"A ladder and a black cat," said Frans. "Fortunately it's not Friday, but Wednesday, and not the thirteenth but the seventh... Fine, Frans the Red is at your disposal."

The boy clapped his hands. "I am Geert-Jan the Treasure-hunter," he said. "Follow me, Frans the Red. Guard us, Ivan the Terrible! We're going on an expedition."

More than two hours later, Frans and Geert-Jan returned to the library; they both dropped into armchairs and sighed. Ivan was no longer with them. He'd left them after just an hour – probably to stand guard by the front door.

Frans lit a cigarette and brushed the cobwebs out of his hair.

Geert-Jan wiped his dirty face with his dirty hand and said, "Well, at least we know this much: the treasure is *not* above the Round Room, or under the Hexagonal Room, and not in the attic above the Small Banqueting Hall, and not..."

"I'd rather know where it is than where it isn't," said his tutor. He frowned when he thought about even more challenging expeditions that might be in store for him. The climbing so far hadn't been too bad, but...

"Next time we'll check out all of the fire escapes," Geert-Jan went on. "There are only four of them..."

"The fire escapes can't be any older than sixty years or thereabouts," said Frans, "so we can ignore them."

"Why?" asked Geert-Jan.

"Count Gregorius lived two hundred years ago," Frans explained. "The fire escapes weren't there when he wrote his prophecies."

"But prophecies are predictions, aren't they?" said Geert-Jan. "Count Gregorius could see into the future. So we can't leave out the fire escapes."

"If we're going to 'scale the heights' and 'head down below', we really can't leave out even one single stair, can we?" said Frans gloomily. "Any of the steps in this house might show us where to go. That's what Mr Thomtidom said."

"Who's Mr Thomtidom?" asked Geert-Jan.

"Don't you know? He's a magician... or at least he claims to be."

"The *magician*!" said Geert-Jan. "Roberto's told me about him. Do you know him? Did he... Did he send you to me?"

"A lot of people sent me to you," replied Frans. "But I actually came here of my own free will. In response to your uncle's advertisement." He struggled out of his chair and said with a sigh, "And what exactly have I taught you this afternoon? Not even how to read a map, because you could already do that." He gave his student a long, hard stare and then said, "Your face could do with a wash."

"So could yours, sir," said Geert-Jan.

"This is ridiculous!" said Frans. "I'm a schoolmaster and a tutor, not a treasure-hunter."

Geert-Jan frowned thoughtfully and muttered something to himself.

"What are you saying?" asked Frans.

"The lines of the poem," replied Geert-Jan. "There's a lot more to it than the steps. *All the Children must be your Friends, if you are to beat the Foe...*"

"Well, the children in my class certainly consider themselves your friends," said Frans. "They all told me to say hello, by the way."

Geert-Jan's eyes gleamed. "That's nice," he whispered.

From somewhere in the house came the sound of footsteps slowly approaching.

"Come along!" said Frans. "First let's wash our faces and then we'll do some work. I mean schoolwork this time, some grammar and arithmetic..."

Not very much schoolwork was done though, that Wednesday afternoon. It was late by then and both the tutor and his student were both tired.

The children in Frans's class were a little jealous when he told them that the next day.

"That Geert-Jan's so lucky," muttered Maarten, saying what all his classmates were thinking.

Frans looked serious and shook his head.

His thoughts had taken him back to the House of Stairs. He was remembering his dinner in the gloomy dining room, with Count Grisenstein, whom he didn't trust, and Geert-Jan, who had withdrawn into a sulky silence again. After dinner, Selina had appeared. She was in a terrible mood, so Frans had offered to put Geert-Jan to bed. The housekeeper had given an unfriendly sniff; Count Grisenstein had spoken in an icy tone about spoilt little boys who were a burden to others and to themselves; and Geert-Jan had haughtily remarked that he was old enough to put himself to bed. Frans hadn't taken it to heart though.

Now he could see Geert-Jan's bedroom again, which was far too big and grandly furnished – the four-poster bed, the old-fashioned paintings on the wall... But two very different pictures hung on the wall at the foot of the bed: photographs of Geert-Jan's dead parents. He remembered how the boy, suddenly confiding in him again, had shown him something: a small gauze bag, filled with dried herbs. "Take a sniff," he'd whispered. "I got it from Aunt Rosemary. She secretly gave it to Jan the Coachman. She picked them in her garden, just for me..." He kept the little gauze bag under his pillow, as if it were as precious as the treasure he was seeking.

But Frans didn't tell that part to the class. He just said, "You really shouldn't feel jealous of Geert-Jan. Quite the opposite, in fact. He's missing out on so many things that you have. Try to imagine how you'd feel if you were in his shoes, and then maybe you'll understand."

He does some teaching and risks his life

THIS IS TWO

On Saturday mornings, Mr Van der Steg the schoolteacher always made his students write an essay. This time Marian put up her hand and asked if she could write a letter. Letters and essays were almost the same thing anyway, she said.

Frans agreed and asked if she wanted to send her letter to a real person.

Marian looked at him almost reproachfully. "Of course, sir," she said. "I'm writing to Geert-Jan."

Frans smiled. "That's very kind of you," he replied.

"A letter to Geert-Jan!" said Maarten, sounding a bit grumpy because he hadn't thought of it first. "That's what I was going to do too, sir."

Then all the children wanted to write to the boy in the House of Stairs. Frans said they could, but he did give them a few instructions. "You have to write as neatly as you do in your exercise books," he said, "and the letter must be the same length as an essay, at least one and a half pages."

The class had never worked so keenly before. At the end of the morning, Frans collected all the sheets of paper and put them in a big yellow envelope. It was only then that he realized he couldn't mark the letters. He couldn't even read them, as he believed that it was wrong to look at letters that are meant for other people.

That afternoon he cycled back to the Grisensteins' house, struggling to pedal through wind and rain. Autumn had really set in now; Mr Thomtidom and Roberto would have to pack up their tents for a few months, and the last flowers in Rosemary's garden would soon be wilted and bedraggled.

Count Grisenstein could have easily sent his coach to fetch me, thought Frans. *After all, that was the agreement! So it seems he's not too happy with Manus's skills as a coachman...*

As he approached the metal gate at the rear of the estate, he saw two men standing there. Manus was inside the fence and Jan Tooreloor was outside; they were looking at each other through the bars and seemed to be having a difference of opinion.

"Just clear off, will you!" Manus snapped.

"I'm on the public highway," said Jan Tooreloor loudly and solemnly. "This is a free country and I can stand here if I want to, even if I want to stay here all day."

Frans got off his bike, but neither of the men paid any attention to him.

"You're just lurking around and peeking through the gate," growled Manus.

"I'm standing and looking," the sacked coachman corrected him. "No one can order me to close my eyes."

"And no one can order me to open the gate," said Manus angrily. Then he saw Frans and forced his face into a friendlier expression – which didn't make him look any better.

"Ah, but you'll have to open the gate for him!" said Jan Tooreloor with a smirk. He gave Frans a slap on the shoulder and added, "Cheer up, Manus, you've no need to worry about me sneaking in. I'm not setting foot on that cursed land; I just want to keep an eye on it. Strange things happen there, you know!"

Manus pursed his lips. Slowly and hesitantly, he opened the gate.

"You see! You let *him* in!" Jan Tooreloor cried cheerfully. "But he's more dangerous than I am! He goes around with loaded pistols. There, now that's taken you by surprise, hasn't it?"

Manus gave Frans a rather alarmed and suspicious look. He didn't say anything though, but just let Frans through.

Jan Tooreloor walked away, striding through the puddles with large steps.

The count's soon going to start getting suspicious, thought Frans. And he wondered what kind of reception he would have at the House of Stairs.

Berend, dressed as a butler, opened the door, took Frans's wet coat and accompanied him to the library. Geert-Jan was sitting obediently at the table; it seemed that this afternoon would pass very normally. Frans said hello and was about to launch straight into his lessons, but Geert-Jan looked eagerly at him and asked if there was any news.

"The children in my class send their best wishes," said Frans. He didn't tell him yet that he'd brought along a thick envelope full of letters; he was concerned that he wouldn't be able to get his student to start work at all if he did. It was already difficult enough. The boy seized every opportunity to stray from the subject he was supposed to be concentrating on.

"Geert-Jan," said Frans after a while, "I don't think you're being very fair! On Wednesday I helped you to look for the treasure, and today I'm here to teach you something. There's a time for everything, and you must aim to do everything equally well."

Geert-Jan nodded. "Yes, sir," he said, "you're right. I haven't behaved *nobly*."

"*Noblesse oblige*," said Frans.

"What's that mean?" asked Geert-Jan.

"It's an expression. It's from France," replied his tutor.

"Frans the Red?" asked Geert-Jan.

"No. And we're studying grammar now, not French," said Frans. "Analyse this sentence again."

Geert-Jan did as he was told. For an hour, they worked very hard, and the mood was pleasant.

Then Count Grisenstein entered through the hidden door. "I'm not disturbing you, am I?" he said with a smile. "I'll just go and sit over there in the corner and keep quiet."

Geert-Jan frowned, so Frans gave his student a stern look. Then they went on with their work, but the pleasant atmosphere was gone.

Geert-Jan kept peeking at his uncle, who was silently leafing through a book. He did his best to be cheeky and unpleasant again, although he seemed to find it more difficult now. He clearly didn't want the count to realize he'd made friends with his tutor. Frans could understand that, and he was torn between sympathy and irritation. This was a situation that called for tact and wisdom!

The count hardly seemed to be paying any attention to them, and his face was an inscrutable mask. Yet Frans felt as if he really were a secret agent now, right in the middle of the enemy camp.

An hour later, Manus came in with the tea tray. He didn't say a word, but there was a gleam of triumph on his face.

"I believe," said the count, "that it's time for a little refreshment for body and mind."

Manus put down the tray and disappeared silently. Geert-Jan stuck out his tongue behind the servant's back.

"And are you making progress, Geert-Jan?" asked the count, when they were drinking tea. "Do you have any lines to write this time?"

"I don't know yet, Uncle Gradus," replied the boy. "The afternoon's not over yet."

"Well, I think Mr Van der Steg will be leaving soon," said the count. "He may well have a social engagement on a Saturday evening."

"Aren't you staying tonight?" asked Geert-Jan, turning to Frans.

"Mr Van der Steg can't devote all his time to you," said the count before Frans could reply.

"He stayed last week," said Geert-Jan, trying to hide his disappointment.

"My dear boy, you don't want to work on Sunday, do you?" said the count. He looked at his nephew with a smile, but his eyes were cold as ice.

"I thought it might be nice for me to have some company," said Geert-Jan smoothly.

"I've had an idea," said Frans. "Maybe you and I could go out together tomorrow morning to... to look for fungi."

"Fungi?" repeated the count, raising his eyebrows. "Out? In this weather?"

"As long as it's dry, of course," said Frans quickly. "At this time of year, there are always lots of mushrooms and toadstools after a rainy day like today. One of the subjects I'm teaching your nephew is natural history."

"It's very kind of you to give up your free time," said the count. "But there's really no need for you to come in on Sunday."

"I'd be happy to," said Frans amiably. "You have to take the opportunity while it's there. If we want to study mushrooms, we'll need to do it tomorrow."

"That's fine by me," said the count. Frans was certain though that the count didn't think it was fine at all, particularly when he added, "But only if the weather's good."

Geert-Jan took a worried look out of the window and Frans said, "Just as long as it doesn't rain. Your nephew can wrap up warm."

"My nephew needs to think of his health," said the count with a sickly sweet smile. "And if his tutor doesn't pay attention to his wellbeing, then I shall have to." He rose from his chair and concluded, "We'll see you tomorrow, then, Mr Van der Steg, wind and weather permitting."

Both Frans and Geert-Jan breathed a sigh of relief when he'd left the library.

"What if it rains?" whispered the boy.

"I'll come anyway," said Frans firmly. "Even if it's raining, it could always dry up later, eh?"

"We have to be very careful, sir," said Geert-Jan. "The Fiendish Foe probably already suspects that you're my ally. He didn't even ask you to stay for dinner! But you'll have to sleep over again next week. I'll invite you."

"You're not in charge here, Geert-Jan," said Frans quietly.

"But I'm still inviting you," said the boy. "And it's my birthday a week tomorrow, so Uncle Gradus won't be able to say no." Thoughtfully, he continued, "When I'm eleven, I'll only have another seven years to search for the treasure..."

"Oh, that's long enough!" said Frans. Then he remembered that not one single child in the past few centuries had ever been able to find the treasure, and he thought anxiously, *What will happen if that wretched ebony chest can't be found? Imagine if the boy remains locked up in the House of Stairs for another seven years...*

"It'd be nice if I could find it within the next year," said Geert-Jan. And then he asked, "What do you do when it's someone's birthday in your class?"

"I draw a flag on the blackboard," replied Frans, "and we all sing a birthday song."

"Hmm. So it's all a bit childish, then," said Geert-Jan. "And what do you do if someone's birthday falls on a Sunday?"

"Then we celebrate it on the Monday," said Frans.

"I'd like to celebrate my birthday too," said Geert-Jan. "With a real party, I mean. But I'm sure Uncle Gradus wouldn't approve..."

"Well, I'll come round to wish you happy birthday anyway," promised Frans. "But now I have a little something for you..." As he glanced over at the hidden door, he tutted at himself, as he realized that he'd begun to fear spies everywhere too. Then he took the large yellow envelope from his bag and said, "There are some letters in here for you – from all the children in my class."

Geert-Jan blushed. "Thank you," he said, taking the envelope. "I'll read them tonight, when I'm alone in bed."

"But don't go to sleep too late," Frans advised him. "You need to watch your health, don't forget."

The next day it was raining, but Frans kept his promise and went anyway, armed with an old box for collecting botanical specimens, which he'd found in Aunt Wilhelmina's attic. And he was in luck, because just as Berend, now wearing his gamekeeper's uniform, opened the gate, it stopped raining, and as Frans reached the House of Stairs, a watery sun emerged.

Frans was about to head up the stairs to the front door, but a shrill voice stopped him in his tracks. Manus appeared around the corner of the building, waving his arms and shouting breathlessly, "Sir, Mr Tutor, sir! H-help me, please!"

Frans walked over to him. "Whatever's wrong?" he asked.

"It's that wretched boy!" said Manus. He looked a little green about the gills. "He won't come down. It's not my fault if he falls to his death."

Frans gasped. "Where is he?" he asked in a sharp tone, and he followed Manus at a run.

At the side of the house, by the foot of a metal fire escape, they stopped and looked up. Geert-Jan had climbed the ladder, and had then shinned further up a drainpipe; he sat dangling his legs on a ledge, a good thirty feet above the ground. When he saw Frans, he leant forward and called out cheerfully, "Hello, sir! Why don't you come up and join me?"

"I've got a better idea! Why don't you come down?" Frans called back. "You won't find any mushrooms growing up on the roof."

"I already have, sir!" Geert-Jan called down, as he got to his feet. "There are mushrooms on this wall, some very fine ones!"

Frans was terribly afraid that he was about to see the boy come tumbling down. "Please! Sit down!" he ordered, as calmly as possible.

"I'll go and tell the count," said Manus beside him. "The boy's risking his life."

"Just wait a moment," said Frans angrily. "I'm sure he'll come down soon."

But Geert-Jan didn't seem at all interested in coming back down. He was still standing up there on the ledge and examining the wall above.

"Geert-Jan!" Frans shouted furiously. "Come down here. This instant!"

He dropped his specimen box on the ground and climbed up the fire escape after Geert-Jan. Soon he was up at the top, but Geert-Jan was still some way higher, and Frans knew he didn't dare to climb the drainpipe.

The boy turned to look at him now. "You don't need to climb up the drainpipe," he said, apparently reading his mind. "You're much taller than me. If you stand on the railing there, you can easily pull yourself up onto the ledge, and reach me that way."

"Not a chance," said Frans angrily. "Come down. I'll catch you."

"But I'm not scared of heights," said Geert-Jan, leaning perilously far forward to him. "Come on, sir," he went on quickly, so that Manus couldn't hear him. "There are all these loose bricks in the wall here, and there's a little alcove too..."

I wish, thought Frans, *that I'd never come here*... It wasn't just because he was scared of heights; he really was concerned about Geert-Jan's safety.

"Is he too scared to come back down?" Manus called from below.

Geert-Jan's face lit up. That was a good idea!

"Oh nooo!" he cried out, pretending to be frightened. "I'm so scared. I'm too scared to climb back down. Help me!" As he spoke, he looked at Frans with an amused glint in his eyes.

"Can you manage, Mr Tutor?" called Manus. It didn't look as if he was planning to venture up there to join them. "Or should I go for help?" he added.

"No," replied Frans. "You'd better stay there and catch us if we fall."

"Help!" wailed Geert-Jan.

Frans gritted his teeth, climbed up onto the railing, and took hold of the ledge. He closed his eyes and pulled himself up...

A few endless moments later, he was sitting next to Geert-Jan; the boy took hold of his arm and whispered, "Well done, sir!"

Frans carefully found a more comfortable position, wondering how long the ledge would take the weight of the two of them.

"We'll have to examine the wall quickly," whispered Geert-Jan. "There really are mushrooms growing on it, sir. And there could easily be a secret hiding place up here. You have to help me. You promised!"

"Fine," said Frans in an icily calm voice. "I'm up here now anyway, and I'll look at your wall. But I'll promise you one more thing: when we get down I'm going to give you such a hiding that you won't be able to sit down for three days."

When Frans said it, he really meant it. But when he was back down at ground level with Geert-Jan twenty minutes later, he'd changed his mind. He was just happy that they'd both survived in one piece, and he was more interested in stopping to catch his breath than giving anyone a hiding.

Geert-Jan didn't know that, of course; he could just see that his tutor still looked angry. "I knew I'd have to take risks," he said a little uncertainly. "But it's a shame to get it for nothing."

"To get what?" asked Frans.

"The hiding you're going to give me," said Geert-Jan, taking a step back. "I wouldn't have minded the punishment if we'd actually found the treasure, but..." He looked back over his shoulder. "Where's Manus?"

"He's gone to tell your uncle," said Frans sternly. "I'm sure he'll be angry too."

"No, he won't," said Geert-Jan. "Uncle Gradus wants me to find the treasure, so he lets me climb wherever I want. He wouldn't even care if I fell, as long as he already had his hands on the treasure."

"That's enough!" said Frans, furiously interrupting him. "Your behaviour today has been disgraceful and you deserve to be punished."

"Yes, sir," replied Geert-Jan. "But please beat me now, before Manus gets back here with Uncle Gradus."

"Oh, it's too late now," Frans said with a sigh.

"So you're not going to do it?" whispered Geert-Jan. "Or do you mean you're putting it off until later?"

"I'm not going to do it," said Frans. "Even though you deserve it."

"Better never than late," said Geert-Jan with a sigh of relief.

Now Frans was furious again. He put his hands on his hips and started yelling at his student. He did such a good job of it that he'd have silenced an entire class of troublemakers. Geert-Jan just gaped at his tutor.

Suddenly Frans stopped, right in the middle of a sentence. "That's enough," he said, completely calm now. "I wish you hadn't had Count Gregorius as an ancestor – he's to blame for all this misery. Come on, let's go."

"Really?" said Geert-Jan, his voice trembling a little. "Oh, look out!" he added. "Here they come."

Count Grisenstein strode towards them, with Manus following at a distance.

"Is there some problem?" asked the count. "I understand my nephew wanted to inspect the wall up there."

"Yes," said Frans. "But he's safely down again now, as you can see."

"Obviously," said the count coldly. "All Grisensteins are excellent climbers." Then, in a suspicious voice, he added, "The question is, though: what exactly was he looking for up there?"

"Oh, you know, fancies and fabrications," replied Frans in the same tone.

"Mr Van der Steg was really angry with me!" Geert-Jan chimed in. "He gave me such a hiding that I won't be able to sit down for three days."

"Surely not!" exclaimed the count. Frans couldn't quite tell if he was shocked, sceptical or pleased.

Geert-Jan picked up the specimen box and said, "So are we still going to look for mushrooms, sir?"

"Yes," said the count, "you have to take the opportunity while it's there, don't you, Mr Van der Steg? Have your natural history lesson while the weather's still dry. Please don't stray outside the fence though, will you? And, Geert-Jan, mind you don't get your feet wet."

He looks for mushrooms and finds them, but Ivan finds something else

THIS IS THREE

The sun was shining brightly now, although more rain-clouds were piling up in the distance. The woods around the House of Stairs were bronze green and golden brown. Some branches, though, were completely bare, with crows cawing away on them. Geert-Jan and his tutor walked slowly along the paths, searching for mushrooms and toadstools. They found plenty, in the shade, among the roots of the trees, and on the damp moss.

Frans talked about spores and mycelium as if he were a professor of botany. Geert-Jan listened closely, even though he'd probably imagined this outing would be very different. He didn't ask any questions that weren't about mushrooms and he hunted eagerly for good specimens.

"I think we have enough now," said Frans after a while. "Don't put your fingers in your mouth. As you know, some fungi are poisonous."

They stopped. There was a sound of wings flapping somewhere, and drops dripping from the trees. "We're not going back now, are we?" said Geert-Jan. "Look, what a fat earthworm! We could study worms too, sir. And spiders... But," he went on, "there are spiders in the house too, hundreds of them. When the weather's bad, will you teach me about spiders, sir?"

"I'll think about it," said Frans.

There was a rustling sound nearby. Geert-Jan looked around, this time as if he were searching for something other than mushrooms, worms or spiders.

"I think it's a squirrel," said Frans, looking up.

"No, it's not," another voice answered unexpectedly. "It's only me."

Geert-Jan dropped the specimen box. "Roberto!" he exclaimed in delight.

"Hey, keep the noise down, you!" said Roberto from his high perch on a branch. "What are you two up to, with your toadstools, spiders and worms? I'm not sure whether to come down or not. Before I know it, I'll step into a fairy ring. Or a magic circle!"

"What's a fairy ring?" asked Geert-Jan.

"Didn't your teacher tell you?" said Roberto. "Then you'll have to ask the magician. He knows everything there is to know about fairies and magic circles and such things." He slid down the trunk and took off his hat with a flourish. "Hello there, Seventh Conspirator," he greeted Frans. "Geert-Jan, your mushrooms are all on the ground."

The three of them knelt down to put them back in the box. Geert-Jan stared at Roberto, then at Frans.

"Now I know why we went out looking for mushrooms," he whispered.

"Frans the Red would like to try out some magic arts for once," said Roberto. "And you need toadstools for that, don't you?"

"No," said Geert-Jan. "We came here to meet you, Roberto. I'm right, aren't I? I know all sorts of things about you, sir. You've travelled the Seven Ways and..."

"He's done more than that," said Roberto, with a grin at Frans. "He's a wild one! He plays cards in drinking dens, he threatens innocent people with pistols, he rides around in old coaches at some ungodly hour..."

"And on scooters," Frans added.

Roberto grinned. "He even sneaks through barbed wire fences," he continued, "and trespasses on private property..."

"Which is exactly what you're doing at the moment," said Frans, looking around. "I'd watch out if I were you."

"I just wanted to say hello to Geert-Jan," said Roberto. He took off his hat again and tried to tuck a particularly fancy mushroom into the worn-out ribbon around the crown.

"That's such a great hat," said Geert-Jan. "Can I try it on for a moment?"

Roberto handed him the hat and went on talking, "I also have a message from Headquarters: will the Secret Agent please report to the President this evening?"

"Does Mr Van der Steg have to go and see Aunt Rosemary?" asked Geert-Jan.

"You'll get your turn too," said Roberto. "It's just too dangerous for you right now. But she sends her love."

"Dangerous..." said Geert-Jan. Then he jumped up and said, "But it's dangerous here for you! Now that Jan the Coachman isn't here..."

"Jan's at the front gate, having an argument with Manus," said Roberto. "He's going to keep him talking until I'm back out. As for Berend, I'm not scared of him, even if he does have hands like hams – and arms like a wrestler's. He never notices anyone until they're standing right under his nose."

"But don't stay too long," said Geert-Jan anxiously. "The Fiendish Foe is already suspicious." He looked accusingly at Frans. "It's your fault that Jan the Coachman was fired," he said.

"How do you know that?" asked Frans.

"They said so in their letters," replied Geert-Jan, "Arie, Kai and some of the other children."

"It was all a misunderstanding..." began Frans.

"I know," said Geert-Jan. "But it's still a shame. Hey, Roberto..."

"Can I have my hat back now?" Roberto said.

"Here you go," said Geert-Jan. "Hey, Roberto, will you come back next week? It's my birthday."

"In that case, I'll definitely come," said Roberto, putting his hat back on. "Maybe I'll even come all the way into the house! See you!"

He was about to walk off, but Geert-Jan stopped him. They stood whispering together for a moment. Then Roberto hurried away and disappeared.

"Have you told your class everything?" Geert-Jan asked his tutor, when they were on their way back and approaching the House of Stairs.

"Nearly everything," replied Frans.

"Including about the Sealed Parchment?"

"Nothing that you told me in confidence," said Frans. "I'd already heard something about it before... because of Miss Rosemary."

Geert-Jan was silent for a while. Then he whispered, "You can tell them everything. I wrote back to them, last night in bed."

Frans looked at him, feeling rather worried. "It really isn't good for you to get to sleep too late," he said. "How are you feeling now? Not too tired, I hope. And you haven't got your feet wet, have you?"

"No, not at all," replied Geert-Jan cheerfully. "I'll give you my letter later, sir, and –" He stopped.

They could see the House of Stairs through the trees and had a good view of the fire escape they'd climbed a couple of hours ago. Up there, on the ledge, stood a tall figure... "Uncle Gradus!" whispered Geert-Jan.

Frans took hold of his hand. "Quiet," he ordered. "Act like you can't see him. We'll just keep on walking calmly, as if everything's perfectly normal. Got it?"

Count Grisenstein stood up there, as calm as you like, with his back to them. He was slowly running his hands over the wall.

Frans tore his eyes away from the count and began talking to his student. They walked towards the house, pretending to be deep in conversation, without looking up again even once.

This is proof! thought Frans. *He really is after the treasure. He knows we didn't bring anything down, but he's checking, just to make sure we didn't find something and leave it up there... He must be as superstitious as Geert-Jan and the other conspirators. I wouldn't really have expected that from him...*

The house appeared to be empty. Selina was working in the kitchen, but she didn't come out; Manus and Berend were both patrolling outside. Frans and Geert-Jan arranged the mushrooms in an old flowerpot and took them to the Rococo Room, so that the count would be able to see that they'd made good use of their time.

Geert-Jan poured his tutor a cup of bitter tea from the cold teapot and ran off to fetch his letter for the children.

When he returned, Frans was looking at the painting of the beautiful lady in the hoop skirt, with the white, long-haired cat.

"That's my great-great-great-aunt Griselda," said the boy. "She was a witch."

"A witch?" repeated Frans. "So why didn't she have a black cat?"

At that very moment, Ivan appeared from behind a curtain. He jumped up onto a chair, stretched and blissfully sank his claws into the expensive upholstery.

"Here's the letter," said Geert-Jan. Frans took it and tucked it away in his inside pocket.

Ivan jumped down from the chair and started prowling around the room, stalking an invisible prey.

"What's that cat looking for?" asked Frans.

"He can smell a mouse," replied Geert-Jan.

So the House of Stairs had mice as well as spiders!

The boy sat down and asked, "Would you like some more tea?"

"No, thank you," said Frans. "I need to get going soon."

Ivan darted between his legs and pounced.

"He's caught a scent!" said Geert-Jan.

The black cat crept under the cabinet beneath the portrait of great-great-great-aunt Griselda; only his tail was still sticking out. There was a rustle, followed by creaking and scratching. Geert-Jan leapt up and, within a second, he was lying on his stomach, peering under the cabinet too.

"What is it, Ivan?" Frans heard him whisper.

And then, more loudly, "There's a hole here."

"Probably just a mouse hole," said Frans.

"It's much bigger than a mouse hole," said Geert-Jan. "Did you make it, Ivan?"

The tip of the black tail twitched.

"I can get my hand in there..." said Geert-Jan's breathless voice. "I can feel something... Oooh!"

"What is it?" asked Frans, half afraid that a mouse had bitten Geert-Jan's finger.

"There's something in there," said Geert-Jan. "Something hard... It's square. I've got it!" he said triumphantly.

He sat up and showed it to Frans. It was a beautiful Morocco leather box with a clasp made of two sparkling stones, as green as Ivan's eyes. The cat came back out from under the cabinet and gave the box a cautious sniff.

"What do you think is in there?" said Geert-Jan excitedly.

"Open it very carefully," said Frans. "I don't know much about such things, but it looks very old, and it could be valuable."

Geert-Jan began to fiddle with the clasp. A few moments later, they were both staring in amazement at what was lying there inside the box, gleaming away on a cushion of black velvet: a small golden key.

Geert-Jan sighed and whispered, "The key! *Greeneyes has found the key...*"

They turned to Ivan, who looked smugly back at them.

"If I'd made this up," murmured Frans, "and told it as a story, people would think it sounded too unlikely." Then he paused. He could hear something. "Quick!" he said. "Put the key back in the box and..."

Geert-Jan had heard it too; someone was coming. "Uncle Gradus," he whispered, closing the box. "I have to hide it..."

"Give it to me," said Frans. "I'll look after it for you."

Luckily Geert-Jan agreed immediately. The precious key was safely inside Frans's pocket when the count entered the room.

It was almost impossible to imagine that this elegant gentleman had recently been climbing high up above the ground on a shaky, slippery ledge. He must have changed his clothes, as his suit didn't have a single crease or mark on it.

"Aha, Mr Van der Steg," he said, raising his eyebrows as Ivan began to sharpen his claws on a table leg. "I thought you'd already gone..."

"Your nephew offered me a cup of tea, Count Grisenstein," said Frans. "But I..."

"Oh, I'm pleased to see you're still here," said the count, interrupting him. "I'd like to speak to you if you have a moment."

"How do you like our mushrooms, Uncle Gradus?" asked Geert-Jan. "We found some really good ones. Some of them are poisonous."

"Poisonous..." the count said under his breath. He regarded the mushrooms with a scowl and said nothing for a moment. Then he turned to his nephew. "Say goodbye to your tutor, Geert-Jan," he ordered, "and be on your way."

"Just a moment, please," said Frans. "There's something else I wanted to say to him." He smiled at the boy and said, "I'm going to give you some homework, Geert-Jan. Do all of the sums in your maths book in section seven – I'm sure you can remember that number. And while you're at, do the next section too. I'd also like you to write an essay about fungi, seven pages, including illustrations. And... copy out the grammar exercise we looked at, and analyse all of the sentences."

Geert-Jan didn't exactly look pleased, but he meekly said, "Yes, sir."

Frans repeated his instructions. "You have to finish it all by Wednesday," he added. "See you then." He put one hand in his pocket and nodded at the boy. Geert-Jan gave him a wink and left the room.

Good, Frans thought with satisfaction. *I've given him so much work that he won't have time for dangerous expeditions and climbing escapades.*

Count Grisenstein interrupted his thoughts. "Mr Van der Steg," he said, "why did my nephew undertake that pointless climbing exercise? Was he off searching for the treasure again?"

Frans hesitated before answering. "Yes, sir," he said. "He was. I couldn't talk him out of it."

The count peered at him through half-closed eyes. "Do you believe it?" he asked.

"That there's a treasure hidden in this house? To tell the truth, no, I don't," lied Frans. "I know just as well as you do that it's only a story. Not that I want to forbid Geert-Jan to look for it! But I think it's rather foolish for him to go climbing fire escapes and walls. Not to mention dangerous."

"I'm sure such high-up places make you feel dizzy," said the count in an amused tone. "But," he continued more seriously, "I have noted your concern for Geert-Jan's wellbeing."

He looked at Frans as if expecting an answer, but none came.

"And I believe you have also succeeded in gaining my nephew's trust," the count continued. He waited a moment before going on, "So I probably don't actually need to ask you to keep a close eye on him. His behaviour worries me deeply though. It truly does! So please do keep me informed about his activities, Mr Van der Steg. Can I count on your help?"

"Of course," said Frans, "if it's about Geert-Jan's wellbeing..."

Count Grisenstein flashed his cold smile. "I thank you, Mr Van der Steg," he said, holding out his hand. "Berend is waiting to let you out. We shall see you on Wednesday. If you don't receive news to the contrary, my coach will come to pick you up. Manus has proven to be a decent coachman, and I'm sure it's much more convenient for you. You'll stay for dinner, I hope."

First he didn't trust me, thought Frans, *and now he suddenly wants to be my friend*. But the longer I know him, the less I like him...

With a frown on his face, Frans left the House of Stairs, sunk deep in thought.

*

It was already getting dark when the gate closed behind him. He stopped and watched Berend until he'd disappeared from sight. Then he jumped on his bike and quickly rode onto the Seventh Way – that was the shortest route to the Herb Garden.

It was nice to see Miss Rosemary's house again, so neat and snug, with friendly lights in the windows. And it was even nicer to go inside and be greeted as a welcome guest. Aunt Wilhelmina and Roberto were there too, and the table was laid.

"We were waiting for you before starting the meal," said Miss Rosemary. Then she gave him a searching look and asked, "So? What news do you have? Any developments?"

"Yes," replied Frans. "But it's nothing bad, so don't worry!" He took out the leather box.

"Ivan... Greeneyes has found the key."

After dinner, Mr Thomtidom and Jan Tooreloor arrived; Miss Rosemary had phoned and asked them to join them. All the conspirators had to meet for a council of war, now that the key had been found.

The magician took off his jacket, so that everyone could see his green sleeves, and then subjected Ivan's discovery to close scrutiny. "This is most certainly Sir Grimbold's key," he said. "It's six or seven hundred years old. The box is from a later date; I think it belonged to Count Gregorius. The clasp is interesting: these two stones of the mineral quartz, with a cabochon cut, are commonly known as 'cats-eyes'. It's so strange and wonderful to see how the prophecy's coming true, step by step..."

"What I'd really like to know is what steps we should take," said Frans rather impatiently. "Let's not talk about prophecies – I'm more interested in Geert-Jan. I'm afraid the boy really will be in danger if he remains at the House of Stairs for much longer!"

"Well said," said Aunt Wilhelmina, with a nod for Frans and a look of disapproval for the magician. "I couldn't care less about all that hocus pocus. We should be thinking about that poor little child."

"But Geert-Jan isn't a 'poor little child' at all," Frans objected. "He's really rather enjoying the situation, as you well know. He's not scared, but that's also why he doesn't see the danger. I wish he lived here instead..." He looked at the President.

Miss Rosemary twisted a curl around her finger and said thoughtfully, "It's his birthday next week."

"It's only his eleventh birthday. He can keep on looking until he's eighteen," said the magician reassuringly.

"Yes, I'm sure you'd be happy if he doesn't find the treasure until he's got a grey beard, just like yours!" exclaimed Roberto.

"Well, I for one don't want to wait that long," growled Jan Tooreloor. "The count has to be defeated and exposed – and that is our goal."

"Geert-Jan must be freed – *that* is our goal," said Aunt Wilhelmina.

"All our paths lead to the same goal," said the magician solemnly. "We have only one wish and one will, and where there is a will, there's a way – and in our case there are actually seven ways. And all those ways lead to..."

"To Sevenways!" Frans said, interrupting him. "Let's stop wasting our time with useless wordplay. What I really need is some good advice!"

Roberto quietly began to hum the Song of Seven and the magician said, "Good advice does not come cheap."

Frans looked around the circle of conspirators. He realized they were all staring at him as if they were expecting to hear good advice and words of wisdom from *him*!

"You know," he said slowly, "that at first I didn't really believe in Count Gregorius's prophecies, but I have to admit now that there could be some truth to them... The question is: how can all of it come true? I agree with Mr Thomtidom that we have only one goal: Geert-Jan must find the treasure, and in such a way that the count can't take it from him..."

"Exactly," said the magician. "When Geert-Jan has the treasure, he'll be free, because the count will no longer be interested in him, and he won't want to keep him prisoner anymore."

"Precisely," said Frans. "The treasure has to be found, and as soon as possible. But where will Geert-Jan find it, and how?"

"I do wish," muttered Aunt Wilhelmina, "that Gregorius the Mad had been a little more specific in his Sealed Parchment."

"It's clear enough," said the magician, taking another look at the key.

"Then explain it to me!" said Frans angrily. "*The steps will show you where to go* – if we have to search every staircase and ladder, it'll take us years! And where are we going to find someone with green hair? Do they have to travel your Seven Ways too?"

"That is not your problem," said the magician calmly.

"Your way leads to the House of Stairs," said Roberto.

"That's right," said Jan Tooreloor, "whether you like it or not."

"Just imagine," continued the magician, casting a sidelong glance at Frans, "that there was a set of traffic lights on the road to the House of Stairs. What would you do if they were red?"

"I'd stop and wait," said Frans. "But..."

"Exactly," said the magician. "And when they turned green, you'd drive on, wouldn't you? Well, your job is just as simple as waiting when the light's red and driving on when it's green. And that's all I can say." He put the key in the box and closed the lid.

Now Miss Rosemary finally spoke. "That's because there is no more to say," she said. "We have appointed Frans the Red as our Secret Agent. Let him complete his mission as he sees fit; he won't disappoint our faith in him." She took the leather box and handed it to Frans. "We're all behind you," she said.

Frans felt very honoured. His worries and irritation vanished as if by magic. "Thank you," he said.

But Jan Tooreloor grumbled, "So we're all behind him, are we? I still haven't worked out why I'm even part of this conspiracy! No one ever listens to me and I..."

Miss Rosemary told him to be quiet. "And with that," she said, "I conclude this meeting."

He gets ready for a birthday party

THIS IS FOUR

TO MR VAN DER STEG'S CLASS, Geert-Jan had written, followed by the names of all the children.

> *Thank you very much for your letters, I'm writing back to all of you in one letter, and Frans the Red will secretly take the letter and deliver it to you. He'll also tell you what's in the Sealed Parchment, which is top secret and confidentual and you're not allowed to tell anyone else about it, but maybe you can tell me what you think. Then Frans the Red will report back to me and tell me what you have to say and maybe I'll write to you again. I was really pleased to receive your letters. It's midnight now and everyone's gone to bed except for Ivan. Tomorrow we're going to look for mushrooms but I think that's just a trick. Ask Frans the Red!*
>
> *With best wishes from,*
>
> GEERT-JAN GRISENSTEIN
>
> P.S. *Arie, would you tell him to take your pistol? The Fiendish Foe already hates him.*

P.P.S. *I didn't know Jan the Coachman's real name was Tooreloor either, but he really, truly is a nice man.*
P.P.P.S. *Marian, the secret passageway has been sealed up, but I'll go and look in the cellars anyway.*
P.P.P.P.S. *I didn't know you'd been to Aunt Rosemary's. He didn't tell me about that.*
P.P.P.P.P.S. *What's all this about the Biker Boy?*
P.P.P.P.P.P.S. *You've worked out who Greensleeves is by now, haven't you?*
P.P.P.P.P.P.P.S...

Frans gave this letter to his students on Monday morning, after they'd finished their sums. Marian read it out, but when she reached the seventh P.S. she stopped and blushed.

"Is that the end of the letter?" asked Frans.

"Yes, no, sir," replied Marian. She wasn't very good at fibbing. "But this... this is confidentual..."

"You mean 'confidential'," Frans corrected her, and he didn't ask again. But he wasn't entirely happy about it. *I don't see why*, he thought, *they're being all secretive again. And just when I'm about to tell them everything... even about Greensleeves and Greeneyes and Greenhair.*

In the afternoon he did exactly that – he even showed the children the golden key.

When he went to the House of Stairs on Wednesday, he took another envelope full of letters with him. His class had also given him plenty of good wishes and words of wisdom. Arie had offered to lend him his pistol again, but Frans had said no. "I have to fight the count with cunning," he'd said, "not with violence."

"So what are you planning to do, sir?" the boy had asked.

Frans had had no answer for him. He had just one plan for the time being: he was going to ask the count if Geert-Jan could invite a few children for his birthday...

On Thursday morning, his class bombarded him with questions. Had he had a nice afternoon at the House of Stairs? How was Geert-Jan? And what about the treasure?

"You seem to think that it's fun searching for something that no one's been able to find for centuries," said the teacher, raising his eyebrows. "Well, I sincerely hope that this treasure will soon be found, and then at least all the wandering around abandoned rooms and sneaking down narrow corridors will be over... not to mention all that climbing up and down! And then maybe Geert-Jan will finally be able to learn something..."

"Had he done his homework, sir?" asked Maarten. The expression on his face said that he expected the answer to be no.

"Yes, he had, Maarten," replied Frans. "All of it!" He didn't mention what a mess Geert-Jan had made of it, except for the essay about fungi. But he did add, "And he also found time to check out the other fire escapes with Ivan. He sends you all his best wishes, and he gave me another letter too – sealed with real wax, just like the Sealed Parchment, and apparently just as top secret and confidentual."

"Confidential," Maarten corrected him. "May I open it, sir?"

"No, not now," said Frans. "Now it's time for work. We're not in the House of Stairs now!"

*

At twenty-five past three, as usual, he told them more: "So Manus took me in the coach to the House of Stairs. He drives much more carefully than Jan Tooreloor, but I didn't feel very safe with him either... I saw Berend walking through the woods with a gun – no, Arie, I don't know if it was loaded. Selina answered the door and Count Grisenstein said hello to me when I saw him in the Small Banqueting Hall. At half past two, I stepped into the library. Geert-Jan was not sitting at or under the table, and he wasn't in or on a cupboard. He'd left his homework out on the table for me. He seemed to think I could check it just as easily without him there. But, of course, I didn't agree, so I went to look for him..."

Frans gave a sigh. "I know one thing for sure, chaps," he said. "When I've completed my mission, I never want to play hide-and-seek again!" He nodded at Marian and continued, "It was thanks to you, Marian, that I finally found him. I remembered that Geert-Jan had written to you that he'd go and search in the cellars, so I went to take a look. And yes, down there in the basement, I finally found my student, with a candle in his hand, cheerfully chatting away about promising alcoves and dead ends. Ivan was with him, but he was hunting for mice and nastier creatures, and he didn't seem at all bothered about the treasure."

"Wasn't Geert-Jan scared?" asked Marian.

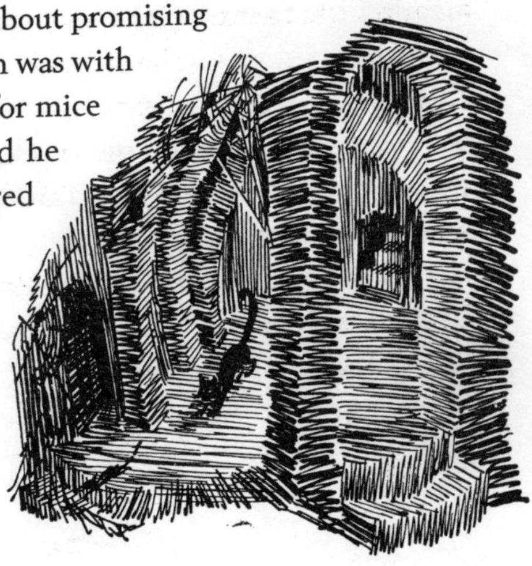

"No," replied Frans slowly. "Of course, that doesn't mean that he's completely fearless. It's just that damp cellars and dark corridors are the most ordinary things in the world to him."

And he went on with his story: "Mr Van der Steg the tutor gave his student a good telling-off, but Frans the Red couldn't bring himself to take him straight to the library. There was a ladder in that cellar, you see, a worn-out rope ladder, half nibbled away by the mice. Frans the Red stamped on the ground, and knocked on the wall, and tapped on the ceiling... but all that happened was that some plaster came falling down; there was no chest of jewels hidden away in there. Then he led Geert-Jan, or Geert-Jan led him, through lots of arched vaults, lit only by the flickering candle, accompanied by the black Ivan and by shadows that were even blacker... until they came to a staircase that would lead them back up again. There were many, many stairs; they climbed them slowly and then suddenly both stopped at the same time.

"Right in front of them they saw a pair of legs, long legs, in a grey pair of trousers with sharp creases... They went on climbing. At the top of the stairs, Count Grisenstein stood waiting for them, as still as a statue, his face rigid with anger..."

Frans paused for a moment. "But maybe we just imagined that," he said, almost apologetically. "When we reached the count, he grabbed me by the arm and said in a low, threatening voice, 'Whatever possessed you to go wandering around down there? These cellars are highly dangerous. Some parts are ready to collapse.'

"'But Uncle Gradus,' said Geert-Jan, 'you've been down there plenty of times yourself – and you even took me with you, just after we moved in.'

"'I know my way around,' the count said abruptly. 'It's quite unacceptable that your tutor had to go down there looking for you.' He turned to me and twisted his mouth into a smile. 'I'm afraid,' he added, 'that my nephew has not responded well to your discipline as yet.'

"I promised him that I'd start Geert-Jan's lessons immediately. In the meantime Geert-Jan ran on up into the room where the stairs came out – which, as it happened, was the Great Banqueting Hall, where I'd never been before. It was a huge room, but it also looked like it was about to come tumbling down.

"It seemed that they were planning to do something about it though, as there were planks, hammers and saws all over the place, and pots of paint, bags of plaster and sacks of cement. There were a couple of ladders too, which, of course, was what Geert-Jan was most interested in. But I grabbed him by the scruff of his neck and dragged him to the library. We spent the rest of the afternoon studying, and there's not much to say about that..."

"What about the count?" asked Marian.

"Count Grisenstein was as pleasant as he could be," replied Frans.

"The big fat sneaky liar!" exclaimed Maarten and Arie.

Frans agreed with them, although he didn't think it was wise to say so out loud. Later, after dinner, he'd cautiously asked the count if Geert-Jan could invite a few children to visit on his birthday. The count had firmly refused though, and he hadn't been at all pleasant about it.

If he only knew, thought Frans, *that his nephew is exchanging letters with twenty-five children. All the Children must be your Friends...* Friendships can develop at a distance too.

When the bell went, he gave his class Geert-Jan's letter.

"If there's anything important in there," he said, "I hope you'll let me know."

But apparently there was nothing important in the letter – or it was all very "confidentual", because none of the children told Frans anything about it. He also received a letter from Geert-Jan, but in the usual way, by post, with a P.S. from Count Grisenstein. Nephew and uncle invited him to spend the weekend at the House of Stairs, to celebrate Geert-Jan's eleventh birthday.

On Friday afternoon, Frans asked if anyone in the class wanted to bring in a little something for Geert-Jan, as it was his birthday – a letter or a small present. The children thought that was a great idea, but he almost regretted telling them, as they started to behave really badly. They whispered, nudged one another, giggled, and whispered some more. Unfortunately, he couldn't make them stay behind after school, as he had something to do at half past three. He wanted to take a present for Geert-Jan himself, of course, and he knew he wouldn't find what he wanted in the village.

So he cycled into town to buy a wide-brimmed straw hat, the same kind that Roberto had. It took him quite a while to find the right hat, and then he decided to stay in town. It was Friday, after all, so he could finally go back to his evening class.

When he set off for home that evening, he was not in the best of moods. He hadn't made a very good impression on his teachers – which was understandable, as he hadn't looked at his books for three weeks. He hadn't even got his books back yet!

"And I'm worried I'm not going to get them back for a while," he said to himself. "Mr Thomtidom has probably spirited them away somewhere."

As he approached a junction with traffic lights, he remembered what the magician had said. *Self-important piffle!* he thought grumpily, and he braked as the green light turned amber and then red.

A second later, a motor scooter pulled up beside him.

"Hey," the Biker Boy said. "I know you!"

Frans looked at his mocking smile and calmly replied, "Good evening. I see your scooter's working again."

"This is that bloke who believes in ghosts," said the Biker Boy to the long-haired lad who was sitting behind him, with a guitar under each arm. "You remember?" he said to Frans. "You were meeting your date in that abandoned pub..."

"I remember it very well," said Frans. "And you and I have met since then too. In another pub, the Thirsty Deer."

"I never go to the Thirsty Deer," said the Biker Boy with another sneer. "They don't even have a jukebox there."

The red light turned green, and he roared away.

Frans set off on his bike, with the scooter getting farther and farther ahead and finally disappearing from sight.

This Biker Boy business is starting to get on my nerves, he thought. *You'd better watch out, Rob or Roberto, or soon you'll forget which one of the two you are...*

The next morning he told his class that he'd had a really bad dream. He couldn't remember exactly what had happened, but he knew the Biker Boy had crashed into the count's carriage and so the count had taken Roberto prisoner and locked him up in the cellar beneath the Great Banqueting

Hall. He also told them that in his dream Geert-Jan had found the treasure, but it was just a jukebox playing awful music.

Frans was a little disappointed by the children. They hadn't brought in anything for Geert-Jan except for a thin envelope, which Maarten handed over to him.

"Is that all?" asked Frans.

Maarten replied that yes, that was all, but Kai said in a loud whisper that there was more to come, and Marian almost jumped up out of her seat and told him to be quiet.

Frans looked rather suspiciously at the unruly bunch of children and said he hoped they weren't planning on getting up to any silly tricks.

"Oh, no, sir," said Marian. "Miss Rosemary said we mustn't."

And I'm sure they'll obey Miss Rosemary, thought Frans, *even though they don't always listen to me*.

Then Arie put his hand up to ask if Frans had a pistol yet.

"No!" said Frans impatiently. "No one at the House of Stairs has a pistol." Then he banged his fist on the table and started the lesson.

Aunt Wilhelmina also had a present for Geert-Jan, not a thin envelope, but a parcel with a ribbon around it. And just after lunch Jan Tooreloor turned up. He'd brought a large suitcase, which he put down at Frans's feet.

"For the lad at the House of Stairs," he said. "A present."

"My goodness!" said Frans. "What on earth's in there?"

"It's a surprise," replied Tooreloor. "He mustn't open it until tomorrow. You'll take it, won't you?"

"Of course," said Frans.

"And there's this too," said Tooreloor, taking a small white parcel from his pocket. "From Mr Thomtidom. With the message that Geert-Jan must open it today, as soon as he's alone in his room."

"Why today?" asked Frans, taking the parcel.

"Because this has to be the very last present that he receives in his tenth year," replied Tooreloor. "Look, that's what Mr Thomtidom's written on the package."

"Jan Thomtidom always comes up with something special," said Aunt Wilhelmina. "No parcel from Rosemary?"

Jan Tooreloor slowly shook his head.

"Oh, I'm sure Rosemary won't forget the boy," said Aunt Wilhelmina. "I think she'll probably go to visit him herself."

"Will the count let her see him?" asked Frans.

"Of course not," said Jan Tooreloor. "But she has her ways."

"How?" asked Frans.

"Don't look at me," said Tooreloor. "All I know is she never forgets the child. And she's certainly not afraid of the count." He suddenly frowned. "What's that I hear?" he said. "It's not my coach, is it?"

"Count Grisenstein's coach," Frans corrected him. "It's coming to fetch me."

"With that Manus driving it?" Tooreloor said in a menacing growl. "I won't do it now, because you've got so many parcels, but someday soon I'm going to wring Manus's neck and throw him off the front of the coach, where I should be sitting! You mark my words, because I mean it."

"Fine," said Aunt Wilhelmina. "But for now why don't you help Frans to load his parcels into the coach?"

"No need," said Frans. "It's better if Manus doesn't see that we're on good terms with each other."

"That we're on good terms?" repeated Jan Tooreloor. "It's the first I've heard of it."

"I mean we're part of the same conspiracy," said Frans.

"You wish we were," said Jan Tooreloor. "I'm part of an entirely different plot... Don't forget my suitcase," he added, with a meaningful look on his face.

It took Frans a while to get everything loaded in and sorted out, but finally he was sitting inside the coach with his luggage. Manus cracked the reins. "Giddy up!" he called in a shaky voice.

Aunt Wilhelmina stood on the doorstep and waved them off. But Jan Tooreloor appeared in the window, clenching his fist at them.

If Manus was surprised about the luggage Frans had with him, he didn't let it show. When they arrived at the House of Stairs, he even helped him to take everything to the guestroom. He gave Frans a friendly smile and, as he left, he said he hoped the young gentleman would behave himself today.

Frans slid Jan Tooreloor's suitcase, which was surprisingly light, under the bed, along with his own present and Aunt Wilhelmina's parcel. He kept three things in his pockets: the box with the precious key, the envelope from the children and the present from Mr Thomtidom. Then he headed to the library. But he got the wrong door and found himself in a different room. He stood there for a moment, trying to work out which way to go, and then he heard a couple of muted voices somewhere nearby...

"...parcels?" he heard Count Grisenstein ask. "Well, well! And do you have my present?"

The answer was an apologetic mumble.

"You can't possibly be so unbelievably stupid," snapped the count. "Is it really that difficult to buy some kind of toy for an eleven-year-old boy? I can't turn up empty-handed tomorrow. Surely you must understand that?"

"I'll go immediately, Count Grisenstein," said the other man. It was Manus.

"No, I'll do it myself," said Count Grisenstein haughtily. "You go and spy on the two of them in the library. And make sure you remember every word they say!"

"What if...?" began Manus. Frans couldn't hear the rest.

"You know what your job is," the count said, concluding the conversation.

Footsteps moved away...

Frans stayed where he was until he could no longer hear any sounds. Then he went looking for the way to the library.

"What is Manus's job?" he said to himself. "Is he Grisenstein's Inspector of Education, or simply a spy? Well, I'm a secret agent and I'm about to do a little counterespionage!"

Miraculously, Geert-Jan was where he was supposed to be; he was sitting neatly at the big table with an eager expression on his face. He wasn't keen to learn more about grammar or sums though – the questions he whispered were about entirely different subjects. But Frans told him to be quiet and said firmly, "We're going to study grammar. I want you to analyse these sentences. Pay attention, Geert-Jan."

"Oh, but you've already made me analyse hundreds of sentences!" Geert-Jan complained. "There's absolutely no point, sir."

"There most certainly is," said Frans, opening a book. "Now pay attention. Or perhaps I should say 'Mind your step'... This is the first sentence. I hope you understand: *Spies like to listen in on conversations.*"

Geert-Jan understood right away. He gave his teacher a cunning look and obediently said, "*Like* and *listen* are verbs, and *spies* and *conversations* are nouns and... Can I come up with a sentence too, sir? *The secret agent knocked out the spy with a devastating punch*... How do you spell 'devastating', sir?"

And so Geert-Jan's lessons began, and for the whole afternoon they did nothing but grammar and spelling, multiplication and division.

So it turns out that spies are good for something, thought Mr Van der Steg the teacher. *I'm finally getting to do the job I was hired for.*

But Frans the Red said to himself, "No, I was taken on to do a very different job indeed... I have to defeat the count, or beat the Dragon, as the prophecy has it. And to free Geert-Jan! But how am I going to do that?"

He didn't get the chance to talk to Geert-Jan privately, just the two of them, until after dinner, when he went to wish him goodnight. It wasn't really just the two of them though, as Ivan was there too, sitting on the foot of Geert-Jan's bed.

The boy was already under the covers, but he was wide awake. He was rather excited, because, of course, it was his birthday the next day. And he was finally free to talk about all the things that were on his mind. He wanted to take another look at the golden key and reluctantly agreed that it was safer with Frans than with him. Then he asked if there was any news from the children.

"They gave me this envelope," said Frans. "But I think it's for your birthday, so you can't open it until tomorrow."

"I don't think so," said Geert-Jan, sitting up in bed. "I know the message I was waiting for was going to arrive today. Give me the envelope now, sir. Go on! Please!"

When Frans finally handed it over though, Geert-Jan didn't open it immediately, but slid it under his pillow.

"I also have a present from Mr Thomtidom for you," said Frans, "the magician, as you know. It seems like a most mysterious package. As soon as I've gone, you may open it – but then you have to promise me you'll blow out your candle right away and go to sleep."

"Yes, sir," said the boy, looking longingly at the parcel.

"Goodnight, then," said Frans. He patted Geert-Jan on the head and then Ivan too, and he left the room.

He spent the rest of the evening in the library, playing backgammon with Count Grisenstein.

A few hours later, he went to bed. As always, it seemed as if invisible creatures were scuttling and scurrying all around the house. He popped round to Geert-Jan's room, quietly opened the door and slipped inside.

The boy was asleep, but he hadn't blown out the candle on his bedside table. It had burned almost all the way down; an empty envelope and the crumpled wrapping paper from Mr Thomtidom's present lay beside it.

As Frans tucked his student in, he spotted something poking out from under his pillow. It looked like a letter. Suddenly a worrying thought occurred to him. The children in his class hadn't promised Geert-Jan they'd come to wish him happy birthday in person, had they? They were all in for such a disappointment; he was certain that the count wouldn't let anyone in... He didn't touch the letter though, but blew out the candle and left the room as quietly as he'd come.

Soon after that, he climbed into his bed. He realized that he was exhausted. Which was strange, because he'd thought he'd be wide awake and alert. It was raining outside – a friendly pattering – and he could smell a faint scent that seemed familiar. A scent of pine trees and freshly mown grass, with a hint of something else: pepper and peppermint. For a moment, he was back in the magician's strange, crowded house, staring again at the wooden bird clock. Then he fell asleep and dreamt of phoenixes and garudas, of the roc and the griffin, and other mythical winged creatures.

He is astonished by Greenhair

THIS IS FIVE

Frans was woken by a heavy weight jumping on top of him; he knew it was Ivan even before he'd opened his eyes.

"It's still the middle of the night," he grumbled grumpily. "Well, I suppose it's getting light already... but it's certainly not time to get up yet. Why do you only purr first thing in the morning?"

Ivan purred even more loudly and snuggled around Frans's neck like a giant fur collar.

"Early birds catch the worm," said Frans, grudgingly giving him a little stroke. "But what do early cats catch, eh? Soft-hearted schoolteachers."

Then he pushed the cat away, who did a little stamping dance on his pillow, before finally settling right next to his head.

Frans sat up with a sigh, put on his glasses and looked at his watch. It was only ten past seven. *But*, he thought, *Geert-Jan won't stay in bed for too long on his birthday*. So Frans knew he might as well get out of bed now and get dressed.

He walked barefoot across the room, shivering in the morning cold. It looked like a dreary, drizzly day. Frans peered into the mirror. He froze for a second, thinking he was looking at someone else. But no, it was him.

And his hair was green.

*

Frans's hair was as green as grass, as green as emeralds, as green as Ivan's eyes. It stood on end around his shocked face, running riot all over his head like some strange, wild plant... but it was hair, his own hair, as he could feel when he gave it a tug.

Frans plunged his head in the washbasin a few times, grabbed his towel and scrubbed his head dry – it wouldn't even rub off! He was wide awake – and his hair was green.

In the mirror, he saw the door open behind him; Geert-Jan stood there gaping at him. Frans turned to look at him. "Shut the door!" he whispered.

Geert-Jan did as he was told. As he came closer, he said just one word: "*Greenhair!*" His eyes were sparkling, but not with surprise... or at least that's how it seemed to Frans.

"So," he said with a frown, "you've come to see how well your accomplices' spells have worked, have you? Stop staring at me! Never seen someone with green hair before?"

"N... no," stammered Geert-Jan. "I came... I've come to... Um, it's my..."

"It's your birthday!" Frans suddenly remembered. "Happy birthday, Geert-Jan," he said. "Many happy returns!" He took Geert-Jan's hand and shook it. "I really do mean that," he added. "I'm so sorry I didn't give you my best wishes as soon as I had a chance. This... change in my appearance briefly threw me off balance."

"I understand," said Geert-Jan graciously. "I think I'd have forgotten about birthdays too." He studied his tutor with a look of both awe and approval. "It really is green," he whispered. "You know, it's quite splendid, sir!"

"Splendid?" repeated Frans. "It's dreadful, ridiculous and... dangerous. I have to get rid of it as quickly as possible."

"Oh no, sir!" said Geert-Jan. "That won't work."

"You knew about this!" said Frans. "I think my green hair was one of your birthday presents. That gift from the magician..."

Geert-Jan nodded. "There was a letter with it," he said quietly. "It was just a piece of blank paper at first, but after I'd looked at it for a while letters appeared, just like you told me that time." He rummaged in the pocket of his pyjama jacket. "Here, sir. Why don't you see for yourself?"

So Frans read Mr Thomtidom's letter.

Dear Geert-Jan,

My hearty congratulations on the eleventh anniversary of the day of your birth. I know what your dearest wish is and, although I do not have the power to grant wishes, I can perhaps help yours to come true. In this bag is a very fine powder. Secretly sprinkle this magical medicine on your tutor's pillow before he goes to sleep. The powder is almost invisible, but it holds great power. And tomorrow Frans the Red will reveal exactly what those powers are.

GREENSLEEVES

"Well, I can hardly call myself Frans the Red anymore, can I?" said Frans, handing the note back to Geert-Jan. "But it'll take a lot more than this before I'll allow anyone to call me *Greenhair*!"

"But red hair and green hair are basically the same thing," said Geert-Jan. He sat down on Frans's bed, gave Ivan a stroke and went on, "That's what Roberto told me. Do you know what he said? The redder the hair, the stronger the green. He heard about it from the magician, from Greensleeves. 'It's just like traffic lights,' he said. Do you understand?"

Finally, Frans understood a great deal. The conspirators had been planning this all along. That's why Mr Thomtidom had sent him to sleep on that first visit: so that he could take samples of his hair! The magical medicine was practically invisible, but yesterday evening he'd smelt it for the second time... that scent of pine trees and freshly mown grass, with a hint of something else: pepper and peppermint...

"Just like traffic lights!" he murmured. "So now I'm supposed to continue on my way? But how? I have no way to beat the Dragon. I don't have a sword to fight him with... I haven't even brought a pistol with me." He looked in the mirror again and gave himself a worried frown; his knitted brows were green too.

Green means safety, he thought. *But it's the opposite for me. I feel anything but safe.*

Then he briskly turned to Geert-Jan. "We'll cross that bridge when we come to it," he said. "But now it's time for you. You've already had the present from Greensleeves, and the one from Greeneyes too – the key that I'm looking after. Greenhair, I mean Frans the Red, doesn't want to be left out." He knelt down and took his present from under the bed. "Here you are," he said.

"Thank you," whispered Geert-Jan. "Thank you!" he said again, when he'd unwrapped it. "It's just like Roberto's. Great!" And he put the hat on straightaway.

"Does it fit?" asked Frans. "Isn't it a bit too big?"

"Not at all," said Geert-Jan. He really did look very happy indeed, even though Frans didn't think the hat particularly suited him. Then Geert-Jan opened the parcel from Aunt Wilhelmina, which turned out to be a box of chocolates.

"And finally, this," said Frans, putting down the suitcase next to the bed. "From Jan Tooreloor. I'm curious to see what he's given you. I don't think it'll be a magical medicine, but it could be something that's equally dangerous. That's just the kind of thing he'd do."

Geert-Jan knelt down beside him. It took him a while to open the suitcase. What was inside didn't look dangerous, but bright and happy: the case was filled with colourful paper chains and streamers and shiny party blowers and funny little paper hats.

"This is exactly what I need!" said Geert-Jan, rummaging around in the case. With a flush of excitement, he looked at Frans. "To decorate Gregorius's Small Banqueting Hall," he whispered. "And... oh, it's going to be a great party..."

"Party?" Frans repeated slowly. "Hmmm, yes, of course, a party..." He paused for a moment before asking, "And what did you get from the children?"

"From the children?" said Geert-Jan. "Um, I don't know... Oh, err, a letter..." He lowered his eyes and wound a streamer around his fingers.

"A letter to say they're coming to see you today!" guessed Frans. "Did you invite them, Geert-Jan? Look at me!"

Geert-Jan did as he was told. "Yes, sir," he admitted. "All of them, your whole class."

"But... but you can't just do that!" said Frans, rather shocked. "Your uncle..."

"Uncle Gradus doesn't know anything about it," said Geert-Jan. "And I'm not afraid of him anymore. I'm ready to do whatever it takes!" He gave one of the party blowers a little toot. "And there's nothing you can do to stop it," he continued, looking defiantly at his teacher. "It's a conspiracy. Jan Tooreloor and Roberto are helping us. All of them are coming, today at twelve." He laughed. "Uncle Gradus doesn't know that Jan still has a key for one of the gates. He's going to have such a surprise! But," he concluded, "the biggest surprise is going to be *you*."

"I don't like this at all!" said Frans, as he got to his feet. "All these conspiracies and plots are going to end up backfiring on us! What on earth is your uncle going to say when I turn up with hair as green as grass?"

"He'll have a fit!" said Geert-Jan gleefully.

Ivan jumped down from the bed and into the suitcase, where he found himself a spot among the hats and the streamers.

"No, he'll just fire me," said Frans. "If he sees me like this, the Conspiracy of Seven will be exposed and betrayed."

He plunged his head into the washbasin again. He was really worried about the situation, and he meant what he'd said. *Why didn't the magician warn me?* he thought. *By taking matters into his own hands, he's just made things all the more difficult for me. I can't put all my faith in prophecies... What am I supposed to do about the count? I don't trust him, but I don't have any evidence against him that anyone with any sense, like the police for instance, would believe...* He vigorously rubbed his head dry and then gave a sigh. His hair was green – and it was staying green.

"Sir..." said Geert-Jan. He was sitting on the bed again, still wearing the straw hat, which really was a little too big for him. Now he had a worried expression on his face too. "You're right, sir," he whispered. "Uncle Gradus is going to be furious!"

"You don't think I'm scared of him, do you?" said Frans. No matter how Frans really felt, he didn't want Geert-Jan to be worried. As cheerfully as possible, he continued, "I just need to make sure he doesn't see my hair until I think the right time has come." He smiled at the boy. "The present I gave you is going to come in handy," he said. "Can I borrow your hat?"

Some time later, they got ready to head to the dining room for breakfast. Frans put Geert-Jan's hat on and pulled it down as far as he could. "If I stretch it or damage it," he said, "I'll get you a new one."

"No, sir," said Geert-Jan. "This is a special hat now, and I want to keep it, even if it is far too big."

The last time I wore a hat like this, thought Frans, *I ended up with a bump on the head and a sprained ankle*. And he said, "A crash helmet might be a better choice."

"That's what Roberto wears when he's on his scooter, isn't it, sir?" said Geert-Jan. "I hope he comes to the party as the Biker Boy."

"The Biker Boy?" said Frans. "You can't be serious! Things are already complicated enough. I'm afraid this is going to be the most peculiar birthday ever..."

Geert-Jan studied him closely. "But honestly, you really don't look all that peculiar," he said. "You can barely see your eyebrows and eyelashes because of your glasses. Uncle Gradus won't notice a thing."

But he's going to wonder why I'm wearing a hat indoors, thought Frans.

Geert-Jan appeared to be thinking the same thing, because he said, "I'm going to wear one of these paper hats, and then it'll look like we did it on purpose. You know what? I'm going to order everyone to wear a hat on my birthday. I'll take some along for Uncle Gradus, Berend and Selina, and the silliest one of all is for Manus."

"Don't forget Ivan," said Frans, looking at the cat, who was still lying inside the suitcase.

"Oh no, Ivan is far too dignified for that," said Geert-Jan. "Come on, beastie, you need to get out of there. You're squashing everything."

Ivan reluctantly did as he was told and left the room with slow steps, his tail in the air.

"Come on. Let's go too," said Geert-Jan.

At breakfast, the atmosphere was rather tense. As the birthday boy, Geert-Jan was the most important person in the room, and he let it show. He was very talkative, bubbling over with glee, and as cheeky to his uncle as he dared. Count Grisenstein did not forget his dignified composure for a moment, although he clearly wasn't enjoying himself very much. He made no comment about what his nephew and his nephew's tutor were wearing on their heads, but firmly refused to wear a hat himself. He did, however, give Geert-Jan the present that (as Frans knew) he'd dashed off to buy the day before. It turned out to be a couple of toy cars. Geert-Jan thanked him rather frostily, but then he started driving them around his plate and talking, with twinkling eyes, about traffic lights. Luckily, Selina then turned up and once she'd put on a paper hat – while loudly protesting – that dangerous subject was forgotten.

Frans was happy to leave the table. He'd felt the count's cold but keen eyes lingering on him several times. He'd barely dared to look at him and he was sorry that he hadn't thought of making his eyelashes black or brown, with shoe polish, for instance.

"Now we're going to decorate the place," said Geert-Jan.

"Decorate the place?" said the count. "I think we should go out to celebrate your birthday. I'll have the coach made ready, and then we can go out for a ride and stop somewhere for an ice cream."

"I don't want to go out," said Geert-Jan. "It's raining far too hard. I could get wet feet. I want to decorate the Small Banqueting Hall and play games."

"Aren't you a bit old for that?" said the count.

"I'm eleven," said Geert-Jan. "And eleven's my lucky number, so I want to have fun."

"As you wish," said the count with little enthusiasm.

"Mr Van der Steg brought a lot of streamers with him," said Geert-Jan. He obviously couldn't say that Jan Tooreloor had sent them. "Are you going to come and help with the decorations?"

he asked Frans. Then he hurried out of the room, loudly singing "Oh, where did you get that hat? Where did you get that hat? I made it out of paper. And some whiskers from a cat!"

"You can take your hat off now," the count said to Frans.

"I'd actually rather keep it on, Count Grisenstein," he replied brightly. "It fits me just fine, and it's what Geert-Jan wants."

"My nephew is in particularly high spirits today," said the count. "I do hope you'll make sure he doesn't get over-excited. It's not good for him."

"Surely he's allowed to be happy!" said Frans.

"There's a big difference between happy and over-excited," said the count in his chilliest tones. "Over-excitement can quickly tip over into unacceptable behaviour. My nephew is ten years old plus one more year today. He's almost a teenager – and I'm sure you're well aware that teenagers' parties can become very rowdy. I am of the opinion that only a decent upbringing can keep modern youngsters in check. Those who are young and green need a firm hand to guide them."

"I couldn't agree more," said Frans, taking a step back at the word "green". "But you really have no need to be concerned about your nephew." And he wondered what the count would do when the children turned up later.

"I trust you," said Count Grisenstein, coming closer, "not to disappoint my faith in you."

"Of course I won't," replied Frans, automatically bringing his hand to his hat. "I'll go and help Geert-Jan with the decorations." Luckily the count didn't go with him when he headed off to Gregorius's Small Banqueting Hall.

Geert-Jan had already got to work; he was cheerfully giving orders to Berend and Manus, who were staring at him with bewildered expressions. One of them was wearing a pink pointed hat with gold dots on top of his bald head, while the other had a purple fez with a tassel perched on his curls.

"The yellow and orange streamers need to go around the banisters," said Geert-Jan, "and the long green ones have to go across the room. Berend, maybe you should go and fetch a ladder."

"Yes, but I'm supposed to be patrolling outside," he began.

"It's my birthday," said Geert-Jan. "And you have to do as I say."

Then Frans realized that Count Grisenstein had followed him after all. He had appeared in a doorway between two suits of armour and was beckoning Manus. The servant hurried over to him, and Berend went off to fetch the ladder.

"Hello, sir! Come over here!" called Geert-Jan. Frans helped him to hang up some streamers and to wrap the suits of armour with garlands of paper roses. When he looked around, the count and his servants had all gone.

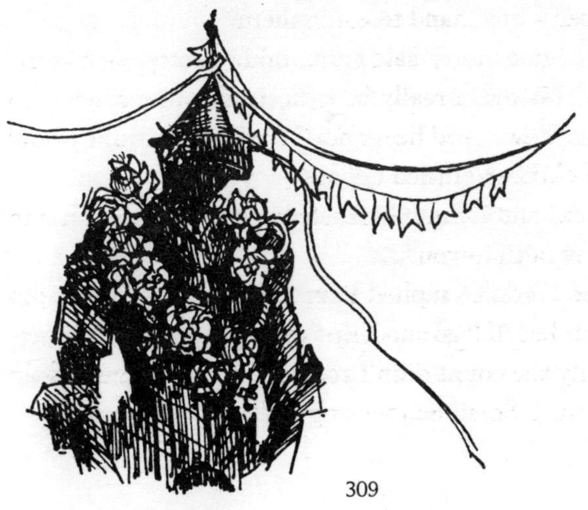

"Hey, where have Berend and Manus got to?" said Geert-Jan. "They're supposed to be helping me. It's already past ten. We don't have much time."

Goodness me, thought Frans. *The festivities are about to begin... but how's it all going to end?* Berend returned, still wearing the pointed hat, but without a ladder. He turned to Frans and said quietly, "The count wants a word with you."

"Why don't you get started on the banisters?" Frans said to Geert-Jan. And he followed Berend with a sinking feeling in his stomach.

Count Grisenstein was waiting for him in the hall by the back door.

"I have a small issue I'd like to discuss with you," he said to Frans. "This is my house, and I expect my guests to..." – he reached out his arm – "...take off their hats!" As he spoke those words, he snatched the straw hat off Frans's head.

For a moment they stared at each other.

"So my suspicions were correct!" said the count. He dropped the hat on the floor, crossed his arms and continued, "You, sir, tricked your way into this house with sinister motives."

"Whatever makes you think that?" said Frans, trying to act both calm and completely surprised.

"Do not try to fool me," said the count coldly. "I have torn off your mask, or rather your hat. Clearly I can no longer permit your presence in this house. You are fired."

"But why?" exclaimed Frans. "I haven't done anything wrong!"

"I do not wish to employ a tutor with green hair," said the count.

"You've never mentioned that before," Frans began.

"You're not suggesting I should have specified it in my advertisement, are you?" the count interrupted him. "No sensible person would do so. It's obvious that no one has green hair."

"But why should it be a problem if someone's hair is green?" said Frans. "And besides, I didn't choose this colour myself."

"I'm afraid I don't believe you," said the count. "That green hair of yours is deliberate! I don't know what else you've done to make my nephew fall for your tricks. But I know what you're planning to do, what you're hoping and wishing for..."

"My only wish," said Frans, "is to help your nephew."

The count held up one hand. "Silence!" he said. "You have abused my trust and are a danger to Geert-Jan. I am firing you with immediate effect and if you do not leave immediately I shall have you thrown out."

"I won't stand for this!" said Frans angrily. "You're the one who's putting Geert-Jan in danger! And you can't just dismiss me like that, and on his birthday too. The boy's counting on me and I will not abandon him."

"Berend..." said the count.

Frans followed his gaze and saw the big man standing in a corner of the hall, waiting for instructions, his enormous fists clenched.

"Berend used to be a bouncer," said the count with a smile. "I meant what I said, Mr Van der Steg. If you do not leave of your own accord, he will throw you out." He put his hands in his pockets and added coldly, "Or possibly employ more drastic measures..."

Frans put his hands in his pockets too – unfortunately he had no weapons; all he could feel was the little leather box.

And what could he have done with a weapon anyway? He could hardly risk a fight, and not just because he was facing more than one man, but also because Geert-Jan might become involved too. And then the boy really would be in danger...

He looked at the count and said, "You know as well as I do that I'm only thinking of Geert-Jan."

The count responded to his glare with a menacing glint in his eyes. "Never speak my nephew's name again," he said. "He'll forget you soon enough. You can be sure of that."

"No, he won't," said Frans. "And I'll be back!" He stepped to one side, as Berend had suddenly appeared beside him.

"In order to return, you will first have to leave," said Count Grisenstein with a mocking sneer. "Berend will let you out. The coach is waiting with your coat and luggage. You see, I've thought of everything." He opened the back door and gave Frans a polite bow. "Goodbye, Mr Greenhair."

"Farewell, Fiendish Foe," said Frans in the same tone. With Berend on his heels, he stepped outside.

"You've forgotten your hat," said the count.

"The hat belongs to Geert-Jan," replied Frans. "You can tell him from me that I'll find my way back here. That's no great challenge for a man who has travelled the Seven Ways."

Then he quickly headed down the stairs and climbed into the waiting coach, with Manus sitting up front. Berend jumped up behind – and away they rode.

He climbs a long ladder and... the party begins

THIS IS SIX

The coach went very slowly, but Frans knew there was no point trying to jump out, with Manus up front and Berend at the back. Furiously tugging his green hair, he cursed Mr Thomtidom. Thanks to the man's meddlesome magic, everything had gone wrong. Greenhair had not defeated the count; instead the count had defeated Greenhair and fired him as well, just as he'd done to Jan Tooreloor.

The coach jolted around the outside of the house. It seemed he was to be sent packing via the front gate. Frans looked gloomily at the strange building. Geert-Jan would be waiting for him inside. The boy would remain imprisoned until the treasure had been found, and the count would...

Then he gasped. There was a ladder leaning against the house. It was just an ordinary wooden ladder, but he'd never seen it there before...

Frans completely forgot that he shouldn't put all his faith in prophecies. A window cleaner had probably left the ladder there; there was a bucket hanging from it. But it could hardly be a coincidence that it was there now of all times, on the day his hair had turned green... Maybe Gregorius the Mad had been right after all! Maybe these were the steps they were looking for!

Frans watched the ladder for as long as he could. He hoped Berend and Manus hadn't noticed it. No, they probably hadn't – the first man seemed too stupid and the other was too occupied with the reins and the whip.

As the coach left the House of Stairs behind and rolled faster and faster down the driveway, he frantically began forging plans. He had to make good on his challenge to the count and return to the house – today! When the gate had closed behind him, he'd act as if he were leaving, but he'd simply walk around the outside of the estate and sneak back in through the gap in the fence... One way or another, he was going to free Geert-Jan from the clutches of his uncle, who had now revealed his true colours.

The coach suddenly juddered. Frans leant out of the window and saw that Berend had jumped off. He strode away and disappeared into the trees. Oh, that was right, he was on patrol outside. Soon after that, the coach came to a stop; they'd reached the gate. Manus jumped down and went to open it.

As he was unlocking the gate, a tall figure appeared on the other side of the railings.

"Hey, Manus! Chief cook and bottle-washer!" called Jan Tooreloor. "And now it would appear that you're daring to drive my coach around too!"

"I'm Count Grisenstein's coachman now," snapped Manus, and he looked at Frans.

Then Tooreloor spotted him too, and his jaw dropped.

"Would you please stand aside?" asked Manus. "Then I can let the tutor out."

Jan Tooreloor didn't move. He just went on staring at Frans, who opened the door and got out. "That's incredible!" he cried.

"They were all talking about your beautiful red hair, but I'd never have believed it would turn so green!"

"Indeed," said Frans curtly. "So green that Count Grisenstein has fired me. That's something else you and the other conspirators would never have believed!"

"Fired?" repeated Tooreloor.

"Yes," said Manus spitefully. "Just like you."

As the gate swung open, Jan Tooreloor charged through, pounced on Manus like a tiger, and held him in an iron grip. "You disgusting little spy!" he roared, giving him a good shaking. "What have you got to say for yourself?"

"H... h... help!" groaned Manus, struggling to free himself.

Jan Tooreloor laughed. "And now I shall take the reins!" he cried. He lifted up the struggling spy like a sack, threw him into the coach, and slammed the door. Then he hopped up front.

"You deal with things here!" he called to Frans. "I'll go and let the others know." With a crack of his whip, he drove out through the gates.

"Halt! Stop right there!" shouted a furious voice, and Berend came running up, waving his arms.

Jan Tooreloor didn't even look back.

Frans was still standing in the same spot. He watched in bewilderment as the coach rode off, with Berend shouting and running along behind. They disappeared in the direction of Langelaan.

Frans realized that Count Grisenstein had lost both of his manservants and his coach. He didn't stop to wonder how it was all going to work out, but turned around and ran back to the House of Stairs.

*

The ladder was still there. It was a narrow ladder, a very long ladder, which ended at a roof window, high up in a tower.

Frans didn't hesitate; he barely even stopped to think. He scaled the ladder without looking down once, quickly and steadily, rung by rung. The window was open; he swung his legs over the ledge and was inside.

Wiping his forehead, he looked around. He was in some kind of junk room, with a low, sloping ceiling. As far as he could remember, he'd never been there before. His first impression was that these steps certainly hadn't shown him where to go... What could be precious about battered suitcases and shabby old chests, broken chairs and damaged bric-à-brac? An old junk room...

But wasn't that the perfect place to hide something that was very valuable? Who knew what he might find in those cases and chests? What might be concealed behind the threadbare velvet curtain in that corner?

Frans stepped over a heater, almost knocked over a jug, and peered around. Cabinets... cases... chests! He spotted a large black box with gold corners; it had a chair on top of it and a broom leaning against it.

"*I know that the treasure is kept in an ebony chest. And legend has it that only one key fits the lock...*" The golden key that he was looking after!

Frans took the leather box from his pocket and opened it with slightly trembling fingers. A moment later, he was standing beside the chest, lifting down the chair, moving the broom...

He knelt down, with the key in his hand. *I must let Geert-Jan know*, he thought. *But first I'll just see if it fits...*

But before he could put the key in the lock, an unexpected sound made him freeze.

An icy voice said, "Don't move."

A footstep creaked on the floor. "Look at me," the voice said. "Hands up or I'll shoot."

Frans turned around. Count Grisenstein was standing in front of the threadbare velvet curtain, and he was aiming a pistol at his chest.

Frans slowly stood up, still clutching the key in his hand.

"Hands up!" repeated the count. "So, will this little plaything make you do as I say?"

One look at the pistol was enough to convince Frans that this gun wasn't a toy at all, and he did as he was told, speechless with fear, regret and helpless rage.

Count Grisenstein smiled. "I told you I'd thought of everything, didn't I?" he said. "Your hair is green, you've travelled the Seven Ways... and so I thought it would be a nice idea for Berend to leave a ladder out so that you could scale the heights. Manus was given the job of driving past very slowly, so that you couldn't miss it. I hardly dared to believe that you would fall for it, but you see, your faith in the Sealed Parchment has proven even stronger than I thought. You've forgotten just one thing: that you'll never find the treasure on your own."

Frans said nothing. But he could have hit the count – and himself even more so.

"Don't move!" the Fiendish Foe said again. "Or my pistol could quite easily go off. You've fallen into my trap, Mr Van der Steg! You were caught red-handed breaking into my house! Just give me that key – I don't know how you got your hands on it, but it belongs to me."

"This key belongs to Geert-Jan," said Frans, breaking his silence.

"Which makes it even worse," said the count calmly. "You've stolen from a poor, innocent child! And that is exactly what I intend to tell the police."

"The police?" said Frans. He lowered his arms, but clasped the key even more tightly.

"Hands up!" the count ordered sharply. "Yes, the police," he continued. "When I get rid of someone, I do it permanently. Soon you'll be under lock and key – and then try proving that you didn't break in here!"

He came closer. Frans stepped back, almost stumbling over the chest, and had to let the count take the golden key from him.

The count quickly backed away to the window, keeping his gun on Frans the whole time. "I shall lock you up in this room," he said. "And soon, when you're all alone, you can take a look at what's inside the chest. It may be black, but it's not locked." He slipped the key into his right inside pocket and, without taking his eyes off Frans, reached his left hand out of the window and gave the ladder a push.

Frans clearly heard the thud as it hit the ground.

"So that's that," said the count. "Now you won't be able to escape that way. And I'm off to inform the police."

"You can't do that!" said Frans. "You know very well that I'm not a thief."

"Tell that to the police!" sneered Count Grisenstein. "Go on! Tell them everything: the legend of the Hidden Treasure, the fairy tale of the Sealed Parchment! Tell the police you dyed your hair green and climbed the ladder because it was all in the prophecy – the prophecy of Gregorius the Mad! Do you think they'll believe your story? And they certainly won't be surprised to hear that I dismissed you from your position as my dear, beloved nephew's tutor."

Frans bit his lips and said nothing. Count Grisenstein walked to the curtain, pushed it aside and opened the door behind it. He waved his pistol. "Goodbye, Mr Greenhair," he said, and he disappeared. The door closed, and a key turned in the lock with a clunk.

Even though he knew better, Frans walked over to the door, but all he could do was confirm that he really was locked in. It was the only door in the room, made of heavy wood, with iron fittings. Count Grisenstein had beaten him and, more than ever, Geert-Jan was in his power.

I've done a wonderful job of completing my mission! Frans thought bitterly. *I've let everyone down. I've messed up everything. First I stumbled into a magic circle and then into a trap...*

He looked at the black chest and realized now that it wasn't even made of ebony. He lifted the lid; there were blankets and mothballs inside.

"You idiot!" he cursed himself. "The count's right. The police are never going to believe the truth."

He walked to the window and looked outside.

Count Grisenstein came around the corner of the building, walked up to the ladder, stepped over it, looked up and raised his hat in a mocking show of politeness. Then he walked towards the front driveway and disappeared from sight.

Frans suddenly remembered that there was no telephone in the House of Stairs. The nearest police station was in Langelaan, and the count would have to go there himself, on foot. Berend and Manus were away, of course, with Jan Tooreloor and the coach.

Oh, if only he could escape now! It could be half an hour before the count returned... and if Frans wasn't in the room, the police wouldn't be able to do anything. What if he started banging, yelling and shouting in the hope that Geert-Jan would hear him...?

What had the count told his nephew? Did Geert-Jan know that his tutor had been lured into a trap and was shamefully imprisoned?

No, thought Frans. He didn't want to start calling for help. But he couldn't let the count have his way; he had to do everything in his power to free Geert-Jan!

Frans looked down. Count Grisenstein knew that heights made tutor Van der Steg dizzy, and of course the same must be true of Greenhair.

But then maybe Greenhair was more like Frans the Red – and Frans the Red knew no fear! Frans the Red would not allow himself to be locked up; he was going to escape through the open window, no matter how high it was.

He studied the face of the precipice, checked that his glasses were firmly on his nose, and then lowered himself out of the window. He clung on to the windowsill until his feet were on a protruding ledge. Then he moved carefully along the wall and, reaching out his hand, he grasped a drainpipe. He slid down it some way, then climbed over a canopy before clambering down a rough section of wall. Then he hit a dead end. He almost fell, but was able to grab hold of a gutter just in time. He tried not to think about how high up he still was; swinging his legs, he pulled himself up and rested on top of a bay window. Then he realized that he didn't have to get down to the ground at all; he could just as easily climb in through another window.

"You deal with things here," Jan Tooreloor had said. He didn't have a clue how, but he knew he had to do something. He looked at his watch – it was half past eleven. With a shock, he thought the children might arrive at any moment, and the count and his servants weren't there to send them away. There was no way to predict how the festivities would turn out but, he said to himself, it was essential for him to stay there and keep an eye on the situation.

He slid down a column to the nearest window, but it turned out to be locked and barred. There was nothing else for it but to start climbing again, which required a certain amount of willpower. First he went back up and around a chimney, startling a crow, which flapped around him for a while, cawing angrily. Then he covered some distance by drainpipe and, after a little swinging on a balcony, he finally reached a window that was open. And he was back inside the House of Stairs.

Frans wondered if his green hair had turned grey by now – he'd certainly skinned his hands and ripped the knee of his trousers, and he'd also virtually dislocated his shoulders. He couldn't stop and rest for long though; he quietly began walking through the building, into rooms and out again, heading upwards whenever he could, looking for the attic above Gregorius's Small Banqueting Hall. From there, he'd be able to keep an eye on events without being spotted. A steep, narrow staircase finally took him to his destination. He stopped for a moment... it was so quiet! Then he walked silently to the arched opening and looked down.

He could see the stairs and galleries, decorated with paper chains and streamers, and far down below, all alone, was Geert-Jan. He looked very small and vulnerable, but Frans couldn't see his face. Was he anxious and disappointed, or filled with excitement and anticipation? He saw that the boy was holding his straw hat in his hand. Had Count Grisenstein given it back to him? Geert-Jan didn't think his ally had abandoned him, did he?

Then Frans raised his head to listen. He could hear noises outside – as bright as birds in the morning, as warming as the sun in springtime, but also as worrying as clouds in a summer sky... the children!

He turned around, walked across the attic and looked out of a window. There they came – so the gate at the back was open. Jan Tooreloor had probably been standing at the front entrance to divert attention. It was a real parade, a cheerful procession, in spite of the grey and drizzly day. The children didn't seem at all shy or intimidated; he could hear them chatting and laughing. As they came closer to the building, they got a little quieter. A few of them looked up and Frans quickly pulled his head back inside.

He went back to the arch and looked down into the room again. Geert-Jan had disappeared; he'd gone to meet his guests, of course. Now Ivan wandered into view – he strolled across the room and hopped up a staircase opposite.

Frans wondered if the cat could sense the atmosphere of anticipation that seemed to fill the house. Soon the children's voices would echo around its walls...

But, he suddenly thought, *that surely can only be a good thing, can't it? The children are Geert-Jan's friends, aren't they? And the more lines of the prophecy come true, the better!* He smiled.

Now they were inside the house. He could hear them arriving, their voices mingling with the sound of Selina's grumbling protests, which were soon drowned out.

But then another sound wiped the smile off his face.

He left his lookout again to take a peek outside.

Of course... Roberto was coming too; he'd promised, after all, even saying that he might dare to venture all the way into the house. It wasn't Roberto, though, that he could see approaching along the driveway. It was the Biker Boy himself, wearing a crash helmet and with his scooter roaring away.

Frans frowned and twitched his green eyebrows in disapproval. He could have expected help from Roberto, but the Biker Boy would only cause even more confusion. The boy had brought his guitar with him too – this was going to be interesting!

Frans left the attic; he went through the arch and down the stairs without a handrail. He stopped on the top gallery and leant over the balustrade. No one saw him, except for Ivan, who was sitting directly opposite him on another balustrade.

The people in the room below were only paying attention to one another. Geert-Jan (wearing his hat) was the centre of attention; all of the children were crowding around him with birthday wishes and parcels large and small. Frans soon had to duck down though, as the children were starting to wander around, climbing the lower stairs and looking at everything. For a while he sat crouched behind the balustrade, wondering if he should stay hidden or not. He decided to keep on hiding, as he didn't have any better ideas, no matter how hard he racked his brain. He couldn't see much through the railings, but he could hear plenty. They were all talking at the same time, so he could only catch a few words. He heard Maarten ask about Frans the Red. And a little later, Arie demonstrated his cap gun. That reminded him of Count Grisenstein. Frans worried that it might be irresponsible to allow his students to remain in this room, where the master of the house might appear at any moment with a loaded pistol in his hand...

After a while, the children gathered around to give a new arrival an enthusiastic welcome.

Frans dared to stand up again now, and he tiptoed down another flight of stairs, as he'd be able to see and hear more from the second gallery. He hoped for a moment that it was Roberto who was receiving this warm welcome... but one look told him it was still the Biker Boy. He was a little annoyed that his students hadn't shown better judgement. The children were actually welcoming the Biker Boy with something like awe and admiration. Marian was the only one who didn't seem entirely happy.

"Isn't Roberto coming?" she asked in a clear voice.

Geert-Jan had taken off the straw hat again and was turning it around in his fingers. "I... I think so," he said uncertainly.

"Roberto can't come," said Maarten, "because the Biker Boy's already here."

"And the Biker Boy has a guitar!" cried Kai. "Come on, it's time to start the party."

Lots of loud chattering, all at the same time... Then Marian said – *What a nice girl she is*, thought Frans – "No, we have to wait for Frans the Red to get here."

Again, more yelling...

"...Frans the Red..."

"Why isn't he here?"

"Frans the Red!"

Greenhair's name wasn't mentioned.

Frans took a step back, and when he looked again, he saw that Geert-Jan was speaking, but the boy was talking so quietly that he couldn't hear a word. Just as he was wondering if he should show himself after all, the Biker Boy spoke up. He'd taken off his crash helmet and was making a big show of combing his hair. "That is such rubbish!" he said slowly and painfully clearly. "It's much more fun without old people around, don't you think?" He brushed aside the paper hats that the children offered and added, "How are you ever going to have any fun with a schoolteacher here, watching your every move?"

His fingers had started to pick out a scale on the strings of his guitar.

Then there were lots of raised voices; some agreeing with him, others disagreeing.

The Biker Boy ignored them – he walked around the room, going up and down scales and tuning his guitar. The children followed him as if he were the Pied Piper of Hamelin.

Frans watched it all with a disapproving frown. His frown grew even deeper as the Biker Boy tossed back his long hair, started tapping his foot on the wooden floor and launched into a song – although it was barely a song, thought Frans, as it had no real melody. Most of the children seemed to know it though, and they sang along with the chorus.

"Pah!" Frans tutted at himself. "Who cares what they sing, as long as they give it their all?" Slowly he crept down another flight of stairs, to the lowest gallery.

The Biker Boy began a new song, tapping his foot on the floor, faster and faster, and making the strings of his guitar ring out. The children swayed in time to the music, their paper hats wobbling on their heads. Geert-Jan moved through the crowd with a hop, skip and a jump, handing out chocolates from Aunt Wilhelmina's box with one hand, and streamers with the other.

Frans glanced over at Ivan, who was walking restlessly to and fro on a balustrade. *Any minute now, he's going to join in,* Frans thought.

Roberto sang; he didn't have an unpleasant voice, even though it cracked occasionally. The children seemed to think it was great. Frans began to listen more closely... He could understand the words of the song now; they felt both ancient and brand-new...

Go up the stairs
and down again
and dance a happy dance!
Around the house
and back again.
This could be your lucky chance!
Rosemary, Rosemary, have a fine day!
Knife-grinder's daughter, toorelay!
Tooreloor, Tooreloor, skip and dance,
Jan Thomtidom, hop and prance!
Up the stairs
and down the stairs
All the day and night!
Around the house
and back again.
We'll all be merry and bright!

High up on the balustrade, Ivan opened his mouth wide and let out a yowl that he usually saved for wild nights with a full moon. But his wailing was lost in the noise down below.

All of the children sang the song again, stamping hard on the floor.

Geert-Jan and Kai began to do a kind of war dance and Arie fired his gun again. Maarten tooted a party blower and Marian threw a streamer in the air. Other children followed their lead. Selina came dashing in, horrified, and was soon tangled up in ribbons of coloured paper. Undeterred, the Biker Boy started the song again, even though his voice could barely be heard above the din. One of the suits of armour toppled over with a thundering crash. More and more streamers flew across the room, twisting into a tangled chaos.

Frans watched the pandemonium, open-mouthed.

Rosemary, Rosemary, have a fine day!
Knife-grinder's daughter, toorelay!

A door opened on one of the long sides of the room, and Miss Rosemary appeared, in her elegant coat with white dots. She took a couple of steps and then stopped, with her eyebrows slightly raised, but otherwise very calm. After her came Aunt Wilhelmina, who looked shocked, Jan Tooreloor, who seemed delighted, and Mr Thomtidom, who viewed the scene with a scholar's interested gaze.

Tooreloor, Tooreloor, skip and dance,
Jan Thomtidom, hop and prance!

Then a door opened on one of the short sides of the room, and Count Grisenstein appeared, closely followed by Berend and two almost equally hefty policemen. For the first time, the count had lost his cool composure; his mouth kept making strange noises and he was waving his arms around. But he didn't have a pistol in his hand now. One of the policemen looked hesitantly at his truncheon, but the other one had a better idea. He put his whistle to his lips and gave it a loud blow – the shrill note cut through everything.

And immediately there was silence, broken only by the rustling of paper and a deep meow from Ivan. All of the children turned to stare at Count Grisenstein, who had pulled himself together and was staring back at them with ice-cold eyes in a face as white as marble.

He gets into the party mood and a song fills the House of Stairs

Frans was still standing motionless by the balustrade. *I've got to do something,* he thought feverishly. *But what? I need to make sure this party ends well...*

With a sudden flash of inspiration, he raised his voice and said, "Roberto!"

Now everyone turned to look at him, and a cry went up among the children: "GREENHAIR!"

Frans leant over the balustrade and said, in a loud and commanding voice, "Play another song, Roberto. The Song of Seven!"

Roberto obeyed immediately, slowly strumming the first chords.

Do you know the Seven, the Seven,

Gently and a little hesitantly, the tune echoed around the room.

Do you know the Seven Ways?

Frans glanced at the count, who had turned even paler now, with fear or fury, and he quickly headed down the final flight of stairs.

People say that I can't dance,
But I can dance like the King of France...

Roberto strummed a loud chord and the children sang, their voices soft and trembling with excitement:

This is one.

Frans stood on the bottom step and raised his hand, as if he were standing in front of the class and giving them a singing lesson. And then the children sang it again, as he beat time:

Do you know the Seven, the Seven,
Do you know the Seven Ways?
People say that I can't dance,
But I can dance like the King of France!

Roberto tapped his foot. *This is one*. The children stamped on the floor. *This is two*. And then they went straight into the song for the third time. Roberto sang along with them, playing as if his life depended on it.

People say that I can't dance...

Geert-Jan took the lead; he held Marian by the hands and skipped happily around.

But I can dance like the King of France!

The song went on, accompanied by loud stamping:

This is one – This is two – This is three!

All the children danced along to the next verse. The floor creaked beneath their feet.

This is one – This is two – This is three – This is four!

They were all whirling around together; hats flew off, and the stairs seemed to be trembling and shaking. Jan Tooreloor sang along and even did a few dance steps.

This is one – This is two – This is three – This is four – This is five!

Now the party had descended into complete chaos again. Count Grisenstein stood frozen, unable to utter a single word. The policemen stood by helplessly and forgot about their whistles. Berend was so confused that he joined in with the stamping:

This is one – This is two – This is three – This is four – This is five – This is six!

Frans was rather startled by the violent reaction he'd unleashed. He took a step into the room, half afraid the roof was about to come falling down on them. But Roberto went on playing and the Song of Seven still rang out, louder and louder, faster and faster... They stamped on the ground to the beat of the music.

Do you know the Seven, the Seven,

The children had formed a circle that Frans couldn't get through, and Geert-Jan was leaping about in the middle, waving his hat in the air. "Stop! Stop!" cried Frans, but he couldn't even hear his own voice. The floor seemed to be moving... and triumphantly the tedious tune played on:

This is one – This is two – This is three –

The floor really was moving!

"Geert-Jan!" cried Frans. "Stop it! That's enough!"

This is four – This is five – This is six –

The wood beneath Geert-Jan's feet began to crack...

THIS IS SEVEN!

And the floor gave way, splitting apart and collapsing.

Roberto's guitar strings snapped with a *ting*, breaking the sudden horrified silence.

The wood gave another creak, and everyone stared at the gaping hole into which Geert-Jan had disappeared.

A cry went up and everyone in the room crowded around the hole. Then there came another cry, a shout of delight, surprise and joy. It was Geert-Jan's voice shouting: "I've found it! The treasure! The treasure!"

A moment later his head popped up from down below, through the splintered floorboards, his face dirty but beaming.

"I've found it!" he panted. "The Song of Seven... you all found it. The chest is here, under the floor..."

It took a while to bring Geert-Jan and the chest up out of the hole. Then they all stood around the chest in awed silence. It was a small but heavy chest, a chest of ebony... very old and with a golden lock.

Geert-Jan knelt down beside it; he stroked it affectionately and looked up with gleaming eyes at Frans, who was standing beside him. Count Grisenstein stood on the other side, with the two policemen just behind him. They stared in surprise at the chest and then at Frans and his green hair.

Mr Thomtidom was the first to speak.

"Well, well," he said, stepping forward. "It seems that we've witnessed a great event: the Treasure of the House of Stairs has been found."

"A great event indeed," said Count Grisenstein with a stony face. "But who, may I ask, are you?"

Mr Thomtidom bowed and replied in a quiet voice, "Police... plain clothes. Um, just between the two of us, I'm a detective." He held up his hand; a badge glinted in his fingers.

The policemen politely tipped their caps.

"You came here to deal with a disturbance of the peace," Mr Thomtidom said to them. "But now you can be witnesses to a far more important matter!"

"Yes," Frans chimed in. "The treasure has been found, which by right belongs to this child, the heir of the Grisensteins."

The count bit his lips. "That's if it is the treasure!" he said frostily. "We won't find out until the chest is opened."

"But you'll open it right away, won't you?" said Mr Thomtidom with a smile. "We're all very eager to see."

Geert-Jan held his hand out to Frans and whispered, "The key, sir."

Count Grisenstein smiled. "I would like nothing more than to allow my nephew to unlock the chest," he said. "But perhaps you are unaware that there is only one key that fits... and we don't want to force and damage the lock but should wait until it too has been found. Gregorius the Mad's golden key."

Geert-Jan sat up and said, "Greeneyes already found it!"

"Oh yes?" said the count. "So where is it?"

Geert-Jan looked at Frans again, who was staring at the count. "The key," he said calmly, "is in your right inside pocket."

The count glowered at Frans, as if he hadn't been expecting this response. But before he could reply, the magician had conjured up the key.

"Yes, here it is," he said cheerfully, handing the key over to Frans.

Frans waved the key at Ivan, who was still sitting high up on a balustrade, and then he passed it to Geert-Jan.

In the background Miss Rosemary said in a singsong tone:

Greensleeves will cast the Spell.
Greeneyes will find the Key.
Greenhair will beat the Dragon.

In breathless silence, Geert-Jan put the key in the lock, turned it and opened the chest. Everyone craned their necks to look inside, but what they saw didn't look very impressive at all. Inside the ebony chest was a smaller metal box, and inside that was a parcel wrapped in a faded green cloth...

"There's a letter too," said Geert-Jan, "from Count Gregorius."

It all started with a letter, thought Frans, *and that's how it's ending too...*

He heard the children sigh and wondered if it was disappointment – they'd probably been expecting silver and gold, precious stones and jewellery.

As Geert-Jan looked at the letter with a serious expression, something fell out; three coins rolled across the floor.

The magician picked them up, studied them closely and said, "These are very old coins, bronze ones from the Holy Land."

"Ha! And there are only three of them," gloated the count.

"All good things come in threes," said Mr Thomtidom.

He gave the coins back to Geert-Jan, leant over the letter and slowly read out the first lines:

> *I, Count Gregorius Grisenstein, hereby give this treasure to my grandson, or to his child, or to his child's child, and so on. I shall also account for how I came to find it and why I hid it again. But anyone who wishes to understand me fully must read this Book, from A to Z.*

"A book, a letter and three bronze coins," he added under his breath.

Geert-Jan had in the meantime taken the parcel out of the metal box and carefully unwrapped the faded cloth. The book appeared; it was bound in leather and looked very old.

Frans closed the chest, so that Geert-Jan could rest the book on its lid. The boy opened it and let out a surprised "Oooh!"

The pages were made of parchment; they were not printed, but written in graceful letters, and on every page there were beautiful capital letters inlaid with gold leaf, and drawings of mythical creatures, with colourful miniatures of wonderful castles and knights on horseback with plumes on their helmets. Every page was a masterpiece of art and calligraphy.

"This is very precious indeed!" said Frans. "A genuine medieval manuscript, Geert-Jan!"

The children came closer to take a better look.

"Don't touch it with your fingers!" Count Grisenstein said sharply. "Geert-Jan, be careful! If it's genuine, it'll be absolutely priceless."

"It's just a sort of comic book," mumbled Jan Tooreloor.

"But very artistic," said one of the policemen.

"And most certainly authentic," said Mr Thomtidom, turning the title page. "Can you read it, Mr Van der Steg?"

Frans bent more deeply over the book and read:

> *This is a True and Faithful Account of the Escapades of Sir Grimbold, Count Grisenstein, how he went on a Crusade and sailed across the sea, and suffered a Shipwreck and became stranded in the Land of Torelore, of his Adventures in Torelore, and his Journey back, which ended at the Seven Ways.*

Twice he hesitated – at the word *Torelore*. He'd always thought he'd invented that land himself, and it was very strange to discover that it really existed, or had once existed... *Does that happen often?* he wondered. *That the stories you dream up aren't just fantasy, but came from somewhere and really happened, in another time, in another place, without you knowing it?*

Geert-Jan picked up the book and looked around with an expression of delight. Suddenly, though, he almost dropped it. Frans quickly took the book from him.

"Aunt Rosemary!" cried Geert-Jan, flying into her arms. "Aunt Rosemary, what an amazing birthday!"

"I beg to differ," said Count Grisenstein coldly. He turned to the policemen. "I withdraw my accusation," he said. "You may leave."

"But you can't just send them away," said Aunt Wilhelmina unexpectedly. "We might need them. And, besides, we should give them something to eat. I've brought cakes and, whether you like it or not, this is a birthday."

Jan Tooreloor stepped forward with a big box.

"How dare you show your face here again?" growled the count. "Where's Manus?"

"I threw him out of the coach not far from Roskam," replied

Tooreloor. "But I don't think he started walking home straightaway. He's probably recovering at the Thirsty Deer."

Count Grisenstein shifted his angry glare to Frans. "I should have suspected you from the very first," he said. "I believe a conspiracy has been hatched against me..."

"You're right," said Frans calmly. "There were seven conspirators. And now there are even more people who know who you are: the Fiendish Foe of the rhyme on the lintel."

"And the Dragon in the Sealed Parchment," added Mr Thomtidom, passing the police badge from one hand into the other.

"However did you..." began the count.

"You know very well!" said Frans. "Why else did you object to my green hair?"

The children whispered his words like an echo: "Green hair. He's Greenhair..."

The count looked at them, a flash of concern on his face. But then he recovered. "I don't like this one bit," he said. "I'll have nothing to do with this party." He turned and strode off.

"Good riddance," said Roberto. He took a cake from the box Jan Tooreloor was holding.

"I don't think it's quite that simple, Roberto," said Miss Rosemary, who had come to join them, with Geert-Jan. "As far as Gradus Grisenstein is concerned, he may well be the Fiendish Foe, but he's still one of us!"

"One of us?" said Frans, rather surprised.

"Absolutely. After all, he believes in Gregorius the Mad's prophecies too." Miss Rosemary watched the count go; he was just disappearing through the door that led to the spiral staircase up to the Rococo Room. "I'll go and have a quiet word with him," she continued. "We need to settle this whole business once and for all, don't you think?" She patted Geert-Jan on the shoulder and dashed after the count.

Good, thought Frans, *she's probably the best one here to convince the count that he's lost.*

He looked at Geert-Jan and said, "I'm sorry I was a little late to your party, but..."

"Oh, I knew right away that you had a plan, sir," said Geert-Jan. "When Uncle Gradus said you'd left..."

"Ah, so that's what he said, is it?" muttered Frans.

"Yes... but I knew it was just one of your tricks," said the boy, with a look of delighted approval. "Mr Greenhair..."

Frans didn't reply; he was touched by Geert-Jan's faith in him.

"I think red hair suits him better," said Aunt Wilhelmina. "Green hair is rather unusual... just as unusual as this party, in fact. My goodness, what a mess! It's going to be such a lot of work to clean it all up. But first let's have something to eat and drink."

And assisted by Selina, who was still in a state of utter confusion, she set to work. Meanwhile Mr Thomtidom returned the badge to one of the policemen. "Thanks for the loan," he said.

"Don't mention it, sir," replied the policeman, and then he exclaimed in surprise, "But I didn't lend you anything!"

Frans had sat down on the chest, with the precious book on his knees.

"I have your books too," said the magician, sitting down beside him. "Here, in this bag. I thought you might want to get back to your studies."

"However did you guess?" said Frans.

Calm had returned; the children sat contentedly around the hole in the floor, surrounded by all the debris. They ate cakes, drank lemonade and talked quietly together. Roberto ate a second cake, looked at his guitar with a frown and started to restring it.

"So the prophecy turned out to be true," said the magician. "Well, almost... Thanks to your bright – no, brilliant – idea, Geert-Jan and the children found the treasure, and the song sealed the count's sorry fate. But there's still one thing that's bothering me..."

"Me too," said Frans. "I think my idea, no matter how bright it may have been, wasn't really that brilliant. Allowing the children to demolish a room just doesn't seem right..."

"Demolish? I wouldn't exactly call it that," said the magician. "It's really not that bad."

"They danced a hole in the floor," said Frans, "and as a reward for their bad behaviour, they found a treasure!"

"They found a treasure," repeated the magician. "And that's what's bothering me. What about the steps that were supposed to show us where to go?"

Yes, something wasn't quite right! Frans thought about the ladder that had almost proved his downfall, but he really didn't feel like talking about that. "Oh," he said, "I suppose not all parts of a prophecy have to work out. I didn't get my green hair because it was predicted, for instance. I have you to thank for that."

"That was a bright idea too," said the magician. "It was traffic lights that gave me the brainwave: if they can switch from red to green, then so can hair. Red and green are complementary colours, as you probably know."

"But how long am I going to have to go around like this?" asked Frans.

"I think your hair will turn amber first," said Roberto, looking up from his guitar. "And then it'll probably go back to its old colour."

Mr Thomtidom had returned to his own problem. "*Scale the heights, head down below, the steps will show you where to go*," he mumbled.

Roberto strummed his new strings, testing them out.

"Hey, play something else for us!" cried Geert-Jan, jumping to his feet.

"Only if you all stay sitting down!" said Aunt Wilhelmina sternly.

The magician suddenly stood up. He looked at Roberto and sang quietly: *Do re mi fa so la ti*... I've got it!" he said. "The Seven Ways... the seven notes of the scale... Roberto played his guitar, the children sang a song... You can't make music without a scale... That's the meaning of Gregorius's prophecy. Scale the heights! He meant a musical scale!"

"A musical scale?" repeated Geert-Jan.

"Yes," replied Mr Thomtidom. "And the 'head down below' – that was your head, Geert-Jan, looking up at us from the hole. 'The steps will show you where to go'... Oh my goodness me, of course! The steps of the dance. And 'Together you must beat the Time' – it wasn't about the time limit at all. It was all about the music!"

Roberto strummed his guitar. "Well, I'd never have thought of that," he said.

"I wish someone had worked it out sooner," said Frans, thinking back to all the steps he'd scaled for nothing.

"I've said it before and I'll say it again," said the magician with a look of satisfaction. "Prophecies always come true, notwithstanding and in spite of our efforts."

When Miss Rosemary returned to the room, all the children were standing around and looking at the pictures in the old, old book. She went to join them and said, "At home in the attic I have a glass case that this book would fit inside perfectly. You can bring the book with you, Geert-Jan, but your uncle has set one condition: you have to keep the book in the case."

They all looked questioningly at her.

She smiled and nodded at Geert-Jan. "Yes," she said, "Count Grisenstein thinks it'd be better for you if you came to live with me at the Herb Garden."

The children responded to this news with a loud "Hurrah!" Except for Geert-Jan – he didn't shout; he just looked very happy indeed.

"What about the count?" Frans asked in a quiet voice.

"I told Gradus he should return to The Hague," replied Miss Rosemary. "After all, that's where counts belong. You know the old song: *In The Hague there lives a count...* And he can't stay here. He's made it impossible for himself, and he must realize that too."

"So the House of Stairs is going to be empty," said Frans.

Geert-Jan looked around the room. Ivan had come downstairs and was rolling around in the streamers. "But I do love the House of Stairs," said the boy pensively.

"Later, when you're older, it will belong to you," said Miss Rosemary. "Then you can come and live here – if you like."

Geert-Jan nodded and turned to look at Frans. "Sir..." he began, and then he gasped. "Sir, your hair isn't green anymore... it's orange!"

"You see! I was right," said Roberto. "Soon it'll be back to red again."

Geert-Jan threw his hat in the air and cried cheerfully, "Three cheers for Frans the Red! Hip, hip...!"

And that was the end of the party.

The children said goodbye and went home, and the policemen went on their way too. Selina and Berend cleared up the mess and headed off to the kitchen, taking the leftover cakes with them. Count Grisenstein returned, calm, cool and polite, as if nothing had happened. The conspirators were waiting for him.

For the first time, all seven of them were together: Frans the Red and Roberto, Miss Rosemary and Aunt Wilhelmina, Jan Thomtidom and Jan Tooreloor, and Ivan the Terrible, who was winding around Geert-Jan's legs.

The count called his nephew and repeated what Miss Rosemary had already said: that he would be going with her to the Herb Garden. "Miss Grysenstein can take better care of you," he said, "even though I'll still be your guardian."

"Yes, Uncle Gradus," said Geert-Jan. "And what about the treasure? Will it have to stay inside the glass case forever?"

"Until you're eighteen," replied the count. "The book is yours, but it's far too valuable for a child." He paused for a moment and then said, "You may take a look inside now and then, as long as you wash your hands first. And only on Sundays." He turned to Miss Rosemary. "You may leave now," he said.

"And when are you leaving?" asked Frans.

The count glowered at him. "I'd like to leave as soon as my bags are packed," he said. "But I need to make sure that the house is locked up properly."

"There should be a caretaker," said Mr Thomtidom. "Someone to make sure no trespassers get in while it's empty."

"What would be the point?" said the count. "There's no hidden treasure now."

"But it has a story connected to it," said Miss Rosemary.

"It's always been a dangerous house," said Aunt Wilhelmina. "I don't think it should be left unguarded."

"Ah, is that right?" said the count angrily. "Fine, then you can find a caretaker! I always have problems with my staff. I can't even trust the tutors I hire."

"I know a very good caretaker," said Mr Thomtidom. "Jan Tooreloor is perfect for this job, and he just so happens to be out of work."

"An excellent idea!" Roberto cried.

The count didn't share his enthusiasm; he just scowled at the conspirators.

Jan Tooreloor grinned. "That's fine by me," he said. "As long as the pay's good."

"That goes without saying," said Mr Thomtidom. "Well, hasn't that worked out well? And Jan's a good handyman too. He can get to work on repairing that hole in the floor."

"I'll do that for free," said Tooreloor.

"Then I suppose I shall have to agree," said the count grumpily. "But first you can do something else for me, Tooreloor. Manus hasn't shown up, so I think it's your responsibility to drive Miss Grysenstein and my nephew to the Herb Garden."

Jan Tooreloor grinned again. "Right you are, sir," he said. "If we go along the Seventh Way we'll be there in no time."

The count turned to Frans. "You, Mr Van der Steg, have been dismissed," he said coldly. "You'll understand that Geert-Jan no longer needs a tutor, as he'll be going to school. Fine. Good day, everyone."

"What about Ivan?" cried Geert-Jan. "What's going to happen to Ivan?" He looked anxiously at the cat, who purred and gave his leg a bump.

"Ivan's welcome to stay here," said Tooreloor. "He loves the House of Stairs, and I'm sure we'll get along just fine!"

A funny scene popped into Frans's head: Jan Tooreloor waltzing around Gregorius's Small Banqueting Hall, while the black tomcat watched him from the stairs.

"That's true," said Geert-Jan slowly. "All right, then." He bent down, stroked the cat and whispered, "Bye, Ivan. See you soon! I'll come and visit you every now and then, okay?"

The count gave Miss Rosemary a bow. "I shall, of course, have to come and pay you a visit from time to time," he said, "to make sure my nephew's doing well."

"You're welcome, Gradus," said Miss Rosemary, "but only if Geert-Jan invites you himself."

Count Grisenstein looked at his nephew, who was still saying goodbye to the cat. He remained silent.

Before long the coach was trundling through the open gate; Jan Tooreloor was sitting up front and his passengers were Miss Rosemary and Geert-Jan, Aunt Wilhelmina and Mr Thomtidom. Frans couldn't fit inside, but Roberto said he'd take him home on his scooter. So Frans climbed up behind him again, with his bag of books under one arm and Roberto's guitar under the other. They raced past the coach, tore onto the Seventh Way, and drove back to Frans's village via Sevenways.

"Would you like to come in for a moment?" asked Frans, when he'd got off. "Aunt Wilhelmina isn't here yet, but she always leaves the back door open."

The boy shook his head. "I have to get home on time."

"Where are you going?" asked Frans. "To your tent in the woods, or to your house in town?"

"Into town," replied the boy a little sadly.

"Yes, the adventure's over," said Frans. "But it's been fun, don't you think?" He hesitated for a moment before saying, "Which one were you today? Roberto or the Biker Boy?"

"I don't know," said the boy, shrugging his shoulders. "Just call me Rob." He smiled briefly and added, "But Roberto works too..."

"Ah, it's not really your name that matters," said Frans. "Bye, then." He watched him go – Biker Boy, Rob and Roberto – until he'd disappeared from sight. Then he thoughtfully weighed the heavy bag of books in his hand, and slowly headed inside.

The next morning, Mr Van der Steg the teacher stood at the front of his classroom as usual. Greenhair had disappeared for good, but the same couldn't be said for Frans the Red. The teacher's hair had gone back to the colour that Mr Thomtidom was so fond of... *a proper dark red, not that carroty colour. But,* Frans thought to himself, *I don't think I'll ever tell another story with Frans the Red as the hero.*

He looked at his students, his gaze resting on the boy in the front row – next to Kai, who had always sat alone... Geert-Jan Grisenstein! *Maybe,* he thought, *there are other stories to be told* – the treasure of the House of Stairs had given him the idea: stories about Gregorius the Mad, and about Sir Grimbold, who had been to the Land of Torelore...

But it was Monday morning now, and the timetable said there was work to do. Mr Van der Steg turned to the board; he didn't write any sums on it though, but drew a flag, a fluttering flag with a long green pennant. And he said, "Yesterday someone in the class had a birthday. You all know who. Let's sing a birthday song for Geert-Jan Grisenstein."

When the song was finished, Marian put her hand up. "Sir," she asked, "could we sing another song? The Song of Seven?"

Frans smiled. "Fine," he said. "Just once and that's all."

A little worried, he added, "And please sing it quietly, very quietly indeed!"

Their eyes gleaming, the children began their song. They did as they were told and chanted the words quietly, almost mysteriously:

Do you know the Seven, the Seven,
Do you know the Seven Ways?
People say that I can't dance,
But I can dance like the King of France.

THIS IS ONE
THIS IS TWO
THIS IS THREE
THIS IS FOUR

THIS IS FIVE

THIS IS SIX...

But then they couldn't hold it back any longer, and they ended with a resounding note, a triumphant yell and a thunderous stamping of feet – so that the walls shuddered, the windows rattled and a cry shook the whole school:

THIS IS SEVEN!

Yes, that was seven, and now the story's done.

TONKE DRAGT writes and illustrates books of adventure, fantasy and fairy tales. She was born in 1930 in Jakarta. When she was twelve, she was imprisoned in a Japanese camp, where she wrote her very first book, using begged and borrowed paper. After the war, she moved to the Netherlands with her family, and eventually became an art teacher. She published her first book in 1961, and a year later this was followed by her most famous story, *The Letter for the King,* which won the Children's Book of the Year Award and has been translated into sixteen languages. She was awarded the State Prize for Youth Literature in 1976 and was knighted in 2001. Pushkin also publishes *The Letter for the King* and the sequel, *The Secrets of the Wild Wood.*

LAURA WATKINSON studied medieval and modern languages at Oxford, and taught English around the world before returning to the UK to take a Master's in English and Applied Linguistics and a postgraduate certificate in literary translation. She is now a full-time translator from Dutch, Italian and German, and has also translated Dragt's *The Letter for the King* and *The Secrets of the Wild Wood* for Pushkin. She lives in Amsterdam.

PUSHKIN CHILDREN'S BOOKS

We created Pushkin Children's Books to share tales from different languages and cultures with younger readers, and to open the door to the wide, colourful worlds these stories offer.

From picture books and adventure stories to fairy tales and classics, and from fifty-year-old bestsellers to current huge successes abroad, the books on the Pushkin Children's list reflect the very best stories from around the world, for our most discerning readers of all: children.